THE SURFACE

BLACK CARBON #2

A.J. SCUDIERE

The Hunted - Black Carbon #1

FIRST EDITION

PRAISE FOR A.J. SCUDIERE

"There are really just 2 types of readers—those who are fans of AJ Scudiere, and those who will be."
-Bill Salina, Reviewer, Amazon

For *The Shadow Constant*:

"The Shadow Constant by A.J. Scudiere was one of those novels I got wrapped up in quickly and had a hard time putting down."
-Thomas Duff, Reviewer, Amazon

For *Phoenix*:

"It's not a book you read and forget; this is a book you read and think about, again and again . . . everything that has happened in this book could be true. That's why it sticks in your mind and keeps coming back for rethought."
-Jo Ann Hakola, The Book Faerie

This book is for all the Renegades out there. The ones who joined my newsletter at DragonCon when we met. The ones in the Facebook group, who post the most wonderful, ridiculous, scientific, and fun things for me! The ones who write back to me when you get an email.

When I started writing as a kid, I wanted to be a published author. When I was published just over a decade ago, I wanted to sell books and make a splash. Now, I realize that awards and movie options are great, but what I really love is knowing that you're out there, whether we've met in person or not. I love that you're waiting on the next book. I love knowing that you're there each time I sit down to write. And I love that you take the time to reach out to me and tell me.

THANK YOU.

ACKNOWLEDGMENTS

As always, this book—by the time you hold it in your hands—is more than just my brainchild.

It has been through first round edits (and all the publishing!) Thank you Eli. (Seriously, y'all should thank Eli, too. There are no A.J. books without her.)

It has been through beta readers. Thank you, Dana, Victoria, and Julie.

It has been through the editor. Thank you, Kimberley!

Then it goes back through me... there's usually drinking at this point. Then it goes to the advanced copy readers who often send comments and find any typos trying to weasel their way through into the final copy. These guys are warriors! Thank you to my ARC team!

Lastly, this book in particular deserves a shout out to Wade de Gottardi. (Yes, if you read the NightShade books, *that* Wade.) He's a Stanford grad himself and he put up with several months of me randomly asking him questions ranging from the perfectly reasonable to the bizarre. Yes, I took some liberties with the campus and the water, but that's what stories are for. Wade kept me in line and directed me to all the "Stanford speak" and things I should know about being a student there. Thank you, Wade.

1

Joule looked down into the dark water that puddled at her feet. It seemed shallow here, but she didn't step in. That was the problem with dark puddles: Sometimes, they were deep.

A movement flicked at the surface of the otherwise still water. Maybe it was a bug. She was no fisherman, but there was something about the ripple that told her it had come from under the water, not on top. *It was definitely bigger than a bug.*

Gingerly, she stepped one foot into the saturated grass at her feet. This was why she'd worn her rain boots: They covered her almost to her knees. *I'll be okay*, she told herself and took another step.

The water slid across the smooth rubber of her boot—navy with small white polkadots. It was still shallow enough that she could see her feet. Taking another step, she lost sight of the toe of her boot. The water only reached to her ankle now and there was plenty further to go, if it didn't get too deep too fast.

Glancing outward, the vast pool of water reflected

upside down campus buildings to her. It would have been just a puddle, if not for the size. The rains had come hard all last week, with very few gaps in the showers. Sometimes, they'd come heavy and dark, with thunder shaking the buildings. And other times, they'd come light and misty, seeming almost enchanted. But the clouds and their water hadn't stopped.

The average rainfall in the Bay Area was just over twenty-four inches annually; this storm had dumped almost ten. Sliding in from the ocean, the storm had seemed to skid to a stop over the famed university. Now Stanford squished in all the places it wasn't fully underwater.

Today, the showers had lightened to a mist and the rain was predicted to—*finally!*—stop, but it hadn't yet. Joule could feel the unruly waves of her wet hair tightening to ringlets, but she had a curiosity to satisfy.

In front of her, the surface rippled again and she stepped forward slowly, letting her boot sink into the loose ground. Behind her, she carefully lifted her other foot, holding her ankle rigid and making sure the mushy earth didn't steal her rain boot.

Once she had her feet planted again, Joule breathed easier. From her back pocket, she pulled blue nitrile gloves she'd inadvertently stolen from chem lab and snapped them on. She'd likely get water inside them, but if she touched anything... well, she didn't want to actually *touch* it.

"Are you okay? Did you lose something?" a voice called out behind her.

Not wanting to move her feet, Joule twisted slightly, catching sight of a professor behind her. She didn't know him. But it figured. A few other students had walked by, but no one had spoken to the young woman wading out into the crap.

"No," she called back. Then she turned her head again and looked him up and down. Wool pants, jacket with patches on the elbows. He couldn't look more like a young associate professor if he tried. Maybe he was just a TA. But this puddle was in the middle of the science buildings, so she took a chance. "I thought I saw something in the water and I wanted to see if I could figure out what it was."

"Oh. That doesn't necessarily sound safe."

It wasn't. But he didn't know what she'd done last year. Her smile was wry. "I'll be fine."

"What if it's a water moccasin?"

Oh, good try, she thought, but kept it to herself. She called back over her shoulder as she took another tentative step forward. "Water moccasins are common to *southern* California, not up here."

"Yes, they *were*. But I have two in my lab that were locally caught. They're moving northward."

So he wasn't a student. He'd said "my lab." Most likely he was probably a professor. She moved another foot forward and saw the ripple again. It didn't have the "S" shape of a snake in water. "What are my chances this is a fat water moccasin?"

The water was now halfway up her boots, deep enough for whatever was swimming around. She pushed forward, watching as each step took the water line higher on her boots. If it got within three inches of the top, she'd call it a wash and turn back.

She took another step forward but frowned when she heard the water moving behind her. When her foot was planted firmly, Joule turned to see the man high-stepping his way through until he was even with her. Her mouth fell open.

"You don't have boots. You just ruined your shoes." *What was he doing?* "And your pants."

"Well, whatever you pull out of here, I want to see it. And if you get bit by a water moccasin, someone will have to carry you out and call for help."

"I'm *wearing* boots. You're the one who's going to get bitten."

"Ah. Yes. Supremely bad choice on my part, then." He only shrugged and she thought, *He was probabaly already wet from this never-ending drizzle.*

He looked her up and down and she was about to frown at him again when he asked, "Are you stronger than you look?"

A harsh burst of laughter exploded from her lungs, and she was glad she could at least say, "Yes. I am."

"Alright then." He turned his gaze to the surface of the water and didn't move his eyes as he spoke. "I'm Dr. Dean Kimura. Marine sciences."

"Well, that's lucky of me. Joule Mazur. Freshman. Undeclared."

She, too, was watching the water intently. Neither of them had moved. She had four inches of clearance to the top of her boots, but Kimura was standing in his loafers... or maybe his socks?

Perhaps his hasty arrival had scared away whatever it was. Now she waited, with a stillness and patience she'd learned the hard way. She was relieved he was here. What if it *was* a water moccasin? That was a threat she hadn't considered.

She had pushed the sleeves of her hoodie up until they stayed put around her elbows, as she fully intended to plunge her hand into the water. But she watched as the professor slowly unbuttoned the cuffs of his shirt. He'd lost the jacket. Probably tossed it away somewhere back at the edge of the puddle/pond.

The water had been here for enough days now that she'd begun to think of the edge as "the shore." *His books and his bag must be back there, too, soaking up all the water they can.* She refused to feel guilty.

Producing his own blue lab gloves, he registered her raised eyebrow and only shrugged. He probably really *was* a marine sciences professor. She looked back to the surface and waited. Smooth and reflective, it showed her more of the endless gray sky, the tops of a few trees, and the sharp rooflines of the nearby buildings.

At the edge of her vision, his now-blue finger flicked and she followed the point fast enough to catch the ripple at the surface about ten feet away.

It was still here.

But, even as she thought that, his finger flicked again and her head snapped the other way catching another telltale mark on the otherwise placid surface. "There are two of them," she said, hoping she didn't whisper like an idiot.

"At least."

She didn't like the tone in his voice.

2

Joule's eyes flicked to the right, her normally steady heartbeats stuttering.

Was that a shadow just under the tree? She'd been seeing them everywhere after yesterday's foray into the water.

Figuring she could prove to herself there was nothing there, she leaned in closer. She didn't see anything. Then again, what *could* she see? The water was dark and, in places, so muddy that something might be just below the surface and no one would know.

"Joule!" The voice called from further down the street. Startled at getting caught staring into the giant puddle again, Joule cautiously moved a few inches further away from the water that hugged the sidewalk she stood on.

In the distance, she saw a figure waving wildly at her. Though she was too far away to discern the facial features, it was easy to tell the young woman wore her tightly curled hair pulled up in a messy ponytail, shooting like a fountain above a perfectly symmetrical face. That alone made Joule certain it was Gabby approaching.

She waved back, hand high over her head, the movement large enough to be seen as she kept walking forward. Maybe it *wasn't* Gabby, but it would be more embarrassing not to wave back. Again, though, Joule's eyes darted to the side as a ripple formed in the standing water at the ditch. The water's color was deep, somewhere between the darkest evergreen and black. She reminded herself that any number of things can be alive in the water—things that *should* be alive in the water.

It might be something as simple as a current carrying a stick. After all, the ditches and gutters had been made for drainage. The water had simply gotten high enough that no current flowed now and they all stood still, backed up and waiting for something further down on the line to let them drain again.

Focusing again on the figures down the street—definitely Gabby—she recognized the other person then. Tall and reed thin, Marcus would always stand out in a crowd, even though he most certainly didn't want to. The deep red Stanford sweatshirt didn't help. His parents, so proud of their son's achievement, had spent their money on a bag full of school merchandise for him.

Marcus was here on scholarship, like Joule and Cage. Unlike them, he didn't have a backup savings account, so he didn't have the money for white Oxford button-downs, designer jeans, or even a hoodie that didn't have a huge "S" emblazoned across the front.

"*Max*. No!"

Cage's shout gave Joule only a moment's warning before she felt the large body slam into her from behind. She would have been thrown to the ground if strong arms hadn't wrapped around her, lifted her up, and swung her in a circle. Her feet passed ever so slightly over the edge of the standing water in the ditch. She yanked them back, her heart freezing at the thought of landing in the water.

Her body clenched in response to being yanked backward and swung around, even though her brain knew this wasn't a random attack. This was Max—Cage's roommate and possibly the worst football player on the Stanford team, but dedicated to his physical regimen and surviving the academic rigors of the school.

Somehow, Max and Cage were a perfect match. After almost eight months living on campus, it remained well beyond Joule's comprehension how this worked. But Cage liked his roommate enough to bring him along when everyone met up. Joule would have chosen otherwise.

College was supposed to be a time when she and her twin possibly went their different ways, learned different things for once, ran with different friends. But they didn't. Max was the thing they differed on. Go figure.

"Put me down, Max."

Joule tried to utter the words without irritation in her voice. Max had never quite outgrown the idea that torturing someone was fun, so she tried not to let her aggravation show.

"Jesus, Max. How many times do I have to tell you, she *hates* that?"

Her brother's words were firm, but unfortunately, so was Max's head. Joule sincerely doubted that the message would get through this time. It certainly hadn't penetrated his brain any of the times before.

Still, slowly and gently, she felt her feet touch the ground. Whatever he wanted to accomplish by rushing her was over and Max would now be a sweetheart again.

As she sucked in a breath, grateful at being back on terra

firma, she saw that Gabby and Marcus had almost arrived at the corner.

It was Gabriella who scolded, "Max, you big idiot. You realize she can kill you. Right?"

"Sure," Max said, the death threat not fazing him in the slightest. "But she's most deadly at a distance. That's why I gotta get in close."

Joule just shook her head. Max wasn't entirely wrong. She was best with a bow and was just as deadly—if not as quiet—with a nine-millimeter or a shot gun. But she hadn't killed *people*.

Some days, Max had her rethinking her position on that.

The five of them stopped and waited on the corner. It would be at least a handful more minutes before Sky and Roxie showed. The two remaining friends coming to their little conglomerate were identical in their long, narrow faces, large blue eyes, and ability to geek out over something scientific. Every other thing about the Baker twins was radically different.

All around her, the group chatted while Joule remained quiet. Today had bothered her. Though the new rain was concerning, it was the water on the ground that bothered her most.

Then again, it might be the date. April wasn't going to be her best month. She could already feel it creeping up, and she was hoping to bury her feeling of unease into a Psych 101 text book.

She'd lost both of her parents, tragically, a year ago. That had changed her, during her last months of high school, from a carefree, nerdy kid eager to claim her scholarship to the school of her choice, to a fighter who would become a killer.

Lately, things had seemed so normal. Though she and Cage had odd moments—going to visit their grandparents' for the holiday breaks, instead of returning to their own home— most of her life passed as it would have had her parents been alive. She still would have been at school several hundred miles away. She wouldn't have seen them every day, anyway.

The loss should have remained in the gaps. Instead, it wove its way into her whole life. Grief stalked her. It appeared when she least expected it, and she became paranoid that sadness was lurking around the corner... even when it wasn't.

Though most of her friends had come through tragedies of their own, it wasn't the same. Max's family had been caught in an avalanche, but they'd all *survived*.

Gabby had come from the south. She'd lost her home, but not her family. The water on the beach had finally risen high enough that her family's multi-million-dollar seaside house had been washed away. That had happened a year and a half ago. Her family was still fighting the insurance company to cover the loss. They'd been struggling financially in the meantime.

But they'd all *survived*.

Marcus, having grown up in a poor area of town, had seen a massive crime increase before he graduated high school. He'd actually killed a person—forced to shoot a home invader one night in self-defense. Joule didn't know for sure, but could easily guess that the incident had changed him.

Certainly, others here had lost family members. The country was in upheaval. College was an attempt at normalcy, though California cities were still turning off power intermittently and running burn rings around the populated areas in an effort to keep the raging wildfires at bay.

As Sky and Roxie finally approached from down the street, Joule almost smiled. They spotted their friends and began running—as though their tardiness were unexpected or could be corrected with an apology and a dash.

"Oh, wow. We made it!" Sky fanned her hand in front of her face as though that would cool her off from her run. As her hand moved, Joule noticed the jacket had embedded sparkles. Of course it did. That worked with the sleek hair, pulled into a perfectly straight pony. It was Roxie who motioned them on with no fanfare and, as a unit, they turned and headed down the street toward the cafe.

This, at least, was comfortable. Joule started breathing easier with everyone accounted for. She always breathed easier with the confirmation that her fear was rooted in the past and not the present. The conversation of the group around her meant that her new world had maintained some level of order.

Despite what had happened last year, she had a good life. Joule loved what she was learning in her classes. She liked most of her professors, and even a few of the TAs. Her parents would have been proud.

All of those things were wonderful, but she couldn't stop the deep thudding of her heart. Or the memory of what Dr. Kimura had pulled out of the water. It wouldn't have seemed so strange if Kimura hadn't known enough to classify it. And now Joule knew, too.

Beneath the surface, something in her world was wildly out of control.

3

"What was it?" Cage asked Joule.

She had pulled him aside after leaving the café, telling their friends she needed him to run an errand. It had only taken her twin half a block to see that Joule didn't need anything from the convenience store other than the opportunity to separate from the group.

"It was a red-tailed goby," Joule told him. Her serious tone told him the presence of a local fish concerned her more than it should have.

Cage had found his own thoughts turning morbid over the past few days, but his worries seemed more reasonable than being upset about an aquarium fish. "Do you think it's *not* about the fish? Maybe it's really because of the date. Because of Mom. Maybe the fish is just the easier thing to worry about."

His sister shook her head for a moment, but then she tilted it side to side and raised one eyebrow thoughtfully. "Maybe. Part of it *must* be. I mean, how could it not?"

That, at least, Cage understood. This year had gone mostly as planned. Last year had not. But now, each day, he woke up and things were okay. The world had not turned on its head. A hurricane had not ripped through the school. There had been no tornadoes here, no wild animals. No crises. He attended all his classes and was grateful for the consistency and mediocrity of his days. Things had happened, of course. School had already been closed for rain on more than one day. One of the buildings had lost the use of its lower floor to flooding, and the classrooms had been moved elsewhere until some kind fix could be implemented.

But those, Cage thought, were minor crises. Max didn't question that his roommate clipped the curtains tightly closed at night and slept with a dead silent stillness. No one really commented that he didn't like to pet dogs, ever. And he went on as though things were normal. He could pretend his parents were simply away, not gone forever.

"Here's the problem," Joule said, breaking into what was pushing to become a deep melancholy. "Even if it *is* about Mom and the anniversary, it's also about *the fish*."

Okay, he would bite. Clearly, his sister needed to bounce this idea off someone. "Why is the red-tailed goby so concerning? I mean, the water was plenty deep, right? So why wouldn't there be fish?"

"But it was a *nine-inch* fish."

It was his turn to look surprised. "You measured it? With what?"

"The scanning electron microscope." The sarcasm showed she was growing frustrated with him. Maybe she had a right to be.

She had interrupted his studying to ask him to check out what was swimming in the puddles. He hadn't told her *no* —he didn't think he would ever have the ability to straight up say *no* to his sister again. But he had pushed her off, effectively canceling her request.

She was rightly irritated. "I wasn't out there alone. I mean, I *was*, but this professor came up. It turns out he's in marine sciences. He's the one who caught the fish. Apparently, he carries a small tape measure and specimen bags in his pocket because... marine sciences"

"Okay..." Cage was relieved that she'd had someone out in the water with her. He hadn't thought she'd give up on him and go alone. *Dammit, I should have found the time.*

This was his *twin,* and she was his only remaining immediate family. "Still, it was standing water and if it came up to your calves, that's really plenty deep for a fish. Right?"

"But they weren't baby fish, Cage. The water wasn't there long enough for them to grow that big. Even with an abundance of food, it wouldn't have happened that fast."

Cage nodded again, trying to follow her reasoning but relatively certain that it was slipping through his grip.

She didn't give him time to catch up. "So *how* did the fish get there?"

Oh. He was getting it now and the surprise showed on his face. She had a solid point, but just as he was arriving where she was, she darted ahead again.

"So, let's make it worse: The red-tailed goby is a bottom feeder."

Damn, another word that rang only inside his own head.

She was right. How did *any* fish get onto campus? And a bottom feeder, at that? They would have needed a path of some sort, a river or stream. Maybe it was a runoff ditch from all the water. That made sense. All the sewers had been running high since the rain started, almost ten days ago. The rain had only stopped yesterday. He tried to work it out. "Are they from a nearby lake?"

"Nope," she replied immediately, meaning she'd already thought it through, before she even pulled him aside to tell him what she'd found. Her answer made everything even more strange. "They're from the bay."

"A goby got here from *the Bay?*"

He felt like an idiot, repeating her words, but what else could he say? The Bay was too far. *How did that creature get into a puddle?* If she was talking, he couldn't hear her. His heart was thumping hard, shutting out all the sounds of the cars on the streets, the people passing by, doors opening and closing, music from someone walking by with their phone turned far too loud.

Stuck in his thoughts, Cage churned through the obvious connections. The Bay had almost as high a salinity as the ocean at large. *Shouldn't the puddle be mostly fresh water? And how did the fish come so far so fast?*

He latched on to the one idea he could handle without getting squeamish. "It must be an anomaly."

"No." Joule's tone was clean, even. Whatever he was scrambling through, she was already out the other side.

Joule pushed her way into the convenience store. She walked ten feet to the counter, grabbed a pack of gum, paid for it, and pocketed her change while he tried to solve the complex algebra of the fish in the puddle.

Somehow, it wasn't an anomaly.

"After Dr. Kimura caught a specimen, we stayed still and watched. We counted at least three more that couldn't have been different surface ripples from the same fish. So that means at least three separate animals, *plus* the one he'd bagged. And Dr. Kimura was convinced there were more. We just couldn't *prove* it."

"Well shit," Cage replied, finally uttering his words out loud. It didn't matter that it was the anniversary of their mother saving their lives at the expense of her own. It didn't matter that it was one year since the last day they'd truly had their father.

Maybe Joule had been right to invent a fake run to the convenience store. He and his twin knew things their friends didn't.

Cage had always loved marine biology and had considered taking it up as a career, but after the events of last year, he'd decided perhaps evolutionary genetics would be wiser. Or maybe a broad-spectrum biology degree would give him more to work with as the world's changes rolled in.

One way or another, he needed to get on top of these damn fish before they became a problem. He, too, would begin researching the goby and the rainfall and the watershed. He needed to change course, but he could easily pivot.

If the night hunters had taught him anything, it was how to adapt.

4

The scrape of the key gave Joule the only warning before the door began to push open.

"You're here." The flat sounding words fell from Ginnifer's lips and hit the ground between them as though her irritation was a thing. Cleary she was upset that Joule was actually in their shared dorm room.

Joule was counting down the remaining time. She had roughly two more months, and then she could put her name back in the hat and spin the wheel on another roommate. The chances of anyone being less savory than Ginnifer were low.

She admitted to being jealous that Cage had been matched with Max. They'd decided to room together again next year. Everything wrapped up neatly for her brother, while her living arrangements were still up in the air and would stay that way until she walked into the room next September and found out who the lotto had paired her with.

Cage and Max at least liked each other. For whatever reason, their levels of messiness and their neuroses lined up.

Gabby was with Melanie, and though they went their separate ways 90 percent of the time, they got along fine. Sky and Roxie were twins, too, but being same gender, they were allowed to room together.

Joule could almost hear her mother's voice telling her, "Ginnifer is helping you grow as a person!" At her roommate's appearance of disappointment in Joule's very existence, Joule decided she wasn't becoming any better version of herself.

Joule and Ginnifer—despite their cute-sounding, matchy names—did not share anything else, except maybe a mutual dislike.

She considered replying with, "Yes, shockingly, I am in my *own* room." But she held her tongue and instead offered a hard, blank stare until the other girl looked away. She'd won, but she was never sure exactly *what* she won or lost in these showdowns.

Slouched on her bed, Joule had her knees pulled up and her tablet across her lap. Without the note papers and pens spread around her, she would have looked as though she were lying in bed, simply slacking.

Once she'd told herself she'd done enough of whatever she needed to study, she usually stopped for the day. But she'd worked her way through her homework for Modern Socio-economic History of the US. The professor had started them off with the factors that led to the AIDS crisis, and now they were in the middle of the War on Drugs.

She should have studied more, but shoved aside the DEA and Nancy Reagan and plowed headfirst into her own research.

What she was discovering about the red-tailed goby was making her feel a little better, at least. The Goby was relatively populous in the Bay. The individual fish weren't that hardy, but the species was. They were wily as well, having been found in a number of streams and tributaries where they had no business being—places where the salinity was all wrong.

If anything was going to come out of the Bay and into the standing water at her school, the red-tailed goby at least seemed to be a harmless intruder. Gobies were small, colorful, innocuous fish and populated many a home aquarium. Only a few river and ocean varieties reached the size she and Dr. Kimura had pulled from the water.

The only thing that bothered Joule about them was that gobies, in general, were carnivorous.

Holly had trailed into the room behind Ginnifer. Had Ginnifer not been her roommate, Joule would not have been able to tell the two apart. Though they weren't wearing identical clothing, she was certain that, whatever one wore, the other had the same outfit somewhere in her closet. More than once, she'd heard Ginnifer on the phone to Holly in the mornings talking wardrobe. It sounded as though they had to make an effort to *not* look exactly alike.

In return for Joule's disdain at their efforts, Ginnifer often scoffed at Joule's simple uniform of jeans, black boots, camisole, and flannel. But Joule brushed off her fellow student's up-and-down visual check, thinking to herself, *I'm fucking adorable. And I don't have to call my friend every morning to be sure I don't look like her.*

Her interaction with Holly this time was the same as it often was. One would spot the other, be clearly disappointed in the other young woman's continued existence, and stare until someone conceded. It wouldn't be Joule today. She sat quietly waiting out the interruption, while Ginnifer and Holly scooped up whatever items they needed and headed off to find a more suitable location for whatever they were going to do.

Joule didn't know what kind of grades her roommate was getting, although she'd overheard one terse phone conversation in which a tearful Ginnifer had been in tears about a near-failing mark in economics. Joule's sympathy had bubbled to the surface, until Ginnifer turned around and glared at her.

Maybe Ginnifer wouldn't even be back next year.

Joule felt the dark thought of *one can hope* cross her mind. By the time the room was hers again, her mind had wandered away from the red-tailed goby.

Having found enough information to make her think that maybe the handful of the fish in the standing water *had* been an anomaly, she became more interested in the professor.

Dr. Kimura had left her standing in the shallow pool while he sloshed his way out, before running in wet stocking feet back to his building. He'd probably splashed a wet trail across the floor for someone on staff to clean up later. She'd stood alone, watching and counting the ripples for a good twenty minutes until he returned with a janitorial mop bucket and a net that was clearly specialized to this task.

If she'd wondered whether he was lying about his title before, this sold her.

He'd splashed right into the water this time, scaring away all the ripples she had counted. She'd felt better once he'd identified the Red-Tailed Goby, and she'd also been calmer knowing that he had stood beside her for several minutes and no water moccasin had taken a liking to one of his ankles.

Once he was beside her again, they'd stood still until, with an expert hand, he suddenly plunged the net into the pool at their feet. She'd seen nothing, but he came up with a fish. He held it wriggling in the net and asked her to scoop water into the bucket, then turned the net inside out, leaving the fish thrashing inside. Only then did he speak. "I wanted to catch two, but with that kind of movement, they'll pop right out of the bucket before I can bag them. I guess I can settle for one."

Then, excited with his find—which was really *hers*—he suggested they leave the large puddle behind. Though he'd splashed his way out again, she'd walked much more gingerly, not wanting to slosh water over the top and into her boots. Joule had no desire to walk home in a puddle of her own.

She'd left him then, thanking him and turning her own direction. Kimura would study the fish. She had answered her question.

It was just a regular fish. Nothing too strange. And he'd recognized it right away. There was no "Holy shit, they've evolved!" Nothing that would keep her awake with nightmares.

She pushed the notes on fish aside and tapped around her tablet, opening her homework for her Fundamentals of Civil Engineering class. She had told Kimura she was undeclared, and officially she *was*, but she was toying with this idea.

If she decided to pursue engineering, she would want to get a solid grade in the intro class. Joule reminded herself of this, as though she needed extra incentive to get good grades.

When the light faded outside and she was still studying, her eyes drifted closed. She slept without disturbing the tablet on her lap, the papers around her, or even the pen laced between her fingers.

But her dream was disturbing.

The streets of the school were dark and large, fish-like creatures ran the paths and chased the students looking for whatever their carnivorous tastes could consume. Though she fought them until she was weary, they didn't die.

Joule woke with a gasp at three in the morning, suddenly sitting upright in the dark and empty room. Though her eyes darted, frantically looking for a lump under the covers of the other bed, there was nothing there. Ginnifer had not returned. *Okay,* Joule reminded herself, *but this is not unusual.*

What was odd was the nightmare. She thought she'd left them behind months ago, but now she'd awakened almost screaming into the dark at three a.m.—on the anniversary of her mother's death.

She told herself, *It's just a bad feeling, just a memory coming to the surface on a significant date.*

But she knew.

As the world came into focus around her, Joule heard a sound she'd come to know too well. Turning her head toward the light coming through the window, she put the sound and sight together. Rain was splattering on the window. It was back.

5

C age stepped out the door into what had become a deluge.

The water had begun rushing in the gutters and starting to fill the low areas when he and Joule had walked into the restaurant for a late brunch. Their mother had made them pancakes when they were little—made-to-order flavors with blueberries, chocolate chips, pecans and cinnamon. So they'd come here, to gorge on breakfast food and order individual pancakes of as many combinations as possible in tribute to her.

Feeling stuffed and sluggish now, he pulled up the hood of his heavy jacket, happy that he'd invested in raingear at the beginning of the season. His lace-up duck boots had cost a pretty penny, but they kept his feet dry.

As he peered out from under the awning, he saw they would be put to the test on the way back.

He and Joule had gotten up early, taken two buses, and walked almost fifteen blocks to get here. Now, he wondered how they would make it back to the bus stop.

Joule unzipped her tiny backpack and pulled out an even tinier umbrella, impressing Cage when it unfolded to full size. She shrugged the pack over her shoulders and said, "I thought we were skipping class today, but it looks like everything is going to get canceled anyway."

Again. He nodded in agreement.

Scanning the road in front of him, he could see the water had bypassed simply sheeting on the street and was now rushing down the roadway with seemingly no end in sight. The intersection one block down was starting to flood. Behind him, he heard the staff from the restaurant lock the door, causing both him and Joule to startle and turn.

"I guess we are going to be the last customers for today..." she let the words trail off. "Should we call a ride?"

They'd been planning to walk back to the bus, but the rain had been only a drizzle then. Cage had noticed the drops hitting the window with greater urgency while they'd eaten, but he hadn't realized it had become this bad, or that they might have gotten themselves stuck...

"I don't think we can." He waved a hand at the street where only a few vehicles even attempted passage. The ones that did were trucks, jacked up on kits and sporting all-terrain tires. Not many of those in the Bay Area.

Down the street, he spotted a white station wagon that must have parked to avoid driving in the rain. But the water was coming up past the wheels now, and a frantic mother was getting soaked as she pulled her kids from the backseat. As he checked, he saw the other businesses on the street had already closed up shop. The restaurant was the last.

"Then we walk." Joule's voice was grim, and she stepped out from under the awning into the downpour. The rain rolled off her umbrella in waves. Individual drops spattered her jeans, and her boots sank into the sheet of water sluicing across the sidewalk.

It was the speed of the water that concerned him. It rushed up and over the tops of her boots rather than finding an easier path around. As he stepped out from under the awning himself, Cage saw Joule searching along the gutter, checking for a place that was shallow enough to cross.

She didn't find one.

"Here," she finally declared. "This looks like the best option." She pointed to a spot away from where the sewer grate sucked the water down below the surface of the street.

Even though the sounds were a rush of white noise, he could tell the water wasn't dropping very far anymore. The underground system, already heavily taxed from last week, was about to fill up.

The rain hit his jacket with small, forceful splats, but he reached out a hand toward hers, watching as she shuffled her umbrella. He linked them together to step into the rushing river in front of them. Holding tightly, Cage turned his head and looked at the sidewalk, still rushing with its own layer of rain that was now pushing at the lip of the restaurant door behind them.

His hand jerked, instantly pulling his gaze back toward his sister. She was fine. She'd stepped off the curb and was standing in the water. He could see it was only ankle deep. *Not as bad as it had originally looked*, he thought. But it hit the sides of her legs fast enough that if she went down, it might sweep her away.

He ground his teeth, clenching his jaw a little tighter, and stepped into the rushing stream. The pressure hit his ankles in a constant and steady push that he had to fight against. Putting one foot in front of another, Cage turned his head from side to side to see what might be coming at him. The little visor fitted inside the hood protected the upper part of his face, but it definitely obscured his peripheral vision. The rain sheeting down around him did the rest.

He looked for oncoming cars. The water really was too deep in places for safe driving. But as he looked around, he felt the eerie feeling sink into his heart that he and his sister were alone in the middle of the rising flood.

Step by step, they lifted their feet out of the water, taking only one stride forward each time by an unspoken agreement. They moved like a four-legged animal, three legs on the ground at all times. Joule clenched his fingers so tightly that his hand ached and he didn't doubt hers did, too. But he didn't dare let go even enough to adjust his grip.

"Oh good," Joule said as they approached the middle of the four lanes, where the water was lower. The slope was a normal feature of city streets and allowed for runoff. Right now, he was glad it meant the middle of the pavement wouldn't be a problem. Their next big challenge would happen when they had to cross another rushing gutter.

Cage was grateful that his sister's boots came almost to her knees. His did not. He was pretty certain his legs and feet were going to be soaked before he made it back to his dorm. For a moment, they stood in the center of the road, seeing no oncoming traffic, as both of them scanned for the easiest place to step up onto the opposing sidewalk. The water in the gutters was deep enough now that it became difficult to see where the curbs began and ended.

"There," he pointed. "That's our spot."

His sister nodded in agreement. The area had a slightly lower current and hopefully, shallower water. It was so hard to tell. So, one foot at a time, they began moving toward the other side of the street. Then he saw his sister's head snap hard to the right and he couldn't avoid the loud, solid sound of her voice. "Oh, shit."

Following her gaze, he looked down the street and saw a rolling wave of water coming right toward them.

"Go!" Cage yelled, tugging harder at his sister's hand. His feet already running, he left no room for her to refuse. Not that she would.

They could no longer afford their careful one-foot-at-a-time movement. His boots splashed through water that remained remarkably steady in height and force. But that wouldn't last long, because nothing could change the wall of water coming at them. Something must have broken, some levy overflowed, or a lock let go somewhere down the line, because he could see five more inches of height rolling toward them from several blocks away.

How long did they have before it hit them?

Five inches of water shouldn't feel deadly, but Cage knew it was—especially at that speed, especially all at once. He leapt faster, no longer racing beside his sister but out in front now, tugging at her hand.

He would have been dragging her along with him if she hadn't been so frantic to reach the other side herself. As short as the distance was, it was exhausting work, lifting their feet and fighting the current.

It felt like a bad dream, in which he ran and ran but got nowhere. The kind where the wind and the air and his own very existence fought to keep him from moving forward. Even despite all the physical effort and the mental frustrations, he kept his eye on that moving section of water coming toward them.

He quickly calculated they'd covered half the distance to the curb. But the water was closer than halfway to them. It was moving far more rapidly than they were.

"*Faster!*" The word came from his sister's frantic lips, stolen from his brain just as he would have yelled it himself. Cage felt her pace pick up and he, too, tried and probably failed to move with any better speed.

Even though the wave hadn't hit them yet, the water was getting deeper and the current faster as they approached the side of the road. The task of moving became even more difficult, and the speed they needed to get to higher ground as the wave now barreled at them wasn't going to happen.

The water was close enough to force a decision. Cage bet everything and took a final leap.

He wasn't agile enough in his clunky boots to do it well, but he tried. Shoving off hard with his back leg, he stretched forward, his hand still locked tight with his sister's. He aimed for the upper level of the curb that he couldn't quite see. He had to believe it was just below the surface of the water.

Time moved in slow motion. He saw his foot in midair, aiming toward the sidewalk, toward freedom, toward safety... he didn't know. He knew the wave of water racing toward them would wash up onto the sidewalk too, but at least he would be on higher ground. Hopefully, it wouldn't hit them as hard. If they could make it, the water might still be fast, but it wouldn't be as deep.

Cage waited for his foot to contact the solid cement underneath it. But before it did, his sister's hand yanked hard and spun him around. For a brief moment, he hung outside of time, suspended in that second, and he saw that the water had hit them.

Joule had not leapt fast enough, and the force of the water caught her ankles. As he watched, her legs were taken out from under her. Joule was getting swept away, her fingers still locked tightly in his.

7

The water slammed into Joule. Only five extra inches, but they hit her with the force of a barreling bulldog, yanking her legs out from under her. If she hadn't been ready, it would have sent her spinning, feet over head.

In reaction, she'd automatically gripped Cage's hand even more tightly, as if that were possible. She only wished they had latched on to each other's wrists instead of this childish and friendly hand clasp they'd taken, thinking it was enough.

As her feet jerked from under her, her body yanked to the side, and she felt the force in her shoulder. Cage splashed through the depth of rolling water and stomped onto the hard top of the sidewalk. Even so, he stumbled as he landed, pulled off balance by her flailing weight.

The dark water covered everything, obscuring his boots up to the ankles. But even as her body was tugged one way, and her hand reached out to hold on to him, she could see he'd managed to get his feet firmly planted.

Thank God, she thought, but had the wherewithal not to

waste her energy saying it out loud. Her feet touched nothing as the water yanked her sideways, trying its best to steal her from her brother's grip. He was turning to face her, trying to stay planted firmly on the sidewalk neither of them could see anymore. If he tumbled, they would be pulled down the street, thrashed by a feckless current and smacked into cars and curbs and who knew what else.

Flexing her fingers to maintain their grip despite the rain seeping between their hands, Joule felt the cold rush of water, up and over the edge of one boot. It sank inside, quickly soaking her sock and rapidly stripping the boot from her foot.

Her arm tugged again, the pain radiating through her shoulder and down to her wrist, letting her know she risked dislocating her arm. Her fingers hurt and she couldn't tell why. Wrenching her head to the side, she saw that she'd dropped the arm holding the umbrella and the water had caught inside the bowl shape. It was one of the strongest forces trying to pull her away.

Instinctively, she let go, watching as the water quickly turned the fabric arc inside out. It didn't wash away. The sharp burn at her wrist told her the strap was still caught and she shook at her hand until it let go. She yelled at it the whole time.

"Joule!" Cage shouted, sharp and quick, his words muffled by her diatribe at the caught strap. The rain filled his head with a roar as each tiny drop smacked into the surface. The water rushing by had its own angry chorus as it tried to wrench her away from him. "Don't wiggle. I can't hold on."

She had to move. He couldn't hold on if the umbrella caught the water and yanked her downstream. She flipped at her wrist again. And again.

"Joule! Stop!"

But she couldn't. He didn't understand. One last shake and she felt the strap slide free, the nylon of the cord almost scorching a friction burn as it slipped away. Once it was free of her wrist, the water stole the whole contraption quickly, leaving the back of her hand burning and throbbing. At least she was no longer being pulled sideways. She breathed a sigh of relief when she felt Cage's grip begin to slide from her fingers.

Ignoring the cold wrapping quickly and silently around her wet foot, she slammed her free arm up and over, aiming her hand for her brother's wrist. The move tugged hard at the fragile grasp she already held. Joule was trying desperately to get both hands clasped firmly on Cage, the only anchor she had. She could feel his responding tug.

Even as she lurched forward to grab onto him, Cage pulled the other way, planting his feet against the tide and hauling her back toward him. He was using his upper body strength to pull her closer, trying to get her feet onto the same ground where his stood.

For what seemed like a slow eternity, Cage fought the water. Walking one hand over the other, he tried to hold onto her wrist and then her arm, forcing her in closer. Several times, his grip slid, but he gritted his teeth and held on tighter. She didn't complain.

Joule moved her feet, trying to find her way below the rushing current and onto the sidewalk beneath her. If she could just find the ground, she could stand upright. Her wet foot moved frantically through the water, feeling for the edge of the curb.

"Swing me this way!" She nodded with her head which direction.

For a moment, Cage frowned, but he slowly began to

twist the two of them into the current. Though his feet stayed planted, the water tried and tried again to yank her away.

"Son of a shitbiscuit!" she yelled as something hard struck her shin. Joule felt her teeth tighten together and her face contort, but she quickly smoothed her features back out for her brother. Had she been in their old living room, she would have hopped on one foot, offered a full string of colorful swears, and glared at the offending furniture. Here, obeying her pain did no good. She couldn't even look to see if there was a bone sticking out—not yet. At least she was convinced it wasn't quite that bad

Cage didn't ask. Joule shutting her own mouth told him enough.

And he seemed to have realized the problem she'd just discovered. She *wasn't* over the sidewalk. That's why she couldn't find any ground with her feet. Her boot and her wet, sock-covered foot were sweeping down into the water over the gutter, over the sewer grates. Into the deepest water with the fastest current.

As soon as he had her aimed the right way, her sock foot made contact. She planted it hard, wishing she had the grip of rubber beneath her, and grateful that pain didn't shoot up her leg. So she mustn't have sustained any serious damage from the hit. In the next moment, she swung her boot into place behind her foot and slapped it through the water, down to the hard surface of the sidewalk.

Instantly, the pressure eased in her wrists. The force she was applying to her brother's grip lessened as she finally stood on her own. Still, Cage refused to let her go.

"Just loosen up enough to let the blood flow again. Thank you," she said, breathing heavily.

Cage barely acknowledged her words, but moved his

hands and switched his grip letting the feeling surge sharply back into her hands. He was breathing heavily. The fear of Joule being stolen had seeped into him, just as the water did. "Now what?"

She could see that they were both soaked, almost head to toe. They would get cold soon. If there was any sun, it was blocked by the clouds dumping water on top of the city, leaving the air humid and cool. So that wouldn't help them.

Flicking her eyes back across the street, she saw the pancake restaurant was closed up tight. Even if they could make it back across, no one would answer if they banged on the door. Where had everyone gone? Was there a back alley to the businesses that was simply drier than the streets? The whole area felt eerily deserted.

Looking up to her brother, she only said, "We have to get back. We need shelter, heat, and high ground."

He nodded and once again adjusted their grip. This time, he wrapped his hand around her wrist, forcing her to grasp his in response. It created a tighter—if more awkward —bond.

One foot at a time, they began moving in tandem down the street. There was no time to pay attention to the fact that she was now wearing only one shoe and her sock-covered foot was unprotected. She might step on anything and injure herself.

"This way." He pointed with his free hand, suggesting they take a slightly longer route on streets that should be higher than where they were.

Joule nodded, but looked off after the rushing water. At least they were now aimed away from the current. Her boot, already halfway down the block, swirled and twirled in the eddies, bumping around the cars the water ambushed.

She harbored a brief moment of stupid hope that she

could run after it and somehow fetch her boot. Her sock would remain soaked and soggy, but at least she'd have the safety of rubber surrounding her foot. But the polka dots only bobbed farther and farther down the street, making it clear there was no way she would catch up.

Cage was already pushing them around the corner, away from the wonderful pancakes and the moment of terror that the water would win. For all that they'd fought and won, they'd only made it across one street. Even that short distance had been perilous.

Joule was already recalculating the path back to the dorms. The buses had to be down, didn't they? What if she and Cage couldn't make it? What might they do instead? Where could they go? Because staying here was not a safe option.

"Are you okay?" Cage asked as he continued sloshing through the water that was thankfully only ankle-deep on the sidewalk.

"Yes," she answered honestly. *I am okay.* As of yet, she had not stepped on any rocks or broken glass. None of the branches and twigs they'd seen tumbling along with the water had struck her hard enough to cause pain—again. But if he was asking, *will* you be okay? She honestly didn't know.

Slowly, one painstaking step at a time, they turned the corner to the right. As they began to pass out of sight of the street behind them, Joule turned and looked again for her boot.

The brightly colored dots were easy to spot, though they were already another block down, moving faster than she would have expected. Just before she lost sight of her shoe, she watched it tug slightly underwater. Once. Twice. And then it was pulled beneath the surface.

8

"Cage," Joule said, pulling her foot high out of the water. She had to work too hard with each step. Despite being much shallower on the sidewalk, the water still fought her every move. "We don't know what the university looks like. It could be just as flooded as here."

She thought about the red-tailed gobies and wondered what else might be on campus that shouldn't be. Though she'd never pulled up a topographical map of the school, she knew Stanford had flooded before. There was no reason to think the school would be dry—or even simply *dry enough* to get to their dorm—if they were stuck in this much water here.

Her brother easily followed her line of thought. "You're not wrong," he replied, but offered no real answers.

Joule walked on until her muscles burned and her foot was sore. She couldn't say how many rocks or bumps in the sidewalk she'd stepped on. She'd stubbed her numb toes more times than she could count.

She felt lucky though. Nothing had slashed her foot open or even ripped her sock off. She'd been careful, stopping to check several times, certain her foot was cold enough that she might not even notice a gash and bleeding.

But the foot was only part of her worries. Everything had begun to hurt. Her hand ached because she wouldn't let go of her brother. Her arm ached at her wrist because he wouldn't let go of her. He was squeezing far too tightly, but she couldn't tell him to stop.

Her thighs burned from the effort of lifting her feet above the passing water with each step. High-stepping was an unusual movement for her, and the repetition was killing her. To make it worse, she fought against the water which sucked at her remaining boot with every step.

Luckily, the water was only ankle-deep where they now walked. The sidewalk ran with the water that quickly sluiced down over the curbs and into the gutters. But it didn't stop coming, so there was nowhere they didn't have to fight the pressure of the water.

At least there was no more wave streaking toward them. No more streets that were deadly to cross. However, while they'd escaped the immediate danger around the diner, they were now slightly farther from the school.

Joule was certain that, for all the distance they'd covered —which honestly wasn't much, at this speed—they weren't any closer to where they needed to be. And they weren't closer to the bus stop... if she harbored any fantasies that it was the one vehicle still on the road.

Cage at least had his raincoat. Joule, without her umbrella, was now soaked to the bone. She was weary, exhausted, possibly getting sick, and uncertain of which direction she should be going.

Her brother's silence indicated he was likely still tracking her thoughts and agreeing. Even talking was too much effort over the white noise of the battering rain. The silence should have been soothing, but it was terrifying. There was no reason another wave of water couldn't come down the street again. They didn't know what had broken or let loose to make that happen. She couldn't even get her phone out to call someone—her phone would get soaked, and then where would she be?

Had they been talking, Cage would have told her about what was happening in his classes that she didn't share. He would have mentioned something dumb that Max had done, but that somehow most of them would find endearing. Instead, he stayed silent as they pressed forward.

"Holy crapballs," Joule said as she looked up for a moment. She was as startled by the sudden lack of rain as she'd been by how much there was when they stepped out of the pancake restaurant. "We've got a break."

Looking down at her feet, she watched as the water ran off the sidewalk. Slowly, the depth receded as quickly as the sky stopped sending it. She wasn't sure if that was a good sign or a bad omen.

"Look." Cage, too, was staring at the cement beneath their drenched boots. All that was left was a sheen of wetness that wasn't building or moving.

"Oh my god." She breathed it out, not sure if she should be this happy or if the break was anything worth commenting on.

Sure enough, Cage was fighting a smile as he looked up and around and pointed. "Don't get too excited." His warning was likely as much to himself as to her.

Joule noticed how clear he sounded now, as he now only had to talk over the water rushing by in the gutters and along the street. They no longer had to shout over the relentless rain. The sky had cleared enough to let a brief ray on sun hit them.

But it wasn't hard to see that the sun was only a gap in the relentless rain. A line of thicker, darker clouds was aimed toward them at high speed.

Joule stood still and focused, trying to discern if she could see rain actually falling from those clouds in the distance. Could she and her brother possibly get back to campus before it caught up to them? "How long do you think we have until it gets here?" she asked.

Cage shook his head as though he had no idea, but he said "Soon" with the same kind of certainty she felt.

This wasn't going to get any better, and they still had a way to go.

Just as he turned and asked, "What's the plan?" a truck rolled toward them down the street.

Though not the kind of jacked-up truck Joule had encountered in the past, this one sat high enough to splash through the standing water in the street and not worry about flooding the engine. As they watched, it passed right by them and made a U turn, tightly cornering back and forth in the narrow space until it had pulled up right next to their position on the sidewalk.

At last, they weren't the only two humans on Earth. It was hard to see inside the heavily tinted windows, but Joule could hope. Maybe it was a rescue.

As the bright blue door flew wide, a young woman in a dress entirely unsuited for the weather popped out of the passenger side. No one seemed to notice the two drenched college students as the woman and the driver exchanged a rushed goodbye.

Her ballet flats, perhaps the worst possible decision for the weather, landed in the layer of water on the sidewalk and were instantly soaked.

She looked down, the long red waves of her hair

bobbing in the blessedly clear air. "Thank you. Thank you so much!" she yelled to the driver. Then she slammed the door, spun around, and only missed barreling into Cage and Joule because they managed to step out of the way. The truck was already taking off down the street.

"I'm so sorry!" She looked back and forth between them, frowning. Only then did Joule realize they must look like the rainstorm refugees they were. Though she was probably only a handful of years older than they were, she was dry. And that made her the top of the pecking order here.

"Oh my God." As she examined them, Joule could see the realization dawning just how badly they'd been caught in the weather. Then the redhead looked up and down the street, as though someone should appear and claim these urchins.

Joule felt her mouth quirk. Had anyone been around, they would have been dry. There hadn't even been a safe awning to hide under.

Instead, Joule only pointed away, toward the sky. The woman was still looking at the street, but she needed to be checking the wall of clouds.

They all needed shelter, fast.

"You are a mess," the woman said, as though this was their fault. Then she pointed to an unassuming door set between two businesses. It led to a flight of stairs Joule could just make out through the less-than-clean glass.

"I live here." She looked again up and down the street. "It seems they shut off all the power. But I have a roof and I can offer you some dry clothes."

Turning to her brother, Joule mentally calculated the odds that the woman was a crazy psycho-killer. In their favor, they outnumbered her. Also, Joule figured they had already encountered worse than whatever this woman could bring.

"I have food," she offered, as though now trying to bribe the two ragamuffins inside.

Joule's first thought was that they had just come from stuffing their faces with pancakes. But that had been a while ago now, and she was suddenly hungry again. She must have burned off every sugar molecule she'd eaten.

The lure of dry clothes was winning out over the likelihood that an underdressed-for-the-weather serial killer had just popped out of a truck in front of them and was sizing them up as targets.

It was only then Joule realized the woman with the bright red, perfect spiral curls was still darting her gaze back and forth between them, waiting for an answer.

Cage finally spoke for both of them. "That would be wonderful."

With her hand still clenching his more tightly than necessary, Joule followed her brother and the stranger through the door and up the steps.

9

Cage was fascinated by the woman's springy, red curls, the skin covered in dark freckles, and the wide, green eyes. He was probably just as fascinated that she was dry as anything else.

Leading them up the narrow stairs, she stopped at the first landing where four doors with old, chipping paint—each in a different color—greeted them. The tiny floorspace was hardly big enough for the three of them to stand, and Cage tried not to crowd her. She turned what looked like an inefficient lock.

He'd learned last year about using proper bolts. Whoever she was, she hadn't.

She pushed the door open and flipped the light switches several times, as though the dead silence of the apartment wasn't a clue that the power was well and truly out. Her ineptitude was somehow reassuring. *She might simply be too dumb to be an axe murderer*, he thought.

She stood in the middle of the room and turned a circle, almost as though it wasn't her place and she needed to see what was around her. But then she went back to eyeing the two of them up and down again. "I'm going to get you both some dry clothes. Obviously, the dryer isn't going to be working, so it'll be a while before we can dry what you're wearing now. But at least you won't be actively wet in the meantime."

Or dripping on her carpet, Cage thought, even as he noticed that her words were stronger than her demeanor. She didn't sound as flighty as she looked.

She spun away as though she had her task, and nothing would hold her back. Walking through one of the doors from the small, main room, she headed into what must be a bedroom. Before she closed the door behind her, she quickly turned back around as though she'd forgotten something. "I'm Moonbeam, Moonbeam Winchester."

Well, that is some name, Cage thought, but he stuck his hand out. "Cage Mazur." Before he could introduce his sister, Joule's own hand came out, finally releasing the small, soft grip on his. "I'm Joule. I'm his twin sister."

"What were you all doing out in that rain?" Moonbeam asked, no longer focused on whatever she'd dashed into the bedroom for.

"It was an accident," Joule answered, all the while dripping a puddle onto the living room carpet. She explained how they'd gotten stuck, her words carefully measured. Maybe she was waiting to see what Moonbeam Winchester would offer rather than asking. "We weren't ready for a downpour like that."

Cage nodded along, thinking at least now their hostess had an explanation for why *his sister wasn't wearing a raincoat and was standing in one soaked sock.*

This time, Moonbeam headed into the bedroom and made it. "Let me see what I can find." The door swung shut behind her and she left the twins waiting to see what would happen when she returned.

Though he wasn't willing to walk around and ruin the carpet, Cage did move. Only then did he realize he was still holding onto his sister's hand in a tight clench. Dropping his overly firm grasp of Joule's wrist, he flexed his hands and worked through the pain to bring back the sensation that he'd lost some time ago.

Even as he and his sister silently made claws of their hands, Moonbeam popped out of the back room. She'd changed into a pale blue sweat suit and pulled her hair up, perhaps just tying the mess directly into a knot. In her arms were two color-coded piles of towels and clothing. Black for Cage, baby yellow for Joule.

Moonbeam Winchester didn't seem to mind that they left a trail of wet footprints as they went to change. A few minutes later, Cage breathed a sigh of deep relief as he emerged from the bathroom in a sweat suit that didn't quite reach his wrists or his ankles. She'd included thick socks— Moonbeam Winchester apparently thought things through. He didn't feel fully dry, but he was so much better off than he'd been five minutes before. The stress that rolled off his shoulders told him just how much he'd been carrying out in the rain.

He wasn't surprised to find that Joule was already dressed and waiting for him in the main room, her own hair now pulled up in a scrunchie that matched the pale yellow of her sweatsuit. Another Moonbeam Winchester thoughtful gesture, Cage could only surmise. Joule certainly didn't own anything like a puffy hair tie—or any pale yellow anything.

Their hostess was in the tiny kitchen, leaning over something that was making a clicking sound. It took him a moment to realize she had a laboratory lighter and Bunsen burner.

His eyebrows raised in a question and, instead of explaining her cooking arrangement, she simply said, "Coffee" before she turned back to the Erlenmeyer flask on the three legged laboratory stand.

He and Joule waited patiently while she got it lit, adjusted the height of the flame, and turned back to them. "I mean, I guess I can do tea, too. Oh! I have hot cocoa, but getting milk would mean we we'd have to open the fridge."

Her scattered conversation didn't go with the hospitality she offered or with the laboratory-grade setup she had on her kitchen counter. She must have finally taken in the looks on their faces. "Oh, sorry! I'm a chemist. Post-grad." She paused. "Stanford. Mudd." She spoke in the shorthand that, as students, they had learned to understand. She was in the Mudd Chemistry building.

Well, Cage thought *I didn't see that coming.*

"Freshmen," Joule replied quickly, getting her head wrapped around the anomalies in front of them faster than Cage did.

"Oh, wonderful. I remember being a freshman."

He waited for her to go on. But when she didn't, he decided that as his hostess, she deserved to let conversations drop. Instead, she simply shifted the topic. "Where are you from?"

He explained, giving only the general area, and in exchange, she replied, "I'm from Aspen and here." Then she pulled the hot water off the Bunsen burner using a pair of lab tongs, and poured it through a gravity filtration system and over the carefully measured coffee grounds. Cage was glad she'd mentioned she was a chemist, or he would have wondered if she had some kind of obsessive compulsive disorder.

After waiting the gravity system out, she divided the brew into mugs and offered them milk, even though it meant getting into the fridge. Then she surprised him by opening the fridge and plunging a hand in without looking to snatch out the half-and-half.

Moonbeam didn't seem to think this skill was unusual, so Cage kept his mouth shut. What she did say, as she handed out the coffee—which smelled far more wonderful than anything he'd had in a long time—was, "Well, this rain is much better than the blizzards and avalanches we were having in Colorado. What did you have?"

10

Ginnifer stomped out of bed, slapping her feet across the floor.

For the life of her, Joule could not figure out how her roommate woke up each mßorning already in a tizzy over something. But as Joule rolled over and opened her eyes, she caught Ginnifer's narrow stare.

"I'm using the bathroom." It was always announced like a proclamation, and maybe it was. Lord knew the girl spent enough time in there.

"Whatever." Joule managed to fall back asleep, but when Ginnifer began ransacking her own dresser drawers, it was enough to wake her again. She'd barely opened her eyes again before Ginnifer started speaking.

"Yesterday was full bullshit."

Why the girl insisted on both glaring at her and sharing whatever latest gossip she had, Joule didn't know. Ginnifer was a conundrum, and Joule was greatly looking forward to finding a new roommate next year. Maybe she should see about Gabby?

But her attention was pulled back to her clearly upset

current roomie. Gin often got mad if Joule didn't reply. It was easier to just say, "Oh?"

She expected to hear some hot news about a frat party or whatnot. But no, Ginnifer could not be that predictable. "There are still fifteen students missing from the flooding."

Joule sat upright, suddenly wide awake. *Students were missing?* "Who?"

"I mean, I don't know any of them personally," Gin gestured with the shirt in her hand, regally holding court with a towel on her head. "But a handful were in the basement lab at one of science buildings."

There was a pause for effect, and an eye roll that seemed to say no one should be in a science building voluntarily. This was the Freshmen-Sophomore dorm, affectionately called FroSoCo, and known as "nerd heaven." Joule and Gabby had had more than one conversation speculating on what Gin had done to get placed in this dorm where she clearly didn't belong.

"So, they seemed to have left the lab—the building security shows all of them leaving at about four yesterday afternoon—" *How does Gin even know this?* "But none of them made it back to their rooms." She shrugged. "They haven't been found."

She delivered the punchline like she was relaying the plot of a cozy mystery, in which someone stubbed their toe on a dead body and was delighted to have a puzzle to solve rather than being horrified there was actually a *dead body*. Ginnifer had slid into her clothes while she talked, but now turned and headed back into the bathroom, ready to apply her makeup. She was done lighting the kerosene she'd artfully poured.

Joule jumped to her feet, her flannel pajama pants and black T-shirt not rivaling the matching set Gin had left folded over the foot of her own bed. Standing in the bathroom doorway, she asked her questions. "How did you find this out? Is there a list? A search party?"

Missing students. Joule could feel her teeth clench. She'd been petrified of getting swept away. When the wave had barreled down the street and hit her, she'd felt the force of it. Had Cage not been holding onto her, she could have been one of the missing herself.

Ginnifer seemed happy to have the answers and talked while she applied her makeup, diligently replying to Joule's rapid-fire inquiries until a knock came at the door. "That's Holly. Can you be a dear and get that?"

Joule had never been a "dear" a day in her life, but Holly's arrival signaled the end of anything useful from Ginnifer. Opening the door, she waved her hand in an empty gesture. But as soon as the two disappeared, she climbed into her own clothes and headed out the door.

She found Max and Cage exactly where she expected to find them, in their dorm room, out cold. Their beds were in parallel, as were their soft snores. They had not had the benefit of Ginnifer applying whatever Hollywood *feng shui* had happened in her own dorm. They also didn't lock their door.

"Get up. Time to end the snorgasms!" she announced and watched as their eyes blinked open. It wasn't necessary to wake Max, but it hadn't been necessary for him to barrel into her on the street yesterday, either.

As the guys rolled over and looked at her through slitted eyes, she quit playing. "Cage, there are fifteen students missing from the flooding yesterday."

That was all it took. Both were out of bed in a flash, asking questions that she was forced to answer with Ginnifer-gleaned intel. The guys got dressed with little sense of moral decency, only ducking into the bathroom but leaving the door open so they could pester her with more questions she couldn't answer.

"I'm on my way to the student union. I figure I'll join a search if I can."

"*We*," Cage corrected. "We will join the search."

She smiled and turned to lead the trio out the door. "Let's get Gabby. I already texted Sky and Roxie."

They gathered near the student services building fifteen minutes later. Their arrival doubled the number who had shown up. Mostly, the volunteers seemed to be friends of the missing students. One couple was obviously parents, waiting to talk to someone. Taking point and talking to officials, Joule found herself quickly rerouted to a separate location.

Soon, they were on yet another quadrant of campus, where a volunteer in a fleece jacket stood handing out crackers and bottled water in front of a tent. It seemed like a legit operation and Joule saw that it was manned by the Palo Alto Search and Rescue Team.

"Hello, how can you help us?" the woman in the red fleece asked a little too brightly.

"We're here to help search," Cage offered, "but we are just students and not trained."

"*We're* trained," Roxie interrupted him, explaining that she and her sister had volunteered for S and R in the past. She quickly began asking about grids, dogs, number of searchers, and last known locations.

The woman in the fleece, despite Roxie's clear knowledge, addressed the entire group, including the newbies. "That's why we're here. Honestly, a good number of students with unknown whereabouts is normal at any given time on a campus this size. The school has been reaching out, and there's a system in place that's locating everyone. The problem with this group is that they left that building—" she pointed across the open grass to the science building Ginnifer had mentioned. Score one for the roommate's intel. "after four yesterday."

Another point for Gin.

"The footage is unclear, because of the rain. But there were six who left together. None have had any contact that we know about since they left the building. Their cell phones all track to a variety of points one mile northeast of here. But one by one, the signals disappeared, and the phone company was only able to ping one—which we recovered."

Joule couldn't stop her heart from pounding as she listened. For a moment, she wondered if the night hunters had come back, if people were being stalked and killed again. But that didn't make any sense. Fast-moving water did. Deep waters, feet getting shot out from under them, heads hitting something and getting dragged downstream— that made more sense.

She tried to fight her rising heart rate but failed until Roxie turned and looked at them. "Okay, Sky and I are going to lead our group. We're going to help with a grid pattern search. We have to do a check-in first, though."

Grateful to have someone more knowledgeable in charge, Joule trailed along and soon found herself holding hands with Cage on one side and Roxie on the other as they carefully moved, step by step, across campus streets and up against buildings as a single line.

"Usually, we do this in the woods," Roxie informed them. "I'm used to going around trees, not running into buildings."

"Aren't you usually searching for people, though?" Joule asked.

Their task was not to find the students, but missing pieces of plastic, scraps of clothing, a shoe, a wallet— anything that might indicate the students had passed here. She swallowed down memories of other bits of evidence she'd seen in the past. Torn scraps of fabric. A watch. Even a foot. All reminders of the people that had been stolen from her neighborhood. But now wasn't the time to see the past. She kept her eyes on the ground, scanning the grass, telling herself she was a robot.

"We always search for any kind of evidence," Roxie said. She was looking down at the grass, her eyes scanning only the space directly in front of her.

Joule did the same, but noticed that the water seeped up around her boots with each step. They left footprints full of standing water behind them, making it harder for the next round of searchers to find anything in the grass.

Everything will be alright, Joule repeated the words in her head until she saw it.

"Roxie, Cage. In the bushes."

"Don't get ahead. We don't look in the bushes until we get there." Roxie didn't even lift her eyes.

"No, it's this angle. I was looking around occasionally, like you told us, and I don't know if we'd see it when we're on top of it."

She'd seen some serious shit before. But it had been a while. She wasn't prepared for the open eyes that stared back at her.

11

"Let's go back to the dorms." Cage reached for Gabby's hand and slowly pulled her away from where they'd finally stopped their search.

Beside him, Joule was also herding her friend away. Sky and Roxie seemed unfazed by the death, mostly because they'd participated in SAR—search and rescue—in their hometown. Apparently, their town had needed a huge upsurge in SAR in the past three years. Cage didn't ask why or how bad it was that they were taking on teenagers.

Max was unfazed by the death, but mostly because he was Max. He had moments of brilliance, Cage had seen. Still, the vast majority of what flew at him didn't sink in. At least Max wouldn't have nightmares. Gabby would. He didn't know yet whether he and Joule would.

"Come on, we need to eat something besides energy bars." His sister stepped up beside her best friend, shielding her from the bushes where they'd found the first head.

"I don't think I can eat anything," was Gabby's response. But thirty minutes later, they were crammed around a too-small table eating burgers in the Old Union building. Gabby was stuffing fries in her face as fast as any of them.

Once they finished the food and the conversation waned, one by one, they fell away. Max got a call and headed out to see "a girl he liked." Sky and Roxie had a project to finish. Cage and Joule walked Gabby to the intersection nearest her dorm and then headed across the way to their own dorm complex.

He and Joule had chosen this dorm, the Freshman Sophomore College, from the pictures online. They'd read glowing recommendations from the students who lived there—surely the school had cherry-picked the glowing reviews. He didn't figure Stanford was any different from any other school, but he hadn't known then where his friends would live, or even who they would be. He had wanted a dorm in which he and Joule could stay close.

They'd always been together—both science-nerdy kids raised by science-nerdy parents. Their whole family had fit together, snarking at each other over the dinner table. Commenting on the denaturation of proteins in the chicken and just how much that meant their mother had overcooked it was relatively common Mazur dinner talk. But that had all dissolved over the past year.

He was trying to make a point to do casual things with his sister—share meals, go for walks, the kinds of things one would do with their only remaining immediate family and *twin*. Unfortunately, their last several outings had included almost getting swept away in a flood and now finding dead bodies.

Or rather, dead body *parts*.

"How much is that going to bother you?" He decided it was better to ask, point blank.

She shrugged. Then she looked sideways at him. "It doesn't bother me that he was dead. It's that his eyes were open—or the one I saw was. It's that he seemed to be looking out from under the bush." She paused for a moment and Cage felt the importance of what she was about to say taking shape. "At first, I thought he might still be alive."

He'd not realized that. Joule had been the first to spot the student. Roxie had been trying to keep his sister's group on track, apparently misunderstanding and thinking Joule had seen a scrap of cloth or piece of evidence. Well, it was evidence all right.

He'd watched from the other side of the wide, green lawn, where he was part of his own chain of hands that Sky commanded, as Joule had broken rank and run toward the side of the building, yelling "I see him!"

But then, she'd suddenly pulled up short. By then, Cage was already chasing after her as though they would pull the missing student, unharmed, from the well-tended bushes in front of the sociology building. The flowers had bloomed with the abundant rains and clung to the hardy plants despite the deluge. The colors—pink and red and vibrant green—had obscured the student beneath the foliage.

Joule's hand had whipped out, smacking him across the chest the way his mother used to if she'd hit the brakes too hard. She'd whispered, "It's just the head..."

He'd seen it then. As the words had washed over him, so had the knowledge that the color came from the hair and the scrap of a collar that wound around the neck. They'd all carried their phones, now holding pictures given to them by the Search and Rescue crew, so they could identify if they found something from one of the missing students. The hair and the fabric clearly identified Steven Wasby.

Gabby had run up beside Joule to see what they'd found and promptly lost her lunch.

Fifteen minutes later, the students had been turned away from their find. But they'd kept going, Sky and Roxie insisting that they were trained searchers. Before either of their groups found anything else, they heard whispers about a foot. Then, not long after that, the message came. Someone had found a foot. It was not Steven Wasby's foot. Most likely Ted Hatter's.

It was Roxie who spotted the third piece... an arm. Not Steven's nor Ted's.

The police were too busy cataloging the finds to participate in the search themselves. That was left to the volunteers, many of whom were clearly regretting signing up. One by one, they'd begun to tap out as this horror story proved it would have no happy ending.

Cage had seen a human foot being carried through the woods before. Still, he wasn't immune to the sick sensations that rolled through a person when the brain finally realized this wasn't a plastic piece but a real human limb... no longer attached to its human. So he wasn't surprised that the search team's numbers dwindled with each new find. But he told himself he could handle it, because these weren't people he knew.

He was getting ready to spout something innocuous into the air between him and Joule when she beat him to it. He would have said it was shame to waste the only sunny day they'd had. But as their boots squished through the still-soaked lawns of the otherwise pristine school grounds, she said, "You know what? It's not even that it was just his head. It's that everyone was wrong."

"Wrong?" He stopped walking but had to jump to catch up when she didn't.

"It wasn't the current that killed him. I don't know if they were saying that so we wouldn't worry or if they really believed it was the water. But there were bite marks on his neck. And his other eye was gone, probably eaten."

Cage was nodding along. He'd thought the same thing. "But it's not like the hunters."

"No," she agreed. "They bit and tore things to shreds. This was more like... fish."

"But don't fish eat things *after* they're dead? Then maybe the cops are right. Maybe the current did kill the students, and the fish just scavenged them." Cage was following the chain of his own logic as he spoke it, but his sister was already shaking her head, blond curls tossing with the vehemence of her conviction.

"So the current killed them immediately, and then the fish ate enough to sever the limbs and head? It doesn't make sense."

"Well, maybe—"

She was already cutting him off, turning around and staring back at him. "Look where we found those... parts! They were in parts of campus that were under at least a foot of water yesterday. Low parts that connected through to other standing water. When the water receded, that's where the... leftovers would have been beached."

She sucked in a trembling breath that told him even she didn't like what she was saying. "The water would have been high enough long enough for a school of fish to sever the limbs."

Oh, shit. He was starting to see her point. "You think it was the same fish that you and the professor found in the puddles on campus."

She didn't nod, just turned and resumed walking toward

the main entrance to their dorm. "I don't know. But the water wasn't *puddles*, Cage. We had *ponds*. And those gobies? They're carnivorous."

12

J oule headed across campus with a cloth bag tucked under her arm. It was full of color-coordinated sweats, washed and folded, ready to return to Moonbeam Winchester.

The chem lab where Moonbeam worked was somehow as far as it could possibly be from her dorm, yet still be on the same side of campus. Joule trudged the distance, listening as her feet squished into the still wet ground and wondering when it would finally dry out.

Five days, she thought as she looked up at the gray sky. It hadn't rained in five days, but it had been an unholy deluge, and today was the first time she'd been able to wear anything other than the rain boots she'd had delivered to replace the ones that had been ruined in the deluge. Still, the ground wasn't solid beneath her feet yet.

She and Cage had known about the foggy and rainy weather the Bay Area was known for when they chose to attend Stanford—or they thought they had. It turned out that understanding it in the academic sense was very different from living with it. There was enough sun that she would make it through the four years to get her degree, but she had not truly been prepared for the feeling that came with seeing real daylight so infrequently.

Maybe it was partly her own lingering trauma. Sunlight had been the only thing that kept the night hunters at bay. In her old world, bad things happened in the dark. For her and her brother, it wasn't just a dark fairy tale or an irrational fear. It had been their painful reality and it had torn their family apart.

Joule now found herself looking at the sky and desperately wanting to see the sun.

Still, they'd had five straight days with no rain. That was a bonus and she would have to take it. The grass was growing lush and green from the downfall and the careful tending of the school grounds teams, though standing water still remained in wide patches from the flooding.

She entered the Mudd Chem building, finding her way around only through logic. She'd never been in here before. The campus was plenty big and, being a freshman, she'd not yet started the chemistry courses she'd need for that possible engineering degree.

Checking out the elevator buttons, she chose the floor that matched the first number on Dr. Bang's lab. In a few minutes, she found herself pushing open the door. It was exactly where Moonbeam had told her it would be. Still, it was a little nervewracking walking into a lab where she didn't know the experimenters or what they were doing.

Reminding herself, *I hand-fought a vicious new species and survived to name it,* she straightened her back. She could walk into an unknown lab with a bag of folded clothes under her arm.

Weird? Yes. Survivable? Definitely.

She breathed easier as, for a moment, the lab seemed

empty. But then a student walked from around the corner a vial in his hand. The clear liquid he held was more threatening than any colored, TV-style scene could have been, and so was the bizarre glare he gave to Joule just for entering the lab as an unknown person.

"I'm looking for Moonbeam." She offered a smile, though it did nothing to change his expression.

"Oh, hi Joule." The chipper woman was a stark contrast to the serious Asian student who was still staring her down. Maybe she'd interrupted a timed experiment. But he rolled his eyes and went back to working in his own tiny lab space as though her mere presence was cause enough for his attitude.

Joule quickly handed over the bag. "Thank you for taking care of us during the flood. It's entirely possible you saved our lives."

"That sounds a little extreme," Moonbeam offered with a smile. Joule didn't elaborate on how the water had swept her feet out from under her.

They chatted for a few more moments and then Joule extracted herself from the lab and the borderline awkward conversation, offering up a parting comment. "My brother and I owe you one. Seriously. If there's something you need, please don't hesitate to ask!"

She was answered with a genuine smile and a, "You're so sweet. Maybe I will." Somehow, Moonbeam remained just like her name, even in this lab that seemed cold and sterile. Her bright ginger hair was rivaled only by her almost over-sweet attitude.

On the way back across campus, Joule now worked her own agenda. Other than avoiding Ginnifer, she wanted to linger a little longer at the puddles. She couldn't get too close without her boots, and she regretted not wearing them.

Then again, not getting close meant that she wouldn't find any stray body parts of missing students, either. She was wondering if the fish would have consumed most everything but the bones by now.

She was scanning the surface of her third remaining puddle when she saw it. Strings of bubbles wound their way through the dark water.

Shit, she thought. *This is going to ruin my shoes.*

She almost did ruin them as she stepped gingerly into the water, moving slowly until it just kissed at the fabric above the thick soles. She leaned over, trying to get a better look, and almost fell in.

With a sigh, and knowing her agenda had just increased, Joule backed away, managing—barely—to keep her feet dry. Still, she pushed close and examined several other small pockets of standing water on her way back to the dorm. By now, she was nearly running. The need to stay ahead of the world's emerging problems wasn't something she thought about anymore. Her quest was soul deep, burned into her very definition of herself after last year's fights and losses.

She veered to the right and headed into the corner store, where she bought herself a three-pack of plastic containers with snap-on lids. Back at the dorm, she filled her backpack with supplies and traded her shoes for her boots before heading back out.

Forty-five minutes later, she and three full sample containers were knocking on the door to Dr. Dean Kimura's lab.

13

"Why didn't you call me?" Cage heard a force behind his words that he hadn't intended. Only then did he realize he was far more upset than he'd recognized.

But Joule shrugged it away. "You have Max. You're busy."

He was shaking his head. "Max is always around, but I definitely have time for you."

Her eyes narrowed at him a little bit. *Didn't she have Gabby? Sky? Roxie?*

His sister was still shaking her head at him. "I just saw something, and I went after it. We're not barricaded into the same room at night anymore, brother. We're not the only two people in our house. And nothing was going to attack me. So I went."

She wasn't wrong. Not necessarily. But fifteen students had gone missing. Two had been found alive but injured. Three were still missing. The rest had been found in parts. Cage did not think being alone was as safe as Joule was making it out to be.

Did she really believe everything was fine? Or was it just

an attitude to cover that something was very wrong with the last rainfall?

Still, he wasn't convinced it was a good thing that the two of them weren't the only ones anymore. They'd been very careful about their safety when that was the case. She was his only remaining family. Though he let his anger drop, he added, "Take me with you next time."

She shrugged. "If you can be ready."

"I will." He meant it, but he wasn't going to fight over whether or not he should go. He tried to change the topic. "So what did you find?"

"Eggs." She said it with a little emphasis of pride. "That's what I thought they were, and I was right."

He frowned. "How do you know that you're right?"

"Dr. Kimura confirmed it. I was right but, also, I was wrong. I didn't find two kinds of eggs. I found five."

Cage was getting alarmed. As small and harmless as the eggs were themselves, this was becoming a terrifying scenario. Then he relaxed. "Surely, they were just insects."

But Joule vehemently shook her head. "No insects, no arthropods at all."

He thought for another moment. "Amphibians, then."

It made perfect sense. Amphibians would, *of course*, in the spring, be laying eggs in standing water that they found —especially if the water had been there for a handful of days.

"Yes," Joule nodded. And he was starting to say "Oh, good," and breathe easier when she cut him off. "But only one was amphibian."

"Fish?" He asked it with trepidation. It was an emotion he'd never thought he would associate with that word.

"All the other four were species of fish." She laid the

words out there, like she was turning over a winning hand in poker. But she wasn't happy about it. "It's not right."

"No shit," he replied, his hands rubbing at his face as though that would change anything. "We're not supposed to have fish on campus, except in the labs. I mean, they didn't just spontaneously generate in the puddles. That doesn't make any logical sense."

"Agreed." She wasn't as frustrated by this as he was. Maybe it was because she'd had time to process what fish eggs in the standing water on campus meant. Her words were calm and measured. "It means that we have a direct link from the Bay to campus."

"Aren't we too far away?"

"It feels like we *should* be. But the only other option is spontaneous generation of adult fish on campus last week. So has to be *something*, some path that when the water comes up, is giving these species an opportunity to get into our water."

Cage had to stop and think for a moment. The chatter had died down about the missing students. They were mourned, memorials had been held, and small piles of cards, flowers, and trinkets adorned the front doors of their dorms. But the general word on the street was that they had been caught in the flash flood and died because of the currents.

That isn't necessarily wrong, he thought. But Joule's little discoveries were becoming disturbing. "Do you know what kind of fish they are?"

"Not yet." She said it with confidence, so he wasn't surprised when she filled him in on what else she already knew. "Dr. Kimura said that two of the kinds of eggs, though different, were both plausibly goby eggs. So it's likely that we have several kinds of gobies—red-tailed and some other variety. There are apparently a metric crap ton of goby species."

"So it could just be that one kind of fish?" Cage asked. "Aren't these the same fish that you're suggesting ate the students?"

"I don't know anymore," Joule replied. Her tone and expression were easy for him to read. She was confident about the eggs and about the problem they presented. Now she was less confident about her initial theory that red-tailed gobies had been nibbling at the dead bodies of the missing students or even dismembered them. "When I lay it all out, it feels ridiculous. But I did just return our borrowed clothes to Moonbeam, because we almost died in that flood ourselves. And I did see large, live fish in the flood on the street and on campus later."

Cage was shaking his head, wishing the bad thoughts would dissipate. Joule's words were creating a sinking feeling deep in his chest.

"I'm beginning to think I need to stop researching. Since it just keeps getting worse the more I look," she said.

He almost laughed. There was no way his sister would ever stop investigating the world around her. Anything small or strange, anything she could pick up and put in her pocket, then learn all about it. That had always been her way. Given that their mother had never flinched at earthworms or dirty frogs hopping across their dining room table, Joule had never let go of the habit. In fact, she'd merely grown into it. Now she used plastic containers for her samples and took them to scientists for confirmation.

"I'm beginning to think," she offered up cheerfully, "that we should simply invest in kayaks."

When he frowned at her change of subject, she added, "I saw a few students tooling around campus in them the last time we flooded. It would certainly be safer than what we were doing when the water hit."

He didn't say it out loud, but he thought, *Good. She had something else to focus on.* Let Dr. Kimura follow up on the fish. Let the dead students disappear from their daily thoughts. They could just be an anomaly, dead from the flooding, eaten by the fish that had somehow gotten onto campus and taken advantage of what was in the water.

Even as his thoughts tried to dismiss what had happened, it didn't sound logical and didn't make him feel better. Cage told himself that it did both.

But just then, both their phones began beeping a harsh sound. He saw the expression on Joule's face as she managed to reach hers first. But the yellow bar flashing across the screen told him that they had just gotten a severe weather alert.

14

"What is this?"

Ginnifer's sharp voice pulled Joule from her unpacking and she looked up to where her roommate pointed to the writing on the whiteboard near their door.

"Gabby left it for you." Joule tried to shrug off the rude tone and turn back to the box she was cutting the tape on. It was large enough to take up half of her bed. The delivery man, having struggled with it himself, only got it as far as the front door of the dorm. She and Gabby had hauled it the rest of the way up, holding the awkward shape between them.

"She called me *Djinn*?" Ginnifer pointed again to the sign, her disdain clear. "*Really*?"

Joule just shrugged. Honestly, she hadn't thought Ginnifer would get the reference of that particular spelling. But her roommate tossed her dark ponytail over her shoulder and kept going. "I know what a *djinn* is. It's an evil spirit, and that's why I don't like being called *Gin* at all."

Joule almost smirked, but she tried to hide her humor

behind a complacent expression. Ginnifer was enough trouble, even without getting so easily offended. "A gin could be an evil spirit, too. You know, G I N."

"Funny." But the tone made it clear that Ginnifer thought it was anything but. As her roommate's lip curled and her eyes narrowed, Joule realized she wasn't certain if she'd ever seen Ginnifer with a true smile on her face.

"I'm heading out." Ginnifer offered this as though this might be information Joule needed to have.

"Have fun," Joule called back merely for something to say, and returned to using the side of her scissors to slice again at the overzealous tape job. Inside the box were three other boxes wedged tightly together, one much smaller than the other two.

Jamming her fingers down the side, Joule pulled the smallest box out. Even as she did, she heard the rain hit the dorm window yet again. This time, she didn't have quite the foreboding sense of dread. The boxes were probably the reason she was calmer.

Slicing the smallest one open, she found high-end, rubberized rain gear. Two sets.

"Excellent," she whispered to herself as she pulled all the pieces out to double check the sizes. She'd ordered a coat with a hood and a bill for each her and Cage. In addition to that, they now had waterproof pants with elastic drawstrings around each ankle. The pant legs were designed to fit over or down inside the rain boots she had. She'd insisted Cage order his own *real* rain boots last week. The lace-up duck boots he'd insisted on the first time were not going to survive any more severe weather.

Excited about her purchase, she held up each piece and shook out the gear for inspection. Then she put it all on, modeling it in the full length mirror Gin had insisted every dorm room needed. The head-to-toe yellow suit still had the fold creases pressed into it.

She looked like a complete nut.

But, she thought, after having had her feet swept out from under her and her umbrella yanked away, this was exactly what she'd wanted. When she'd placed the order, she was curious if she was simply wasting money.

Still, she'd managed to talk herself into it. It wasn't a waste if it made her *feel* better. And having the rain gear at hand now certainly did take some of the pressure she'd been feeling off her shoulders. While the rain on the window made her feel worse, the fact that she was prepared this time slowed her heart rate. Hadn't she learned she could do anything if she was prepared? Hadn't her father inadvertently taught them that being unprepared might mean death?

She pushed her morbid thoughts aside and peeled the rain gear off before hauling out the two remaining boxes and laying them sideways on the bed. She sliced the tape on each and poked at the folded rubber inside but didn't open them any further. Carefully, she folded the tops back down and slid them into the small space that remained under her dorm bed. They barely fit, but that was good enough.

Not kayaks. Joule thought she'd ultimately found a better solution. Though she'd initially figured she could order kayaks online, she had not been able to figure out where to store one. It certainly couldn't live in the dorm room. There simply wasn't enough space, even if she stood them up against the wall. Getting them up here and then down again when she needed them would be just as much of a challenge. Turning the corners in the stairwells with one of those things would have been prohibitive.

Keeping it outside would have meant she either had to

find a way to lock it up or risk getting it stolen. Joule had no issues with being the nutjob who had a kayak locked to the bike rack. She just hadn't figured out a way to secure it. The searches and the pictures and Q&A she'd found online hadn't been any help. So the heavy plastic kayaks were a no-go.

Inflatable ones had been available. But having a punctured kayak was the same as not having one at all. Maybe worse. Once she'd moved on to the idea of an inflatable— something she could store in a relatively small space—she'd also moved to the idea of being able to hold more than just herself inside the vessel.

What she had now were two eight-man, inflatable boats. They were made of extra thick rubber intended for ocean rescue and recommended for personal seafaring vessels. She breathed easier knowing they wouldn't be punctured by sticks or rocks floating along on campus. Even if the water was shallow, she could trust they wouldn't rip or puncture. She breathed easier and pulled the fabric of her oversized comforter down to cover the cardboard under her bed.

She'd spent hundreds of dollars on her new equipment. Then again, she'd decided that high-quality materials would be worth the cost.

Joule closed her eyes and felt her lips press together. She had not told Cage about the purchase yet, though she should have, long before now. For a moment, she entertained the idea of waiting out the thirty-day return window. But another thought followed immediately on the heels of that one: She would be angry if Cage had bought something this huge without telling her. So she hauled the now-empty delivery box down the stairs to the recycling bin and then headed to the other end of the hall.

Cage answered almost immediately when she knocked.

His face showed obvious concern at from misreading her expression. Wanting to get this over with and seeing Max lounging in the room, she pulled him into the hallway to tell him what she done.

She'd expected to defend her purchase, but all her brother did was look out the window at the end of the hall and say, "I'm glad you made me get the boots. And honestly, I think rest was a good idea, too."

Though she'd noticed when the rain started earlier, Joule hadn't looked out the window after that. Now she saw water pouring down in gray sheets so thick, she couldn't see the building next door.

15

J oule crossed campus more than a little bit irritated. The rain was merely a light mist today, the severe weather alert of three days ago never having quite panned out. Still, the air swirled wet and cold around her, making her jeans damp to the touch and the breath in her lungs a little icy.

That it was only mist was a good thing, she'd reminded herself as she'd grabbed her new, sturdier umbrella. She certainly would look like she'd fallen off her rocker, if she'd worn her full rain gear in this.

She and Cage and their friends had stayed inside during the hardest part of the rain. Luckily, it had passed in a few hours, and they hadn't had to trudge across campus or leave to get food before it had let up.

Despite the light quality of today's rain, her boots were still necessary. The already saturated ground was now splashing, rather than just squishing, under her feet. The land was doing its best to run off all the excess water, but it couldn't handle the volume.

Having grown tired of waiting for results, she'd emailed

Kimura this morning, asking if he'd found out anything else about the eggs.

His quick reply of "Yes" had irritated her further. He'd added, "I don't have a full species identification, but I do have more information. And I've been incubating them. If you'd like to see, come on up to the lab. I'll be here today until six."

If he had more information, why hadn't he reached out to her? She understood that she'd given him the samples for his research. But didn't he understand that she had a stake in this, too?

She stepped from the grass onto the concrete patio surrounding the Bass Biological Sciences Building and noticed the patio was covered in an inch or two of standing water. The flat surface had created an ideal location for pooling. Picking her foot up and setting it back down, she noted how muddy the water was and wondered if it had been here long enough for anything small to be swimming around below the surface.

Then she wondered if Kimura would still be here. It was going on four in the afternoon. She headed into the building, leaving her wet footprints behind and arrived at the professor's office, only to find it empty. Luckily, a sign hung on his door saying he was in the wet lab.

Great, she thought. *If only I knew where the wet lab was.* It took ten more minutes to find out that Dr. Kimura's lab was in the basement. She headed downstairs, figuring she'd come this far and didn't really have anything to lose at this point.

As she cautiously pushed the door open, she was thinking of the glare she'd gotten entering Dr. Bang's lab to look for Moonbeam. Joule was a little more cautious, but Kimura immediately popped his head up from behind a row of small aquariums and said, "Joule. I'm glad you came in!"

For a moment, her irritation at not being kept up-to-date fled.

"Did you come by to see the eggs?"

Maybe he just didn't have the social graces to know that he should have reported any results he'd gotten from her samples—not that she could have incubated anything in her dorm room. And not that she could trust Gin not to flush them down the toilet, or at least just glare at her every time she walked by. She decided to let it pass. "What did you find?"

"Well," he said as he walked across the room, pointing to a few specific aquariums among at least a dozen. All looked sparkling clean, with filters and running water. "I carefully split up some of the strings of eggs."

Kimura then motioned to the other side of the lab, where microscopes of various sizes and qualities stood. "I checked under the microscope to see if I could ID the species. But only of a few chosen eggs. I split the remaining eggs into three, roughly equal groups and incubated them in fresh, brackish, and salt water." He motioned across the rows to each tank as he mentioned the water type.

There were possibly a hundred different twenty-gallon aquariums lined up side-by-side here, each labeled on the end with masking tape and poorly handwritten dates and notes. The water in each of the aquariums was a slightly different shade. Joule had brought him seven strings of eggs from five locations that she'd put into three containers. It had turned out she had five different kinds of eggs. Surely, even if he divided them all up, it didn't account for everything in the room. But she nodded along as he talked. "What am I looking for?"

Joule rubbed her hands down her jeans, only then remembering that they were still damp and slightly uncomfortable. In here, the science pulled her mind away from the physical sensations bothering her.

Kimura walked her through his process, excitedly showing off each of the different portions of his experiment with her samples. Joule couldn't help but appreciate that he came off more as a teacher than a researcher.

"These are the gobies. There seemed to be two different species here, and I can't be positive they are both gobies. Still, that's what I think. Given that the fish we pulled out of the puddle were red-tailed gobies, we know that's the most likely possibility."

He was talking a mile a minute, and Joule was just as excited to keep up. "What other kinds of gobies could there be?"

"Yellow. The yellow gobies in the Bay are relatively large and also carnivorous." For a moment, his expression pulled to one side. Perhaps her question was slightly out of range. He turned back to another aquarium. "This is where I have them in freshwater, but even in just a few days, I can see they don't seem to be developing as well as those in the brackish water." He walked to a third aisle. "Here's salt water, and these aren't doing as well, either."

Joule was noticing that the filtration systems in each tank were slightly different. She'd leaned down to examine them when he turned, still frowning. "Why did you ask about them being carnivorous?"

For a moment, she paused. Maybe she was crazy. Then again, maybe she was traumatized. She had found a student's head in the bushes... and then later, an arm. But she thought if she didn't ask now, she'd never know. It wasn't as if she could look these things up on the internet. "The student that we found, Stephen—"

"We?" Kimura interrupted.

"Yes, I was out with a search party. A friend of mine is an SAR specialist—search and rescue. So she had a team and I was on it. We found Stephen... or we found his head."

"Wow," Kimura said, standing upright and tapping his fingers on the desk beside him. It seemed to create the sound of his thoughts. "I heard that they'd found parts of some of the students, but I didn't really believe it. I thought it was just sensationalist rumor."

"Oh no," Joule said. "It was real. And I found it, so I looked up close." She watched as he made a face. For all that he clearly loved science, maybe forensics wasn't his thing. Still, she continued. "I noticed that the neck area looked like it had been *chewed*. So I wondered if the gobies could do that. *Would* they do that while the student was alive or only if he was already dead before they started eating him?" She didn't really give him a chance to answer. "I know fish will eat soft tissue particularly quickly, and some fish will eventually eat everything but the bones if a body is found underwater."

She was now reciting the things she had read online, when she'd been curious about what might possibly have happened to Steven and Ted and the others. Kimura was nodding along.

"All of that's correct. But the head was severed?"

"Yes. As were the lower leg and the arm we found later." She watched as he grimaced again, but he'd asked.

"Where the bones broken or cut?" He kept digging, and she realized he was asking around something specific: Fish didn't bite through bone.

She thought about it. "No, I think just the connective

tissue around them was gone, and that was enough to take the bones apart. All the bones I saw looked whole." She shuddered that she could even say that.

He nodded. "But you asked about bites."

"Yes. It looked like something had been chewing on him. Maybe." She added the *maybe* at the end in case she remembered wrong. *Maybe I'm just crazy.*

He turned to her now, his attention completely removed from the bubbling aquariums beside him. "Gobies wouldn't leave bite marks."

16

C age had mostly shaken himself off by the time he reached to the basement lab in the Biological Sciences Building. Joule had called him in a rush. Luckily, he hadn't been up to anything to important.

It was Joule who swung the door open wide and looked him up and down as he peeled off the rubber rain jacket that she'd gotten for him.

"This works wonders. Thank you." It wasn't like they had a mother or a father to buy them these things anymore. But Joule's eyes stared hard at him for a moment.

"You're very wet."

It was a ridiculous statement, and it took Cage a moment to process it. "It's coming down harder now." He watched as she absorbed that, and he realized she'd not worn her full rain gear over here. She was in a jacket and her jeans.

Still, she led him into the lab, draping his wet jacket over a nearby chair and introducing him to Dr. Kimura.

Cage held out his hand. "She told me you were helping with the eggs she'd found and that you helped her catch the fish the first day."

Kimura nodded. "I'm hoping she'll major in biological sciences. She has the head for it." But he didn't seem to make that statement as an ego piece for Joule, merely as a commentary on what he'd been thinking. He launched into an explanation of what he'd done with the eggs.

Joule occasionally added her own punctuation. "I found these over on the oval." And later, "Those two were pulled from the same standing water, over between Campus Street and Galvez. By the visitor center and the stadium."

Cage blinked a little at the information. He thought his sister had been picking up things as she passed them. Seeing odd occurrences and following through. It now sounded more as if she'd been conducting a carefully organized survey of the water on campus.

"These two are the ones Dr. Kimura is following most closely."

Kimura chimed in, "I think they are likely elasmobranchii, but right now, their development isn't far enough along to identify anything more than that." He paused and sighed, "Honestly, that might even be wrong."

Cage was opening his mouth to ask what that word meant, but Kimura and Joule were both already talking. He held up a hand as they were verbally tumbling over each other, well past his ability to follow. "I thought there were five species she brought you. One amphibian, two possible gobies, and the remaining two were unidentified."

He watched as Kimura slowly nodded along, thankfully not offended by the pointed questioning. "Yes, they are. Would you like to see each of them?"

Cage was surprised at Kimura's candid openness, but he followed the man over to an aquarium and peered in, unsure what he was looking at. Joule seemed to already know what was happening, but wasn't that the way this whole season had gone? Joule seem to be slightly ahead of him on everything. Now, looking into the aquarium, Cage took a moment to locate the small section of eggs in the twenty-gallon space.

The glass was only half full and had a yellowish brown assortment of relatively natural looking rock on the bottom. The small, squarish eggs were not what he was expecting. Joule had shown him pictures of what she'd found, but the first ones hadn't looked like this, and he must not have paid enough attention as she'd flipped through all of them for him.

He'd been expecting clear, gooey balls with dark centers, strung together almost like pearls. They'd had a pond in the back yard at one house and he and Joule had caught the fingertip-sized frogs when they hatched in the spring. He'd seen those eggs, and he'd seen caviar. So the two clusters of small, whitish eggs, one with black dots inside, had seemed normal to him. But these were strange.

On a string that looked almost like seaweed, they were neither a chain nor a cluster. More like the way a fisherman strung up fish in a bunch. And they weren't round. These were flat and had a stringy, almost dry-looking texture. "I feel like I've seen this on the Discovery Channel or something."

Kimura smiled. "Exactly. The entire class of elasmobranch fishes uses an egg case like this. They vary a good bit and I'm trying to look up this particular color and size, and what's local to the area. No luck so far, though."

Cage was nodding along. At least he could follow this. "So, there's nothing particularly alarming about these eggs?" He gestured at the whole room, still not sure which aquariums were housing his sister's samples.

"Exactly." However reassuring the word was, Kimura's expression was still grim. "It's not the eggs themselves that are alarming—"

It was Joule who burst into the conversation then. She, too, motioned to the aquariums as though the whole room, bubbling behind them, was part of her evidence. "What the five kinds of eggs mean is that there's a link from the Bay to the campus—just like I thought. And that it's more than just one or two enterprising red-tailed gobies that made it here. Wherever the tunnel or sewer or valley is, it's channeling bay sea life all the way here. Anything that can handle brackish or fresh water has been invited onto campus with the rainwater!"

Her words hit him the way the cold water had the week before. A feeling of dread took hold as he realized the ramifications of what she was saying. She wouldn't like what he added, but he looked to Dr. Kimura. "It's not just the campus."

Joule's expression changed as he said the words. Had she forgotten? Pushed it out of her memory? They hadn't talked about it, but was it possible she hadn't seen what he saw?

Cage decided to tread carefully. "We were out—off campus—when the levee broke. We got hit by a crash current. We were over by Evergreen Park, trying to walk home, when the rush of water almost pulled us under. It could have killed us." He looked to Joule, still not sure if she'd seen what he saw when they were out. He'd not mentioned it again, just glad that they'd gotten through okay. "There were fish in that water, too."

Joule nodded, not surprised by what he said. "I think they were decent-sized."

"What's *decent*?" Kimura asked and waited while Joule

held her hands up to indicate. Clearly, Cage was not the only one who'd seen the dark bodies writhing in the water as it rushed past. He hadn't been certain enough to count it until now. He should have been talking to his sister more.

"Well then." Kimura crossed his arms as his eyes glazed and stared into the distance. "We have a problem." When he looked back at the twins, he seemed to have made a decision. "Joule has presented several options, and I think she's right. Either the students who went missing were washed away and died before the fish got to them or they were still alive when it happened. Were there any wounds on the arm that might have looked like the student fought something?"

Joule shrugged. "I don't know how we would know. All the parts were pretty bashed up, but they'd been in strong current on campus and down the street. There were cars, curbs, and who knows what else the water might have crashed them into."

"You're right," Kimura conceded, his eyes glazing a little again as he thought. "So, we won't know about that, but we do know that the fish got to them, and your sister says she saw bite marks on the body parts that were found."

Cage hadn't really thought about it. She'd told him the gobies were carnivorous, and he knew fish often ate bodies left in the water. But then Kimura told them something that didn't seem to faze Joule at all.

"When we think of carnivorous animals, we think of teeth. But many carnivorous fish are scavengers or eat their prey whole, and teeth aren't part of the equation. Gobies wouldn't leave the kinds of marks your sister saw. They're *relatively* small, and a human body left in the water is free food for most anything that comes by. Hell, even goldfish will eat a dead body."

Though it was silly, the comment about the goldfish let

Cage slow his heart rate a bit. Anything could have eaten the bodies. Even goldfish. He didn't like that image, but it did make him breathe a little easier.

"We now have two major problems. The first is the path from the Bay to the campus, and the surrounding area. Wherever it is, it's big enough to let multiple species through."

Cage thought about the walk over here and about how the rain had picked up. The ground had filled in behind him, every step leaving a footprint with several inches of water in it. But Kimura hadn't caught that concern and was still talking.

"The second problem is that we have something with teeth—"

Just then, Joule stopped the conversation with a sharp wave of her hand. Her face scrunched up, her eyes shooting up and to the left as her head tilted. "What's that sound?" she asked, then clarified, "Like dripping?"

"It's the aquariums," Kimura brushed her off. But Joule wasn't having it.

"No, I don't think it's the filters. It's different, and it just started a while ago." She turned away from them and began walking around the room, her head cocked to one side as she obviously searched with her ears and not her eyes.

Stopping suddenly on the other side of the room, she stood still under the bank of high, horizontal windows that looked out at the ground level of the campus. She first looked down and then up and then down again. Then, as Cage watched, she leveled her gaze at Kimura. "There's a puddle on the floor over here. And it looks like it's leaking from that window..." she pointed up.

Cage followed her gaze and saw that the water outside

was several inches up on the window. In the basement, they were well below the ground water level.

The building was beginning to leak.

Still, his sister's voice was remarkably calm as she announced, "The lab is flooding."

17

"**N**o, really. The lab is *flooding*."

Joule didn't yell it or flip out. She simply pointed out their potential demise without turning her head to look at either her brother or Dr. Kimura. Instead, she watched as the puddle rapidly expanded at her feet, encircling her boots as it moved across the linoleum flooring. Then, she followed the water trail up from the floor to the bottom edge of the window. It traced the mortar in the cinderblock, skipping over the not-quite-white paint.

As she watched, the small trail grew just a little wider.

Still without turning around or taking her eyes off of the tiny river on the wall, she added, "The leak has gotten faster. Even in the few minutes since I found it."

"Shit."

She heard the muttered expletive behind her and felt Cage's presence as he came up to stand next to her. The nice, high rubber boots he was now wearing meant he was in no danger from the puddle. It flowed past, barely brushing the blue polka-dotted rubber of her heels until it encompassed the entire area around her.

"It's the window," she announced, not that it really mattered. Leaking was leaking and they couldn't likely fix it now. "The casing isn't holding."

Because of the thickness of the basement-level walls where the construction crew had sunk the Bass Biological Sciences building into the ground, the window was set back in a deep recess. She could see the water running over the ledge, but not the bottom edge of the casing. Slowly, Joule walked backwards, knocking her hip into the corner of one of the long lab tables that held all the aquariums. She ignored the sharp pain and continued stepping back until she could see the black metal around the window's edge.

"It's not made for this," Kimura added, the tone in his voice telling her he, too, was examining the leak as carefully as he could.

Joule shrugged. "Well, it's not your ordinary rain."

Though Kimura was not a tall man, he was still just a little bit taller than she was. It was Cage who was able to stretch up and get the clearest view. "The water outside has risen above the bottom level of the window. It's not just raining hard against the glass, there's actually a rising water level outside."

Joule finally turned away from the window and looked at her brother and the professor. There was a very real possibility they were going to be stuck in this building. That this room would flood.

For a moment, the three of them only looked at each other as though someone would think up a quick, easy answer. None came.

Finally, Joule asked, "If it's an inch over the bottom edge of that window, what does that mean for the outside depth?"

Kimura thought for a moment. "The bottom of the windows should be right at ground level. So, whatever you see, that's how deep the water is outside."

"Which means, in some areas, it's probably already much deeper," Cage added, and Joule saw an unmistakable message in his eyes. He thought they should get out of here. *Now.*

"What about the lab?" she asked.

Kimura shrugged, but it was a false answer. As his eyes darted frantically around, he took stock of the bubbling filters and glass rectangles of fish and eggs, clearly trying not to panic.

The water level outside, if it was allowed into the lab, would be well over their heads. That was the major fallacy of putting important or dangerous things in a basement room. Every experiment would be ruined, and everything in the aquariums would wash away in the water. Because the rain and outside water were most likely fresh, a good number of the specimens would survive.

"What exactly is in the aquariums?"

"Too many species to name—"

But she pushed him, morbid curiosity adding force behind her tone. "Do you have sharks in here?"

He laughed. But he didn't say no.

Her eyes darted to the side and caught her brother's return glance, he'd caught the omission as well. *At least,* she thought *the aquariums are small.* If the sharks did get out, they wouldn't be big.

"I don't think anything would be able to get out of this room," Kimura offered as a small comfort. "Still, I'll need to be certain the lab is locked down as safely as possible before I leave."

"Even if you lock it up tight, it could still flood, and the aquariums could overflow. If the room is full of water, how would you ever get back in? Or how would the cleanup crew know what to do? I'm thinking they would open the door and find sharks on the other side."

But Dr. Dean Kimura was already shaking his head, seemingly not concerned about the thin layer of water that had already covered a third of his lab floor. "It's not sharks that I'm concerned about. I do have a few elasmobranchs in here, but they're not harmful. They're already found in the Bay, anyway, as is everything you brought me—I'm assuming." He looked pointedly at Joule as though she should realize her samples could "escape" too.

"The problem," he continued, "is that I haven't yet identified some of the eggs that you brought in, Joule. I have a few unknown samples of my own, too." He took a hard breath, thinking for a moment. "There are a few things that aren't native. So I don't know if they would survive. A lot of it wouldn't survive the fresh water. But clearly, more things than we thought *can* survive it."

Even as Kimura made her more and more concerned, Joule thought, *Cage is right. We need to get out of here fast.*

But Dr. Kimura was right, too. They needed to do something about the lab.

She'd heard of cities dealing with floods. When the zoo flooded, the animals died. But when the aquariums flooded, things escaped. "Do we have to kill all your specimens?"

There was a pause and she tried to soften the idea. "Or maybe just sacrifice the ones that might hurt someone if they had a random encounter with a human."

Kimura was shaking his head. "Hopefully, the water won't ever get that deep."

But the puddle was already halfway across the lab, creeping steadily further while they argued.

It was Cage who made a decision. "Forget the aquariums. Everything in here that is from the Bay, can get back to the Bay without harming the ecology. It would be no worse than jumping in the water out there."

Kimura had nodded along until that point. "Well, it's more like jumping directly into the Bay itself. That's a lot more species to encounter. And not everything is from the Bay originally."

Cage pointed up to the window, not really putting stock in Kimura's words. "We are about to get stuck in this building. And the question is—"

Joule was catching on now, and she easily picked up her brother's train of thought. "Where are we going to get stuck? We are going to get stranded *somewhere*. We probably have another ten or fifteen minutes before we don't get to choose. Before the water level gets too high outside to safely cross. We have that long to figure out where we want to go *and* get there."

But as Joule looked out the window again, she wasn't certain they even had that.

18

"I don't think it's wise to stay here," Cage told the professor, wondering, even as he said it if he would be taken seriously. Maybe he was out of line—just a freshman, trying to tell one of the professors what to do. Still, he pushed the issue. Kimura wasn't *his* professor or even his friend. "Do you have food here? Showers? Running water?"

"Yes, to all of it. We have a faculty lounge."

"Not on the ground floor," Cage stated it, but it was mostly a question. He realized his tone was more harsh than he intended. But every minute they stood here deciding shaved the odds of getting out safely.

He'd given his own raincoat to Joule. She at least had her boots on, and looked to have mostly dried out from the misting she got on the way over. In return, she'd handed him her umbrella. Kimura had dug an old jacket out of his office and handed it to Cage to replace the one he'd passed off to his sister.

"I have another. Here," Kimura had said, as he held it out to Cage. Cage found the sleeves were slightly too short.

But with the rain coming down like it was, he was not going to be picky.

Kimura continued, "I'm going to hang out here and watch the lab. Then I'll get to my car when I can."

Joule must have raised her eyebrows at him or something, because the professor quickly jumped back in. "I'm not staying in this lab, just in the building. Remember, the ground floor is above this one, and we've got another two feet before the water gets there."

"Is there even anyone else in the building?" Joule asked.

"Probably," Kimura said, though he didn't sound like he believed it.

Cage turned toward the door to motion Joule through it. Someone else *had* to be in this building. So the professor wouldn't be here alone. That's what he told himself.

Cage was leaving. They'd tried to convince Kimura to come with them, but he'd made up his mind, and it wasn't their place to save him.

Joule had argued in favor of heading to the dorm rather than staying here. Their building was several stories tall, and their rooms were both on the third floor. The water would have to get very, very deep before anything would affect them. Cage agreed.

"There will probably be a lot of students there and not much food," Joule said, "and we'll get soaked getting across campus but at least all our dry clothing is in the dorm."

But what was Kimura going to do?

"I don't know about getting to your car..." His sister managed to use a nicer tone than he would have as she tried one more time. "The weather report says we're looking at more rain for the next several days."

"I'll be good here." The professor shrugged her off. "I've got the faculty lounge. This is a really good excuse to eat everybody's food. There are vending machines and a microwave."

By the time Joule agreed, Cage was already out the door and heading down the hallway. Surely, she'd come quickly behind him.

He stepped forward at each doorway and put his face up to the glass. Cupping his hands around his face to shield the glare, he tried to see into the labs that populated either side of the hallway. The basement of the Bass Biological Sciences Building was dark, and it was hard to see. Still, he could see enough.

"Joule!" he called out, motioning her along, even as he pointed to the window of the door as he walked past. "That one's flooding, too."

"It's possible they are all are. This one's too dark to check." She was stepping up behind him and glancing into the labs to get her own view. The she took a few running steps to catch up. "Do we detour for food?"

Shit, he thought. "We're going to get soaked."

"Right. But the water's not as high as it was the other day when we were on the streets and the campus isn't like it was down in Evergreen. If it's going to rain for days the dorm will get ugly if we can't get out."

"Lots of students have food in the rooms," Cage pointed out with a frown as he headed into the corner and up the staircase.

Her words wove through their echoing footfalls. "Yes, and lots of students are probably not *in* their dorms."

He was nodding along. It was a Saturday, which meant the student population on campus would be a little lower. Also, the school officials had warned of hard rains and possible flooding. They'd told the staff and students to go home for the weekend if they could.

Joule was still making her case. "If the students are there, they're going to eat their own food. If they're not their dorm rooms, their doors are most likely locked. So those of us who are in the dorms can't break into anyone else's food stash unless we take an ax to the hallway."

She had a valid point. They should definitely hit up the small convenience stop inside the cafeteria and load up on whatever they could carry. "We need chips and drinks," he said with a sigh. He rattled off a list as he thought of things, instead of just openly agreeing.

His sister nodded along, having brought him around to her point of view. "No sandwich meats—nothing that requires refrigeration."

He almost said, *I have a fridge,* thinking of the mini unit that he and Max shared, but she was right. If the power wasn't already out, it would be soon.

Finally, they reached the building's exit door and threw it open against the pressure of the water pooling at the base. This time, Cage held his sister's hand firmly in his from the moment his foot hit the water. He was not up for a repeat performance. Being the last person in his family was something he wasn't even ready to contemplate. He held on tight as they splashed their way across the patio.

It was almost too dark to see which direction they were going. He reconsidered the idea of stopping for food, but Joule passed him by and tugged him along on their predetermine route. She was not stopping, and she wasn't giving up.

"We'll be fine." She said it as though she read his thoughts. Probably, she'd just read his hesitation, but she tugged him toward the cafeteria and brooked no argument as she rattled off what she knew. "We'll be high up. We'll have running water. And we've got to have *food.*"

Cage felt her hold jerk against his hand as her foot passed the edge of the patio and plunged into the grass of the lawn. Despite the warning of her sudden jolt, it was a surprise as his own foot sank into the squish of the soft ground he couldn't see.

He followed right behind her, one of his hands clutching hers and the other grasped tightly around his umbrella. The rain descended in sheets, pummeling him as he told himself they'd made the right decision and—despite getting soaked —the longer route was necessary.

"Sidewalk!" she announced, stepping slightly up and keeping him from stubbing a toe.

Her pace is too slow. The rain was getting heavier even as they headed for food and safety. So he stepped in front of her as he reached the other side of the wide walkway.

When his foot stepped off the edge, he found he'd sunk into much deeper water than he had anticipated.

19

"Just carry it over yourself." Joule pushed at her brother's hand that held the umbrella between them. Joule controlled her breathing, or she tried to.

It was too much like the last time they'd been caught in the rain, with the floods swirling at their feet. *When I almost died.* Though she'd thought she was ready, once again, she was unprepared for the water.

Her jeans were now soaked, and the two of them were only halfway to the store. Luckily, Cage was holding the umbrella with relative ease. There was no high wind today and no current rushing past her feet here on campus. But the still water was even more disturbing.

She held tight to Cage's hand with her right, leaving her left, dominant hand free, even though she didn't know quite what she would need it for. Still, she wanted to be ready. Her fingers itched for the grip of her bow. For the feel of the string pulled tight against her skin as the nocked an arrow and prepared to let it fly.

She'd put the bow away after the Night Hunters had

been taken care of, but now she wished for it again. It might not provide much defense against anything in the water, but she wanted the feeling of protection the bow and arrows afforded her. She wondered if her brother was still carrying the gun he'd kept at his side last spring. It shouldn't be possible for him to get the firearm onto campus, but Joule didn't put anything past Cage.

She didn't ask, just focused on the walk in front of her and lifted her feet out of the puddles that deepened with each step. The water in the middle of the quad was more than a foot high, threatening to pass the tops of her boots in a few more minutes if it kept rising.

They moved as fast as they could with the water fighting them the whole way. It sucked at their feet and attacked them from the sky.

Joule's eyes darted upward to check if the rain was maybe waning. It wasn't. The gunmetal color told her this was just the beginning. She looked down into the water, in case anything was slithering past her feet, and steeled herself for something to bump her. Next, she checked in both directions.

To the right, she spotted something.

Watching as the shadow moved, she tried to discern if it was a human form or just a shadow from a cloud. Her brain could be making up the shape she saw.

Joule watched as the shadow trudged several feet forward. If it was a person, maybe he was heading for the safety of one of the buildings. She couldn't tell what his path was, only that he was alone.

There was definitely safety in numbers here, and she was glad to have her brother's hand tightly in her own. Her eyes darted back to the right and saw the shadow had grown smaller. As she frowned, she saw what looked like hands flailing into the air as the shadow—*man?*—slipped under the water.

"Cage!" She was tugging on his hand, pointing to where she'd seen it. "I think I just saw someone go under."

She was splashing through the water, tugging him along behind her, aiming toward the now-empty space where the man had once stood.

"Where?" His head turned rapidly as he looked for what she'd seen. "There's no one here."

"Not now." She was still high-stepping through the depths, fighting gravity and the suck of the water as she went. "But he was there."

Cage tugged back. "We can't go over there for nothing. We have a goal." He pointed upward, his finger aiming along the shaft of the umbrella he still clutched. "And the water is still coming down."

"I know, but if someone went under, they need help." She was frantic. Minutes were passing. If he was under, he'd be dead. Struggling to take more steps, she tugged against the anchor of her brother's unmoving body. He'd planted his feet, refusing to go farther.

"How certain are you that you saw someone?" As gray as the day was it was hard to see anything more than twenty feet away.

Taking a breath, Joule confessed. "Maybe eighty percent."

"Is that enough?"

Shit, she hated when he did that. He wouldn't tell her no, but he'd make her call off the dogs. He'd been doing that since they left the house behind. "No. Maybe. It's a life. He was alone."

"Who would be out here alone?"

She didn't know the answer to that. She took three more

steps and this time he followed. She practically ran, until something bumped at her feet

Whatever it was, it had slithered away as quickly as it had come, and Joule fought the roll in her stomach. Still, she kept pushing forward. Now she was almost jumping, leaping to one foot then another, making enough of a splash that she somehow managed to get even wetter than she already was. *Oh well*, she thought. She'd known she wouldn't be dry by the end of this.

She was much closer to where she'd seen the figure go under the water when she realized the water was sloshing up and over the edge of her boots. It was getting deeper with every step. Even as she thought that, a tug pulled her arm and her brother hauled her backwards, stopping her forward momentum.

"It's too deep here," he told her.

"Yes." Joule had stopped abruptly, but she didn't turn to look at him. Her eyes kept scanning the open water in front of her. There was no main current, but underneath the relatively serene top layer, swirls and eddies appeared to be working on some secret plan. It was probably only water running down into now-hidden drains, creating eddies they couldn't see from above.

She examined each spot where the surface rippled or swayed, looking for any kind of clue.

"There!" Cage pointed and her eyes flicked to where he motioned. "What is it?"

She didn't know. Lumps of something moved slowly together in the water as though pulled along by an unseen force. Whatever it was, it didn't look alive.

Her foot lifted as though to take another step of its own accord before she consciously remembered how deep the water was getting. In one more step, the water would be pouring into her boots. But she had a different thought.

She looked back at Cage. "Hold tight."

Twisting her hand and wrapping her own grip tightly around his wrist, she nearly forced him to do the same for her. Once it was secure, she leaned slowly forward, using him as her anchor. Joule tried to keep the tops of her boots above the surface, but her main focus was her hand, reaching out gingerly as she put several fingers into the water and tried to create a small current to bring the item closer.

Whether or not it worked, she didn't know. But slowly, the object moved and as it came nearer, she saw that it was a lump of swirling brown fabric. "It's a coat."

She might have just left it at that, but the coat was still moving, a little bit of forward momentum helping it drift closer and closer to where the twins stood. With their four legs planted side by side, they watched as the piece came almost within grasp.

At last, Joule leaned over one more time. Using her brother as a counterweight, she reached out and touched the edge of the fabric. She scraped at it several times before finally managing to snag a piece and pull it forward. The fabric dragged in the water, heavy and wet, making her frown until the garment slipped and revealed what had been weighing it down.

Joule saw what was left of a torso.

20

I t was pure reaction: Cage yanked Joule's arm. It was only after he did it that he stopped to think that he might pull her shoulder out of the socket. *The last thing they needed was another injury.*

The first words out of his mouth were, "I'm sorry!"

The second words were, "We have to get out of here."

His sister nodded back, a small tight move of agreement interlaced with fear. She turned and opened her mouth, looking like she was going to speak. Instead, she squeaked, "It was chewed."

Just like the others, he thought.

The idea that something in the water was chewing up human beings and leaving leftovers was more than Cage could handle right then.

He turned and began trudging away. The water was as deep as his boots, easily more than a foot. *But certainly less than two feet...* he thought. Estimating flood level heights wasn't a skill he'd ever imagined he'd need. Though after last year, he should have realized that nothing was off the table.

"What could survive in eighteen inches of water?" Cage mused as he pushed forward. He didn't realize at first that he'd asked the question out loud.

Joule looked at him almost as though he was nuts. "A lot of things, apparently. The red-tailed gobies were in less than a foot of water... and they were thriving." She paused and then answered his next question before he could ask. "And no, this wasn't the gobies. Remember? Gobies don't leave bite marks."

The best course of action right now, as they stood in the drizzle, was not to think about the body. Cage had far more pressing matters. They walked on, leaving the torso tangled in the jacket floating slowly away from where they stood. What else could they do? The rain was coming down just a little harder now.

In unison, the twins aimed themselves toward the cafeteria, reworking their original path.

"It makes more sense," Joule offered up, her voice now sounding as though this were an ordinary trek to stock up on chips and soda, that something else is happening to the people—something not in the water. Then the floods are dislodging the bodies."

"Body parts," Cage corrected, high-stepping carefully and thinking that even if the water did slosh up over their boots, it would be okay. The water might seep in, but anything swimming around would have to chew through the thick rubber to get to him.

It was small comfort. But he took it and raised his eyes to the gray horizon, looking for landmarks. He was familiar enough with the buildings on campus now to navigate by watching the corners and the faint colors that penetrated his vision. That was all they could discern through the dark day and the water in the air.

They were almost there. The squarish shape in front of him had to be the Coffee House.

Just as he took a step forward, something bumped at the side of his boot. He plowed forward, gritting his teeth and telling himself to ignore it. He would not try to determine whether his foot had touched an inanimate object or a live one.

The water was dark—a deep, deep green, so dense it was almost black. Not muddy, or silty. The color was probably a testament to the high quality of the Stanford groundskeepers. But right now, Cage would have preferred dirt in the water. It might have shown him better where the things were moving underneath.

Had there been any sunlight, they would have seen it reflected back to them. Instead, the surface gave them only the gunmetal gray of the rain coming down.

The building materialized in front of him, and Cage began to pick up his pace. He would have tugged his sister along, but she was already right beside him, maybe even a foot in front. Both of them rushed ahead, anxious to get inside somewhere.

Only as he stepped onto the cement patio did it occur to him that maybe the building would be locked.

He still held the umbrella over his head, a meaningless gesture, since he was already soaked. He still held Joule's hand firmly in his and wasn't going to let go.

"You've got to get the door," he told her and watched as her slim hand reached out, grabbed the handle and tugged, only to hear the click as the heavy door denied her entry.

She tugged again, but the door held firm.

21

N o, she thought. *No!*
     Joule yanked three more times at the door,
     only to be thwarted by the heavy bolt. Surely
someone had been caught inside, just as they had been at
the science building. But as she peered through the door
glass, the hallways seemed too dark to be holding people
at all.

Was the darkness because the building was shut down,
or simply because the power was already out? The water
was high and getting higher. Surely the whole campus was
already experiencing problems.

Reaching up her free hand, Joule smacked her fist
against the glass, harder each time, and watched as Cage
folded up the umbrella. He set it aside as if the small awning
they stood under was enough protection now. She feared
the water might sweep the umbrella away, but the move
freed his hand so he could help her beat on the glass. They
made enough noise to alert anyone who might be inside.

Her brother stopped for a moment and cupped his hand

around his face as he peered in to see if their noise had brought them any progress.

"No," Joule said again, only this time it was a a sigh of defeat than a rail against an unjust universe. Still smacking at the thick, clear barrier that guarded the building, she felt the entire middle of her chest sink.

Slowly, she began to catalog what food she might have had stashed in the dorm. What things of Ginnifer's she might eat... maybe the lovely fruit on the bottom of her Greek yogurt. Or a handful of chips made out of some kind of designer root, but certainly not potato. The weird juice blends made with whey would go bad quickly. Joule wondered how hungry she would have to get before she broke into those, too. But her plan only worked if Ginnifer wasn't in the dorm eating her food herself. Joule didn't think her roommate was one for sharing.

The rain was supposed to come down for three straight days. Maybe more.

She found herself praying that the weather report was wrong again.

Smacking the glass one more time, Joule felt the hit hard enough to bruise her hand. Hope flickered with the dot of light she spotted wavering down one hallway. She began shouting "Hey!" and banging on the window harder and harder, watching as the small puddle of light grew larger and larger until, at last, it came around the corner.

It was a flashlight followed by a tall, thin man in uniform, keys dangling from his pockets. Clearly, someone from the grounds staff.

He must have come down some stairs to see them, because the first floor was covered in water sloshing at his feet. This building was higher up than the Bass Sciences building and higher than the middle of the quad where they'd just passed. Her feet weren't in danger of the water topping her boots here, but his black-soled sneakers were getting wet as he waded toward them.

Luckily, he didn't tell them the building was closed. He just turned the key, opened the door, and said, "Come inside." Then he looked pointedly at the floor and added, "Get as dry as you can."

Joule nodded at his wry tone. Normally, she would have had a comeback, but not today. As she crossed the threshold, she realized the relentless drumming noise from the outside quieted as he pushed the door against the water, locking it behind them.

"Why did you lock it?" Cage asked. "Other people might be out there."

She'd barely been forming the same thought herself. But the janitor—or superintendent, or whoever he was—merely glanced at them sideways as he headed back down the hall, his flashlight now lighting the way for all three of them. "I don't trust what's out there. If it's people, I'll let him in."

His tone brooked no argument and seemed to shut down the conversation, but Joule felt her eyes flick toward her brother and wasn't surprised when his gaze met hers.

They weren't the only ones thinking disturbing things about what might be under the surface.

"We came to get food," she offered as sweetly as she was capable, which probably wasn't very much. "We're on our way to our dorm."

His eyebrows raised and he pointed almost too casually down the hall. "Coffee House is under three inches of water, too," he said. "And there's no one there to ring you out."

Joule reacted immediately and felt her brother's hand twitch where she still grasped it. Even safe inside the building, even in the very low water, they weren't letting go. But rather than get irritated, she forced herself to a more subtle approach. "We're starving. We'll pay for it. We have our cards and we can ring ourselves out." When he seemed about to balk, she added carefully, "We really need food."

His face had stayed hardened until the last two words, as though he considered protecting the building more important than feeding the students, but then something shifted. "There's no power. Can't ring you out now anyway."

"We'll come back and pay for it when the rain stops," she volunteered quickly, hoping that she'd put enough confidence behind her voice that he would agree.

He took a moment thinking, and Joule watched as her brother pointedly turned and stared at the large, floor-to-ceiling glass windows behind them. The water was still coming down.

What would happen to them if this man denied them food? Surely, if he stayed here, he would have access to everything in the coffee shop. She glanced down at the keys on his waist for a moment, hoping she was obvious. He had the place to himself. He could can get into everything and eat whatever he wanted. He might even be able to open the professors' desks upstairs in their offices...

"Make a list of everything you take," he barked, his words abrupt and harsh as he pulled a key from the giant ring and unlocked the door.

They didn't have to be told twice. The twins rushed frantically around the store, but it still took longer than she had hoped. She'd had to go behind the counter and find bags so they could carry everything. They got bottled drinks—juices that would hold up until opened.

"Water," she called out to her brother, thinking that while they might have a running tap and be able to shower and wash things, drinking that water might very well become another story, and fast.

Nodding, he opened a third bag and stuffed it full of pre-packaged sandwiches and bags of chips. The trip from here to the dorm was not just going to be wet, it was going to be heavy and awkward.

Once they'd gathered everything they could hold, they took it to where the security guard waited at the counter. Joule would have preferred to go right out the door. *Time is wasting.*

He was already standing at the counter with a pen. Instead of letting them note their purchases, he catalogued each piece himself. Though Joule wondered how well the plain printer paper with the Bic pen's blue ink would survive this flooding. It would be so easily ruined by a little water. She had no intention of stealing this stuff, but his careful documentation seemed like overkill.

He turned the paper toward them when he finished. "Print and then sign your names and add your dorm Names and room numbers."

She did this as quickly as she could, realizing as she swished her signature at the bottom that she'd unlaced her fingers from her brother's a while ago to grab the food. She handed him the pen, then uttered a quick "Thank you."

She turned to leave before remembering that the janitor had them still locked into the building. After reading their information, he folded the paper and stuck it in his pocket, then turned the other direction.

"This way," he motioned, leading them to the other side. "It's a shorter path to FroSoCo out this way."

Joule smiled. This time, her "Thank you" was soft and sincere as they followed him across the floor to the back door. The janitor frowned as he fitted one of his keys into the large bolt and turned the lock. Even as he did it, the surge of standing water outside pushed the door open against him, almost knocking the three of them onto their butts. If not for the counterbalance of the weight of all the food she carried, Joule would have gone right over.

"You should stay here," the old man said suddenly seeming worried for their safety.

The twins looked to each other and didn't have to say anything. Joule knew they'd communicated. It was a no. They were going back to the dorm.

"Thanks anyway," she said, turning to trudge through the water again. She stacked the bags up one arm, knowing it would hurt like a bitch inside of five minutes, and reached out her other hand and locked it with her brother's. Then together, they stepped into the rushing water, and back out into the gray.

Cage had brought the umbrella inside and carried it out into the rain again, but as he tried to open it, the wind kicked and fought him. Muttering "Fuck me" as he tucked it under his arm, he instead pulled the hood of the jacket Dr. Kimura had lent him closer around his face.

They tried to hold on to everything as she put one foot forward and felt the water surge against her.

22

"Oh my god."

Joule watched Ginnifer's expression turn to horror as she pushed past and entered the dorm room, not caring if she brushed up against her roommate.

She and her brother were soaked head to toe. The plastic bags from the coffee house, heavy with the food they had picked up, were still dripping water even after being carried up several flights of stairs.

Ginnifer had looked at them as though they were visitors from an alien planet as she quickly stepped back and let them into the room.

The twins had come to Joule's room first. She'd explained to Cage, "My clothing is there, and I can change. Then we'll go settle in at your room."

Slipping into the bathroom, Joule rapidly gathered what was necessary for an overnight bag. She would conceivably be staying stay with Cage and Max for several days. While she figured she could come back here to grab what she needed, the rain pounding at the windows was beginning to make her question that idea. She shoved a handful of extra items down into the bag.

It took five minutes for Joule to get as dry as she could and slip into a warm change of clothing. Rolling up another pair of black jeans, she added them to several pairs of dark socks and a fistful of T shirts she shoved into a cloth grocery bag.

Her hair was still dripping when she stepped out and gathered up the food she'd left on the bed. The bags had soaked small patches into the foot of her bedspread where Holly was now spread out on the comforter as though she owned it. Holly glared rudely as Joule picked up her own things off her own bed.

Her roommate's "bestie" was not Joule's favorite person, and she didn't even give her a second glance as she and her brother headed out the door and down the hallway to friendlier quarters.

At Cage's room, Max must have heard the doorknob start to turn because he pulled it wide, almost yanking Cage into the small dorm room as he began gushing at their arrival. "Oh, thank God, man. I've been texting you, hoping you were holed up in the science building."

"We were there," Cage said, starting to set the bags down onto the floor. Here, they wouldn't get the beds wet. They'd be staying. "But we realized we needed to grab food and come back this way. If it does last the three days the weather is predicting, we'll be without power—"

"Already out!" Max said, looking up and around the room as though that explained everything.

The light that was coming in was natural and brighter than what Joule had expected, given the grayness of the day outside. But Max was right. That natural light was all there was.

For a moment, Joule hoped that was a good sign and the storm was turning. She sent Cage off to change out of his wet clothes as Max dove in to unpack the bags.

She'd bought as much food as she could carry, not really thinking about feeding the big, beefy food-bin that was Max. But it was what it was, and they'd planned to share.

He lined up the juices by color, saying, "Let's figure out what we need to do first and then only open the fridge once."

Joule nodded along. The plan was solid, though the color line-up of the bottles was unnecessary. It reminded her of her father, and she pushed down the lump in her throat. "Good idea," she told Max, knowing that the dorm-sized fridge unit—though large enough—was now no better than a cooler with the power gone.

She helped Max situate things, clearing space on a shelf to create a makeshift pantry. Thinking that maybe if they watched *the food supply as it diminished, they'd be more careful about it.*

At last, she sank down onto the nearest bed, Max's, as she wiggled her toes. Her skin still felt wet.

Joule was contemplating whether she would ever get her feet dry as Max looked over at her and asked, "Is the lobby dry?"

"No." She shook her head.

"I was wondering. I mean, I went down to clear out the vending machines while the power was still on. The water was starting to creep under the door then. That was a couple of hours ago."

Smart, Joule thought, even as Max added, "I only got a few things. Unfortunately, I wasn't the only one with the idea to raid the lobby for snacks. Good news, all the food got bought. So nobody's going to starve while food's trapped on the other side of the Plexiglas." He grinned.

Joule didn't think a little clear plastic was going to stop anyone in their dorm complex, but she didn't say so. She looked at the bathroom door, where sounds from the shower offered a more consistent rival to the rain. Cage was still taking his sweet time. Apparently, he'd decided to enjoy a shower while the hot water still existed.

Max turned and looked Joule in the eyes. "Cage told me you were going to go visit some professor who was studying the fish that came in with the flood."

Joule only nodded, somewhat surprised that Cage and Max had had these conversations about her. But Max kept pushing. "He said the professor said some of the fish were *carnivorous*."

He wasn't wrong, though she didn't know how much of a problem that was. She relayed to Max everything they'd learned and breathed a small sigh of relief as she heard the water shut off in the bathroom. Her brother should be out soon.

"But if gobies don't bite, then what did that to the students? Those were bite marks! I saw them myself."

She could only shrug. "That's the problem. We do know it isn't gobies, but we don't know what it is."

23

"We should head downstairs. Check out the lobby." Cage lobbed the idea into the silence that had grown in the tiny dorm room.

Seven of them were crammed into the small square of space. Him and Max, of course, as it was their room. And Joule, since she had arrived with him. Roxie and Sky had shown up not fifteen minutes after the water in the shower had finally run cold.

They arrived with bags of clothing and more food, announcing "We come bearing gifts!" Their dorm, while relatively close by, had started shorting out as soon as the water went under the door. Several vending machines on the first floor were plugged into sockets recessed into the floor, and those had been the first to suffer from the water.

Cage had watched as Joule's eyes widened and then rolled toward him. He was grateful that their dorm was much newer. Maybe someone had anticipated flooding. There were, after all, college kids on campus.

"We went out a window," Sky told them, as though it

were an everyday occurrence to try to avoid getting electro-cuted in the shallow water in your dorm lounge.

They had arrived wet, but with waterproof packs, carrying their dry clothes and food. It was Roxie who grinned. "We almost literally jumped ship."

Gabby had shown up not much later with Marcus in tow. The seven of them had spent a while shuffling around, setting up camp, rearranging the growing food stores, and figuring out where and how to sleep.

It was Max who found an open door down the hall and a room with no one in it. "If they don't come back, it's free beds."

Cage had agreed. The floor wasn't a good place to be, and for all that they had managed to amass, no one had brought sleeping bags or pillows. But for a while, his heart was a little bit lighter. His friends were all safe, even if they might not have enough to feed them all.

It was Gabby who'd unpacked the biggest arsenal, announcing, "I stole it from my dorm fridge."

Though Cage wasn't sure why it would be stealing if it was her fridge, he didn't ask. She unpacked item after item from her duffel bag, and Cage was grateful to see it.

Gabby next handed out slices of meat and cheese. "Roll them up... or something—" she instructed as she watched Max open his mouth and drop the slices in. "It's now or never. There's no fridge."

After they'd sorted the food by what would go bad first, they chatted about mundane things like classes and acted as though the day outside wasn't horrifying. But it had only grown darker. Though there had been enough light to see by when he and Joule had come in, now the only light came from their cell phones.

Eventually, the room had grown quiet. It was almost

completely dark. Max had nodded off to nap. Cage had read for a while. Without any verbal agreement, all of them had turned the brightness down on their devices in an attempt to save battery life.

Several hours later, Joule spoke softly over Max's snores. "We might be here several days, and we don't have battery backup for all of us." Cage's eyes had flitted to the pile of double-A batteries and portable chargers. For a moment, he wondered if anyone was holding out, keeping back something valuable without telling the others. But he shrugged it off. He didn't think his friends would do that.

Joule was right and he spoke up. "I think we should turn off half the devices and share the rest."

No one argued. Only Gabby held up her phone and slowly pressed her thumb until it went black. Roxie and Sky looked at each other, and Roxie quickly followed suit, holding hers up and clicking it off. Cage went next. That made half. It felt weird to not have it on. But they'd all heard the weather reports; they were gearing up for at least several days.

It only took a few minutes for his mind to wander away. "Someone needs to go check out the lobby. See if there's anything worth salvaging, or any news about the campus..." He didn't wait for responses, just began pulling on his boots, even though the sensation made his muscles curl. Bad things happened when he was wearing these boots.

"I'll be back in probably ten to fifteen minutes." He was standing up and about to walk out the door, but Joule was shaking her head at him.

Sky moved swiftly in front of him, staring him down. "No one goes alone."

He watched as Roxie stepped up beside her and tipped her head in agreement.

The movement of their identical faces, the way they lined up like a wall against him, made Cage wonder if something had happened to them on the way over... something that made them doubt their safety.

"I'll come with," Max volunteered from where he lay on the bed, suddenly awake. But as much as Cage loved Max, he knew his roommate wasn't the best head in an emergency.

Joule seem to catch on. "You should stay here, Max. If Cage leaves, then you're the one who knows where everything is in the room."

Cage was grateful when Max took Joule at her suggestion and nodded. It looked almost as though he had volunteered bravely but didn't really want to go.

Even as she was talking, Joule was pulling on her boots. Roxie was joining them, the two having seemed to decide that Sky would hang back. Silently, the group split into two.

Marcus was the last to step up, but Joule put her hand out to stop him. "Do you have boots?"

His bag was almost the size of a small suitcase. He grinned. "Oh, yeah," and pulled out a pair of Army surplus waders, the likes of which Cage had never seen before.

A few minutes later, they headed out the door and down the hallway. Their first steps felt like breaking the seal on something big. Cage suppressed a shiver. The group headed toward the lobby, all quiet for once in the dark staircase. Pulling two flashlights from his pockets, he held one out to Roxie. "Use this. Don't waste your phone light."

There should have been more light in here. It wasn't the emergency stairs, but the main route, spotted with windows. However, the light outside had shrouded almost as though it had been snapped off. The flashlights were all they had.

Though a few heads poked out of dormitory doors and

watched as they passed the second floor, no one said anything. That alone might have been the most telling.

When they hit the bottom floor, he gingerly lowered his foot into the water until he found the solid floor beneath. He'd come down this staircase hundreds of times this year, but with his vision obscured, his sense memory of the distance from the bottom step to the ground level was gone.

Holding hands, the four waded through the water that had seeped into the lobby.

"It's not up to the outlets," Roxie informed them, making careful note of what had gone wrong before. She pulled out a small tape measure and unspooled it, sticking the end into the water at their feet. "Nine and a half inches."

Then she let go of Marcus's hand and she and Joule— still linked—headed toward the front doors as Cage and his friend turned to check out the furniture and look down the hallway.

Cage was peering into the vending machine to check if Max had been right. But even the rows for black licorice and off-brand Skittles were empty now. Behind him, he heard the water slosh as Joule and Roxie moved around the lobby.

"It's at least three inches higher outside," Joule called back. Cage glanced over his shoulder and watched as Roxie planted her metal ruler into the water once again, this time measuring what she could see on the other side of the glass.

"The seam looks watertight, but it can't be. Or else it's leaking in from somewhere else. But the water indoors is noticeably lower than that outside."

"Then the doors are doing something," his sister said to him, turning to face him as she pointed behind her to the layer of water that pressed against the glass door.

He jolted backward slightly as he saw a dark shadow slither by his feet. Was he bumped, ever-so-slightly? Was that why he had looked down just then? But with the water swirling around his ankles in the lobby, he couldn't see anything clearly. He couldn't even tell if there was something near him, other than his imagination.

Just then, Roxie screamed.

Before Cage could register the sound, a human form smacked the glass door from the outside.

Hands high on the glass, the person clawed as though they could tear their way inside. "Help! Help me!"

The person pawed at the door as the four students raced forward as best they could through the heavy water. It seemed the woman—it took Cage's brain another half second to register that fact—didn't see them. Then she did, and for a moment she looked relieved.

As he watched, her mouth flew open and she screamed again as she was dragged backward in a rush of water.

24

"Nooooo!" Joule felt the word rush from her almost like a curse as she charged toward the door. As if her cry could change what she'd just seen.

She screamed for the others, and the four of them fought the water trying to get forward. What had been an odd and interesting expedition had quickly turned into a nightmare, complete with the inability to move.

"No!" She yelled it again, as she splashed several steps forward. The water was only nine inches deep, but it was enough to fight their every step and feel as though it was actively dragging them backward.

Cage, who had must have learned in the last few days to pick up his feet with inhuman speed, bolted past her.

Reaching out, she grabbed the back of his shirt and prayed that she didn't wind up yanking them both backwards onto their butts. Sitting down in the murky lobby water would be a bad move.

The water itself was a rich, silty red-brown inside the dorm, not the dark green they'd seen in the Science and

Engineering Quad. Joule couldn't be sure that there weren't things already making moves to bite her feet.

"No," she told him again as Cage tugged against her grasp. Marcus and Roxie looked at her oddly, even as Roxie dove for the door. Joule yelled out, "You can't!"

Cage stopped pulling against her and slowly turned. There was a look in his eyes that told her he remembered when he had made this decision once before... for her. He'd held her back when she wanted to move. This time, he'd listen to her.

But not everyone did.

Roxie leapt forward.

"It doesn't matter that we don't know who it is, Joule!" she protested as she pulled at the door handle.

"That's not what it's about," Joule countered in a low, deep voice that she knew revealed her fear as she slowly unclenched her fingers from the back of her brother's shirt. "But we don't know what's out there, or what attacked her. We don't know if that woman is still alive. We need to be ready if she gets to the door again." She paused then for a moment. "If we open the doors, we might not ever get them shut again."

"Why would you think she's not alive?"

Roxie turned, but she didn't look stunned, even as she worked alone to tug the door open. But she worked alone. Marcus had stopped and was now still, looking back and forth between the twins and the darkness beyond the doorway. Roxie tugged harder. "Didn't you hear her scream?"

It was Cage's voice that said what Joule was thinking, and she was grateful he had turned his attention from his immediate reaction—to run outside and perform a rescue— to a more logical approach of thinking things through. "It looked like something pulled her away from the door. If we go out, we have to be ready to fight it, whatever it is."

They weren't ready.

Joule knew that much.

But she tried to counter Roxie's determined force. "I'm not saying we don't go rescue people. She needs help. But how do we even get the door open?" It clearly wasn't budging with just Roxie working at it. "And how do we get the door closed once we're all back inside?" Her words were short staccato hits on the need for action.

At least this made Roxie stop wasting her energy against a door she wasn't able to move alone. She looked up at the other three, taking a deep breath and planting her hands on her hips.

"If we can brace the doors," Marcus motioned as he stepped forward, "Then they'll only open so far. That'll at least give us less distance to push them back closed."

Cage, too, approached the door and checked it. "This lock is a turn bolt," he said, looking as though he was ready to flip it, but not quite doing so. Joule watched as Roxie rolled her eyes, realizing that she'd been shoving at a locked door the whole time. Panic did that to a person. Joule knew.

"Roxie," she asked gently, trying to distract her friend, "Do you see her?"

Maybe Roxie would look out into the dark. Joule was not quite willing to put her own face against the glass and check; she'd seen too many things in the past couple days to want to look at the water any more than she had to.

"No." Roxie cupped her hands, blocking the light. But then she turned back to the group. "I don't see her anymore. If we had a chance to save her, we lost it."

With the four of them inside, working by the glow of the two flashlights, Joule looked around at the darkened corners and still water. She didn't like the idea that their light reflected off the glass rather than showing her what was beyond it. Her own reflection was growing more and more disturbing.

Distracting herself with the problem at hand, she asked. "What can we brace the doors with?"

The four of them looked around the lobby.

"The chairs are too lightweight," Roxie threw out. Marcus commented almost immediately that anything heavy enough to brace a door would take too much effort to move.

"Maybe *we* brace the doors," Joule thought out loud. "Two of us inside holding position, while two of us go outside searching."

No one told her no.

It took a few minutes to get the plan down. Joule could tell by the look on Roxie's face that she hoped the same thing Joule did: that whoever the woman was, she hadn't wandered too far away.

Joule's mind churned through the details of what she'd seen. There were only a few things she could be certain of. One—there was a woman in a raincoat and two—her hands had been bare.

The guys agreed to brace the door, and Joule felt the thought pass through her brain that it was rare for her and Cage to split up. Even Roxie and Sky, also twins, didn't seem to quite have the bond that she had she and her brother had. Then again, maybe they hadn't faced the same ordeals.

"Hold my hand," she told Roxie. "If one of us gets tugged suddenly, the other one will have to act as anchor."

Roxie offered a quick nod and slapped her hand into Joule's. They were in no way dressed to go out in the weather. They'd planned to check if they'd missed anything important, see if anyone else was down here, and raid any last items from the vending machine.

Cage and Marcus braced themselves, one on each door, as though they and not the lock were holding them closed. Joule stood ready as Cage reached out and turned the bolt.

Instantly, the doors began to give way under the force of the higher water outside. What little light there was from their flashlights glinted off the now rushing water. For a moment, Joule thought she saw blood on the door, but she didn't let it stop her.

Though the water and wind tried to push her and Roxie backward, they braced themselves. It took a moment of just standing, one foot in front of the other, leaning into the onslaught before they could move. As she managed her first step, Joule could tell the water inside the lobby of the dorm was already visibly rising.

"Go!" Roxie told her, and together they took three steps out into the wash of grey, into the rain coming down on them and the water trying to push them back through doors.

Still, when the arm bumped up against Joules leg, she didn't scream. Not at first.

25

C age heard the scream, his body recoiling before he registered all the information contained in the sound.

The harsh noise was less about terror and more of being startled. Though it still made his blood curdle, it wasn't his sister's voice. For a moment, he hated himself for being grateful that it was Roxie who was screaming.

Roxie was a good friend, but if he had to choose, there wouldn't be a choice. He pushed that thought aside as Roxie and Joule began retreating. They were only a few feet beyond the open door—enough to get drenched from the rain darting in under the overhang that should have protected them. But in this, nothing would keep them dry.

The two turned, switching hands in a move Cage would have advised against. For in the brief moment that they let go, he saw the flooded land just behind them. Something dark thrashed in the water.

"Run!" he yelled, even as he motioned to Marcus to brace the door. They had to be ready to push it closed against the water that would surely fight them even after Joule and Roxie were back inside.

"Run!" He yelled it again, his voice going hoarse on just the one word as the wind tried to steal it from him. In his sister's eyes, he could see her moment of clarity—her understanding that his reason to yell meant she was in immediate danger.

She moved faster. The water swirled around her and sucked at her feet. He knew she was clenching her toes in the boots, trying to fight the heavy pressure that wanted to suck them off. But they were her only protection against something that might want to bite.

And it was apparent now that there were things that might want to bite in this murky hell.

Water in the sink was clear and non-threatening. Water in the bathtub, though deep, still wasn't enough to knock him over. Even full of bubbles, the lack of sight below the surface wasn't scary. But this water? Its very existence was a threat. Gravity and volume made it lethal.

Marcus nodded in reply as he set his shoulder against the door. His hands already braced, though he didn't start to close the door; he seemed ready to follow Cage's order, but didn't yet realize that Cage had seen something menacing.

"Run!" He shouted it a third time, thinking it shouldn't take them so long for the young women to get just a few feet. But the water slowed them down, and the adrenaline sped him up. He'd likely not paused at all between his orders. Still, he yelled again and watched as the two young women leapt, jumping out of the water as best they could.

They stomped downward, splashing through, seeming to be in slow motion. The water thrashed around them thought it seemed to be only ankle-deep.

Whatever was behind them was several feet long. And

whoever had been out here—whoever she was who had smacked up against the door—was long gone. Whether she'd escaped or been killed, he couldn't tell.

But his sister *had* to get back inside. He and Marcus cleared the doorway as Roxie and Joule splashed inside to the relative safety of the dorm lobby. He would have grabbed his sister's hand and pulled her through, but it was far more important that he shut the doors behind them.

As he and Marcus began their synchronized shove of the doors, Joule and Roxie spun around immediately and began pushing with them.

Did they see it? he wondered. Whatever it was seemed to have stayed behind, lurking in the outside waters, which had gone much calmer since the girls vacated the patio area. *Was that bad? Or good?*

"She's gone," Joule whispered, her hands and feet bracing against the door next to him as they struggled to keep everything out.

Cage began to fear that the Plexi of the door would crack and break rather than hold the water back. Shutting the door should have been something they could do quickly. He'd opened and closed these doors countless times in the months that he'd lived here. But this time, everything fought against them.

It took four of them applying constant pressure against the water but, at last, they got the doors closed. Together, they strained to hold their position as he turned the bolt.

With a glance between them, Marcus reached up and pushed the slide bolt into place at the top of the door. "There's another one at the bottom," he added and Cage nodded.

"Brace with your feet," Marcus told them, and they all put one foot back and one foot forward, flush against the edge as they pushed at the bottom of the door. Though no one could see it under the water, they had to line up the bolt so the metal rod could slide into place.

Marcus' hand disappeared into the silty murk and the three of them held their collective breath as he felt around and finally found the piece. It took a few moments to make it move. When it was in place at last, the four of them slowly stepped back as a unit and watched to see that the doors would hold.

Cage, still watching the seam between the doors and hoping the water couldn't leak through, wasn't looking where the rest of them were. So he wasn't prepared when Roxie screamed.

He jolted his head up so fast that he almost toppled backward and into the water himself, but his hand shot out to brace against the door.

As they saw it, the four of them grew silent, Roxie's scream ending abruptly, as though she had her power cut off. The four of them slowly moved backwards, hands reaching for the doors or the wall. Anything to tell them they were steady as they watched what moved in front of them.

A dark, four-foot monster thrashed just under the surface.

Cage couldn't see what it was, and he didn't have time for any kind of scientific evaluation or identification. None of them did. For a moment, they softly gasped each time it moved in the space between them.

Clearly, the water wasn't quite as deep in here as it was outside, despite the massive inflow they'd allowed when they opened the doors. The creature didn't seem to like it. Shifting and rolling, it darted one way then another, eluding the dimming circles of vision their flashlights afforded.

There were fins, a mouth, a tail... but beyond that, Cage knew nothing.

Before this, he'd thought it was possible that something in the water outside had been eating students. Now he was confident.

His sister said the only logical thing. "Get out, now!"

26

J oule was breathing heavily by the time she hit the landing on the third floor of the dorm. They'd all run faster but with more control once they were six steps up, out of the water and free of the silty murk.

At the back of the pack, Joule turned and looked back to see if she could still spot whatever it was that thrashed in the water. Her breath caught as she saw the movement at the bottom of the steps. Had it been right behind them the whole time?

At least it didn't try to follow them up the steps. So far, the things that were in the water seemed to stay in the water. *Thank God.*

But Joule looked ahead to see that none of the others had stopped. Heading straight up, they took every turn at full speed, not noticing if anyone peeked out of their dorm room this time. She bolted by, passing most of them until, at the landing, she heard them call out. The others had stopped in the doorway to breathe and take a moment, now behind her.

"Joule, where are you going?"

Roxie had even commented, "Cage's room is this way," as though Joule might not remember that. But she was already part way down the hall, her hand already on the knob of her own dorm room, the key fished from her pocket. She was grateful for a moment that she simply always had it on her. With a few practiced twists, she threw the door wide, obviously catching Holly and Ginnifer napping. It was difficult for Joule to think these two were able to doze off in the face of all that was going on, but that's what it looked like.

Moreover, Holly had made herself quite comfortable on Joule's bed, snuggling in as though she belonged there. It passed Joule's thoughts that she and seven others were crammed into one room while Holly merely had taken over what wasn't hers. Joule still ignored the other girl. They weren't friends, and there was something she needed to do now.

Reaching into the back of the closet, she snaked her hand between her clothing until she felt it. It had been here, stashed in the back corner and used only a few times the first quarter. Only once this term. Where did a person go at Stanford to practice archery? There was a club, and there was training, but neither applied to Joule. She just wanted to be able to take out a Night Hunter or two when it was necessary.

"Keeping up my lethal skills" had not been a box she'd been able to check on the form the club asked her to fill out, so she'd left without signing up. But now, as her hand grasped the curved of the bow and the string pressed into her palm, it felt comfortable, familiar. Safe. Even as she pulled the bow out, she plunged her hand back into the closet to retrieve the quiver of arrows. Standing upright, supplies in hand, she was ready to sling the strap over her shoulder like some fucked-up Robin Hood. Joule was out the door before Holly or Ginnifer could wake up enough to make any comments, and Joule didn't have the breath for a snarky goodbye.

Slowing now, she sailed right past her friends and headed back down the steps. She made it halfway down the flight before she realized no one was following her. She had no light save for her cell phone. Stopping, she turned and looked back up the flight, bow still in hand, arrow somehow pulled, nocked, and at the ready. "I need a flashlight. And someone to hold it."

Cage shook his head at her. "What are you going to do?"

"I'm going to kill it. Then we can see what it is."

But her brother shook his head again and raised one eyebrow as if to say, haven't we done this before?

Joule shrugged in response. It had worked last time. Though *worked* was such a strong word for what had happened. In the end, they had won. But what they'd lost in getting there was so great... she shut the thought down and put it away. "Well, what do you propose? I don't have a net to catch it in, and we sure as hell don't want it alive."

"Amen to that, sister," Roxie said into the space between them.

"Let's go back to the room." Cage motioned for her to come back up the steps. Reluctantly, she let go of the tension on the bow string and followed.

"Even if you nailed it," Marcus said, "like with one shot to the eye? You would still have to wade out into the water to bring it back." Then he paused a moment, seeming to think. "Could you still shoot that—" he motioned to the arrow as though he didn't have a name for it, "if it had fishing line attached?"

Joule almost didn't answer. She was trudging along behind, defeated, hurt that her seemingly brilliant idea had been dismissed out of hand. But Marcus wasn't wrong. She took a breath and thought it through. "Maybe. But I've never tried, and of course, I don't have any fishing line."

"I do," he piped up almost too cheerfully. She didn't ask why.

Then Cage was opening the door back to his room. When they entered, Max, Sky, and Gabby only moved a little in acknowledgment of their safe return. For a moment, Joule was stunned. Weren't they glad their friends had survived? The woman outside hadn't.

Then she realized they had no idea what had happened. They still thought the group had gone downstairs, waded through the water, maybe smacked the vending machines or turned over the cushions on the couches to search for loose chips. They didn't know what she'd just seen.

It was Gabby who first noticed the bow and arrow, and her eyes widened. She sat up rapidly, setting her phone down.

"You know, we didn't want to say anything when we arrived, because we were safe inside and we didn't want anyone to get too afraid,"Gabby muttered softly. "But Marcus and I ran into a leg on the way over. Just... *a leg.*"

27

Cage watched as his sister led the way, staying several steps in front of the rest of the group. He held up the flashlight and wished it was his nine millimeter in his other hand instead of the fishing line he held. If he'd had the gun, he would have crossed one wrist over the other—FBI style—and been ready to take all comers. As it was, he had only the light and it was a crappy defensive weapon.

Then again, this little mission was ragtag at best.

Marcus took the stairs beside him, a fishing pole over his shoulder, as though he were out for a leisurely day at the lake. But there was nothing leisurely about any of the rest of them.

Cage's hand clenched. He didn't know what good the gun would do him here or even if he could shoot anything, but he craved the feel of it. He and Joule had left a few of their things in a nearby storage unit, the smallest one they could get. It was barely the size of a closet and only a couple of dollars a month. That's where his gun was. *A fat lot of good it does me now.*

Not that he could bring the gun on campus, even if he called it an "emotional support weapon." Instead he held Marcus's spare spool of fishing line. His friend had dug it out of his dorm room along with the rod, casually explaining that he had a friend with a boat, and they fished on the bay sometimes.

Honestly, Cage didn't care. He'd only cataloged the things he saw in Marcus's closet, thinking about what they might have need of in the future. Unfortunately, none of the detritus has struck him as useful now. The only thing he could do now was hold the flashlight, lighting the way for everyone else, not really part of the action himself.

The group slowed a little bit as they neared the bottom floor. In an unspoken agreement, their proximity to the danger below had made them all draw back just a little until they stood on the lowest of the dry steps and scanned the water.

Next to him, Gabby held her own flashlight and a small dagger.

Cage rolled his eyes at that. He'd been good. He'd not brought his gun on campus because weapons were forbidden on school grounds. Gabby shrugged at him and said, "Oh, I have three of these."

Not only did she have them, she'd had them in her own dorm, then packed them and brought them up to his room. Because apparently, even before she and Marcus had seen the leg while they walked over, she'd become very concerned about what they might find.

"Give me the line," she said, holding out the dagger as though he might just slide a donut or an onion ring onto it. They'd already figured out that the dagger was the only thing that they could fit the line over and allow it to spool out without burning or cutting anyone's hands. The hilt of the dagger even protected the surface of her hand from any friction burns that might happen if the line unwound quickly. Cage thought it might.

"Do you want me to take the light?" Sky asked. As Cage thanked her but said no, he watched as she shrugged and pulled out a light of her own, adding its beam to the collective spot of light. It still didn't add up to enough to light the room in a way that made him feel he could see what was coming.

Cage suddenly wondered if it was wise for all of them to be here. Even though he knew it was good that they all see this thing, it still bothered him that no one was left to stand by in case they needed food or water or some item fetched. No one was prepared to administer first aid...

At least he'd remembered to lock the room behind them.

Gabby had pulled out her own flashlight. "I want the light and the line. I want to be able to shine it where I need. But please keep your eyes peeled, all of you."

Cage was on spotter duty now. "Okay, so those with lights are definitely going to have to be all over the place. Every one of us has to watch for this thing."

There were four lights now, including Marcus's cell, which he suddenly held up and handed backward to Max as they hit the base of the steps. Then he announced, "Here I go."

This was the other part Cage didn't like. As he watched, Marcus baited the hook with a slice of ham from the dorm room. Granted, the meat would have gone bad soon anyway, but the idea that they were feeding their precious store to this monster did not sit well.

Cage's protest had fallen on deaf ears earlier, so he didn't bother to repeat it now. Everyone else agreed that sacrificing a piece of meat was worth it to catch this thing. He stood back as Marcus cast the line out into the middle of the dark room, the flashlights trying and failing to follow the arc of the hook.

It only took a few moments for the line and the wiggling hook to entice movement from the other side of the room. Cage held his tongue, not speaking aloud his fears that they might discover they didn't have one, but actually five or ten of these things. Luckily, only one area of water splashed in response to the food.

Marcus pulled the line in and tossed it back out several times, reeling and throwing until Cage decided that whatever it was it didn't like their slice of ham. It was right then, of course, that the creature began to follow the slowly dragging hook.

Shockingly, everything went like clockwork, exactly as Marcus had said it would. After all, he knew fishing, and he wanted control of the bait and hook. None of them would be able to kill it until it got close. Marcus had been clear that he would catch it, but he wasn't willing to do the final deed.

Sky stepped forward, grasping a dagger—another one from Gabby's set—firmly in her hand. She was ready, even if they hadn't seen the thing yet. Right now, it was all a waiting game.

Cage wanted to hold her back. He didn't want them using the knives unless absolutely necessary. So as the thing swam closer, following the meat and the hook that Marcus controlled, Cage held his light up and watched as his sister slowly planted her boot one step down. She was now one inch into the water. As shallow as that was, he still didn't like it, but Joule was pulling her arrow back and waiting for the fish to get close.

Cage did a quick visual survey as the sounds of water splashing told him the creature was wriggling closer and closer, trying to catch the bait. Visually, he checked that the fishing line was tied tightly to the back of her arrow, so they could use it to help haul in what they caught. But her stance concerned him; the fact that she was in the water frightened him the most. So he did the only thing he could: with his free hand, Cage reached out and grab a fistful of the back of her shirt, just as she started to fall forward.

28

"Let go of me! I need to move." Joule couldn't control the irritation in her tone. He'd almost ruined her shot, yanking her the way he did. But she'd kept her eye on the squirming creature and controlled her breathing.

She pulled back further on the arrow, hardly noticing the cut of the string against her fingers. Her vision narrowed, and she could almost taste her heartbeat.

In... out...

She let go and watched as the arrow flew.

"You looked like you were falling," Cage protested.

Had he said something else? She wouldn't have heard. But, until the arrow hit its mark, she couldn't give any part of her focus to his words.

"I wasn't!" she growled, but though her brother loosened his grip to let her move more freely, he didn't let go of her shirt.

Joule's fingers burned from the string. Despite her solid aim, it had been a while since she'd stood with her bow taut, pressure burning into her hands. The string felt embedded in her flesh, though she didn't see any blood. She didn't have time to argue with her brother. She had nailed the thing.

Reaching quickly into her back pocket, Joule put on her gloves. She pulled the edges of her sleeves down over her hands as well. But it still hurt to haul the catch in.

Fishing line wasn't meant to be tugged on this way. She needed a reel and maybe a spare rod that they didn't have. Cage couldn't help, because he was too busy holding onto her. But as the force of the squirming creature threatened to pull her face-first into the water, she became more grateful for the anchor. The way it thrashed, it was obviously still alive—even though it had an arrow right through its head.

Gabby stepped beside her, adding her own strength and acting as another anchor. Then Sky moved down one foot into the water, then she went down one more step to help them pull the line.

Joule jerked her head up to meet her friend's eyes. "No! Don't go farther in!"

Sky hadn't seen it. She hadn't been down here the first time. But they were all watching now as it flopped in the water, angry about being reeled in.

Roxie had reached out and grabbed onto the back of her sister's shirt, too. Slowly, they all worked together to drag the creature up several steps. Joule's eyes had gone wide and she almost let go of the line.

But she couldn't. Her line was the last one holding the thing, since Marcus had been so stunned he'd simply opened his hand and dropped his fishing pole. With the lessened pressure, the creature slid back a few steps, tightening the line around her fingers.

Joule yelped, but maybe that had stopped her from saying, "Holy shit!"

It was a shark.

There was a shark in the lobby of the freshman-sophomore college dorm.

Her brain hadn't really processed it.

When Dr. Kimura had said some of the eggs she'd brought in had been elasmobranches, she' d thought maybe they were rays, or maybe one of the small fishes that simply classified under the same category as sharks.

Even as she thought that, Sky stepped forward, dagger in hand, and drove the blade directly through the center of the shark's skull. The body twitched for another thirty seconds, and Joule was grateful that she knew that fish did that even after they were dead. She was still dealing with the last surprise.

Sky yanked the blade out, making Joule wince and turn her head. From the way her friend arced her hand up, it appeared she intended to stab it again. But the shark had finally gone still, and Sky stepped backward slowly, ready to pounce if it so much as twitched.

It was Cage who managed the first words since they'd seen it. "I think it's a bull shark."

At four feet long, it was relatively hefty. Though Joule wanted to peel her glove, reach out, and run her fingers over its rough, sandpapery skin, she didn't dare. "We have to get it somewhere where we can get an ID."

"Too late," Gabby said, almost too cheerfully. "It looks like a bull to me." Her phone was in her hand and turned on. She'd begun researching while the rest of them had stood there gawking.

For a moment, they hovered around the lit phone. Though it would have been better to have several of them researching, they were still working to conserve their batteries. So they all looked back and forth between Gabby's tiny screen and pointed. "The dorsal fin matches for a bull shark."

"Mouth, too."

"Same for the shape of the nose."

"Drag it further up," Gabby requested, "And let's take a look at the tail."

Joule didn't think they needed to, but Gabby insisted. "We have to have a solid confirmation of what it is. We have to show people so we can warn them, and they have to believe us."

Joule noticed none of them asked what the chances were that this was a lone shark that had worked its way through the channels created by the rain. No one suggested this was the only bull shark on campus... They'd already seen the evidence.

The bull shark's sharp teeth and aggressive nature explained so much.

"We probably need to get it up to the landing," Gabby said, continuing to direct the group. Turning, she pointed behind her, swinging her light wildly as she went. "We need to get a full picture with something for scale. Then we need to share it."

Joule hadn't considered that. She'd simply been thinking like a scientist: *Find out what it is.* Gabby had been thinking on a much larger scale: Alert everyone

It took several minutes of maneuvering flashlights to find a way to distribute the shark's weight between them so they could maneuver it up the stairs. Joule was grateful that when she held her hands out, her brother simply handed his flashlight over to her and had taken up the job of being one of the people carrying the thing. Her hands were still stinging from the fishing line and the struggle.

She'd thought the Night Hunters had been bad...

They were. They'd been awful.

The Night Hunters had ultimately turned out to be a new species, and they hadn't understood a lot when they'd fought them. A bull shark, however, was a known quantity. Even as Joule and Roxie lit the way at the front of the group, they began exchanging information.

"Aren't they aggressive?" Joule looked to her friend.

"The most aggressive, I think," Roxie confirmed. "Worse than great whites."

Lovely. The movie *Jaws* had given great whites a bad reputation. "But this is fresh water."

Even as she thought back to what little she knew, Roxie answered. "They've been known to move into brackish water."

Of course, Joule thought. "I'm assuming they are a normal thing in the bay."

"Yes." Marcus piped up from the end of their little caravan, slowly grunting as he helped carry the shark up a full flight of steps.

Though they'd been intending to go all the way to the third floor with it—where they would have access to Cage and Max's supplies and where they knew more of the residents—at the second floor, they were met by a group of students nearly blocking the way.

Almost ten of them stood with arms crossed, waiting at the landing until the middle of the caravan came into view. One of the students held up a light, then stumbled backwards as he saw what they carried.

"Where the fuck did you get that?"

Joule tipped her head. "It was in the lobby. We opened the doors to help someone and it came in." She bit her tongue and didn't mention that the someone they'd wanted to help had been far beyond saving by the time they'd gotten the doors open.

There would be time to explain all that later.

Already, cell phones around them were snapping photos and Joule turned her face to the side. This was not what she'd intended. She held her hand up, blocking her image from the lenses. "Wait, let us lay it down."

But the chatter around them had grown too high. No one heard her through the pinging of cell phones all around her. And no one stopped.

As pictures were snapped and snapped again, it became harder to stay out of anyone's camera frame. She looked from the shark to the students and began to think of them as bait. They seemed more interested in a good picture or the newest hot gossip than in being safe.

They reached out to touch the creature without first confirming that it was dead.

The thought that rolled through Joule's head was unkind: *America's best and brightest.* The wonderfully sarcastic tone was her own.

Even as she tried to suppress the harsh thought, Gabby held her phone up and showed it to Joule. "Already."

Her friend had just received one of the pictures taken moments ago. It had gone out to someone else, been shared, and shared again, until someone had thought to alert Gabby about the shark she'd help catch.

Well, this is it, Joule thought. *It has begun.*

29

The shark made a splash as it hit the water. Joule stood at the window and watched as the body caused ripples from entry and then began to slowly sink.

But that only lasted for half a second. Soon, the dead shark jerked one way and then another. It tipped up, the tail reaching high into the air, and then rapidly plunged beneath the water, pulled under by something she couldn't see.

But she had a pretty damn good idea what it was.

The tail popped back up for a moment but, as it fell to its side, she saw that the piece was now disconnected from the rest of the shark.

The water didn't turn red. It didn't have to. The thrashing, the fins surfacing here and there as pieces were ripped apart, the way the dead shark was yanked under and aside was more than enough to make it clear what was happening.

Joule stepped back from the window as her stomach rolled.

Then she shook her head and looked at the ceiling from where she lay on the bed, slowly coming awake. She was lying in Cage's dorm room bed, wedged against the wall. Gabby was squished on one side of her. Sky lay facing the other direction, her feet up near Joule's shoulders.

Taking a deep breath, Joule slowly wriggled onto her side, trying not to wake anyone she hadn't already roused with her bad dream. Had she thrashed back and forth? She didn't know. The problem was, her nightmare—the vision of the shark getting torn apart—was also a real memory. She hadn't dreamed anything that hadn't actually happened. They'd all been stunned by the swiftness with which the body had been dismantled and then disappeared.

She wasn't sure what to do with that knowledge. *Nobody can safely enter any water above ankle deep,* she thought. She'd seen the way the one they'd killed had thrashed about and mostly hidden in the shallows of the lobby.

It had taken them a while to decide to throw the shark into the water. Though Joule didn't think it was the wrong decision, she wished she hadn't seen what happened after. In fact, it had taken the group of them longer to decide what to do with the shark's body than it had taken the students on the landing to decide that they were bored with snapping pictures.

By the time the area cleared, and the original seven were left to make the decision of what to do with the body, more than one of them had been pinged with pictures of themselves. Most had gotten comments or seen posts saying how fascinating it was that there was a shark on campus.

It wasn't fascinating. It was deadly.

And it wasn't just one shark. Apparently, they were everywhere.

It was Marcus who'd pointed out, "If we leave the corpse

here, it will rot. We have maybe six or seven hours before it begins to smell."

They'd all agreed that they were likely to be stuck in the building for much longer than that. None of them wanted to go to sleep and wake up to a stench—even if they were on the third floor, and they'd left the body on the second.

Sky jumped in next. "I would consider leaving it here, but someone will likely steal it."

Roxie had immediately turned to her sister. "What would someone do with it if they stole it?"

Despite her uncharitable thoughts about America's best and brightest earlier, the Freshman Sophomore College was populated by many strange and awesome, scientifically minded students. Joule feared that by morning, they might not be able to find it. Someone might think they should do a dissection.

God forbid someone tried to make shark fin soup with a hot plate. Or even just fill their social media feed with shark selfies.

So they decided to catalog everything they could see and touch. Max ran off and returned with a new lab notebook.

"I'm taking notes on my phone," Sky had already pointed out.

"Pencil." He held up the yellow, old school version. "This record will be waterproof." He began jotting down everything he could see, touch, or smell.

Joule sent pictures to Dr. Kimura, hoping that he might give them some insight. But when she didn't hear back and everyone agreed they had recorded everything they could, they'd hoisted the shark body and carried it to the end of the hall.

Shoved out of a second floor window, the shark had hit

with a rude splash. Joule sucked in another deep breath at the memory, but no one around her stirred much.

Roxie mumbled a little in her sleep. She was still curled up on the floor with blankets she'd stolen from an open dorm several doors down. Though they did know of other rooms with beds available, the seven of them had opted not to split up and instead divided the limited floor space among them.

Max was spread-eagle on the mattress, taking up all of his own bed, while Cage and Marcus also carved out a space on the floor. For a moment, Joule wished she was in the other room alone. But there was probably no way to get out of the bed without disturbing everyone else.

Lying still for a while, she tried to figure out if there was anything she should, or even could, do. She was the one who had brought up the horrible problem that had them all concerned now.

"You know, the weather said it would rain for three days. If they're right, we have two more days of rain." She'd thrown the idea out into the group right before bedtime. She hadn't added, "And that's a conservative estimate."

The water level had already risen well past "flash-flood" level. They'd all been listening to alerts and getting emergency pings on their phones—as if they couldn't see the water outside for themselves.

"The problem I just realized," she'd continued, not adding that it was only one of many problems, "is that we have enough food for three days."

Gabby wasn't the only one who frowned at her.

"We need more than three days of food!" Joule emphasized, as no one seemed to be catching on. "If it rains for three days, how much longer until the water recedes? How long until we can leave? We may be here for a week. Or more!"

She was sure they didn't have enough food for that. Not in this room. No one had an answer when she'd asked it. They'd all gone to sleep without one.

Staring at the ceiling now, reliving all the bad thoughts of the day, she sighed. On any other night, she would have gotten up and grabbed a snack out of her refrigerator. But she was already rationing food, so she stayed put. Her brain called back to a year before, when they'd closed the house tightly every night against the Night Hunters.

As bad as that was, there'd always been the next day. The sunshine had always kept the hunters away. Her family and the whole neighborhood moved about freely while the sun was out. They went to grocery stores. They went to school. Now, she had no idea how long they would be stuck in this building. Maybe it was time to start raiding other food stores... if they could find any.

She stared at the ceiling almost blankly, her mind wandering for a while. Joule wasn't sure how long she'd been there when she heard the commotion downstairs.

Slowly climbing out of bed, she tried not to rouse anyone else in the room. But Sky was awake now and stared at her sleepily. It only took a moment before her friend heard the noise, too, Joule had motioned her toward the hallway. Slowly, both crept out of the room, the din from downstairs getting louder as they tiptoed.

As she opened the door, Joule saw students arriving at the top of the steps, arms heavy with seemingly anything they could carry.

"What's going on?" she asked

One girl looked at her with wide, scared eyes and said, "The water reached the second floor."

30

C age surveyed the room. Though, it was the middle
of the day, everything was still dark gray. They
could tell it was daytime simply because it was
not pitch black. There wasn't much he wouldn't give right
now to see the sun.

Why does bad shit always happen in the dark?

Gabby had grabbed a pillow and curled up in the corner
of Max's bed. She was out cold. Max was in the fetal position
at the other end, also dead to the world.

Joule and Sky were playing backgammon on the floor
while Roxie waited to play against the winner. There
appeared to be money involved.

Marcus sat in the far corner, reading, as Cage took a
moment to survey everything around him.

They'd all been up since about three a.m. One good
thing about the dorm: Someone was always awake.
Someone had noticed the water seeping across the floor,
and they were able to abandon the floor before it got too
deep.

Now all the first-floor residents had already been pushed

upward, spread out over the second- and third-floor rooms. It was highly probably that someone had been sleeping on the floor. With the water ruining the second floor too, the students had spent the midnight hours hauling everything into the open and empty rooms. The third-floor residents had pitched in and helped the second-floor students carry whatever they could salvage.

They'd first lined the hallway with blankets, food, and the occasional cooler. There were pillows, clothes, computers, and tech... and boots. So many watertight boots.

Cage and Joule had not been the only ones to understand several months ago that the flooding wasn't going to be a one-time deal. It looked as if most of the students had invested in sturdy rain boots. They were prepared for puddles... but no one had been ready for this.

When his friends had thrown the dead shark out the window, the water had been halfway up to the second floor. He hadn't thought much about it at the time. After all, he was on the third floor. He was still well above the surface.

But this meant that the water was not only still rising, but was now rising at an even faster rate. His heart hammered with the implications. No one had yet asked the inevitable question: What would they do when the water got even higher?

Once everyone had everything they could save brought to the third floor, the students had taken to pioneering for available space. They had broken through the doors of the rooms that remained locked. There had been some discussion, but following a general vote, it was decided that the school was not likely to expel them for saving their own lives.

For now, the spare students huddled together in rooms where the doors didn't quite close because of the splintered doorframes. At least for now, everyone was out of the water. But the third floor was getting crowded and Cage was getting worried.

Hell, he'd been worried before. He was now dialed all the way up to "afraid."

Joule's discussion about "three days of food and three days of rain" lingered in his brain like a hamster on a wheel. And though he'd tried to lie down and go to sleep, he hadn't been able to stop his racing thoughts.

He did a cursory visual search of the pantry. The fridge needed to remain closed, so those items he inventoried by memory. He counted everything edible he could think of. He divided by the seven of them. Then he frowned and did it again.

Joule had been right. It wouldn't be enough.

When Joule lost her game, he called her over, motioning her into the hallway, where he found he didn't have any more privacy than he'd had in the room. Students sprawled and sat against the walls all along the corridor. In the far corner, under the window, a student wrapped in a sleeping bag was huddled and sound asleep, seemingly unfazed by the sound of the rain hitting the glass just overhead. A little further down, a conversation went on in musical tones that didn't reflect his fear.

Did they just think it was an exceptionally rainy day? Or were they actively ignoring the threat?

Cage kept his voice quiet and walked with Joule into the stairwell, even though they wouldn't be going down the stairs. He hoped it would afford them a place to speak with a measure of privacy.

What surprised him was that, where the stairwell took a turn halfway between floors, thin rivulets of water ran across the linoleum. The flood hadn't just reached the second floor. Since the middle of the night, it had come halfway up to the third floor.

Still rising, he thought. But what he said to his sister was, "What do we do? I calculated it out. At this rate, we have another twenty-four hours at most before the water hits this level."

Joule looked up at the ceiling as though she could see through it to a non-existent fourth floor. It wasn't up there waiting for them. She didn't reply for a moment, but Cage waited. After a moment, she asked, "Has anyone gotten any information about rescue?"

He shook his head at her. They'd all been checking in. Occasionally waiting on hold forever, only to hear that the winds were still too strong. Rescue wasn't coming. "Even the Coast Guard couldn't safely get in."

"Then, we've got nowhere left to go but the roof."

"It's raining on the roof," he commented.

"Yes." Her eyes still aimed toward the ceiling; her hands still perched on her hips. "But I have something."

Cage felt his brows pull together as she finally looked at him.

"Do you remember I told you I spent all that money on supplies?"

He nodded. "It was several hundred dollars, if I recall."

"Well," she said, "I think it's time to get into my supplies."

"Where are they?" He hadn't seen anything. Was she hoarding food? And where would she have anything stashed? She'd only brought clothes and food to his room.

"Under my bed. Come on." She motioned toward her own room, the one she shared with Ginnifer.

Originally, the dorm had been set out with males down one side of the hall and females on the other. It had apparently been rearranged from year to year, some years with different floors designated for different genders. Now there were different wings to keep the boys and girls apart. But the flood had put an end to any segregation.

So it was a short walk on the hard floor to the room she shared with Ginnifer on the women's side. She tried the knob and it resisted, but she quickly slipped the key in and opened the door. Cage was surprised to find that Ginnifer and Holly were now hosting a number of other people in his sister's room.

He watched as Joule apologized but waded boldly through the human detritus. Then she knelt down by her bed and hauled a huge box out from underneath. "There's another one," she told Cage. "Grab it."

"What's that?" Ginnifer asked.

Cage didn't know, and Joule acted as though she hadn't even heard the sound.

"Joule?" her roommate pressed, but again, his sister just headed for the door, the awkward weight balanced at her fingertips.

He opened his mouth to ask the same question, but her sharp glare told him to hold it.

He could only follow, waddling with the ungainly, heavy box back down the hall toward his own room. Ahead of him, his sister juggled her own mass, trying to keep it upright as she went.

At his room, she kicked on the door, having no hands to turn the knob or even to knock with. Behind him, Ginnifer was staring down the hallway at him. Still Joule kept up her serious face, continuing to pretend deafness as her roomie called out questions.

She'd awakened most of the group with her kicking, but Cage was now curious enough to not care. Dropping her box unceremoniously into the center of the room, Joule took a deep breath and stood up straight in a stretch. Cage, not knowing what was inside, tried to carefully set the heavy package down. Then he thought about what would happen if he injured his back in the middle of all this shit. So he let it drop the last few inches.

"All right." He put his hands on his hips and stared at his sister. "What's in the box?"

31

"T hey're boats," Joule said, hands still on her hips, as she watched her friends suddenly perk up with curiosity.

"Inflatables," she clarified. "Eight-man. Four foldable oars. Each will hold up to fourteen average-size humans in a pinch."

"Holy crap!" Cage responded, the words bursting out of him.

Joule shrugged. "They said the rains were coming. I still have two months to return them if I don't like my purchase. And I have to tell you, right now, I really like my purchase."

She watched as her brother tipped his head to the side, accepting her argument. "So what do we do with them?"

"That's the big question." Joule shrugged. "I bought them as a backup, but I didn't make any plan beyond simply having them."

"It means we can row out of here if we have to," Sky said as she jumped up. She threw her arms around Joule, as though she had offered them all free candy or free tuition, or maybe even something better.

To a certain extent, she had. But Joule shook her head. "I don't think we can." When they all looked at her oddly, she added, "I don't think we can just row out of here."

Still, no one seemed to understand, so she explained. "We should have rowed away a long time ago. But we didn't think the rain would be as much of a problem as it is. And I sure as fuck didn't anticipate sharks." Joule waved her hand toward the window, as though the fish were waiting just beyond the glass.

"And anyway, we won't have room for the whole dorm full of students. If we pop this baby open right now and drag it down to the second floor and go out the window, everyone will try to fight us for a seat in the boat."

"Maybe not everyone," Marcus said, but then conceded, "But definitely enough to start a fight."

Joule was nodding, still holding court in the middle of her friends. "And I don't even know how to launch this thing yet! It's never been out of the box. Are we going to wade through the water on the second floor and just hope none of these bulls have made it into the building?"

Gabby shook her head. "They shouldn't be inside. We closed the doors."

Roxie agreed. "And we caught the one that was in the lobby."

"Right," Joule said. "But how many students on the first or second floors left their windows open? I mean, it would be stupid, but..."

"Not that stupid," Max noted. "If I was on the first floor and I knew it was going to flood, opening the window changes the pressure, helps preserve the structural integrity of the building. I might have done it before I left..."

"Or..." Marcus picked up the thread, "it could happen

that the pressure of the water broke the glass if they didn't leave it open."

"So it's entirely possible that the second floor already has bull sharks in it." Joule looked each of them in the eyes. The second floor was out as an option.

"Shiiiiit." Gabby drew the word out, not liking this argument. "No one's going wading in any water deeper than their ankles then. Not anymore."

Joule had to agree, but that wasn't the only logistical problem. "If we go up on the roof, we have an almost two-story drop to the water's surface."

"That's way too far," Cage added, joining the conversation for the first time.

No one disagreed with him, it was simply understood that was correct.

"The hall window is closer to the surface, but we'll start a riot if we do that. I think we have to keep the boats hidden, since we don't have enough space for everyone."

Sky was nodding along, but her eyes had gone unfocused. Their logistically oriented friend was thinking, walking her finger back and forth in front of her. By the time she spoke, she'd figured something out. "We first take all of us in the two boats. We may be able to take a handful of other people, but we can't open it to a lottery. We simply have to pick a few people and keep them quiet, and then take them with us."

"Why do we have to take anyone?" Gabby pushed, but Sky still didn't focus on her.

"More rowers. Because we have to go on a search for higher ground. Once we find it, someone has to come back with the boat. Only a few of us. That time, we'll need as many open seats in the boats as possible. We collect as many people as we can and take them back. Then it becomes an issue of making it back and forth."

Roxie chimed in, "We'll need to trade people out, so they don't get too tired. Which means we have to know the path back and forth. Someone has to navigate." While she spoke, she stood up and walked to the window, looking out. "I don't see any higher ground from here..."

Joule was half out of breath, maybe from carrying the heavy box, but more likely from worry. "Exactly. What that means is, we either have to get the box somewhere private and open it there, or we go out this window." She pointed.

"It won't fit." Cage was the first to point that out.

"The windows aren't made to be opened all the way." Sky joined him at the window. They didn't open it, but together they examined the runners and the metal edges.

Marcus stood up and pushed in between them, as he banged the heel of his hand against the top corner. "The framing looks pretty solid."

"They don't want people getting out easily," Sky added. "Suicides." She added the last word as an explanation, though Joule was fairly certain that a third-floor fall wouldn't kill most people.

"If we break the window, the broken glass could slice the rubber of the boat..." Marcus said as he turned and headed back to the box. Reaching in, he touched the material as though he could figure out more from the feel.

"It's made for open-ocean rescue teams." Joule didn't add that it was resistant against sharks. That was a feature she'd never considered she would need. She was grateful now. No one spoke for a moment.

"Holy crap," Joule muttered under her breath. When she'd bought the boats, she'd thought of them as a ridiculous security blanket. Having them under her bed made her sleep better. But she'd thought if she ever felt the need to use one, she'd simply put on her boots, go down to the water, climb in, and paddle away. It had been an idyllic fantasy of saving herself. It was a promise of safety if the water flooded again, a promise of not getting swept up by a crashing current. The boat might roll along, but she and her brother would be safe, paddles in hand.

It wasn't turning out like that at all. Just getting the boat into the water was a tactical nightmare.

Roxie was still going. "We can't put the boat out the window anyway. The water is still a full story below us. It's not as bad as launching from the roof, but it's the same problem. What would we do? Jump out the window and hope we land in the boat?"

Joule shook her head emphatically. That could not happen.

If the water was halfway up the second floor, then it was well over ten feet deep. Who knew what sharks were lurking there? They knew more than enough had gathered for a feeding frenzy on the bull shark body that they'd tossed. It hadn't taken more than a few seconds for the carcass to be gone. Anyone who missed landing in the boat likely wouldn't have enough time to climb in, even if they landed right beside it.

Crap, she thought. "We can't do this now. There's no way."

She looked to Cage, but he was pacing in a small circle, his mind churning, though he wasn't speaking.

Gabby pulled her attention. "So we don't implement this plan unless the water comes up to the third floor. But if it does, then we have to do it. Because once it gets up here—" She motioned to the bottom of the window.

"No," Joule cut her off. "That's part of the problem. How

do we stay in this room until the water gets that high? It will be up to our waists in here, if it's up to the window ledge out there..."

The building was leaking. Even when the doors had been closed and bolted they'd only maintained a few inches of difference between the inside and outside levels.

The circle Cage paced grew tighter. His arms pushed straight down at his side, his hands were balled into fists. He wasn't angry. He was frustrated, and she didn't know what he was thinking. So she waited him out, letting the conversation work around him.

They discussed what would be the ideal water height to load the boat.

"How do we inflate it?" Marcus asked her.

"There's a manual backup, but each boat has a motor attached. There's a switch, so that's easy."

Cage reached down and opened one of the boxes. It took a few minutes for him to unfold the rubber and find the motor she'd mentioned.

Turning his attention, he checked the oar he'd pulled out. He pushed the plastic sleeve off and extended the rods, letting them pop into place from an internal piece of elastic holding the solid plastic tubes tightly in place. That seemed to satisfy him.

When he set the oar down, he pulled back the cover to the small fan and turned on the inflator.

"Don't waste the battery," Joule chastised him as he put his hand in front of the nozzle.

Cage counted to three then flipped the switch off. "This is another problem. These will self-inflate, but it's not going to happen too fast. Not like in the movies where it just pops open, ready to go."

Joule's heart sank. The boats had seemed like such a

good idea—an expensive one, but a good one. She still thought they would use the boats, but she was no longer confident she wouldn't get cracked upside the head from a fellow dorm resident trying to steal her route to safety. She no longer harbored an idyllic dream of putting the boat in the water and pushing off. Even the water itself presented far more problems than she'd foreseen.

The group sat in a circle, ate some of the snacks, and worked on the "boat problem" as Marcus called it. Joule now felt the boats had turned out to be nothing but problems, but she tried to keep her disappointment out of her comments.

"There are emergency alerts going off," Gabby added hopefully. "They will send rescue teams when they can."

Everyone offered small nods at the slim hope. Gabby wasn't wrong, but the current orders had been "Get to the highest point, stay dry, and wait." Help might be coming, but none was coming yet. The crews couldn't get out in the rain. Joule didn't say that. None of them did.

She also knew that the crews would first save the people who were sitting on the roofs of the one- and two-story houses. They'd rescue the people clinging to the tops of trees—not the ones in the three-story building. Not first. Probably not even second.

But she didn't say that, either.

The group talked the problem to death, until they gave up and decided it was time to get to sleep. The water was rising faster and despite all the issues, the boats were likely going to be their only hope. They needed to be rested.

Cage tucked his wooden desk chair under the door handle and Joule caught the look in his eye. This was reminiscent of last year, even though it wasn't the same at all. The very sight of the chair jammed against a door gave her anxiety, but she laid down on her slim, designated strip of mattress and pulled a blanket up under her chin.

They'd set up alarms, so that someone was up every hour to look out the window, check the water level, and look for new issues or use a flashlight to flag any arriving help.

Three hours later, when Joule's buzzer went off, she quietly peeled herself out of the bed. Slowly, so as not to wake anyone, she stood up and went to the window.

The air outside had grown darker. She had to focus one of the high-end LED flashlights out the window with her hand cupped around it to see anything.

The water was already several feet higher.

32

C age was awake before his alarm went off. Standing straight up from his spot where he'd curled up on the floor, he wondered if he'd even slept at all. He must have. He didn't remember the others getting up and checking at the window.

It was four a.m. now. Since no one had told him to wake up, that meant none of them had been too alarmed by the water level. As he stood peering out the window, flashlight in hand, he hoped the reflection didn't wake his cadre of roommates.

But once he caught the light reflecting off the dark surface of the water, it didn't matter. Either the water had been much lower an hour ago, or whoever was supposed to do the last check had missed their alarm. It didn't matter how it had happened.

The water was past the point they'd agreed on. Sleeping was over.

Aiming the flashlight beam around the room, he hoped that would start to wake his friends up. It was Joule who popped up first. Not surprising.

She only asked, "Is it too high?"

He nodded. They'd made their plans, gathered their tools and food and stuffed it into their backpacks. They had bottled water and drinks, plus all their food, a screwdriver, pliers that Marcus had found, rope, and one big bowl.

Gabby had surreptitiously scrounged through the communal room on the floor and found it, thinking they might use it to collect rainwater. Surely, they could drink what came from the sky, if they caught it as it fell. There was no way anyone would drink the water that was swirling around the building.

Max popped up next, making eye contact with Joule first. She offered him a nod and slowly he uncurled himself before reaching up and shaking one of Gabby's shoulders. She, too, rolled awake. One by one, they moved into action.

They'd made their plans last night. They would find out now if it worked.

The chair remained wedged under the door, where Cage had shoved it earlier. Once again, the sight of it tightened his chest. The fact that he had to lock out his fellow residents was concerning, but they hadn't figured out another way to do this. If they started a riot, it was possible no one would survive.

Having slept in their clothes, all seven of them stood up, fully dressed and ready to go.

He leaned over and grabbed the oars where they had already been set aside. Putting them on the desk near the window, he watched as the group silently began pulling the boats from the box. Gabby found the switches and turned on the motors. Slowly, the vessels began to puff up with air. Cage took a little more solace in the fact that they started looking sturdier as more air went into them.

Max and Marcus were ignoring the boats, standing at

the window. They'd opened the bottom sash, pushing it all the way up as they eyeballed the window's dimensions. Cage stepped back as the cold air rolled in and watched from a distance as his friends wrapped their fingers around the sash. They pulled and tugged on it until it cracked loudly. By breaking the metal runners holding it in place, they'd managed to pull it free.

However, that didn't help unless they could get out the upper pane that still blocked half the window. Max quickly pushed at the screen, popping it outward and watching as it fell into the water below. Cage didn't look. He didn't want to see what might leap up to grab at it.

The temperature in the room dropped quickly, and Cage realized they'd all failed to consider the cold. Turning from where he was organizing supplies on the beds, he opened his dresser and pulled on a second sweatshirt before he began handing out his extras. They were going to be wet and cold. Hypothermia was going to become a problem.

Another cracking noise behind him made him turn and watch as Marcus and Max now took small pliers to the window frame. They tugged and twisted pieces until they snapped a piece of the metal molding. Eventually, they managed to remove enough to bust the last pane free. Marcus grinned as he set the window aside. They'd doubled the size of the opening.

Cage's position was as director, and he was doing his best to watch everything. He turned to Roxie and Sky and ordered them to stop inflating the boats. "We still have to get them through that opening."

He pointed at the window as he heard the motors shut off. His heart pounded. It was go time.

Luckily, Joule had bought boats that were sturdy enough for search-and-rescue operation. Reflective yellow rope tied to the rings made a steady pattern around the top edge of the boat. But the friends had scrounged up additional bungee cords, twine, and rope—whatever they could find. There was no telling how much they would eventually need.

Once they were in the water, they would tether the inflatables together. But first, they had to rig the boats up to push out the window and get lowered to the water.

When he had the cords in place, they all added their weight and rolled the sides of the boat up so it more resembled a hot dog. Even so, it was barely narrow enough to go through the open window. At least they didn't have to worry about slicing their rescue boat with broken glass. There had been a contingency plan for if they'd had to break the windows out.

First stroke of good luck, Cage thought. He hoped it held, but he kept his eyes on the boat as it was pushed through the opening and began to unfold on the other side now that no one was holding it tightly. They would never get it back inside.

The inflated boat caught the wind—another thing they hadn't really planned for—but he and Max fought to lower it slowly, letting the far end just touch the water. Another problem occurred to Cage now: *What if the boat flipped over?* It was only five or so feet below them, but it was well out of reach.

Since it wasn't fully inflated, it floated like a lump. The rubber of the bottom was curling and rolling, not stretched out flat like it should be. Whoever stepped into it would sink well below the waterline, surrounded by tough rubber until the ring fully inflated and the boat formed its final shape.

"Alright guys," Gabby said, her small backpack on and ready to go. Last night she'd piped up. "I'm the lightest, so I'm out first."

Joule had protested, saying two people should go first, but Gabby had deftly countered with their current plan. "Tie the rope around me. It would be more dangerous to have more of us in it before it's fully inflated."

At least she would be anchored. As much as it would suck to drag her up the side of the building, they could if they had to.

With Marcus and Max slowly letting out the rope, Cage and Joule each took one of Gabby's hands as they lowered her down the wall. Her feet slowly walked the outside stucco until she at last waved her toe into the open space below her, hooking the boat and stepping down in.

She almost fell anyway and would have plopped into the bottom if not for the rope. Cage was grateful they'd devised a bit of a harness rather than just looping it around her waist. As he'd predicted, her feet sank well below the surface of the water and they all watched, holding their breath, waiting to see if the partially inflated boat would hold her.

But it did.

Gabby found her balance and Cage watched as she crouched down and pushed at the outer ring until she found what she was looking for. Max and Marcus kept the rope harness taut in case something went wrong and they had to yank her back out. Cage hadn't drawn a full breath yet.

"Got it," she said as she flipped the switch and he heard the faint whirr as the motor once again began inflating the boat. Slowly it unfurled, forming its expected shape as Gabby worked to distribute her weight and not jostle anything.

Beside him, Joule stepped up and said, "My turn. Get the harness on me."

His sister was next. Not his ideal plan, but they were going down in order of size. As tall as she was, she was second in weight, the more important measure in the boats right now. Putting her hand in his, she let him take some of the pressure as he helped lower her out the window.

The boat was almost fully inflated by the time she joined Gabby, who was now bobbing along the surface. Had the water risen while they'd been working? He didn't see the difference, but the way the rain was coming down, it must have.

Cage watched from the window. Seeing Joule—his last remaining family member—sitting in the boat in the middle of bull shark-infested waters, tethered only by a single rope, was possibly the hardest thing he'd ever done.

33

The rain came down on her head, tapping a rhythm on the hood of the waterproof jacket. *At least the gear is trying to be waterproof,* Joule thought.

Though she wanted to look up and check out the state of the sky in the pre-dawn hours, she didn't dare. The rain would get in her eyes, hit her face, and run it little rivulets down the front of her jacket despite the hood. Instead, she reached out to take Gabby's hand and wasn't surprised when her friend's grip was far too strong.

It was petrifying, sitting on the surface of the water in only an inflatable boat.

Though the motor offered a soft but high-pitched whine to signal it was working, the pitch was changing as the pressure increased. It was almost full.

She hollered up to her brother, "Start getting the next one out!"

Her eyes darted frantically along the side of the building. Rectangular windows, most dark, stared back at her. A few had blue or yellow lights showing. Anyone who looked out their window would see the boats. She and her friends had to get out of here before someone discovered what they were doing.

Just then, a surprising but familiar face popped out of the window above her.

"Joule!" Ginnifer's voice cut the air. "I'm coming with you."

"What?" Joule asked, wondering how in hell had Ginnifer gotten into the room? How had she even figured out that she to follow them? Joule didn't know.

But her brother always seemed to understand. He stuck his head out into the rain to say, "She knocked on the door. She already knew about the boats... She and Holly are both here."

Joule felt her teeth grind. They couldn't have people barging in, demanding to get in the boats! They'd overflow before they even got the second one out the window.

Ginnifer popped her head out the window again, the rain plastering her hair to her head. For once, she didn't seem to notice. "I didn't tell anyone, Joule. I don't want your operation to start a riot. But we've got to get out of here."

No shit, Joule thought. *But "we" wasn't supposed to include you.*

Again, Joule looked up to her brother, risking the rain on her face and down her jacket once more, but all she saw was a shrug. His voice carried down again, though she could tell he was fighting not to be too loud. "They pounded on the door and demanded to be let in. But we locked the door behind them."

So Ginnifer and Holly were now in the group? It wasn't the time or the place, but Joule couldn't help it. Seven months. For seven months, Ginnifer had ignored her—and those had been the good days. Otherwise, she'd been a pain in the ass. Now, she wanted Joule to rescue her?

For a moment, her roommate's expression changed and Ginnifer called out, "I'm sorry. I shouldn't have been such a butthead to you."

Butthead? That was how she was categorizing it? But Joule didn't have time to dwell; it was all that Ginnifer gave her. Her roommate followed it up immediately with, "You need me. Holly and I are in programming."

As the second boat came out the window, lowered via rope over their heads, she and Gabby had to move from their original position. Still tethered by harnesses stabilized by Max and Marcus, they reached up. Together, they pushed the other boat away and into a position beside them.

Joule switched off the motor on the boat she sat in and motioned to Gabby to cap the open vent as she reached out and grabbed onto the rope that ringed the edge of each inflated boat. Keeping the two rafts close together was of the utmost importance, but she still reached over and grabbed onto Gabby's hand.

Crouching low, she leaned out and maneuvered the other boat around, feeling the partially inflated ring mushy beneath her fingers. It was disconcerting at best, but she had to find the motor and start inflating it again. The longer they sat here, the more likely it was that someone would see them. *Someone else.*

She breathed out a harsh sigh of relief as her wet fingers brushed against the hard plastic of the black motor box. Tugging off the cap, she flipped the switch and listened to the motor start to work.

Her immediate task done, she looked back up at Ginnifer and, over the noise of the motor, the rain, and the people still in the room above her, she almost yelled. "In case you hadn't noticed, there's no power. There's nothing to program. We *don't* need you."

But Ginnifer was ready. "I can make your phones last twice as long."

Crap monkeys. Joule couldn't help it. She *did* need that. Her phone battery was well below forty percent, and she'd been conserving everything she could. They had backups, but how far would they have to travel? How long would they need those phones to hold out? What if they got somewhere safe and dry, but no one knew where they were? The phones would be a lifeline. Maybe their only one...

"And your flashlights. I can make a generator work, if we find one. I'm disturbingly handy."

Behind Ginnifer, Cage shrugged.

As far as Joule could tell, the argument was over. If they shoved Ginnifer and Holly back out into the hall, it would start a fight, and that would definitely start a riot.

"Fine," Joule muttered. From above her in the window, the others seemed to agree.

She focused on her friends now getting ready to come down into the boat, even as she kept checking the second boat to be sure it continued to inflate properly.

The others weren't tethered. Then again, they weren't being lowered into a partially inflated raft. First, they dangled Roxie out the window and then Sky. As soon as they had dropped the last few inches in and were seated in the rocking boat, Gabby tugged at her own tether line and Max let go of her. They had to trust the boat, but they didn't have to trust the sea. Gabby used the now loose rope to tether Sky to her, exactly as planned. Roxie waited for another person to drop into the boat. They wouldn't tie them all together yet.

It was time for the next maneuver. They had this all mapped out and so far—aside from the arrival of Ginnifer and Holly—it was going according to plan.

This move was why Joule was still anchored by Marcus above her. Staying low, she prayed to any deity that might be listening before beginning to climb out of Gabby's fully inflated boat and into the second raft.

Joule didn't like the feeling of the rubber rolling loosely beneath her. It gave way under her weight and she sank below the waterline. She would feel better when it was stretched taut, the ring fully inflated. She muttered under her breath to the little motor. "Faster, faster."

But then Cage was in the boat beside her. She almost chastised him, but quickly realized the ring was already solid beneath her touch. The thick rubber beneath her had stretched taut while she was muttering. The rain had changed, and she couldn't quite hear the pitch altering in the motor, but she could tell it was still working. She lowered her ear closer until it touched the smooth, rubbery surface, listening for the telltale note that said the pressure was high enough.

Behind her, she felt Cage unlink her fingers from where she'd continued to hold onto Gabby and wrap his own hand around hers. As she looked up for a moment, she saw that he'd grabbed Gabby's hand. The two of them were now holding the boats in place together.

Ginnifer and Holly were lowered next, and by the time everyone was down, Joule and Cage's boat was inflated to the proper pressure. She turned off the motor, snapped the protective cover into place, and looked up. With two extra people along for the ride, their division of people, supplies, and numbers had changed.

"Ginnifer's with us," she announced, motioning her roommate to cross into the second boat. "Holly, you stay behind. Max, you stay in that boat."

"You don't have to separate us," Ginnifer protested.

"Yes, we do. We already had the weight evenly distributed. You've messed it up." Joule almost added that Ginnifer needed to shut up and sit down and do what she was told. It wasn't her boat.

Luckily, she didn't have to say it. Ginnifer moved quickly and sat calmly in the corner, her raincoat huddled around her, the rainboots on her feet tucked up, cross style, under her butt.

Max's size and weight in the first boat meant that Joule and Cage got two more people in theirs. "Marcus will be with us," she called out, continuing this twisted game of mathematical Red Rover. "And Roxie."

Then, once they were sorted, Max looked up to the window at the rope still draped over the ledge. The paint was chipped where they'd pushed at the screen and broken out the panes. Joule watched as Marcus slowly climbed out. He was the tallest and therefore the last one to leave.

He hung by his fingertips while the others reached out and grasped onto his feet. The nylon cord he'd draped over his shoulder was attached to nothing. He was just bringing it with him. Though one still tethered the first boat to the window and therefore the building, it was the only thing keeping the boat close enough to the building for Marcus to drop down in. It was the only rope they would cut.

As Marcus climbed into their boat, Max pulled out a knife and began sawing at the cord that held them to the dorm. When it severed, she felt a small jolt as the boats were finally at the mercy of the water.

34

J oule watched as they cleared the corner of the dorm building with four people in each boat paddling. The increased numbers meant that one person in their boat could sit back and thus navigate. It also meant a fresh rower in case someone had to drop out. She begrudgingly admitted the benefit, if only to herself.

The addition of Ginnifer and Holly meant that every paddle was in use at all times. That, at least, was good. Ginnifer hadn't complained when Joule had handed her a plastic oar. She'd merely climbed into place along the side and joined in.

Joule pulled her phone from her pocket as she felt the soft buzz. Surely it was another weather alert. She'd set the tone and vibrations as low as possible, not wanting to use any more battery than she had to. Now she was eager for Ginnifer to do as she had promised and jack up the charge on her devices.

Joule wouldn't have opened the email, except that it came from Dr. Kimura.

"Oh dear God, that is just fucktastic," she muttered as

she read it quickly, then looked up at the others and announced, "I just got an email from the professor who helped with the fish."

Only Ginnifer looked confused.

"He's stuck in the sciences building, on the top floor."

"Do we need to go get him?" Cage asked. But they were all thinking it.

"I don't know." Joule truly couldn't answer that. Being stuck was bad. But if he was in a building, maybe he was high enough to be safe. Then again, the water was rising at a rate no one had predicted.

The plan had been to exit campus as soon as possible. Rowing their way to the Science and Engineering quad wasn't a good idea. There was no higher ground there, only a few taller buildings, and it was entirely the wrong direction. However, there was no way to know how much longer that protection of an added story or two might last for the professor. Joule wasn't even sure if they would be able to break into the building, if they decided it was to be their safe space.

"He's stranded and we know where he is. If we don't go get him, can we live with that?" Joule asked the others.

She was met with shrugs.

Roxie at least offered some insight. "Eventually, we'll be going back and forth and saving as many people as we can."

Cage followed along. "Maybe we should see now if we even can rescue someone. If we can't, at least we won't risk ourselves coming back later for an impossible task."

It was both a hopeful and sobering thought.

If they couldn't rescue Kimura, then—when they got themselves to dry land—they would stay put. They would simply have to hope everyone else did okay.

Joule fought to ignore the fact that they couldn't save

everyone. The water was going to cross the threshold on the third floor of the dorm at any moment. The students huddled there would be climbing on beds and on top of dressers. They would figure out how to get onto the roof or how to launch into the water as she and her friends had. She'd seen the kayaks before. Maybe there was hope.

That was what she clung to. To her friends, she said, "Bass Science building will be around another corner to the right, then aim almost straight ahead."

But as they cleared the other edge of the building, she was stunned by what she saw. The trees had blocked her view from the room. Now they were underwater—some only partially, some almost completely submerged. She wasn't prepared for the stunningly altered landscape in front of her.

They were forced to use various dark patches in the grey as landmarks. It would mean a building was blocking what little light was beginning to filter through. She checked her phone again and saw that the sun should be up, but "up" was well beyond the mass of clouds covering the entire bay area.

They certainly couldn't see the Bass Science building from here, but they could see a corridor, created by upper floors of buildings and the tops of trees. It was as if she was a bird, flying along the rooflines. On some buildings, all that crested the surface was the top lines of the roof.

Other structures were missing altogether. She knew the shorter buildings were fully underwater, but it was disconcerting to see those familiar landmarks had vanished.

As the others rowed, making slow progress, Joule kept an eye out. On her left, they would be skimming over the top of another low, squat building. "Watch out. We don't want to get caught on the roof of any of the Santa Teresa residences."

They rowed an arc around one of the only partially submerged parking garages and aimed for the Allen building. Even shrouded in shadow, its shape was easy to find. Joule typed out her message to Dr. Kumara. "We're on our way."

But then she looked where her feet were tucked up under her. Her butt was not only wet, but she was now sitting in maybe a centimeter of water. It wasn't much, but it puddled where her weight pressed into the rubber. Though she was making an indentation, the rain coming down on them was starting to accumulate.

The boat itself was gathering water. The bowl that they brought to collect rainwater to drink wasn't a bad plan, but they hadn't extrapolated that to the bigger picture. However deep that bowl got was how deep the boat would be, too. Only the water the boat carried would become a massive problem. For all that they tried to get ahead of everything, they'd missed that very important mark.

She looked to her fellow castaways, glancing around both the boats. All oars and rowers were on the outside edges. The boats were lashed firmly together along one long side, tugging slightly against each other as they paddled. Most of the rowers sat up on their knees, allowing them to stack in closely and fit in a neat line. But it meant they weren't sitting down in the water like she was. They didn't see it yet.

"We're going to have to bail the boats out," she shouted as the dorm disappeared further in the distance behind her. If any of her old dormmates was looking out the window and watching them, she didn't want to know. "We won't make it very far with the water coming down at this rate unless we're constantly removing incoming water."

"And we're going to take on another person?" Ginnifer asked, clearly miffed. "How many?"

Joule felt her eyes turn angry. The idea that they might rescue Ginnifer but not Dr. Kimura burned in her gut. "Listen, you undercooked Becky, we already took you on, and you weren't invited." Ginnifer's head snapped back at the insult, but Joule kept going. "You don't get a vote in who we rescue or where we go."

Ginnifer snapped her lips into a tight line and didn't respond.

The others stayed staring straight ahead. No one needed to deal with a roommate fight right now. Which was exactly why Ginnifer and Holly shouldn't be here. At least Holly had the grace to stay quiet. But even so, they were in the boat now, and unless Joule was willing to throw them over the side, she had to do her best to keep the peace.

They rowed on in silence a little farther, and as they cut a wide path around the Allen Building, she saw it. "That's the science complex, Bass Biology is just beyond it."

Joule offered to trade out for someone who was rowing. Not Ginnifer, but one of the others. No one took her up on it.

"We need to trade before we get tired," she pushed. "We have a relief crew now, but it's only one person." She didn't mention that there was a possibility that the non-rower would be sick or injured in the future, and she was once again grudgingly grateful for the extra manpower Ginnifer and Holly provided. They were at least warm, strong bodies. If they rescued Kimura, it would add a second relief rower.

Eventually, Roxie added, "I'll trade soon, but I can go a little farther."

Marcus pointed out, "When we get there, you're going to be the one he recognizes—"

"Right," Joule cut in. "But both me and Cage."

He nodded. "We may need you to grab him. He'll trust you. After he's in the boat, we'll be all hands on deck."

It was later than Joule would have liked. She would have voted for shorter, more frequent breaks. But she'd learned last year that she was stronger than she thought, and her friends were very smart, so she didn't dwell on it.

A few moments later, Gabby, sitting at the front, shouted, "There! That's Bass Biology."

Joule pushed up onto her knees for a better look. Loaded with the five of them, the boat was better balanced, and she didn't feel as nervous as when she'd first climbed in. The looming shape *did* look like the Bass Building.

But even as the happiness at getting close swelled in her chest, the water rippled in front of the boat.

A fin cut the surface of the water just under Gabby's outstretched finger.

Joule was about to say something when the fin disappeared beneath the water and a mouth—open, teeth showing—burst up through the surface aimed straight for her friend's hand.

35

"Gabby!" Cage yelled out as he dove into the other boat to grab her. He launched his way over the middle divider where the two boats were lashed together, snatching Gabby's slick raingear and grasping for purchase. He hauled her backward and they crashed in a pile onto the PVC that made up the floor of their skiffs.

As they landed and he sucked in air to make up what had been knocked out of him, everything rocked. At the edges of the boats, his friends held on to their oars and grabbed for something to stabilize themselves.

Gabby had seen the first shark, of course. But it wasn't the fin that cut the water right under her hand that set him off. That shark was horizontal. Petrifying, yes, but not in position to get her. It was the snout that burst up through the surface of the water that sent Cage flying to grab her and haul her hand out of reach.

The rounded and brownish nose belonged to a second shark, one swimming straight upward, likely aiming for a bite.

Cage didn't know what would have happened if he

hadn't jumped, but the way his heart pounded, it didn't matter.

He was breathing heavily, and it took a moment to unwind his fingers from where they clutched her jacket. His fingers had almost pierced the rubberized material.

"Holy crap, that was way too close." Though he wasn't looking, he could make out Roxie's voice through the drone of the rain still coming down.

As he rolled his head from side to side, checking that everyone was okay, he saw his friends look at where their hands rested on top of the inflatable ring. Even that was now too close to the water. Everyone slowly pulled their fingers back out of reach.

For a moment, he and Gabby looked upward and regrouped. For his own part, Cage was simply deciding to stay safe in the middle of the boat for a minute.

"New rule," Joule announced. "No holding anything over the water."

Marcus, at least, had the wherewithal to smirk his way through an answer. "What about the oars?"

Well, shit, Cage thought. The oars *had* to go over the side of the boat. Also, their hands had to be on the handles of the oars, which meant their hands were mostly over the side of the boat, if they were going to continue to row. They all looked to each other and, for a moment, no one paddled.

The two boats, lashed together almost as a single unit, rocked back and forth. There weren't waves here or a tide, only the rain and the landscape underneath that wasn't used to supporting this amount of water. The wind made the water surface rough, and they would just have to deal with it.

Cage was wet now, despite the waterproof rain gear that Joule had bought for him. He laid down in the indentation he made in the boat. Water seeped up his back. As he set his hand down beside him, he felt that the puddle was now several centimeters deep in the boat. He didn't want to calculate how fast and heavy the rain had to be coming down to make that happen in the time they had been out.

Sure. They'd been out for a while. It wasn't as if somebody overhead had simply poured water into their boat. But still, it was too much, too fast.

He was taking a breath, suggesting that they couldn't just sit here and that they would need to be more careful when he felt it. Something touched him from under the boat. Something big. The lump started at his shoulder and, before he could even move to sit up, it traced a path down his spine across his left butt cheek and toward his thigh.

"Holy shit!" He burst upright, once again rocking the boat. Turning around, he grabbed for Gabby's hands and yanked her up beside him. The last thing he wanted was her lying in the bottom and feeling what he felt. But as he sat up, Cage saw eight other faces just frowning at him.

"Something rubbed along under the boat."

But no one else had felt it. Did he tell them it felt big? Had it been big? Or was it maybe just a stick floating by?

He didn't have any answers, so he didn't say anything and simply let his little outburst stand for what it was.

"Hey," Roxie said softly. "We're drifting away from Bass Biology building." She stuck her oar in the water and pushed.

Whether it was brave or stupid, Cage couldn't tell. But this next stop felt necessary.

They couldn't sit out here. Eventually, the rain would fill the boat. It might not sink, but it would ride low and be incredibly difficult to maneuver. Maybe they could simply go to the Science building and stay stranded with Dr.

Kimura. Although that option was probably out. If there'd been another floor, the professor would have gone up to it. He wouldn't have messaged to Joule that he was stranded.

So Cage nodded and picked up his oar, grateful that when he dove to grab Gabby, he'd dropped it inside the boat. He began calculating that they could lose oars down to about four, but after that, they'd be nearly dead in the water. They had to hold on to them.

They paddled forward another five minutes before he spoke again. "Wait. We need to secure these to our wrists somehow. We can't lose the oars."

"No, we don't!" Joule countered quickly. "What is something grabs it and it's tied to your wrist? We don't want anyone yanked out of the boat by the oar."

She didn't comment on what that "something" was. They knew.

"Okay, so it needs to be able to slip off, but..." He paused to think. Getting pulled into the water was definitely worse than losing an oar, but they couldn't afford to lose oars, either. The more people they loaded into the boats, the more force they would need to row.

"Got it!" Holly piped up for the first time.

For a moment, they all looked at her as if she were bonkers. But she unzipped her backpack and pulled out a fistful of loose hair scrunchies. Cage thought that was the dumbest thing he'd ever seen.

"You can slip your hand out pretty easy. But if you slip this over the oar handle—" she pointed to the T at the top and then to her own wrist as she demonstrated. Holly pulled the fabric-covered elastic over her wrist in a stretchy loop. "—it will hold on to it."

Cage merely blinked at her. She wasn't wrong. It was a good idea. Additionally, it meant they wouldn't have to cut up any of their rope. Nor would a scrunchie burn their skin like rope would if it got yanked. But... "What in God's name are you doing with a handful of hair scrunchies on a mission like this?"

Had he really just called it a mission? Oh hell. They were out in the middle of a flood tide, in the dark, with few landmarks, and something with teeth had just jumped at Gabby's finger. So, yeah, mission was okay.

But Holly was already explaining, seemingly unfazed by his irritation. "I was packing things, checking around the room and grabbing anything I thought might be useful. Seriously, since so many of us have long hair—" She looked pointedly toward Marcus. "—getting it out of our faces seemed like a good thing. So I grabbed everything."

Okay, Cage thought, *it wasn't a horrendously stupid idea.*

He tried to graciously accept the scrunchie that was passed to him. Holly handed them out. And one by one, they looped the brightly colored hair ties around their wrists.

He was liking Holly better and better. She stayed silent until she was useful, even if the scrunchies were a bit weird.

Ten minutes later, they got close enough to the Bass building to see Dr. Kimura on the upper floor. He stood at one of the windows, waving frantically at them as the water approached the bottom edge of the floor-to-ceiling window. Three more feet of water and the top floor of the Building would start flooding.

But how, Cage wondered, *can we get him out?*

They could see him. But the windows didn't open, and the building was designed to keep people from exiting the top floors.

They had arrived. But the professor was just as stuck as if no one had come.

36

A s they rowed in close to the science building, Joule waved to Dr. Kimura. She'd been messaging him so she'd known where he would be.

But after waving back to her, he motioned them to not row any closer.

One by one, they tucked their oars safely into the boat, and stayed kneeling in the water that was still gathering. They watched as he lifted something from the ground and swung it at the plexiglass window in front of him.

It was a sledgehammer. Though Joule braced herself for the window shattering above them, the heavy hammer only made a dull thud and bounced off.

"What the hell is he doing?" Roxie asked.

Joule shook her head. "He didn't mention he had a sledgehammer when I messaged him. He just said he'd find a way out."

"Well, he found it."

"I don't know. Doesn't look like it's working," Sky responded to her sister. Always a little quieter, she sighed and kept her eyes trained on the man they were all trying to save.

"Well, we don't want any glass flying at us." Roxie dipped her oar and tried to paddle the boat sideways frantically. The others agreed, if the frantic speed with which they began rowing and steering out of the way was an indicator.

Joule crouched in the back and clutched at her phone as the boat tried to twist and turn. She needed to begin contributing. She was a logistics coordinator right now, getting them to Dr. Kimura and staying in touch with him, but soon, she would need to contribute some muscle.

Above them, the third thunk changed to a crack and the thick polymer window spidered outward from his hit. It didn't react the way normal glass did, and it took the professor several more swings before he made any further progress.

From where they sat drifting on the surface, they could see he was getting more and more frustrated with his lack of success. But eventually, he cracked the barrier enough to push a triangle out. As it fell with a plop into the water—much too close to the boat—he stuck his hand out and hollered down, "Hey, I got the damn window open!"

Joule hadn't heard him cuss before. Then again, she'd only known him a short while. Her bigger concern was that he wouldn't fit through the small opening he'd created. The dormmates all sat and watched while he took the sledgehammer to the window again and again, until he pushed two more loose pieces of thick plexi out into the water and made a hole big enough to climb out.

But now that he could leave the building, how did they do this? Even as she thought that, Joule watched him pop his head out the hole and propose the stupidest idea ever.

"I can jump from here and swim over."

The entire boat yelled back. "No!"

Dr. Kimura jerked back so fast, he hit his head on the Plexiglas. He frowned.

Joule had quickly crawled to the front of the boat, hands planted on the inflated ring. She leaned forward just enough to yell, but not forward enough to hold any part of her over the water. "Sharks!"

"What?"

"Those elasmobranch egg pouches? Those were sharks." She almost smiled and shrugged.

"Even so," he hollered down, still frowning. "Most aren't a danger to hum—"

"Bull sharks!" She cut him off. She didn't need a lecture, he did. "We've seen feeding frenzies. Do not jump into the water. In fact, you can't even dangle over it or they will jump."

"Are you serious?" He now had his hands carefully wrapped around the Plexiglas, his head having poked back out the hole so he could holler to them and hear her replies. He stood several feet above them. At least that meant the water wasn't already at his feet. Joule was grateful that his question and concerned expression meant he was taking her at her word.

But the whole issue posed logistical problems.

"Can you find a rope? You can climb down the side of the building and we'll position the boat right underneath you." She didn't elaborate on the sharks. Surely, no one would believe them until they saw it for themselves.

He could study the pictures they'd all taken at a later time. Right now, they needed to get somewhere dry. The boats were temporary transportation. Not safety.

"I can't just jump in?"

It didn't seem that far, but Joule shook her head. "We can't risk knocking anyone out. See if you can climb down."

When he nodded and frowned, she wound up hollering at his back as his form retreated into the darkness of the building. "Is anyone with you?"

"Nooo," he replied, but the drawn out word didn't sound confident, making Joule wonder if he was leaving someone behind.

But now wasn't the time to worry about that.

It took ten minutes before he returned, but he held up a coil of rope as though in victory. It took another five minutes, apparently, for him to find an anchor that would support his weight.

But when they saw him begin to exit the window, they began rowing furiously in an attempt to bump the boat up against the building.

"What if he falls?" Roxie had asked.

"I know. Row faster," Joule replied, even as she yelled out, "Wait!" to the professor. The wind must have ripped the word away, because he kept creeping down the side of the building, the rope grasped tightly in his hands.

So they all plunged their oars in and stroked frantically, managing to bump the side of the building as the professor was about three feet above them. A piece of plexiglass still floated sideways, too close to the boat.

Joule didn't know if it could or would cut the rubber or PVC fabric that coated the inflated rings, but she didn't want to find out. Instinctively, Max reached to move it away.

"No," Holly whispered fiercely. "Use your oar."

As understanding dawned, Max gave the large piece of glass a hard shove and watched it drift away.

Joule kept her gaze trained on Dr. Kimura. His shoes were not appropriate for rappelling down the side of a building. His khaki pants were soaked, and his heavy jacket probably covered a button-down shirt and a sweater vest. He was getting wetter by the moment. Most of the students at least wore some kind of rain gear.

As he got closer, Joule noticed that his pockets were heavy. The jacket was stuffed, making him look as though he were several pounds heavier. The question was, What was that extra weight?

She wanted to stand and reach him faster, but instead, she rocked up onto her knees. Reaching up to awkwardly grab at his leg, she helped guide him backward toward the boat.

When she and Sky each had a hand around one calf, he let go of his rope. Flopping backwards, the professor bounced, trampoline-style, off the inflated rings tied together in the middle of the boats. It couldn't have felt good, the knots pressing into his back the way they did.

For a split second, Joule's throat closed as it seemed the boat would fold in the middle. The only thing keeping it open was the weight of the students lining either side. Still, everyone once again ducked down and grabbed for anything to give them stability.

Once the boat stopped rocking, they all sat up. Dr. Kimura did, too. Like the rest of them, he was no longer concerned with being wet. Looking around, he offered up a very heartfelt "Thank you."

Joule smiled, but as she adjusted her weight, her hand settled on something that had fallen out of his pocket... a thick, expensive silver wristwatch.

37

"T hey're what?" Cage asked, staring at Dr. Kimura as the professor reached carefully inside his coat and pulled out item after item.

"Containers," the professor answered with no smile, only a shrug and the word.

As if they would have leftovers they would need to take care of...?

"Your sister said we'd need to bail the boat," the professor added when Cage must have looked very confused.

He almost missed his stroke. That would have hurt Marcus in front of him or Gabby behind. They were having to run like a well-oiled racing crew. They were packed in so tightly that if anyone was out of pattern, they would at least clack their oar against the others, if not worse.

Cage watched as the professor handed Roxie the sealed containers he slid one by one out of his coat, almost like a magician. Occasionally, she would pull the top back and expose various foods.

Cage watched all of this from his position near the back

of the boat. Eight of them rowed. Poorly. The two not rowing —right now Kimura and Roxie—were supposed to be navigating. And maybe bailing.

That's how the system was supposed to work.

When Roxie lifted one lid and frowned at him, Kimura shrugged. "I brought all the food I could find."

Cage almost raised an eyebrow. The plastic box Roxie held contained nothing but cherry tomatoes. Then again, food was food. When they got hungry, no one would turn down plain cherry tomatoes.

He watched as Roxie snapped the lid back on tightly. Maybe they could use it for something else later. But she pulled out bags of chips and more soda cans as she went.

"Raided the vending machine, did ya?" she asked him, and Kimura nodded.

"Also the fridge." He reached into his coat and pulled out yogurts and more. "I hoped between the containers and the food, I might be able to partially pay my passage aboard the Safety Cruise."

Cage barked out a laugh, as though anything about this were a cruise. Or safe.

The rain continued to pound down on his head. On his thighs. On his arms. He felt wet even in places he wasn't. Cage was more than grateful for Joule's foresight in buying them the rain gear. Some of his friends weren't so lucky. Holly and Ginnifer, who wore regular sweatshirt parkas, had to be soaked to the bone. And the rubbery poly-whatever-it-was was doing a second duty holding his body heat in.

Eight of them continued paddling, but they were barely making any progress. And they didn't even really know where they were going. They needed to find higher ground, but they'd gone the opposite way to pick up Kimura. Luckily, they wouldn't need to pass by the dorms again. Cage didn't want to see his fellow students stranded on the rooftops. He couldn't handle that yet. Hell, he could barely handle being here himself.

Once she had the food stashed into various packs and the containers separated and stacked to save space, Roxie pulled out her phone. "Well, hells bells." She paused a moment then held her screen up as though any of them could see it. "The map still shows what road we are over. Apparently, we are coming up on Campus Drive. We need to turn and follow Gerona." Another pause, a sigh, and then, "Well, that's good. I know which way to go... I hope."

"Where are we going?" Kimura asked the group at large.

"Honestly," Cage turned his head as he tried to both answer and keep his paddle going in the right cadence. "We don't really know. We know we need to get to higher ground."

"Somewhere with shelter and heat," Joule added in.

Cage nodded along. She wasn't wrong.

"Maybe food?" Gabby piped up.

Cage watched a little from his spot near the back of the boat, as Kimura took it all in. Then he slowly added, "I think you're headed in the right direction. There should be houses up on the hill over there."

But where Kimura pointed wasn't where they had originally thought they'd go. It took a few more moments of untangling what each of them knew to change course a little bit.

They were working on slowly turning the tied together boats when Roxie yelled out, "Wait!"

His heart stuttering, Cage pulled his oar out of the water, just like all the others. The little orange scrunchie held the oar to his wrist even now.

"We're right over the top of the Enchanted Broccoli building."

Well crap-monkeys, Cage thought. It was hard enough steering the two boats together, but if they ran themselves across a roofline—one that they couldn't see—they could slice one of the boats. The undergrad dorm with the crazy name also had a crazy roof line, and a lot of tall trees around it.

His eyes scanned the water and he saw several of his boatmates turn their heads and start looking around, too. Probably, they were thinking what he was: *There are too many things to get caught on here.*

Tree tops crested the water, the branches sticking up almost like ancient burial mounds, offering a somber warning of where some of the passing hazards were. But there were so many they couldn't see.

Despite the rain still filling the boat, Cage slowly crawled toward the front to rest his hand on the inflated ring. Pointing, he asked his sister, "Do you see the gray lump in the distance there?"

He barely had the question out before they had attacked him. Three of them hauled him backward with brute force, their oars still scrunchied to their wrists, as they shook their hands and tried to get free... all while trying to wrestle him backwards.

He didn't fight, even though he was shocked that they'd taken him down like a rogue football player.

"You don't hang your hand over the water!" Gabby admonished harshly as she let go of his jacket. "Look."

As she gestured—her hand and arm fully over the boat and not the water—a fin cut the surface right in front of them.

Cage felt the boat shift as Kimura scrambled backward

so quickly, he rocked the small vessel. He almost collided with Cage.

"They shouldn't be here!" The professor's eyes were frantic, even though the students around him remained relatively jaded to the disturbing sight.

"Bull sharks. Remember," Joule told him. "We found elasmobranch eggs. They might be bull sharks."

Kimura was getting himself together. On his hands and knees, he scooted toward the front of the boat. Muttering to himself, he said things that Cage could make out less and less, even though the distance between them remained slight. The rain drowned out most of his words, but Cage heard a few things clearly.

"Eggs... most aggressive." Followed by, "This is bad."

At least he thought that's what he heard, until Kimura sat back on his knees, his hands on his thighs, as though he were around a campfire contemplating the meaning of life or choosing a spirit animal. But when the professor turned and looked at Joule, his eyes narrowed.

"We have to get out of the water. This is worse than you think."

———————

38

"Why is it worse? It's bull sharks. We've found parts of bodies in the water already." Joule eyed the professor. "How could it be worse than what we already think?"

Her oar draped across her knees and she sat back, the entire machine of rowers stopped while Roxie tried to get their bearings and not drag them across the roofline or a handful of trees. Either could snag them, and Joule had no idea how much the boat could handle. Though it was advertised as "tough," it was made for open water rescue, not skimming treetops. Would the bottom rip? Would a sharp branch puncture the inflated ring of the boat and destroy their bouyancy? Just how tough was "tough?"

Sitting dead in the water was the last thing she wanted to do, but she couldn't row by herself. If they went forward and hit something bad, that could make things much, much worse. Or maybe the sharks themselves would do that.

The professor didn't quite answer her question, but he looked around, his hand shielding his eyes as though from the sun. But there was no sun. It was rain he was keeping out of his vision. Whatever he saw, it made him frown more. "Is there meat or anything that I can toss into the water? I want to see what happens with a stimulus."

"Oh, we know what happens," Holly spoke up, startling Joule at just how close she was. Aside from the scrunchies, it was about the only time she'd spoken—but she was right.

"I'd like to see for myself." Then he thought for a moment. "It will be better with two pieces of meat, if possible."

Cage only shrugged at her. Joule understood how frustrated he'd been before about anything that wasted even a tiny amount of food, but now he seemed to have accepted it. The meat would go bad anyway.

He crawled through the water that had consistently grown deeper in the boat despite their relatively constant bailing and Joule wondered how much lower they were sitting in the water. *How many more creatures under the surface do we disturb as we float by?* The passing inflatables shifted the water everywhere they went, and that was something the sharks surely picked up on. But her brother unzipped a backpack and pulled out a container of sliced deli meats, and then handed the last few pieces to Kimura.

"Thank you." The man took the roast beef and began pondering it.

At that moment, Joule realized that—though she'd gone out of her way to rescue someone she knew—she'd also invited a new senior-most member into the boat. Up until now, she and Cage had been recognized as the mission's leaders.

When they'd opened the boxes, she'd told their friends that both of them had bought the boats, not mentioning that her brother hadn't known about them until just a few minutes earlier. Owning the boats gave the twins some authority. But now, the professor was the oldest, the most educated, and a teacher at a school where the rest of them were tuition-paying students.

Maybe Cage had handed over the meat more easily because of that. But even as she had the thought, Kimura flung the first piece out into the water as far from the boat as one could sling a floppy slice of roast beef.

Even before it hit the surface, it sparked a sudden frenzy.

Kimura's eyes went wide, but Joule could still see he was watching like the academic that he was.

"What are you testing?" she asked softly, as though everyone in the boat couldn't hear everyone's business.

"I'm counting." His eyes didn't move to look at her.

"Five," she said. She'd been watching the fins, too, trying to see if she could identify individuals or maybe just get a head count. But bull sharks seemed to have the same shape of dorsal fin. There were no real coloration changes on the skin, so there were no markings to catalog. It wasn't like tracking orcas or the tails of humpbacks.

She was trying to use shape as the distinguishing factor, but even then, with their speed, mostly she was counting how many fins she could see at once. She couldn't identify any one individual. It probably didn't help that, each time they got close, she felt more terrified. She'd seen the woman who knocked on the door of the dorm... was it just two nights ago?

But Kimura pulled her attention away from her dawning realization with his clearly professional assessment. "Nine, possibly thirteen."

More than twice as many as she'd counted. None of that was good. The thought of dipping a toe into the water and attracting thirteen aggressive sharks was deeply unsettling.

But he wasn't done. Kimura quickly scrambled to the

opposite corner of the two boats. This time as he sat back on his heels, he wadded the meat up. Instead of flinging it like a fluffy little frisbee, he chucked it overhand into the distance. It sailed through the air, and his hands leaned onto on the ring. As he leaned dangerously forward to watch, Joule placed her hand onto his shoulder. Palm flat, she slowly pushed him back, lest he begin counting sharks under his own nose.

"How many?" she asked.

Kimura shook his head, "They're further away than I can really see, but at least ten."

"Could they be the same ones from over there?" She was calculating the timing even as she asked.

He shook his head again.

Well crap, she thought. *The total grows every time he counts.* But Kimura was willing to explain.

"That was the point of my experiment. I threw the bait in different directions, fast enough that they shouldn't have been able to close the distance. I quit counting new sharks once enough time had passed that the same individual could reach the second location from the first."

He spoke like a researcher. Not like a man in the rain, his sweater vest soaked through, his knees in a puddle of water in the middle of an inflatable raft. None of that made the answer any better.

He sat back, his butt plopping into the water that pooled at the bottom of the boat. Joule was knew it was time to grab the containers he'd brought and start bailing again. Unlike Gabby's big bowl, Kimura's containers were square and squat. They could be scraped along the bottom of the boat, and hopefully yield more water out for every pass.

Between the rowing and the bailing and the rain and the panic, they were going to wear out quickly.

"The immediate area is infested with sharks. Probably worse than you thought," Kimura offered up quietly, making her little existential crisis worse. He pointed in a wide circle around them. "Within a twenty-foot radius of this boat, probably at any time, there are twenty or more sharks. Actually, that's a bare minimum. It's probably a lot more."

He said it with the cold academic interest Joule had come to expect from him, but she had lost the ability to catalog it that way.

"They all came this way because of the rains, yes, but to account for this number? There must be a rich food source. They venture out of saltwater and into brackish water like this only to hunt."

The sharks weren't simply here and the boat was disturbing them. No. They were specifically here to hunt the people. That had to be the food source Kimura had graciously left unnamed. *Them.*

No, she thought defiantly. She had survived the Night Hunters. She was not going to die in this liquid hell.

39

"Well, there's a sight you see right before you die."

The words were whispered a little too sweetly into Cage's ear.

He felt more than heard Holly stop rowing behind him. They'd been rowing for forever, it seemed, and had shifted positions several times. Sky and Gabby were now navigating and bailing the boat, the two designated non-rowers. Cage had filled that position for a time, and it hadn't been the break he'd hoped it would be. They were all wearing down.

When people got tired, they made mistakes.

Kimura had even joined in rowing, and they'd recalculated their weights and how they should be distributed between the two boats. They'd switched sides, to at least allow some muscle groups to relax for a while. But none of it had changed the fact that they were moving slowly, the work was hard, and they were all on their last wind.

Cage looked up to see what had stopped Holly, and what had made her say that. It only took a moment for his eyes to focus on the water in front of him. It was more gray than brown out here, but it was choppier, too. He hated it. Still he saw the fins in front of him.

They cut the surface of the water with no provocation. Just sharks. Circling.

"What does that mean?" Gabby asked. They'd all stopped now, supposedly to check their surroundings, but everyone was breathing a little heavy and they needed a break. If he was worried that they might not have the strength to get out of the water before the sharks got them, now he knew they wouldn't. They'd be too exhausted to climb back into the boat.

Around him, his friends put their heads together to look forward at what appeared to be sharks waiting for them.

"Good sign, bad sign," Kimura told them. He'd been sharing his knowledge and little pieces through the rain and the murk. They've been rowing for quite a while and getting a little bit of a marine biology education.

Cage could only assume they were making really crappy progress. They were constantly held back by the weight of the water in the boat, despite all the bailing they did. The odd and shifting currents of the floodwaters created a need to navigate around buildings, parking garages, trees, and—they quickly discovered—telephone poles and power lines.

Sometimes the lines showed above the surface of the water, but sometimes they didn't, and the group couldn't tell if they were dangerous or not. So they'd been going out of their way, cutting a bizarre, snake-like pattern while trying to stay aimed in the right general direction.

"Bad news?" he prompted the professor.

"Lots of sharks, hungry sharks. The circling behavior is restless. They are waiting for bait, and then they'll fight over it."

Cage felt his stomach clench. From the looks on the faces of his fellow rowers, they felt the same. "Good news?"

"Shallower waters," Kimura murmured to himself, seemingly not catching on that he was upsetting nine-tenths of the boat's occupants. "If they're here and they're not openly in a feeding frenzy, it would indicate they know this is a food source. The food—smaller fish—tend to be in shallower waters. Especially in freshwater species."

"This is deep, not shallow," Holly protested.

Kimura shook his head at her, and Cage heard the professor's response. "It's deep to you, but not to them. They're from the bay. This isn't deep."

Cage disagreed with the fish, but he couldn't fault the professor's analysis.

Joule leaned in closer to him from the other side. The boat rocked slightly, every movement magnified now that they weren't moving to stabilize the system they'd created. "If they're here and they're moving around because there's a food source," she asked, "then it makes it doubly dangerous to go into the water at all, right?" When Kimura didn't answer immediately, Joule continued. "Because as soon as any part of us cuts the surface, we become the food source and they're ready to eat it."

"Yep!" the doctor replied. He sounded completely non-academic for once.

Cage wasn't dismissing what Joule had said. He knew the danger was even higher here, but he felt hope surge in his heart and in his tired muscles. "We're close though?"

"I think so."

They took a few more minutes of break—probably all they could afford—and switched up their positions. Cage was glad when Kimura took a rowing spot and wondered if it would actually keep him quiet. *Probably not.*

Marcus took up their navigation position and pulled out his phone, checked the maps, then held it out toward Kimura. "Is this the neighborhood you were thinking we would go to?"

Before the professor could even answer, Sky asked a question, almost too softly to be heard. "What if these people don't let us in?"

"I'm sure one of the houses will be abandoned." Ginnifer was finding her foothold, contributing more. She spoke with confidence, even though Cage was certain it was false bravado. So far, his only issue with her was that Joule disliked her so much. Her information seemed solid. "I'm sure plenty of people left town."

But other people, Cage thought, toughed it out. Kind of the way the students had. The school had recommended that people leave for the weekend if they could. But they'd missed on demanding that the students leave. There'd been no evacuation. The warnings had been too late, and the last instructions had told everyone to "shelter in place."

People who were likely to tough it out probably felt safe. Maybe they thought it couldn't get this bad. If they'd been ready to leave, it had been too late, and the roads were all washed out.

His other concern was the kind of people that would stay behind. Even though Palo Alto wasn't the place that you would expect to have a large population of preppers and gun nuts, they were here. In fact, they were everywhere, Cage had found. The kind of people who believed they were ready to make a stand—the kind who would stay in their homes in the face of a disaster—were more likely to greet people with shotguns, if at all.

Still, he held out hope that they could find something open. Or at least someone friendly, someone willing. God help them, a shed would be better than where they were now.

He was about to go crazy from the incessant pounding of raindrops on his skull. His hair was plastered to his head and had been for hours, even though his hood was still up. He was bone weary, and his eyes had lost focus a lot of the time. He still couldn't quite see where they were going.

Cage was sure he wasn't the only one at the end of his endurance. But they had to keep themselves together until they had their feet on solid ground. He was growing less and less certain about the plan to return and rescue their fellow students.

"The water will get shallower as we get closer to high ground. Shallow waters are problematic," Holly piped up. Even in the middle of a real disaster, her voice still sounded peppy. But looking at her face, Cage surmised that was due to her vocal chords and not her mood. "Shallow water means more telephone poles, more treetops, and more diffi-culty navigating, because there's less space between obsta-cles. It will also amplify any currents we have to work against."

Cage turned and looked at her. She so infrequently contributed to the conversation, it made her words seem more important. None of what she said sounded wrong, but he must have been making a face of some kind at her.

"Engineering," she offered with a half-smile. "Sopho-more. City planning." Maybe it was her way of saying "I know what I'm talking about."

"So we need to be more careful?" He wasn't sure he could be. He wasn't sure any of them had enough energy to focus more.

"No—well, yes, but... we've had the boats aligned wrong the entire time."

Cage felt his eyebrows go up. They should be rowing, but if they were wrong... ? He didn't even know what she meant.

"Look," Holly continued, waving her hand toward the corners. "They're basically rectangular. They're really just made for rescue operations, or for drifting and waiting to be picked up. This wasn't designed for easy forward movement. By tying them side by side, we've made it worse. We're cutting a wider path. First, it means we have a wider front pushing against the water, which is more work. Second, by being wider, we make it harder to fit between obstacles."

Her eyes glanced one way and then another. Everyone was paying attention. "If we unlaced them—" Everyone started protesting at once. No one wanted to be two separate boats. The thought alone struck fear in his heart, and Cage protested along with the others.

"Listen! If we walk them around and tie them up end to end instead of side by side, then the second boat will draft off the first. The front will be only one boat wide, not two. It will be easier to navigate." She looked among them and Cage felt and saw the protests diminishing.

Still, he had one. "The last thing you want to do now is take the boats apart. Look at what's in the water."

"I know," Ginnifer replied, "but it would be worse to run into a live wire or have something sharp cut one of the rafts open."

Cage looked a Joule, but he could see she wasn't looking back at him. Her eyes had narrowed, and her gaze wasn't on anything in particular. He knew that look. She was already contemplating how to make it happen.

Holly had suggested that the set of boats moving more like a train made them narrower. He wasn't sure why they hadn't thought of that in the first place—or why Holly hadn't piped up hours before.

There was silence for a few moments, and then he watched as his sister took over. These were her boats. She had been the only one smart enough and with enough money to plan ahead. They were all here—and not huddled on the roof waiting for a rescue that still probably hadn't even been launched—because of her.

Joule explained her plan and then listened as her friends made suggestions and amendments.

Once they all knew how it was going to happen, they began to unlash the boats. That wasn't difficult, but it took some time.

The knots had grown as the water absorbed into the rope, despite the fact that it was a poly-based line and not cotton. Together, they tried to push the rope to loosen the knots or dig it out from where each knot had buried into itself. Cage's fingertips felt bruised with the effort and he saw they were wrinkled now and not merely wet.

Though their progress was agonizingly slow, eventually, they got the knots free and unwound the rope from where it held the boats side by side.

It became clear that, without the rope binding them, they might drift apart. But they all reached out and grabbed on to the opposite boat and held tight. Slowly, the group began walking the boats around.

Hand over hand, they shifted until the other boat was still beside them but nearly a full boat-length behind. Corner to corner, they passed the point at which they were the most vulnerable, with only a few hands able to hold on, their connection at its most tenuous.

And then it happened.

Cage and Max were the only ones able to hold on.

Perched in their respective corners, they had to muscle the boats around so they could be dragged into their new positions—end to end. Cage was in the boat that would be in the front, and he and Marcus were looking at each other, discussing adjustments when he felt the line pull across his wrist.

He let go before he looked, already concerned. Sure enough, a fin had surfaced and brushed his skin as the shark cut the small space between the two boats.

"Shit!" Marcus yelled, his own hand suddenly up in the air. He held his wrist with the opposite hand as though he'd been burned.

Cage had jerked backwards at the touch, too startled to think or even keep breathing. But the result was already done. The boats had lurched at the sudden movement and now they began to drift apart.

Reaching out over the water was hazardous, but it had to be done. He and Max scrambled back into place, shark fins be damned. Leaning out, he felt his friends grabbing onto his shoulders, his rain gear, anything they could to haul him back quickly if a mouthful of teeth launched out of the water for his hand.

But even though they both stretched out dangerously far, their fingers didn't touch.

It only took a moment and another fin to make them snatch their hands back for safety. With that movement, the others took action, dragging Cage backward and out of harm's way. He was unceremoniously plopped into the constant puddle that was the bottom of the skiff.

He could only watch as the two boats began to drift apart.

40

J oule's heart pounded in her chest in a way she would have thought impossible just a few moments ago. Despite being exhausted, she'd harnessed her adrenaline surge and launched into action. Now she clenched her hand, feeling Cage's arm beneath her fingertips, grateful that he was still there.

For half a moment, she rested—but only half a moment, because it occurred to her then that she didn't know if he had all of his limbs or if he was bleeding out into the pool of water that had collected in the bottom of their skiff. Lifting her head, she searched him top to toe and saw no glaring red gashes. So she again laid her head back into the water and sucked in a breath filled with rain drops.

The water stung her face. It rolled along the sides of her head, sneaking into her ears, puddling in the corners of her eyes, and making tracers down the back of her neck. Normally, the rain would have irritated her no end. Now, it was the least of her worries.

As the boat began to rock, she scrambled upright like the others. This was no time to relax. She watched as their sister ship moved farther away on the subtle but powerful waves.

Gabby was swearing a blue streak. Marcus was scrambling through backpacks. Kimura was patting at his pockets, as though he might find some some magic rock to save them. And Sky and Roxie were both leaning over the edges of their vessels, hands pushing into the inflated rings though their friends were holding them back.

Joule once again flexed her grasp. Once again, she felt her own twin's hand beneath her fingers and could only imagine what Sky and Roxie were going through at this moment. Then again, she'd been in this situation before...

"The rope!" she yelled, finally sitting upright and beginning her own scramble around the boat. The backpacks were partially underwater. That meant the rope was underwater, too.

She frantically worked to tie knots into the end, the only thing she could think of to do right now. Even as her fingers moved, she looked around. She needed something with...

Though it had taken less than a minute to figure out to use the rope, she was already berating herself for not having the rope between them in the first place. They should have had it in place as a safety feature before they ever started moving the little boats around. But they were all too tired to think of things like that. All they could do now was try to save themselves.

Again.

"Row!" It was Ginnifer's voice, and Joule watched as her fellow boatmates picked up their oars. In the other boat, they were doing the same.

But they'd caught some odd current running between them that kept pushing the boats apart. The rowing, as frantic as it was, didn't move them fast enough.

"Weight!" she called out, hoping the others would understand.

"Here." Roxie set her oar down for a moment and reached into one of the backpacks, and Joule almost burst into hysterical laughter as she was handed a closed Tupperware full of cherry tomatoes. But as she took it, she realized the weight was solid. *There's a pound of tomatoes in this thing...*

She looped the rope around it twice in different directions then tied a knot, anchoring the Tupperware and tomatoes firmly on the end of the line. She looked up, wanting to know who would be willing to throw her little contraption, but she didn't have to ask.

"I've got it." Marcus traded her for his oar and she gratefully swapped positions. He was probably their best shot. Not that playing lacrosse in high school would set him up for slinging bolo lines between boats, but he had strong arms, and she was glad he would try. Her own aim was terrible with anything less than an arrow.

Everyone ducked as Marcus lifted the rope over his head and twirled the cherry tomatoes around a few times as though to gather speed. Joule had no idea if that was necessary, but she wasn't about to argue with the person who was hopefully going to get the two boats back together.

He arced the tomatoes through the air and everyone watched, disappointed, as they splashed just a foot shy of the other boat. It was Sky who instinctively reached out to grab it.

"No!" the entire boat yelled, nearly in unison.

Sky had unthinkingly put herself in danger. Fortunately, nothing below them had noticed and made a lunge for her hand.

"Can you hook it with something?" Joule yelled over, even as she pushed her oar back into the water, but they weren't prepared. No one had brought hangers. No one expected this kind of emergency. They'd left with the boats firmly tied together and the belief that they wouldn't untie them until they hit land.

Movement caught the periphery of her vision and she looked down to see that the splash had brought fins and mouths.

Marcus quickly yanked on the rope, removing any possibility that the other boat would manage to hook the line. "I've got to try again."

But as he towed the weight back in, it became even more interesting to the hungry fish. Quickly, he'd caught a shark. The mouths had come up out of the water in rapid succession, not caring that they were bumping into each other. The Tupperware and its tomatoes disappeared behind one winning set of teeth.

As she watched Marcus tug the line against a shark, she saw that the other boat was still slowly drifting farther away, despite four people rowing against the pull. Marcus should have a better chance of hitting the target on his second shot —but he was now occupied with his tug of war.

More fish seemed to appear out of nowhere, even here in the gray water. Joule had been concerned when the water was brown when they were still on campus. The sharks themselves were a brownish color, and it blended perfectly with the silty water. Even when the water had seemed to have some clarity, the sharks had remained completely invisible. The students spotted them only as they attacked.

Joule had hoped she'd see something now that the water was grayer. Maybe they'd show up as shadows moving under the surface, color changes, anything. Surely the shallow depth would work in her favor. But it didn't. Once again, a mouth popped up as if materializing out of nothing.

"Cut the rope!" Joule yelled, even as she tapped Marcus on the arm to get his attention. They could lose the tomatoes. They couldn't afford to lose the time.

Next to her, Cage flipped open a pocket knife and began to saw at the line. But Marcus continued to tug against the shark and they watched as the teeth cut clean through the rope, taking the Tupperware and the weight of the cherry tomatoes with it.

Joule fought the wildly inappropriate response, *There went the only fruits and vegetables we had.* As if any of that would make a difference.

"We need another weight," she called out and watched as those in her boat began scrambling for anything that would work. What she hadn't counted on was the other boat.

Dr. Kimura, Max, Sky, and Holly had also been scrambling through their bags, searching for anything that would work.

"Batteries!" Joule heard offered up. "No." The reply was Holly, who put a sharp end to that with, "We can't afford to lose them."

"Paddle!" It was Max, oar in hand, waving it around to remind them they still had to row. For a moment he tipped with the movement, and Joule ate the sound that wanted to come out of her throat as she feared she was about to watch him topple into the water. But he regained his balance and rallied his boat members.

Even as she picked her own oar up and slipped the little scrunchie over her wrist, she ignored the fear. They'd already dicked up the boat transfer. They couldn't afford to be upset about anything. They were doing their best.

The bright pink of the hair tie mocked her. It stood out, pretty and frivolous, against everything that had gone wrong with this day. She dipped the blade into the water and worked to push the boats back together. But instead of feeling the press of water against the flat of the blade, she felt it jerk away from her.

She tipped to the side and scrambled, yanking her arm back from where the oar and the little scrunchie wanted to tug her overboard. She was not going to lose the damn oar!

Quickly, she righted herself, oar still in hand—yes!—but the end still remained stuck. Looking down into the water she could follow the line of the edge only a few inches. But that was enough to see the teeth clamped on to the end of her blade.

41

"What is it?" Cage watched as his sister struggled to row. The way she was fighting the water didn't make any sense, but even as the words left his mouth, he felt a tug on his own oar.

Looking down, he saw what Joule must be dealing with.

"Shark's got me," she muttered just loud enough for him to hear.

His oar had not been bitten, but merely bumped. It was enough to twist his blade and catch the water oddly. Just the small amount of movement from the boat gave the body cutting through the water enough force to ruin his stroke.

If what Joule was describing was correct, she had one clamped onto her blade. As he looked over to see if he could help, he felt his blade get bumped again and he began to worry about the numbers. How many were down there, circling the boat?

The students and Dr. Kimura had spread out the way that Holly had originally suggested—five in each boat, two rowing on each side and one left over to navigate, bail, and keep watch for the unexpected. The new arrangement gave them more room, which was good, because as he looked around, Cage saw more of the rowers than not thrashing frantically to keep their oars out of hungry mouths. Some shoved the blades at the water as if to push or hit the sharks away. There were simply too many sharks, too close to the boat

Yanking his oar out of the water, Cage covered the short distance on his knees. Water sloshed around him, reminding him that they needed to bail soon—well, as soon as anyone had a free moment. Once he was close enough to his sister to have an effect, and just far enough away to miss taking an elbow to the face, he swung his oar up over his shoulder and smashed it down flat across the head of the shark biting into her oar.

It didn't let go.

Just fan-fucking-tastic, he thought. Deadly, aggressive, and tenacious. And possibly impervious to pain. All really shitty combinations.

Joule tugged on her oar and it took Cage a moment to catch on that she was bringing the menace closer to the surface. Since the broad side of his oar didn't work, he tried a different tactic. For the second strike, he used the edge of the blade, slicing down with all the force he could muster.

But still, the shark didn't let go.

This asshole was is tough! But Cage was getting more and more determined. He could beat this monster with its mouth full of razors. It might be hungry, but he was hungrier. In a smooth move, he rotated the whole oar. Because he'd practiced slipping the handle quickly out of the scrunchie on his wrist, he was ready.

This time, he didn't swing at the shark, but jabbed it, aiming the tee of the oar handle directly for the shark's eye —or where he imagined it should be.

It worked! The shark finally let go of his sister's oar. In the moment that the mouth gave up a little of its pressure, Joule yanked backward, freeing herself. Maybe she should have let the oar go, but despite his earlier calculations, they needed every blade they could keep. Especially if this was going to be their way of fighting off the sharks.

"Go for the eye!" He hollered above the rain and wind. As though that would help. But he watched as Gabby changed her strike, oar still clutched in one hand, and pummeled the shark with a strange, purplish club.

She smiled and held up the club as the shark that had been pestering her gave up. *An umbrella,* Cage saw. *Good move.*

One disaster averted.

But the boats still weren't together.

Looking up, he saw that the other boat was paddling as frantically as his did. Like his own raft, they were fighting off a swirl of sharks who bumped, lunged at, and even bit their oars. Just keeping the boats moving forward took so much. They couldn't keep this up.

At least they'd managed to move a little bit in the right direction.

Though the distance between the inflatables was now shortened, they weren't close enough. They would have to bump the boats into each other, since they couldn't reach out at all, for fear of what might pop out of the water. No one could afford to lose a hand.

He scanned the grey landscape and realized that even the loss of a finger could mean death. Medical care was nowhere in sight.

The rain somehow managed to come down harder, as though the flooding needed to get worse. It was suddenly diffi-cult to see the other boat, even though they were just a few yards away. It was even more difficult to see the projectile flying toward his head. But he caught sight of it at the last moment, ducking slightly to the side and feeling it whiz past. Too close.

This weight was a bottle of Gatorade. It would have done some damage if it had hit him. But it hadn't. As it landed in the boat next to him, Cage realized what had happened. The other boat had sent the salvo across, and he damn well had to answer it before their tenuous connection slipped into the water. Or before a shark grabbed the rope and stole more of their precious supplies.

Dr. Kimura had stayed at the helm, not rowing. But while Cage and Marcus had been fighting off sharks, in the other boat, Kimura had found a weight—the Gatorade—and attached it to a rope. Cage snatched up the bottle, even though he knew he risked being tugged into the water.

They had to get the boats back together. Wrapping the cord once around his wrist, he held on firmly. His hand was not protected, but at least the rubber of the rain gear covered his arm. A little damage was worth the benefit of getting the boats linked again.

"Have you got it?" he called out to Kimura and watched as Kimura followed his movement, wrapping the cord around his own wrist. That alone pulled the yellow rope off the surface of the water. They weren't out of the woods on this yet—something could still jump up and grab it—but at least it wasn't obvious bait.

Slowly, hand over fist, and with the help of those paddling, they pulled the two boats closer together. Even as they did it, fins cut the water in between them. Other sharks were visible at the surface of the water nearby.

When at last they were close, Cage hollered out. "We need to lash the boats together. All hands on deck!"

All hands. He would have laughed. As though he had any experience in running a crew. But no one scoffed at his wording. Frantically, they all came together. Though they initially crowded the short side of the boat, a few recognized the danger of tipping and scrambled to the far ends as counterweight. Cage stayed put, working in the frantic mass of hands as they tucked raw ends under and around the rope that already hung around across the inflated ring. They tied the rope through the grommets in the pre-punched tabs that the boat had come with. They were here for exactly this purpose.

"Tie them tight, in multiple places." Ginnifer pointed to several spots she wanted anchored. They hadn't done that the first time. Had the rope broken, it could have quickly unwound, and they would have drifted apart. "Here," she said, "and here. It's a failsafe."

When every knot was tied, Kimura put his hands out wide, motioning all of them to stop and stay silent. "Don't move."

The entire boat stilled suddenly. The imminent threat of drifting apart was taken care of, but Kimura's expression said they still had a big problem.

"What?" Joule whispered to him, instictively knowing he wanted them quiet, too.

He whispered loudly in return, checking to see that all of them could hear him. "All our movement has signaled us as bait. We're frantic. That's why they surged around us. They think we're dying."

Cage felt his breathing stop. The frenzy they'd just experienced wasn't random. It was their own fault. *Shit.*

"We have to stop and stay very quiet and very still." Kimura looked at each of them for a long moment.

Cage had never been so grateful to have a professor on his side.

"We have to wait until they find something else to hunt. Hopefully, that will be before one of them bites the ring and the boat starts to deflate."

Though they'd all stilled as quickly as he'd motioned them, the sharks hadn't quite gotten the message. Next to where Kimura kneeled with his hands out wide, Cage saw a mouth surge toward the side of boat, razor-sharp teeth ready to bite.

42

"We're drifting," Joule commented softly, though she knew she was supposed to stay quiet.

Did the sharks hear them? Surely, they couldn't. Her friends could barely even hear each other. But maybe the vibrations of her voice traveled through her body and signaled the sharks under the water. Joule knew sharks and related species had electric field receptors, but she didn't know whether or not her voice transmitted something that could be picked up that way.

Though she didn't know about her voice, she did know sharks were very sensitive to movement. She would have laid down to rest, but underneath the surface, the sharks would know things were moving in the boat. She didn't dare lay back for a second reason as well: only the edge of the boat was inflated. The bottom was a thick piece of PVC rubber coated with some kind of waterproof poly-fabric.

What a laugh, she thought. Waterproof fabric—as though the water wasn't coming in from the skies overhead, or splashing over the sides of the boat. None of the rafts' occupants was in any way dry.

Dr. Kimura nodded back to her. At least they were all close, now that they'd frantically pulled the boats together. He whispered, making her think maybe that sound didn't signal that they were bait. "We'll make up for it later. But if we keep moving around, they'll keep coming after us. And, sooner or later, one of them might bite through that rubber."

He'd pointed at the inflated ring. The shark that had tried to take a bite of it either hadn't been able to cut through or had found the rubber unappetizing. The ring had held. But Joule had no idea what results the next bite might bring. She held her breath and nodded her understanding.

At this point, there was little she could do. She could sit in the boat and wait and watch. Luckily, Kimura was proving to be right. The frenzy had slowly died down. She had no clue of the passage of time now. Was it maybe five minutes before the fins that cut the surface of the water appeared several yards away from the boat?

At last, it appeared that she and her crew were longer the *bait du jour*.

It was a while later when she asked, "Can we row now?"

They couldn't see the edge of the water, and that meant they had a long way to go. They were cold and hungry— most of them had been snacking while they could, but it had been a while since anyone had eaten anything.

Though the map told them where the neighborhood was, she couldn't make out more than shadows in the distance. Joule hoped the shapes were the edges of rooftops, of homes, maybe large trees that grew on the hills.

Though the grand houses up here belonged to people with money, they weren't as tall as the buildings on campus, but they'd been built on higher ground.

Surely, their little crew had passed close enough to a sound structure that had enough of it above water to be useful. But if it was there, she couldn't see it. And no one else had made any frantic gestures of hope while they'd drifted. Joule wasn't up on her fluid dynamics, but she surmised they were drifting away—not toward—the land. Her heart sank a little more.

But they were close. The GPS said so. Surely, they were about to hit an end to this nightmare that they had embarked upon. *For everything this has cost us, we will all make it to safety.* That's what Joule told herself.

Holly had been right about lining the boats up this way. As they all began to slowly row again, Joule realized she could feel the change in her arms. She needed easier strokes now. The boats cut through the water a little more smoothly, and they didn't have to loop as far out of the way to avoid things.

Behind her, in the second boat, Kimura commented softly, "We do move better this way. It's safer, too. Smoother sailing means we disturb the sharks less."

Several of them nodded, but the adrenaline spike of the boats drifting apart had left them all subdued. No one was bailing. No one had specifically decided that, but perhaps the group was holding out hope that they were close, and they could make it to land without the extra work of lifting and dumping more containers of water.

Holly stopped rowing for a moment and pulled out her phone. "We're right over Reservoir Road. If we follow it, it goes up the hill. I've been up here. There are lots of nice, big homes."

Joule was too tired to comment on the irony of heading up a road named for a reservoir, and Ginnifer interrupted her thoughts anyway. "Do they have generators?"

Though there was doubt in Ginnifer's tone, it made sense. Even when they reached higher ground, the power would be out. The alerts had told them the whole area was a disaster. Everything around the bay was flooding, as though the ocean had simply risen. In fact, it had. They had ocean creatures all around them in the water.

The alerts told them to stay inside and stay dry and warm. She almost rolled her eyes at the universe. They would have done that if they could! And for a moment, she imagined her dorm mates huddled together on the roof... but she pushed the thought aside. She couldn't save her father last year. She couldn't save everyone.

Holly quietly motioned for them to make small adjustments that kept the boats over the street. Following the pavement should mean fewer obstructions and much less likelihood of running aground on something they couldn't see.

The treetops and telephone wires acted as additional guidelines. And then, when they could see the roofs and upper stories of the abandoned homes, they aimed themselves between the houses.

Joule found her own second wind. Her friends must have, too, because their rowing picked up pace.

Kimura climbed forward, softly moving up and over the lump between the two boats, his oar still in hand. As he reached the front of the little chain, he leaned out, setting one hand onto the inflated edge, looking for something.

Joule was jumping forward even as Gabby yelled, "Get back!" and smacked at him. "Do not get your hands so close to the water!"

Though he nodded, he only pulled back a little and barely reacted. Instead of climbing back into the relative safety of the middle of the boat, he slowly pushed his oar straight down into the water. When he stopped, the handle of the oar stuck only about three inches out of the water... which meant his hand was close to the surface. Too close.

But he was testing, and the result meant the water here was shallow. Very shallow.

He began talking softly, looking back at them as though this was his classroom, and they were his own students. "If this were any other flood, we would get out and walk the boat in. But right now, it's still deep enough for *them*." He didn't have to clarify what he meant by *them*.

"They might not be here. I don't see fins." His eyes scanned the surface behind the boat, where the water was deeper. "But don't ever doubt they could be right below you. Even if they aren't close enough to get a bite, they can be on top of you before you can even move. They've evolved to be invisible until it's too late. And if they're here, they're hungry."

If, Joule thought, snarking the word through her brain, but she didn't say it out loud. If she'd learned anything over the last umphteen exhausting hours, it was that the sharks were invisible until they didn't want to be and there was nothing she could do about it.

Kimura kept talking. "What we need to do is get close enough to run the front of the boat up onto land, where we can all step out directly onto the ground." The little vessel moved forward while he talked. They pushed their oars in unison, having somehow found a steady rhythm and the energy to make it happen. "The back of the boat will still be deep enough that if you step out from that direction, you aren't safe. Something might get you."

Aggressive, hungry bull sharks were plenty to deal with, if there was anything else in this water, well, Joule didn't want to know about it. She'd already shoved the stupid red gobies out of her brain. They had been interesting, a scientific anomaly, but none had ever tried to grab her oar and drag her into a gaping mouth full of teeth.

Kimura seemed to be suggesting there were more problems...

Five minutes later, she saw the street emerge from the gloom in front of her. First, a slash of pale yellow pointed the direction and her hope surged. The edges of the pavement became clear next, and the homes on either side of her changed from house-shaped blobs, to detailed curb appeal—even if she still couldn't see a curb.

The yellow line was her favorite, though. She followed it, pushing with the paddle now not to get away but to get *to*. The center line was faded from years of minimal upkeep, but it guided her.

"No." Kimura motioned to them to throttle back as the boats began to pick up speed. "Stay slow. Because even though we are about get this boat out of the water, we still can't afford to have it bitten. These inflatables are only way out if we have to leave here."

He was still lecturing them on the importance of slow and steady when the boat jolted beneath them. Joule heard the rubbing noise that meant they'd run the front up onto the pavement.

43

"Joule."

She ignored her name and the voice that said it and took her first deep breath in a long time as she lay back into the soft squishy couch. Looking at her phone, she saw that it had been almost twenty-four hours since they'd launched the boats.

It was almost the middle of the night again, and she hadn't seen the sun once. She was used to gray and fog—after all, she lived in the Bay Area. She had come to expect rainy days. But this? She wasn't sure she could endure three more years of school here.

Then again, she consoled herself, *there might not even be a school here anymore, so maybe it doesn't matter.*

Next to her, Roxie and Sky also leaned back into the love seat that matched the couch, but while Joule stared at the ceiling, they were curled up under a shared comforter, fast asleep.

Breaking into this house had been far too easy—but getting here had not been.

Once they'd run the boat aground, they'd scrambled out,

like ants on crack. It was not the soft, orderly exit Kimura wanted them to make. Everyone wanted out—everyone *needed* out—and they weren't emotionally capable of the clean escape that would have been prudent.

Even as they had fled to the land, fins had appeared near the back of the boat, because they once again signaled that they were thrashing about and that they deserved to be eaten. Still, they'd all turned and grabbed at the ropes along the inflated rings and begun hauling the boats up. Even though she now hated the boat, it represented her only real safety. Joule was not leaving without it. It appeared her friends felt the same and they all tugged hard.

"Stop!"

Kimura once again took charge. "Don't tug! You can't outrun them, not in the water. And the boat is still in the water."

So they'd done the tough thing and put their journey on hold while the sharks calmed down. Joule was about to explode. The stress of waiting was only outdone by the stress of watching the back of the boat as they slowly reeled it in and then inspected it for bite marks.

The bad news was that they found several. The good news was that the ring wasn't punctured—the air hadn't leaked. But there were now weak points on both the rafts.

Her heart heavy and her body beyond weary, she'd helped undo the ropes that lashed the boats together and then hauled the two skiffs between them up the street. If anyone was here to see them, no one popped their head out the window or waved hello. No one called out to ask what they were doing, or why they were here hauling inflatable rafts up the residential street.

But her feet had finally found solid ground. The group tipped the water out of the boats, making them remarkably lighter. When Ginnifer asked, "Do we deflate them?" Joule had quickly countered, "Let's find shelter first!"

Looking back, she wasn't sure if she'd said it because it was a wise thing to do or simply because she was so sick of Ginnifer. Her roommate wasn't supposed to be here. But she'd brought Holly, and Holly had been a help.

They'd hunted across four or five houses and settled on this one. There was no generator, but it was easy to break into. It also had a fireplace and cords of wood piled high outside... under a tarp. The tarp was the deciding factor.

They'd all spent the first half hour settling in. Joule had changed clothes, grateful she'd been smart enough to make them pack a T-shirt and jeans into plastic bags. Looking around, she saw that her friends had done the same, though a few of the bags had ripped and here and there, people had little wet spots on their clothes. But it was so much better than being in the boat that she didn't care.

The fireplace was already hosting a crackling fire. Gabby had been smart enough to point out that they needed to open the flue, even though some rain would come down the chimney. Every once in a while, drops spattered and hissed in the flames. At first, the sound startled her, but over the past several hours, it had grown comforting. Anything that signaled she wasn't still in the boat was a good sound.

She'd used the bathroom and eaten a bag of chips and curled up in a corner of the fluffy couch. Her friends sprawled on the floor, some awake, some asleep, most curled up in blankets they'd raided from the various closets around the house.

Next to her, Ginnifer was using up some of her precious phone battery to reassure her parents she was alive and safe. Just as Joule was hating her for being able to make the call, Ginnifer put one finger in her ear to cancel out the surrounding noise and said, "No, Mom, it's fine. Holly and I are both okay. My roommate Joule saved me. I told you she was good people."

Joule didn't have the energy to jump up out of her seat and deck Ginnifer for saying that. She was *good people*? Ginnifer hadn't been outright mean, but she'd acted as though Joule was a thorn in her side all year, even though the room was as much Joule's as it was Ginnifer's. And Joule hadn't *saved* her; Ginnifer and Holly had bullied their way into the boat.

Her irritation was interrupted by Gabby's voice. "The pantry is full!"

Gabby had not only been willing to build the fire and check the flue, but also somehow had enough energy to scope out the house. "Ooh, fridge, too!"

Joule heard the door close quickly, probably to preserve the fridge as a cooler—because of course, the power was out.

It had been days since the rains had started. Joule suspected the sizes of the houses and the location of the neighborhood indicated the residents had enough money to flee easily. This might be even someone's second home. Possibly, the initial downpour and the warnings the local stations had issued made them decide it was a good time for an impromptu vacation. Whatever it was, it had been several hours since her crew had broken out one small pane of glass in the back window, and no one had yet come around to arrest them for home invasion. No alarms had gone off. No neighbors had stopped by.

She still wasn't sure how illegal their actions were, but she refused to die when there were perfectly good shelters available. Being dry and warm was worth anything they suffered, though Joule was already planning to leave a note explaining their stay here and then return with cash to cover any reasonable payment later. Right now, she was content to look at her friends and be glad they were all with her. Others hadn't been so lucky.

Sky and Roxie were out cold—even Gabby announcing she'd found food hadn't made either of them stir in the slightest. Joule wished she could sleep like them, but found she was starting to doze even as the thought crossed her mind.

According to the time, they'd been here for a while, but she didn't feel like time had really passed.

She was only just now starting to feel stronger, but suddenly, Joule was hearing her name called, and the two feet that appeared in front of her meant someone wanted her.

"Joule." Ginnifer tapped at her toe and Joule was tempted to completely ignore her—pretend to snore, roll over, and wait for her pesky roommate to go away.

But Ginnifer tapped again. "Joule. We need to find a generator. Hopefully one of the neighbors has one, maybe in a shed or the garage."

"What about this house? Is there one here?" Joule instinctively pulled the comforter a little tighter under her chin. She did not want to hear this.

"Marcus and I just went and checked."

Interesting, Joule thought, that Ginnifer would even deign to speak to Marcus.

"No generator, but we did find bolt cutters." She held them up, and Joule couldn't help but think that Ginnifer plus bolt cutters was a menacing combination.

"Why me? I'm not the strongest."

"You have the best rain gear," Ginnifer reply quickly.

"You're one of the few of us who can go out and stay warm and relatively dry."

"Not my fault you didn't buy rain gear," she muttered, but she kept her voice low enough that no one heard. Because, if she recalled, Ginnifer did have rain gear.

"You, me, Holly, Max," Ginnifer said as though she'd assembled a dream team. "We're the ones who can suit up enough to stay dry."

Joule was thinking that Cage had the same rain gear she did, but Ginnifer had anticipated that. "Your brother should stay here in case someone needs to go outside. But it's time to do some recon here."

Joule was now fully awake and looking Ginnifer in the eye. She hated this plan. The last thing she wanted to do was go back outside. She wanted to sleep here with the fire roaring and wait for help, and she couldn't find a flaw with that idea. Except that they would likely be here for several days and they needed power sooner rather than later.

She looked to her brother, who merely offered a short nod back to her that said it was her decision.

But it wasn't really, was it? It was simply something that needed to be done. So fifteen minutes later, after she toweled off her still-very-wet rain gear and her boots, she was heading out the door. Following Ginnifer, of all people... and her bolt cutters.

The sky was somehow darker than it had been before.

44

"Stop pacing," Marcus admonished him, and Cage managed it, but only for a moment. The he started wearing his pathway into the plush carpet again.

He would have liked to have been asleep, but that was hard to do while Joule was out on mission separate from his own. In fact, his mission sucked. "Stay at the house, be ready in case."

So instead of being useful, he was here doing nothing—which included not resting, which would have at least been helpful for later.

"She's got her phone on her. They all do." Apparently, Marcus was trying to bring Cage's agitation level down. It probably wasn't going to work. Besides, Cage *knew* his sister had her phone. That's why his own was on and waiting, draining the battery he couldn't really afford to lose.

There was a slight signal here. Occasionally, it popped up on certain ends of the house. Maybe that's why he was pacing, so he could keep trying to pick up the signal where he could.

"Put the phone on the far end of table. There's better

reception there." Marcus tried again. "You're draining the battery, pacing like that. Every time you get out of range, it tries to search for signal. That uses a lot of power."

Cage hadn't spoken once yet, but this time, he raised an eyebrow, turned around, and did exactly as Marcus suggested.

On his next pass through the house, he saw that Gabby had pulled a variety of things from the kitchen, and now had several high-end, copper-bottom pots over the fire. Clearly, she was attempting to boil water.

"Will it work?" Cage asked.

"It has to," she grinned up at him. "People cooked over their fires for centuries."

"We haven't," he replied. But Gabby merely shrugged and said, "Hey, I've been to historical reenactment villages. I can do this."

He didn't want to argue, and he *did* want boiling water. Because the thought of ramen noodles sounded absolutely fantastic right now. Then again, there was no telling if she'd even found ramen noodles in this house. The plush carpet and art on the walls made him wonder if these people ever ate cheap noodles like college students. He checked his feet to be sure he wasn't leaving any dirt on his walking path. They were squatters here, and the house was nice. He didn't want to mess it up.

He looked up to the clock ticking on the wall. An antique that needed no technology, it alone had kept running when the rest of the house had powered down.

Thirty minutes. He'd hoped Ginnifer and her posse would walk out to the neighbor's shed, find a generator, and be back with power by now. Apparently, that wasn't going to be the case.

He paced back into the living room, then looped around

past the dining room table. The phone remained quiet. On his next pass, he ran into Dr. Kimura. He must have made an odd face, because the professor made one back.

"You might want to stay off your cell," Cage said.

"But we're getting a generator," Kimura replied without looking up.

"We hope we are. We don't know that yet." Cage tilted his head to see what was on the professor's phone but couldn't quite catch it.

Kimura remained optimistic. "I suspect Holly can make batteries from potatoes."

Cage didn't disagree, but he had to point out, "I'm sure she can, but I'm not certain we even have potatoes."

On the next pass, he saw that Kimura hadn't powered his phone down. Instead, his fingers flew rapidly, scrolling before tapping out the next command, whatever it was.

This time, when Cage looked over the other man's shoulder, he only hoped to distract himself. He watched as a text popped up from the man's wife. She and the children were safe and dry. Cage hadn't even known the man had kids.

Kimura quickly tapped out of the text screen and back to the research he was doing.

Cage caught sight of the small screen and blinked. "Why are you looking this up? Do you really need to spend your power researching a Kraken right now?"

Kumara stopped dead still. "I'm not researching mythical sea beasts. I'm researching what naturally lives in the Bay. Because if it's there, it might be here."

Cage stopped cold.

45

"Go ahead, you know what you're looking for."
Joule waved her hand toward Ginnifer, a gesture
that felt foreign. It was odd to step back. As the
boat-owner, she'd been deferred to most of the time, even
Dr. Kimura. Handing the reins to Ginnifer felt wrong in her
heart somehow.

Joule was willing to admit that—though she'd certainly
seen a generator in her past—she didn't know all the things
she might be looking for. This was definitely Ginnifer's
mission: She had called her team, and Joule was willing, if
not perfectly content, to let her lead the way.

Third in line, she trudged behind Holly, happy not to be
bringing up the rear. Max did that, walking quietly behind
as Holly and Ginnifer chattered between themselves.

Joule didn't listen to them. Instead, she heard the leaves
rustling in the distance. She heard the birds twitter and
stop, twitter and stop. The rustling came again off to her
right, and she was too tired to figure out which way the wind
was blowing and what dry leaves might be around to make
the soft scratching sounds. The constant wind and rain

obscured noises that were more than about fifteen feet away. The wind tried to steal her hair from under her hood and whip it, wet and cold, across her face.

She'd had enough of nature for a long, long time. When the sounds of the wind picked up again, and the birds stopped abruptly, Joule was almost glad for the silence.

As she moved by rote pattern rather than desire or destination, she eyed the long, heavy bolt cutters swinging at Ginnifer's side as she walked. These homes were on large lots and none of Ginnifer's team were ready for the hike; rain boots weren't made for distance or harsh terrain. So, they stuck to the street as much as they could. But the houses here were built on hills, and staying on the pavement didn't get them to anyone's garage.

The walk itself was hard. The angles were harsh. The driveways were made of gravel that had washed into divets and missing patches and standing puddles that made Joule's stomach turn.

The first garages they tried to break into were locked up tight.

The houses were dark and empty—no generators running inside. If the residents were home, they'd be running their own power—if they could make it. If they were gone... well, it was a crapshoot whether they would have one and whether or not Joule's little team could get it.

The bolt cutters proved no use against garage doors. These locked from the inside or needed radio signal transmitters to trigger the doors. Trying to overpower them did little but make Max grunt and shake his head.

"Let's try the cute little barn in the back of that one." Ginnifer pointed with the bolt cutters, proving she was stronger, or at least more resilient than Joule had given her credit for. Then again, Joule would not be wasting any energy right now by swinging heavy implements.

The team of four headed down the gravel drive. She was halfway up when she felt the slow slide beneath her feet. Her heart flipped, her stomach dropped. Though the ground slightly giving way beneath her feet wouldn't have bothered her any other day, now it sent her reflexes panicking wildly.

Max's hand suddenly wrapped around her bicep and hauled her upright. She barely even had the energy to say thanks, and she kept walking as though nothing had happened. Because it hadn't, not really. She'd just panicked. She couldn't cause problems now. A generator was a necessity.

As they got close to the little barn-shaped shed, they found that it was indeed closed with a padlock. Ginnifer got so excited, she nearly squealed with delight as she put the bolt cutters to the metal lock. But she quickly discovered she didn't have the arm strength to crack through the hardened steel.

This was why they'd brought Max. He'd probably be the one hauling the heavy generator back to the other house, too. Joule was growing more exhausted with each step. Was something wrong? Or had she just pushed too hard for too long?

Once Max snapped the lock, the others began poking around. They seemed to have an agenda, but Joule wasn't even quite sure what she was looking for. Luckily, Holly took it upon herself to offer an explanation.

"It's going to look almost like a large propane tank. Probably white or silver, but the color depends on the brand. About this big—" she held her hand up to demonstrate something larger than Joule had expected. "Hopefully, it will be on a frame with wheels, because people who need generators need them at different places. We'll also need to see if we can find a fuel source."

Ginnifer chimed in, a smile on her face, though they hadn't yet located one. "I'll be so happy if we can wheel it back to the house and fire it up."

"And get some fucking power," Holly added in with more grit than Joule had expected from the usually reticent young woman.

But as they searched through the old garage, they found only old tires, a random interior door, and a huge TV with a dock for a VHS tape on the front. There were old cardboard boxes of videotapes, both VHS and high eight, all labeled family, TV shows, and exercise.

Someone was a celebrity workout fan. On another day, Joule would have liked to pull the cassette out and watched just for fun. But it had been a rough week, and she was feeling gravity with an extra kick right now. She stepped around a standing piece of plywood and found snow skis all lined up neatly. But no generator.

"I don't see it," Ginnifer declared grimly, with Holly agreeing right on her heels.

"How do we lock their shed back up?" Joule asked. There was no generator and they hadn't taken anything, but they'd just committed a crime. They need to put the barn doors back.

"I'll get a stick," Marcus volunteered, as though that would be enough. But he found a wire hanger and, as they left, he bent it through the holes of the lock, making sure the doors stayed shut. Next, he hung the cut lock onto it, as if he were letting the people know they were sorry they'd broken in.

At the he next shed, the bolt cutters didn't work on the

padlock at all. The lock was cut-proof, with a casing that didn't expose the metal bar enough get the bolt cutters around it. All Max had managed to do with his best efforts was to nick the heavy steel.

"We could pull the pins on the door," Ginnifer offered, but Joule wasn't willing to try anything that required that much effort. Not yet. Not in the rain, and not for a shed that probably didn't even hold a generator.

"Honestly, these are snow-ski-people, not generator-people." The words fell out of her mouth before she stopped to think if that was rude thing to say. Maybe Ginnifer or Holly was "snow-ski-people."

"Sure," Holly replied kindly, "but generators are good for more than just working on your car. They're for roofing your house—"

Joule suspected the owners of the high-end houses on the hill didn't do their own roofing either, but she kept her mouth shut this time.

"—and they're for projects. I promise you, we get some-body with a good wood shop or someone who works on old cars, and we'll find a generator."

That at least made sense to Joule, and the thought kept her going on the long walk back up the rutted gravel drive to the street and then up to the next house.

No one was willing to step into the soggy yards with little puddles here and there. Even though they'd just battled flood waters and won, no one was willing to make even the tiniest splash. So they walked out each driveway, along the street and down the next drive—three times the necessary distance—rather than cutting straight through the soggy yards.

The next house had a garage and again had a door they couldn't lift. Ginnifer stopped and examined it, seemingly tired of being thwarted by such common household tech. "Can we pry the door up? Enough to get one of us under?"

"I think we should leave it be. So far, all we've broken is a pane of glass and a single lock. Garage doors are another class of crime."

With accepting nods, the group walked away again.

They tried several more sheds before, on the seventh try, they got lucky. The doors were simply clipped shut. Joule regretted that they'd cut the other bolt. Together, they pulled the door open and found counters lining the sides of the small space. Tools were laid out on the old plywood built-ins.

It was a hobbyist's tool shop and, exactly as Holly said it would be—and there in the corner was a generator. At least Joule recognized it as one from the description. As no one else was going bonkers, she raised her arm to point it out when Holly jumped up and down and squealed out "Yes! A generator!"

Fifteen minutes later, they'd cleaned off the light layer of cobwebs that had formed around the machine. In fact, there were spiders shuffling out of their way each time she stepped. The moisture must have brought them out. Joule shooed another one away as Max reached for the handle to wheel the generator out of the door.

"It's a hybrid, propane and gas! That's perfect." Ginnifer gazed at the blue and black contraption with an expression she'd previously reserved for whatever hot actor had caught her fancy. "We need to find extra fuel, but we have more options now."

"I think there's a propane tank on the back patio of this house," Max offered up before quickly adding, "I didn't check to see how full it was, though."

Without anything further said, the group began looking around for fuel, but there wasn't any in the garage.

"I'll check the patio for a grill and propane," Max announced as Ginnifer simultaneously said, "I'm heading around the back of the shed," and walked right out the door and back into the rain.

"We shouldn't split up," Joule protested, but her heart wasn't in it. "And you shouldn't go around back. The ground slopes and it's wet." After all, she'd almost slipped in one of the driveways, and that wasn't anywhere near as steep as this back yard was.

Even so, Max headed off in the direction of the house and Holly followed Ginnifer around the back of the shed. Unmoving, just inside the open doorway, Joule scanned the neighborhood.

She was waiting for someone to show up with a shotgun, hold them hostage, and demand to know what they were doing—even though she would have thought it was pretty obvious. When no one did, she forced herself back out into the slow rain that was as obnoxious for constantly hitting her as it was for being wet. She followed Max toward the patio and the grill. He was giving her a thumbs-up sign from the railing on the deck.

He'd found what he needed and didn't require help. Turning, Joule aimed for the back of the shed to check on Ginnifer and Holly.

She was almost behind the shed when she felt her foot slip.

Just as she'd predicted.

The houses were built on the flat spots, but the back-yards sloped sharply away. This one was no exception.

Her breath caught and her gaze darted down the hill, through the thin foliage on the spring trees, to the brown silt swirling at their bases. Water? Again? She was going to slide down the mud and back into the water.

Her ankle twisted slightly and she pinwheeled her arms, as though that would stop her ass from smacking the earth as she slipped away, heading into the flood and the sharks. Joule opened her mouth to scream.

But before she could let out a bloodcurdling sound, Holly grabbed her and hauled her to her feet once again.

No sliding. No crashing into the shallow water that was still climbing up the hillside toward them. "Thank you," Joule rasped out the words. She figured she was getting a workout from her adrenaline alone.

She held tightly onto Holly as they continued the few slick steps behind the shed. She'd lost all concern about seeming weak or unsteady. She was both right now. Was she coming down with something?

Her eyes darted around, the rustling of the wind blocked a bit by the buildings around her, and muffled by the constant rain still coming down. In the distance she could see the houses that had been built lower into the hill. The water had crept slowly up around them, dark and murky. She knew what was in it.

As she turned the last corner, she carefully watched her foot placement. Her rain boots were meant to keep out the water, but weren't built for traction,

"Yes!" Ginnifer called out. "Gas! Lots of people keep it around back near the woodpile."

Well, her roommate apparently knew many useful things. Not that she would ever have known this, the way Ginnifer had shunned her for months.

"Grab these." Ginnifer pointed to Holly and they each picked up a canister.

The weight was too much and tipped her friend. Holly's

feet slipped out from under her, just as Joule's had a moment before. But as Joule reached to steady Holly, it was Ginnifer who screamed.

Max appeared, running at the sound of the piercing cry. As fast as he was, he couldn't get to Ginnifer in time. Holly had managed to get to her hands and knees, and she was looking at Ginnifer, who had finally stopped screaming. But Joule's roommate only sucked in a deep breath and screamed again.

Joule looked her up and down, but nothing was wrong except a spot of blood just blow her knee. Had she fallen and scraped her damn knee?

But then Joule heard the rattles as the snake slithered away.

46

C age held the front door open—the door of the house that wasn't his—as Max carried a screaming Ginnifer inside.

"Get the generator!" she was yelling as though the lack of power source was as concerning as her possibly deadly bite.

Joule followed right behind her, yelling back at her roommate. "Shut up! Take a damn breath, you single - serving clusterfuck!"

At least that made Ginnifer pause. Once she did, however, it became obvious that she was breathing heavily and probably quite scared.

"Good. Now try to breathe slowly," Joule commanded, sounding now like she'd tossed in the swears just to get Ginnifer's attention.

Joule had texted while they were running back to the house that they'd had a rattlesnake bite. Cage and Kimura had suddenly sprung into action. They'd been wound up tight and ready for a crisis all along. Disturbingly, one had materialized.

They now had towels ready and, because of Gabby boiling water over the fire. Kimura had found a clean knife and dropped it into the pot and was now using kitchen tongs to fish it out. He laid it across the towel Cage had set out for just this purpose. It was definitely a stitched-together operation.

Kimura was still on his phone, searching and holding it up to show everyone the emergency procedures for snake bites. Unfortunately, the advice was always the same. Get the victim to a hospital and administer the antivenin.

"Is there even a clinic up here?" Cage asked, and then offered, "If there is, we can break in. Hopefully, one of us can deliver a halfway decent injection."

But as Max laid Ginnifer onto the blanket they'd set out in front of the fire, the professor held his phone out. As though Cage could read the tiny screen from where he stood.

"It doesn't look like it. The closest one is going to be underwater."

Cage nodded, but what he noticed as Kimura held this phone out, was that the red bar across the top indicating his battery life was already flashing red.

Ginnifer didn't like being laid out in front of the fire. She was peeling her boots and yelling, "I need antibiotics!" to no one in particular.

"You have to calm down," Cage said calmly as he grabbed her arm and yanked it to get her attention. But he had already grabbed the knife and begun to reach for the seam of her rain-proof pants.

"No!" Ginnifer yelled again and pushed his hand away.

Gabby intervened, helping Ginnifer peel the pants down her legs. Never mind that the pants had two small holes just below her knee. They couldn't afford to ruin good rain gear while they were stranded in this storm. Ginnifer shoved at her jeans next, unconcerned with anyone who was watching

Putting the knife away, Cage looked up to the group for what to do next.

Ginnifer had exposed the two small punctures on her leg. They were shockingly clear, despite the fact that they were bleeding freely.

Unsure what else to do, Cage poured the rubbing alcohol they'd found into the wound. Ginnifer screamed like a banshee again. This was maybe worse than the frantic, panicked scream when she'd been carried in. But he didn't know what else to do without antivenin available.

Marcus took the knife from him. "Hold her leg."

With the tip of the knife, he made two small X's across the holes that already marred her skin. Ginnifer screamed bloody murder. The sound had changed from pain to anger as Marcus worked quickly.

Cage was almost blown backward, simply by the sound of it. He'd never heard anyone scream quite like that—and he'd heard a lot of things. Then he was almost knocked backward by Ginnifer's thrashing as she tried to fight off the lot of them off. One of his friends caught her wayward fist just before it connected with his jaw.

"Hold her!" Marcus demanded as he put his mouth to Ginnifer's knee and sucked. He then turned and spit blood onto the floor next to him. He repeated this four or five times before he leaned back and reached up to wipe at his mouth. He was the closest thing Cage had ever seen to a vampire.

Cage wanted to ask, "Does that even work?" But it was already done.

Joule at least had thought ahead. She pulled Marcus's arm away from his face before he could rub the bloody mess around and handed him water. Cage watched his sister pour him a generous helping of the whiskey she'd found. "It's better than water, and at least it's got a lot alcohol in it. It's the best we can do."

But Marcus shrugged as though he didn't care. He probably didn't. He had rattlesnake venom in his mouth now. Rather than shooting the drink, he rinsed and spit directly onto a beautiful, white, fluffy towel that they'd set out.

It was much too late to be careful with the things they borrowed from the house and leave them as they'd found them. In fact, that plan had completely bitten the dust. Ginnifer's leg was now bleeding freely through the thin blanket and into the carpet. Rivulets of blood running down her bare skin were bringing out goosebumps near the cuts Max had made. They weren't deep, but they were deep enough.

Next to him, Cage watched as Max swished another shot of whiskey in his mouth again. Needing something to do, Cage grabbed the alcohol bottle from Joule and squirted it a Ginnifer's leg again.

Another high, piercing scream emerged from his sister's roommate, but Cage continued to do the job. Next to him, Gabby grabbed at Ginnifer's shoulder and pressed her down to the floor. Surely, she would pass out from exhaustion any moment now.

Max handed the glass of whiskey back to Joule and stood up. Before he walked away, he motioned her to pour what remained onto Ginnifer's leg as well.

And why not? Cage thought. The carpet was already soaked with blood. What was a little whiskey in the mix? Hell, it might smell better that the coppery tang of blood.

For a moment, Cage wondered if his sister would take some kind of sick delight in pouring the alcohol onto her roommate's open cuts, but from the expression on her face, she didn't enjoy it at all.

"Sorry, Ginnifer," she said as she tipped the glass over the exposed wound.

Another scream. Another kick. Gabby was flung free as Holly grabbed her friend by the shoulders and held her tightly to the ground. She got into Ginnifer's face and growled, "Marcus has done what he can. We've cleaned it as best we are able. The blood coming out of it helped clean it. But you have got to fucking calm down. The faster your blood goes through your system, the faster the faster the venom goes, too."

Cage watched as Ginnifer's eyes went round. Her body stilled, and for a moment, he thought she was listening to her friend and taking some very sage advice.

But then her eyes rolled up and her body went slack.

47

C age sat by Ginnifer's side, watching as her face slowly puffed up.

"Can't let me die, can't let me die." She repeated it like a mantra. He only imagined that it was fear that made her say that.

Honestly, they'd been chattering amongst themselves, and none of them really knew if Ginnifer was going to make it or not. When she'd passed out, he hadn't been sure if she'd fainted or died. Even now, they didn't know if Marcus's actions had been enough. Even Marcus had only raised his eyebrows and shrugged when Cage questioned him.

All his friend had been able to say was that he'd done what he'd been taught to do if this happened during a fishing or camping trip. Cage wanted to question whether the old cut-and-spit method was still the recommended course of action, but all they'd been able to find online was "get her to a clinic." He was grateful for Marcus's knowledge now. But still, there was no medical help coming.

They would have to make it through on their own.

When Ginnifer became pale and feverish, Gabby

began issuing instructions. "We need to move her away from the fire. And someone—" she pointed to Holly, "—needs to search the house for any antibiotics we can give her."

Even as she issued her Nurse Gabby instructions, Ginnifer began to thrash. It was then that her claims of "can't let me die" shifted to "Can't let me die. I'm the only one who can hook up the generator."

Well, Cage thought. Even delirious, she was arrogant. But he kept the thought to himself. No wonder Joule hated her.

Still, he'd grabbed one of the corners of the blanket, wondering if it would even hold the thrashing college student. Gabby issued commands for them to lift, walk slowly, and set her down. They repeated this in steps, barely managing with no help from Ginnifer.

They eventually got her situated in a cooler part of the room. As they laid her into the final position, Cage watched his sister's head snap to the side.

Sky and Roxie also went on sudden alert. The three girls broke into a run, suddenly heading toward the back of the house.

"What is it?" he hollered out as they disappeared into the kitchen. But it was Sky who turned abruptly and motioned him with a strict finger to her lips. Next, she glared at all the rest of them still around the fire. Whatever she'd heard that the others didn't, it was serious. She sent a message with her hand slicing through the air.

They got it. Be quiet. Damn it.

"You got her?" he whispered to Gabby as he motioned down to Ginnifer, who seemed to have wailed herself into passing out again.

Gabby managed to maintain an intelligent response in the middle of everything else going on. "As good as anything," she said, but then added, "I'm keeping an eye on that one, too."

Though her voice was low, Cage heard her clearly. The commotion from the other side of the house had stopped for a moment and then started again. Though he was getting very curious—or maybe concerned—he turned his attention to Marcus, as Gabby had indicated. He saw now that Marcus was blinking and holding one hand to the side of his head.

Shit.

He crawled to where Marcus sat. "You got a good dose of snake venom too, didn't you?"

Marcus nodded. "I'll be fine." He said the words clearly, but his tone wasn't convincing. Now that Cage was looking, he could see that his friend's face looked a little puffy.

He'd been worried about Ginnifer. He'd been fighting off visions of using a handsaw to amputate Ginnifer's leg to save her life. But Marcus took the venom to the face. Had any of Gabby's blood splashed into his eyes? There was no telling. Cage didn't even know if that made things worse or not, but Marcus waved him on.

Unable to help, Cage crawled toward the back of the house, where the heavy rattling noise continued. Was something at the door? No. The window. No. The side of the house was breaking?

Holly returned down the stairs. "No antibiotics... what's that noise?"

Cage made the same motions Sky had earlier and Holly snapped her mouth shut.

The noises were unclear. But he had barely passed through the hallway into the kitchen when he was yanked backward and slammed into the floor.

The crackling and heavy scraping stopped just as he

opened his eyes and saw his sister's face close. Too close. She whispered one word: "Bear."

As he looked up, he saw beyond the large kitchen window and the glass pane door the students had already broken one panel out of. Three large, black bears were attempting to get inside.

And they were about to make it.

48

"They can't get in, they can't get in." Sky softly repeated the words.

Joule thought it sounded more like a chant or a spell than fear, but Sky didn't stop for breath. Reaching out, she put her hand on her friend's arm and squeezed slightly, offering an agreement that she wasn't certain of.

The bears. The rattlesnake.

Weren't the sharks enough?

Clearly, the water affected everything. They weren't as safe now as they thought they'd be.

Motioning to her friends with small taps on the floor, Joule began to move. She used slow steps and low sound so as not to attract the attention of the bears at the window. They didn't let up, pushing on the glass and then testing the corners. The pawed at the door. Whatever they smelled inside, they wanted it. Joule was afraid it was the people. While she wouldn't happily hand over the food in the pantry, it was the better option now.

Together, she and Sky and Roxie slowly backed out of the room. When she was out of sight of the window, Roxie grabbed her arm. "Someone needs to watch them. What if they break through?"

Joule nodded. She'd been thinking the same thing. In fact, it was why she'd pulled her friends back. The crack in the poly-whatever, double-paned glass over the sink let her know the bears meant business, and that the house wasn't capable of keeping them out. It was only a matter of how much the bears were willing to push to get what they wanted.

"We have to move Ginnifer." Joule looked to both her friends, but it was Roxie who agreed first. "We have to move everyone. But where?"

They couldn't run away. Running with Ginnifer would be far too difficult.

"Can we hide her?" Sky asked, but she was already shaking her head in answer to her own question. "She moves too much. If she calls out, she's bait."

None of the three of them were Ginnifer fans, but they weren't murderers, either.

For a moment, Joule wished for her old neighborhood crew. Kayla and her focused determination. Susan, with her bad attitude and her shotgun would serve them well right now. Hell, any gun would serve them well now, though it might not stop a bear.

It was Roxie who peeked around the corner with each sound that came from the deck.

"Do you want to stay sentry and watch?" Joule asked her.

Her friend offered only a thumbs up, and motioned to her twin, who offered the same thumbs up, their two identical faces bracketing either side of the door.

Joule made her own careful movement to see that two of the bears were now pushing on the window. The sharp noise startled the bears and they moved back, but the push had extended the crack in the glass. Joule looked away as they lumbered around the back deck, readying for another try.

Somehow, the bears had climbed the wooden steps and made it onto the raised back patio before anyone had noticed. One bear was dangerous, but this group had three. If they acted in concert... well, it could be the end of Joule and all her friends.

She wouldn't let that happen. They'd come too far. They'd survived sharks, for God's sakes. She wasn't going to get taken out by a bear.

Back in the living room, she checked on Marcus. His eyes were definitely glazed, and the way he'd set his head gingerly back down into his hands concerned her even more.

Moving over another position, she conveyed her questions to her brother, while Gabby slowly crawled over to get in on the action. Max and Kimura paid them no attention as they sat in the corner, huddled over phones they couldn't recharge.

"Marcus got some of the venom when he was working on Ginnifer," Cage told her in a low voice.

She'd figured that out already. He might have saved her life, but now they had two patients to worry about. Twenty percent of their crew was out of commission. "Is he going to be okay?"

It was a stupid question. None of them knew. No one answered.

For all the things she and Cage had done, they didn't know how to solve this. She'd once had stabbed her brother in the leg and left him to superglue it back together. They'd had bites before, but they'd never suffered from venom or poison. And all of that didn't matter if the bears got in and they weren't prepared.

Joule would have told anyone that after the Night Hunters, she could face down anything. And honestly, when the rain started, she'd bought rain gear and boats—and she'd slept better, believing she was prepared. But none of them had been prepared for any of this.

"What was the noise?" Kimura asked.

It was then Joule realized that they hadn't all seen the menace; some of them had just heard the noise. She motioned to group to keep their voices low. They all nodded, even Marcus, though slowly. In the corner, Ginnifer stirred, moaned, muttered something, and rolled over. Joule could only hope that none of them would cry out when they heard what was happening.

"There are three bears at the window trying to break in."

"Three?" asked Gabby as Marcus's head jerked up, suddenly more alert.

"Are you sure they're trying to break in?" he asked.

For a moment she frowned, until she figured out he was asking if they'd just seen bears outside and become frightened. "I'm sure. They are cracking the window over the sink as we speak and trying to open or break the back door."

Obviously surprised, Kimura hopped up and headed toward the archway that led to the kitchen. Joule grabbed him and hauled him unceremoniously to the floor.

Unfazed, he just asked, "Why are they so close to the house?"

As Joule slowly let go of the professor, he pointed to Cage as though he knew something. Certainly, her brother didn't. Or did he?

"I was checking to see what other sea life might exist in the water," Kimura explained softly to them. "I wanted to know what else might have come up from the Bay. We do have large squid."

It took Joule a moment to shake off that crazy thought. She needed to pay attention to what he was saying. If he had information about animals, they needed it.

Kimura continued, "I looked in the wrong place. It's not the water we have to worry about now. It's the land. And I don't know anything about land animals." But already he was tapping furiously on his phone. Using it as though the generator Ginnifer had found would be their backup power supply, even though it hadn't made it all the way to the house. And they were two men down for having tried to fetch one.

He didn't look up from the small screen. "We're up in the hills. The houses are relatively sparse, and the trees are dense. There's a lot of wildlife around here that has been run out of its home. Not only has its territory been disrupted, but so has its food source."

Joule closed her eyes as her heart sank. Kimura made perfect sense.

There was a reason the three bears were at the window. They'd found land, but even the land was disrupted. There was no place in the area that was safe from angry, scared, hungry wildlife. *Jesus*, she wondered, *were the bears grizzlies?*

"Good news," Kimura said. "Not Grizzlies."

She wondered if she'd spoken her question out loud, but there wasn't time to ask. He kept reading off his phone. "Black bears come in black and brown and they are certainly common in this area."

"Well, they're on the back deck," Cage offered up wryly, pointing out that it didn't matter what they found in the archives, or the online information. The bears were here.

"That explains the rattlesnake, too," Joule said as she

leaned back on her heels. "It also probably means we can't go back for that generator."

She'd heard noises in the woods and ignored it as wind. That had been stupid. Wind didn't operate in one small place. They'd been surrounded by wildlife—who knew what was out there, hungry and angry?—and they'd walked along with no concern. She figured they were lucky they'd gotten off with a rattlesnake strike, though Ginnifer probably wouldn't agree.

"We have to move everyone upstairs." They couldn't leave. As well as being an open and clear target, they'd be vulnerable to far more than just the bears. At least she and Cage had experience barricading themselves inside a home.

Gabby and Kimura were agreeing with her. Marcus headed for the staircase, moving slowly, seeming to understand that he was only capable of being in charge of himself. With a few motions, she, Holly, Cage, Kimura, and Gabby gabbed the edges of the thin blanket and began to move Ginnifer again.

But just as they had her roommate lifted, Joule heard a sharp crack from the kitchen and twin screams from their sentries, Roxie and Sky.

"Run!"

49

C age almost let go of the blanket. Ginnifer's weight forced them all to curl their fingers tightly into the fabric in an attempt to move her. They needed handles but, like everything else, they would have to make due. The fact that their charge thrashed and moaned, and basically tried to stop them from moving her, made all of it harder.

Cage had curled his fingers tighter, to the point he thought they might cramp, when he heard the yell.

"Run!"

The single syllable cut through the air. And he jolted. Everyone had, resulting in Ginnifer, somehow, becoming worse. She screamed out as though in pain and her arm flailed and hit him in the ribs. Cage managed not to let go, even as Roxie and Sky ran in, almost toppling the small group.

He did everything he could to sidestep and not drop Ginnifer. Still, he took a hit as Roxie pulled up short a little too late and crashed into him on the other side. He was beginning to wonder what was the lesser of the two evils—

taking the hits and jostling Ginnfer or just dropping his hold.

"Are they inside?" He didn't mean to deliver the words with such a snap.

Sky's eyes flew wide, but it was from terror, not his words. "They broke the glass. One got his head through. They will be completely inside any second now."

"The other one just came through the door." Roxie added the tail to her sister's half-sentence as she skidded around the corner behind the group hauling their invalid. She obviously debated whether to try to help with Ginnifer or bolt up the stairs herself.

Shit, he thought, it wasn't as bad as it could be, but it was still damn bad.

At the bottom of the stairs, the blanket yanked nearly out of his grip, only this time it was Joule. She tugged on her corner of Ginnifer's blanket, as if she could drag the rest of them along.

But Cage was with her. He didn't need to be dragged, only Ginnifer did. With an extra rush of adrenaline fueled by the noises now sounding like they came from inside the kitchen, the team pushed up the staircase quickly if not carefully. He watched as they bumped the poor girl's head on the railing, twice, before she quit squirming.

Had they been smart, or had more time, they would have carried her head first up the narrows steps. Then again, had they been smart, Ginnifer wouldn't have gotten bitten in the first place. They would have been more careful and maybe anticipated the overwhelming mass of wildlife that had been driven out of their homes by the rising water.

But they hadn't been smart. The only thing going right was that Ginnifer had finally calmed the fuck down. Unfortunately, it was likely by way of a minor concussion. Right now, however, concussion was far superior diagnosis to being mauled by bears.

Marcus had hauled his own ass up the stairs ahead of them. It hadn't escaped Cage's notice that his friend still had one hand on his head and the other trailing along the wall, as though he needed it for balance. At any other time, he would be taking better care of Marcus, but right now, they were all hoping to just stay alive.

"This room," Marcus said, holding open the door to the master bedroom. But Joule was already shaking her head.

"Exit? Entrances?" she demanded.

Marcus closed one eye and raised the other eyebrow to question her. Was the venom in his system keeping him from understanding how serious the situation was? Cage couldn't analyze even that as he felt a sudden shift in the weight on the blanket. Joule let go and Ginnifer's leg slid over the edge and hung loose.

It was Gabby and Max, thinking quickly, who curled her loose limb back into place. Ginnifer's lack of response over the mild abuse made him think the concussion might have been worse than he'd originally thought.

But there were noises coming from downstairs now. It sounded like the pretty wood door to the back deck—the old wooden one with nine small panes of glass—was being crushed by massive paws. As if all the little panes in the door were breaking, one by one. Ahead of him, he heard his sister slamming through the room, and calling back. "Yes! This is good."

They shuffled their way in, and he didn't even notice if they bonked Ginnifer's arms or even her head as they pushed through the narrow doorway. Behind him, the sound of heavy footsteps came from the kitchen. He heard the small breakfast dining set topple and probably break.

There were more noises he couldn't distinguish, and he prayed to whatever gods had helped vanquish the Night Hunters that the bears only wanted the pantry goods.

He watched as Joule slammed through the room then dropped suddenly to her hands and knees and scrambled under the blanket that held Ginnifer's heavy body. She maneuvered between their feet, and out into the hallway.

It seemed only Cage wasn't surprised she would do this. She was getting supplies.

Inside the master bedroom, Marcus tilted precariously and then crashed onto the bed as Gabby ordered him around. "Get out of the way! You! Sit!"

The sound was harsh and clear, but she was trying to stay quiet, too. They'd fumbled their way up the steps, leaving a noise trail that any semi-intelligent or very hungry animal would know to follow. Cage was hoping that the bears' own noise in the kitchen had masked their harried flight.

But what would happen when the bears came up the steps? For surely they would. The people were up here. Maybe they didn't want the people and they would stay downstairs. However, if memory served, the bears would come check them out after they ate, and the bears' curiosity alone could kill them all. He looked to the ceiling, praying for easy attic access and pull-up stairs.

They would not be so lucky. As far as he could see, the ceiling was smooth smooth. There was no sign of an attic door.

They'd lowered Ginnifer unceremoniously onto the floor and began frantically looking around the room for help: weapons, weight, or places to hide. Cage itched to pull out his phone and look up anything that might help them stay clear of claws and teeth. But what little battery he had left would not be enough for checking the feeding habits of black bears in Northern California. There was no time.

"On the bed," Gabby said, nodding that direction with the top of her head. Max countered, "No. The floor. Over here!"

No one argued. They lifted the blanket again, moving as a unit. Cage felt his fingers cramp this time, but they worked together and hauled Ginnifer as far inside the room as they could. This time, they'd nearly dragged her along, but she hadn't so much as twitched.

If they'd had time, the move would have been smoother and kinder. As soon as the bloody blanket made contact with the creamy white carpet, they scattered like frantic ants.

"Chairs," Cage told them. "Furniture." He pointed to Max and Roxie and Sky in turn. "Get that dresser. Get ready to push it in front of the door."

He knew how to barricade a room against hungry animals. But where was Joule?

She showed up then, carefully but quickly maneuvering two chairs through the doorway. Her adrenaline overrode her speed, keeping her from bumping the chairs. *No noise.* Another lesson he'd learned not so long ago.

"There's more in the other room!" She lumbered awkwardly into the room and nearly dropped them before grabbing Gabby's hand and hauling her into the hallway. "We're getting more chairs, to brace the doors," she said as she left the room.

Cage started to follow them. But one half-step into the open space, he saw a dark shape at the bottom of the stairs.

Had he caught the bears' attention, or had Gabby and Joule already caught it as they darted across the open hall?

It didn't matter.

"Bear!" He almost yelled it, but pulled the sound back to a wheeze as he thought better of enraging the huge creature that was starting up the stairs toward him. It didn't matter who'd caught its attention. It saw them now.

As he ducked backwards into the master bedroom, he saw his sister and Gabby turn, almost in unison, eyes wide. Then he watched his sister do the only thing she could.

She slammed the door, trapping herself and Gabby in the nearly empty office across the hallway.

50

"Shit. Shitshitshitshit," Joule muttered as she turned her back to the door. She and Gabby leaned hard against it, adding their weight as a barricade. Whether it would be enough, she couldn't say.

It only took a moment of hearing the heavy paws hit the steps for Joule to realize that against the door was the last place they wanted to be. The house was designed to be pretty, not protective. Even these high-end doors were designed for interiors—not like rough storm doors on the outside of the house. And the bears had made short work of one of those.

There was no protection in this position. She hissed at Gabby and yanked at her friend's sweatshirt. "Get away from the door!"

If a bear was on the other side and sensed them, it might take a swipe at the door, its heavy paw could go right through, hitting them before they even knew what had happened. Even if the bear didn't tear through the door, the lock that held it was brass, only slightly stronger than the decorative door frame that held it in place. A thousand-pound bear could push it open in less than a second.

"Chair!" she whispered as she tugged her friend into the open space of the room. She'd just removed half the chairs that had been in here, but she braced one of the remaining two under the knob.

She'd wedged it tightly, but it was an ornate little sucker with a padded seat and curly, ladder-back rungs. It seemed far fancier than purposeful. Joule figured one good shove and the curves in the wood would snap like twigs.

"The desk," Gabby replied, already dragging it from where it was wedged in the corner.

They would have to shove it in front of the door. Though they worked to make that happen, they didn't get the desk more than a foot away from the wall before it became clear that they'd never get it as far as they needed it. Not before a bear—or three—arrived at the door.

"It's too heavy! What else can we add to the chair?" Joule and Gabby moved as quickly and quietly as possible. All the while, the steps in the hallway seemed slow but constant. More feet heavy joined the first.

The burst of panic had given Joule absurdly clear hearing. She she was certain that more than one bear was now headed up the stairs.

Joule and Gabby dragged an overstuffed reading chair to the door. It wasn't wedged into place at all but it served as a little additional weight. They plopped the trash can onto the seat and Joule watched as Gabby began to fill it with the heaviest books off the shelf. Even though books were heavy, the whole setup was laughable in the face of an angry bear.

Checking for everything and anything they might use, Joule opened the closet door. This had once been set up as a bedroom, and that meant there was a dowel across the top of the closet for hangers. Almost two inches wide and made of hard wood, it might be some help. With a hard shove, she popped it loose then tried to maneuver it out of the closet.

She struggled with the shelves and crafting supplies in her way but managed to wrangle the rod out. In her speed, she bumped it into the doorway more than once. Each knock echoed in the pulse of her racing heart.

She took a breath and slowed down. The noise she made was likely harming them more than the dowel could help. She could still hear the bears on the stairs and more sounds coming from downstairs. Was it the third bear? Or had they miscounted before and there were now more of them?

Joule didn't have time to worry about what she didn't know. What she did know was dangerous enough. She slid the dowel sideways behind the both the chair and the fancy door handle hoping it would hold against the bears and buy them at least a few more minutes.

Then she turned to face the room. Should they go out the window?

It was the second floor. They'd likely break or twist something on the drop. An injury would make them even more vulnerable to whatever came after them. They already knew about rattlesnakes and bears.

"Closet," Joule told her friend as Gabby raised her eyebrows, her expression asking, *Is there even space?*

There wasn't much, but Joule motioned to her. Putting a finger to her lips in a gesture that was almost laughable— after all, she'd been the one making a racket just seconds before—she shimmied through the narrow gap beside the shelves and into the only space in the closet.

Luckily, the owner had used pre-fab shelves that hadn't quite filled the space. When she and Gabby were wedged in, her friend reached out to grab the door. But it was too far away.

For a moment, they both froze. Gabby would have to step out of the relative safety of the closet, but they needed the door closed. The bears were on the other side of the office door now. Pawing sounds raked at Joule's organs as the bears tried to push their way into the room.

Holding her breath, she wedged herself tighter against the back wall. Honestly, she wasn't certain that the back of the closet was safer. Certainly, the bears could smell them. What if they got into the room next door and came right through the drywall? The construction of a house like this surely wouldn't hold up against a determined predator. If they knew the girls were here, the bears might come at them from every angle. After all, the girls were outnumbered.

Gabby reached out, lightning-fast, and then wedged herself back into place, this time with the doorknob firmly in her hand. She carefully and quietly fed the click-lock into place behind them, leaving them in pitch black.

With slow and silent but labored breaths, Joule reached slowly backward, her elbow not having enough room to do much of anything, but she managed to touch her back pocket. Her cell phone was still there. Her battery was alarmingly low, but at least she might be able to communicate with the outside world.

Even as she had that thought, she heard the office door crack under the weight of a California Black Bear.

51

C age had closed the door on his sister. At least she'd closed the door first. At least, in his last image of her, she was hale and hearty if scared shitless.

"Now! Here!" he motioned and spoke in a clean whisper, as though the bears wouldn't hear him. As he grabbed the corner of the dresser and began to pull it into place, he fought the ridiculous urge to ask Kimura to look up the hearing range of a California Black Bear. But Max and Roxie were already on the other corners of the dresser, and he suddenly felt it move.

It was a fight to move quickly and yet be quiet. They'd achieved quiet, but they were only as quick as trapped humans could be, and he felt his fingers unclench as the dresser slowly settled to the floor in its new position.

"Push!" Roxie told them, her hands motioning in case her volume was too low.

Together, they leaned into the sturdy piece of furniture and wedged it against the door. The soft tap as wood hit wood reverberated through the otherwise silent room.

Max turned a circle, already looking around. "What else?"

"Side tables," Cage answered quickly. "Lift!"

Each of them grabbed a table and set it on top of the dresser. Once again, the click of the soft, rubberized feet hitting the surface of the dresser and then bumping against the door turned him cold.

He and Max almost jumped out of the way as Roxie and Sky showed up right behind them. Though not as tall as the boys, they still made short work of lifting the other side table up and onto the dresser. It was added weight. Cage didn't know if it was enough.

Stepping back, he examined their work. They'd only maybe kept out the bears. They'd definitely kept out Joule and Gabby. If his sister and his friend needed fast access to this room for safety, they would die. And he'd made it happen.

But he'd learned a while ago that sometimes choices had to be made before the information was available. He could only do his best. Sadly, it appeared this was it.

He was just letting that awful thought pass through his head when he heard the sound of wood splintering as the door across the hall gave way beneath the superior strength of a bear. He stood in the middle of the master bedroom, facing the closed door as though he could eventually see through it.

But he couldn't. He could only hear, and it didn't sound good.

Thump. Thump. Crack.

Everything sounded louder with the added weight of bears inside the house. The floor beneath his feet tremored with each step they took in the hallway, just in case he wasn't already afraid enough. Cage held his breath.

Between repeated hits and cracks of things he couldn't see being destroyed, his eyes darted left and right. There was nothing in here that could tell him what was happening beyond the closed door. Nothing that would let him know if Joule and Gabby would be okay. His eyes searched for something that would make sense, flitting between Dr. Kimura and Max and Marcus.

It was Kimura who looked the most petrified. Were the kids just that jaded?

He didn't know. Maybe the professor was the only one with his wits still together enough to be scared. His own chest didn't feel the fear anymore, just the resignation of helplessness.

He wasn't helpless, not truly—he knew that. But what could he do for his sister? He couldn't fling open the door—they'd finally gotten it barricaded. And even if he did, he would cause more problems by attacking one of the bears. He might even get Joule or Gabby killed. He simply had to sit back and trust that they could save themselves. And he had to be alert for a bear trying to come into this room.

Cage waited for the screams, but they didn't come. He felt Roxie's hand slide into his and squeeze tightly as though offering comfort. For a moment, he almost brushed her off. She wasn't his sister, and he didn't want anyone to touch him, anyway.

But there was no time to do anything , so he squeezed back.

Just then, Ginnifer decided it was time to return to the land of the living. She rolled, flinging one arm wide and hitting the back of her hand against the wooden slat that ran across the bottom of the bed. She cried out, and Cage watched as behind the dresser, the door thumped inward in response to her yelp.

Surely, the bears could hear his heart thumping in his chest. Yet, somehow, he didn't hear Roxie's or Sky's pulses, all he could hear from the others was Marcus's rough, shallow breathing—and of course, the sounds that Ginnifer made as she thrashed around and alerted the deadly predators exactly where they were. He'd be mad, but she was only semi-conscious. Still, it all seemed very Ginnifer-like.

As he watched, Roxie and Sky knelt down next to their sick dorm-mate and covered her face with a pillow.

Holy shit! he thought. Smothering her was not the way to go.

His horrified expression must have asked the question for him, because Roxie frowned back at him as though he were the one holding the pillow. She shook her head as though to say, No, we would never. As she pulled the pillow back, Sky leaned over Ginnifer and held the other girl's face gently in her hands as she whispered, "Shhhhhh. Go back to sleep."

Certainly, the bears could hear that, too.

The door began thumping harder, and it jerked inward a little farther with each hit. Cage waited to hear screams from across the hallway. They never came.

He reminded himself that Joule had survived worse than this before. But had she? He told himself that a hit by a bear to either Joule or Gabby would result in a shriek of epic proportions. It was a terrible thought, but he continued. Either the person getting hit would scream, or the other would, because of what they saw. As awful as that idea was, he was using their continued silence to count them safe.

Cage once again turned his attention to the room he was in. Standing still, trying to make as little noise as possible, he waited. His silence was nearly pointless, as Ginnifer continued to thrash and mumble. The bears continued to thump on the door. The sounds from across the hallway told him that the bears were more than capable of getting through this door. He held his breath and waited.

After an eternity of noise—of bumping and hits and the sounds of bears trying to get into things, or possibly throwing the things they found—the house grew quieter. The bears seemed to be calming down. Then, they seemed to leave. He heard sounds as they thumped their way down the hallway.

His brain however, continued at five-hundred miles per hours. He was counting Gabby and Joule as alive. If the bears continued on their way, he would consider the dresser and night table stack as a success.

There was always the possibility that a bear might turn around. One could be back at the door in an instant. Though he was desperate to pull down the barricade and check on his sister, it wasn't time yet. That sobered his wayward thoughts very quickly.

The heavy sounds continued as the bears shuffled their way down the stairs. A series of sudden and rough bumps made it seem as if one of them had fallen the last bit, and Cage almost burst into laughter. But they couldn't afford a noise, and he was afraid it would turn hysterical, so he swallowed it back and stayed still.

One bear. Two bears. Where was the third? Were there any others?

He didn't know. Quickly, he pulled his phone from his pocket and checked the time.

How long should they wait before they moved the dresser and searched for Gabby and Joule? How long before they had to make a decision about what to do?

They had new and disturbing information now. Bears were in the area and were capable of breaking into the house. What Cage didn't know was whether the creatures had ransacked the place or if they might leave some signal so other bears would know that there was no more food here worth taking. He didn't know if this was the safest house on the block now or the most dangerous.

He didn't dare sit on the floor. If anything happened, it would only make it harder for him to defend himself from that position. Suddenly, he imagined a bear coming through the door to the attached bathroom. Or through the wall that ran the length of the hallway beyond. He didn't think much would stand up to a California Black Bear— certainly nothing in this house. Even their dresser-and-nightstand system wouldn't hold up against a truly determined bear. All they had done was make it not worth the bears' effort.

Hoping for something useful to do, Cage watched as Max slowly crept toward the window and looked out. This window had a view over the back deck. Despite the rain, Max must have seen something, because he excitedly waved to the rest of them. "They're leaving!"

"How many?" Roxie whispered harshly, the fear coming through in the heavy undertones of her voice.

"Three," he said. "All of them."

"All that we saw," Cage corrected and watched as Kimura's eyes grew wider. Suddenly, the professor pulled his phone from his pocket and began tapping on the keyboard. Hopefully, he was learning something of value, because right now, nothing they did seemed to actually save them. It just moved them from one disaster to the next.

Cage set the timer on his own phone with a silent alarm and motioned to everybody to simply wait. They couldn't afford to make noise and attract the bears back. Or, God forbid, something worse. They couldn't take down their barricade and then need to build it again. So he stood there, unmoving.

When thirty minutes was up, he headed to the dresser and leaned against it as he called out across the hallway. They didn't dare open the doors. If the bears were still there, they could come right through the panels. So the first thing was to see if he could get a reaction from the other stranded humans. Pressing his hands to the door, as though that might make the sound travel further, he yelled straight into the wood.

"Joule! Gabby! Are you okay?"

For a long moment, no voices returned an answer. His heart, which had been hopeful that the lack of noise coming from their room was actually a good sign, now began to sink.

But the house stayed silent. The bears were not returning—at least not that he could tell. The only upside to the terror of the bears rattling everything around was that he'd learned they were not always noisy, but they were never quiet. So Cage decided to trust the silence.

This time, he beat on the door and yelled louder into the space that didn't return any message.

"Joule!" smack smack.

"Gabby!" smack smack. He hit with the heel of his hand until it stung. "Tell us you're okay!"

But nothing came back.

52

Cage looked over his shoulder to the others in the room. His skin was cold and clammy, and his fingers had a fine tremor, though he kept telling himself that Gabby and Joule were okay.

Everyone stared at him. Everyone except Ginnifer, who was still lying with her eyes closed on the floor but at least was quieter now, and Marcus, who had now curled up on the bed, his hands on his head. Everyone standing and watching Cage beat on the door had to be thinking the same thing he was: No answer meant bad news.

He gestured to the pile of furniture and, in a soft voice—as though he hadn't just hollered out through the house—he said, "We have to move this."

Piece by piece, they undid their construction. They lifted the nightstands off and moved aside the chairs they'd wedged against it. They cleared the pieces they'd added for weight. Slowly, they gathered on either end of the big piece of furniture.

His gut clenched as he curled his fingertips under the edge. Once they moved this, they would open the door and he would know. Together, they worked as a team, doing their best to lift and then shuffle the massive object out of the way, leaving the door undefended. If anything came back—bears, coyotes, wolves, snakes, Night Hunters even— it could now waltz right through the door. Their only safety feature had just been removed.

But his sister was on the other side of the door, and Caged didn't care about the rest of it right now. He flung the door wide and ran into the hallway before he even thought of stopping and looking around. Luckily, the upstairs was empty.

He hit the other door as though he'd been thrown at it, turned the knob, and put his weight into it. But nothing happened.

Though still closed, the door was splintered right at eye level. How big had the bears been? He hadn't been up close to them, but they must have been huge. Still, he needed to see his sister.

The gaping hole had left shards of sharp wood aimed into the room, where it had lost the fight with the bears. He didn't dare try to even push his arm through the hole. He'd come back with foot-long splinters or slashed arteries. If anything happened to Joule—or Gabby—they would need all the attention. Cage wrapped his hand around the knob and pushed again.

It became clear suddenly why the door hadn't completely given away. Only the top half had caved in because the girls had barricaded their side, too. They probably hadn't had enough material or time to do quite the job the team in the master bedroom had done.

He rattled the knob, wondering why all his noise hadn't made either of the girls call out or ask what he was doing. Had they gone out the window? The bears were outside now. His heart rate kicked up again and he pushed harder.

It didn't give.

Of course it didn't. Gabby and Joule had effectively stopped the bears from getting through. The hole was big enough for a paw or an arm maybe, but not a whole Cage, and certainly not a whole bear. So the bears *hadn't* gotten in. Yet the girls didn't answer.

He tried to peer through the hole. As big as it was, the wood pieces blocked most of what he could see. But the room looked empty.

"Joule? Gabby?" He yelled it and watched as the handle on the closet began to move. Finally, Gabby's face peeked out.

He nearly collapsed in his relief. His deep sigh probably sucked all the oxygen from the room, but he didn't care. When Gabby emerged unharmed, with Joule right behind her, he almost said something. But his sister put her hands to her head and blinked slowly, as if she were confused. Had she hit her head, too?

"You won't believe this," Joule smiled at him, "but we fell asleep."

The anger rushed through him, pushing his organs out of the way and commandeering all of his energy. Cage couldn't remember ever being so angry in his life. Of course, he'd been angry before. He was still angry with his father, and he wondered if he'd ever get past that. But this? When his father had gone off, at least Cage still had Joule. Now? She was the last one. The last Mazur. If something happened to her, he would be alone.

"That was stupid!" he yelled. "You can't let your guard down like that!"

Somehow, his sister took his tirade in stride, though

Gabby looked shocked that he could sound so mean. Joule only raised one eyebrow at him, crossed her arms, and—through the hole the bears had made in the door—stared him down. "We're exhausted. We were waiting in a narrow, dark, confined space, unable to make any noise. We didn't intend to just take a nap in the middle of a bear attack. But once they were gone, we both crashed. Apparently, we must have needed the sleep. So you can back the fuck off."

Her words were calm, and he couldn't get to her to strangle her anyway. Also, she was right.

Maybe he was a little bit jealous. Well, more than a little bit. When had *he* last slept? He didn't know. He should have slept when the small team had gone out looking for the generator. But he hadn't. And thank God he hadn't. He and Kimura had been ready when Max had carried Ginnifer through the door.

"Can you open the door?" This time his words were kinder. The rage had diffused out of his system. He offered no apology for his accusation, though, and no admission that she was right. He just dropped the issue.

It took a few minutes for the girls to undo everything they'd built. It wasn't as good as what they'd done in the master, but it had held. *It was good enough.* The thought lowered his heart rate into the normal range again.

Gabby and Joule didn't ask if the bears were gone and simply took his presence as an absolute confirmation. Once the door was open and they stepped into the hallway, Cage lunged forward and hugged them both. They didn't balk at his near assault.

For most of a minute, the three of them stood in their embrace, relishing the knowledge that everyone was safe. Behind him, most of the occupants of his room had crowded into the hall to see the girls. Everyone was in one piece. That there was no blood—at least no *new* blood—was remarkable. They stood for a moment until the others piled on, and eventually they turned as a group. In a silent agreement, they all headed into the master bedroom.

It was only then that Joule gave Cage a strange look. "Hey guys?" Even the tone of her voice was odd, and Cage couldn't place it. But her words made his stomach drop again. "Marcus doesn't look so good."

Walking over to the bed, she grabbed Marcus' shoulder and gave him a decent shake. She tried to get him to roll over. Talking to him in gentle but goading tones, she shook him harder. As she did, her voice became more and more frantic. "Marcus? Marcus!"

Joule turned and looked at Cage from over her shoulder. Her hand hadn't left their friend's arm. Marcus still had not budged, and Joule's eyes were wide with alarm. "I can't find a pulse!"

53

"We have to leave." Though Joule said it to everyone, no one replied. The silence stretched out around her, and she let it.

She sat on the floor at the foot of the large bed. One leg stretched out in front of her, her elbow turned and resting on her knee, she probably looked as though she were just relaxing on any normal day. She'd let her head fall back against the thick comforter that covered the bed where her friend Marcus lay.

She swallowed and closed her eyes against the images that came to her. She tried to close her ears against the sound of the rain pounding at the windows. This place could have been beautiful. The view would be gorgeous on a sunny day.

But it wasn't sunny. Joule hadn't seen the sun in... she didn't know how long. The door across the hallway had been splintered open by wild bears. And there was a bloodstain on the on the beautiful plush white carpet of the living room from where Ginnifer had been bitten by a rattlesnake.

Behind her, Marcus lay still on the bed. He wouldn't see the sun again.

It felt like she didn't breathe. Like her heart didn't beat. But it must have, because she was still alive. Losing Marcus shouldn't hurt as much as losing her parents had, and yet somehow, it seemed to.

On the other side of the room, Kimura shook his phone as though that might make the battery gain more charge. He'd complained that he was well below the warning charge. She knew the professor was smarter than that, but she also knew that no one was dealing with anything rationally now.

The professor looked at her, confused. "He shouldn't have died."

Gabby had been out in the hallway but was stepping back into the room when Kimura said that. Thank goodness, because Joule didn't have it in her to respond to statements about what the universe should or should not have done. She let Gabby field the answer. "No, he shouldn't have."

"He had rattlesnake venom in his face... in his mouth." Kimura still seemed vexed. "Human mouths are full of bacteria. He should have been able to fight off most of the toxins."

It was Cage who said, "Bacteria doesn't fight venom."

"Maybe he had a cut in his mouth. Or some kind of silent immune disorder. Maybe he was already sick from something," Gabby offered a logical approach. None of it made them feel better.

"He shouldn't have died," Kimura reiterated, only this time he said it to his phone. As he scrolled through, seeming to have gotten his battery going again, Joule found her brain wandering in the fog of her emotions.

She and Cage had talked about how the ten of them had "borrowed the house." They'd discussed how they would pay for the damage they'd caused. But they'd talked about compensating the owner for breaking and entering, for using of all the supplies and eating the food they'd found. At that point, everything could be washed, a glass pane could have been replaced, food could be bought again. Things had been fixable.

Then Max had carried Ginnifer into the living room. Her blood on the carpet was now permanent. What the bears had done was worse. The house needed major repairs.

The kitchen was leaking any heat that a good, high-quality insulation had held in for them. The glass pane Cage had broken to turn the knob wasn't even visible in the detritus left by the bears. Now the whole door was trashed. The kitchen window was shattered. The rain was coming in and making the floor into a puddle.

They had to leave.

Despite Kimura's constant searching of the internet—it seemed miraculous that he could still get a signal up here—no one could find any answers as to whether the bears would return. The group needed a new house, a safe one. They needed to ruin someone else's property. Then they needed to bear-proof it.

They would have to leave Marcus' body here. That was what bothered Joule the most. On the one hand, it was disturbingly logical to abandon this house. Honestly, even the blood on the living room carpet could be explained away by "bears!" Eventually, someone might notice that things had been taken out of the closets, but for the most part, the damage the bears had done probably covered up anything the humans had caused.

Except for the dead body in the master bedroom. That

changed everything.

Not only did it tell the occupants that people had been here, but it told them exactly what people: people who were associated with Marcus Delacroix.

On the emotional side, it pained her to leave her friend behind. But they had barely all made it here. That had been when they were all upright and functioning. Ginnifer still wasn't awake. They'd have to carry her through the rain. Which meant they needed to know where they were going first.

"We have to leave." She said again to the group again. This time, she got a chorus of replies.

"How do we leave Marcus?"

"How do we carry Ginnifer?"

"Where would we even go?"

"We still need a generator."

"How do we get past the bears and snakes outside?"

Joule didn't know what to do about any of these responses. But they were all good questions that needed answers—and quickly.

Her ability to tell day from night sucked lately, because the skies were dark all the time. But she thought she could see a change in the sky that indicated daytime fading. With all the rain and clouds, the sun seemed to set earlier than usual.

As always, Joule felt the loss of the light as a little clench in her heart. Memories of the year before always invaded until she pushed them back. Having Marcus on the bed behind her only made it worse. She looked at all of her friends, though she hadn't moved from her spot sitting vigil at the end of the bed. "I don't know. But we have to figure it out. And we need to find a new place within—"

She checked the time. "The next two hours."

54

"Over there!"

Joule's head snapped sharply to the right at Gabby's harsh whisper. Her body swiveled with her, bow in hand. Though the rain still came down on them, for the first time, she felt steady and real.

She'd hauled this bow and arrow set with her when there wasn't much she could do with it. Joule had envisioned hunting rabbits for food as the worst-case scenario here. It wasn't like she could just shoot the water. But this? This had all been unexpected.

Her feet were set firmly and the arrow was nocked and ready, the string pulled taut in her hand as she tried to sort the sounds of rustling from the steady drum of the rain and constant shushing of the wind.

Was it real? Or were they hallucinating their worst fears?

Joule scanned the area, the tip of the arrow tracking where she looked. She wasn't confident the weapon made her any safer. Just as a gun wouldn't stop a bear, neither would an arrow—unless the shot went directly through the bear's brain, or possibly into his aorta.

Joule was no more confident that she could hit a striking rattlesnake. For all her skill, the easy target—the bear—wouldn't likely even register that she'd hit it, and the target she could take out—the snake—was so small and fast that the likelihood of her aim being true was slim to none. Still, she held the bow at the ready. She would take her chances.

The Night Hunters had been difficult to hit. But they were moving targets. Though small in comparison to a bear, they'd been big and powerful. She'd grown her skill and her confidence on them. Now she pulled back on the string of her bow and waited.

But nothing appeared.

"I don't see anything," Gabby whispered as the small group continued to move slowly along the street. The disappointment in her tone left Joule in agreement. She'd rather see her enemy than deal with mysterious rustling in the bushes.

They trudged down the street, keeping to their pre-set formation. There were only nine of them now.

They'd left Marcus behind—the only thing they could do. Miraculously, they had found another house that seemed safe. It was three houses up and across the street. Being farther up the hill felt safer. Even though Joule believed they were out of the rising water at this point, it didn't hurt to be farther away from the edge.

She looked again at the edge of the road and tried to make out what was happening in the yards behind the houses. But the rain muted everything. "I don't see anything," she whispered to Gabby, despite the fact that the leaves around her continued to move in strange patterns.

It had been a minor miracle that they'd found the place so quickly. And another minor miracle had occurred—Ginnifer had regained consciousness. She was now alert enough that she could walk, although she still stumbled, weak and unsteady on her feet, but mostly alert.

Gabby supported Ginnifer on one side and Sky had her on the other. Together, they helped hold her weight as she worked to stay upright. This was easier than when they'd had to carry her. Though they all had hoods up against the rain, Joule could see all three were sweating from the work. She didn't envy them.

Joule had almost volunteered for the duty, but quickly realized she would have not only dropped her charge at the first sign of danger, but she would have felt trapped the entire time. The bow in her hands meant everything. Though she was truly glad Ginnifer was getting better, there was still no love lost between her and her roommate.

Max, Cage, Roxie, Holly, and Dr. Kimura also walked at the perimeter of the little group. Like refugees, they kept their weak—Gabby, Sky, and Ginnifer—in the center. Those three were the piece that limited their progress. Everyone else was watching for predators.

"Stop!" Joule told them as she caught a slight movement from the right side of her vision.

"Stop!" she repeated when it seemed they hadn't all quite heard her. The group kept shuffling forward, but she planted her feet, aimed an arrow forward, and decided she would let the others run into her back if necessary. She would stop them one way or another. She wasn't losing anyone else.

As the noise continued, Joule stood her ground, narrowed her vision and tried to block out the constant drumming of the rain. Her knees locked and her muscles tightened as her breathing shallowed out. It was an effort to keep calm, but she would need her steady breaths and sharp focus if she had to take proper aim at anything.

She watched as the movement that had seemed almost imaginary became real. The variation in the way the grass in the yard moved became consistent. The slight change in color through the gray of the rain became sharper.

"Holy fuckballs!" She heard the words whispered from Gabby's lips. Her friend was close enough that Joule could hear all the little terrors that every noise brought.

Gabby didn't even have her hands free; she was too busy holding onto Ginnifer. She could only watch as the snakes began to move out of the grass and migrate into the road.

There was nowhere to go. The group was far too massive.

"Stay still!" Joule hissed over her shoulder as she heard the exact same words from her brother. They could not draw attention to themselves. They'd never survive.

As Joule watched, her muscles tightened until they became brittle. Hundreds of snakes were moving out of the grass.

55

"Oh dear God." Cage watched as the mass of snakes had moved across the road in what he could only assume was a migration.

He watched as one wound up Gabby's leg while she stood still, trembling. He was as afraid as she was, as her dark eye caught his and held. He'd nodded slightly, trying to convey, *You'll be okay*. But he'd felt a weight on the front of his boot.

He'd not let go of Gabby's gaze, but he was certain at least one snake was moving up and over his foot.

Gabby would never let go of Ginnifer, though maybe she could have. She and Sky had simply held the other girl steady while the snakes crawled around her. Had she been too scared? Or just that brave? It didn't matter.

The entire group had held their breath until the sandy colored snakes had declared them useless and passed to the other side of the road. Once again, Cage had been certain that his heart would pound its way out of his chest. But it was still attached. And he was still upright.

"Was anyone bitten? he whispered."

"No." It came back on varied whispers, though none of them had yet moved. Maybe these weren't snakes that bit. Maybe they'd gotten lucky. He didn't know.

Like ghosts, the group started moving again. Slowly at first, and then faster, until they were almost racing for the new house. Coming outside at all had been dangerous.

Cage felt his breath whoosh out in relief as he ducked inside the house. The last one in, he quickly shut the door behind him. Then, for good measure, he threw the bolt.

His shoulders sagged, his muscles all finally giving in. All nine of them had made it safely inside the house. He was simply glad that Kimura's phone had finally died and he couldn't stand there looking it up.

"Gotta get started," Max told him as Cage sagged against the door.

Max wasn't wrong, but Cage wasn't ready yet. He needed the moment to breathe, to let go of the fact that one of the snakes had slid right over the toe of his boot. He no longer had the energy for this.

"Let's go." Max seemed to have a hidden reserve that Cage couldn't find for himself.

The original rain prediction had been for three days, but it had been going far longer than that. He wasn't even seeing weather predictions on any of the phone apps anymore, only the bright red alerts. Snake migrations had not even been one of the hazards they listed.

Max shrugged and replied, "At least it wasn't rattlesnakes."

Cage didn't know what to tell him. They'd all watched as the pale snakes had slid by with almost exaggerated movements. He tried to dig up what little he knew... "Red on yellow kill a fellow." But he didn't know if that was right. Black on red, soon be dead. He had to be mixing them up, and these guys weren't banded with bright colors. They didn't blend in here, but they must be camouflaged somewhere.

He wanted to believe that the drab colors meant "not venomous," but the heads... He was certain that the wide back of the head, the almost triangular shape was the mark of poison. He'd stood there with no real idea if he was watching a hundred harmless snakes migrate across the street in a sleepy, Northern California neighborhood, or if they'd all been five inches away from dying where they stood in the road.

Kimura hadn't yet borrowed any of the remaining phones to produce a commentary. He didn't have anything in his hands either, which led Cage to believe that he hadn't found anyone willing to lend their last bit of juice to the research. The rest of them had all been hoarding their remaining power for maps and necessary searches. No one had even checked any social media, as far as he knew. He hadn't gone on because he wasn't sure what he'd find. Cage decided he was better off not knowing on that one...

They were inside again, and they were safe—he hoped—but they still didn't have a generator and they didn't really yet have the person who could cobble any power together.

Max waved a hand in front of Cage's face to get his attention. "If you're not helping, at least don't hinder."

It took everything Cage had to step aside. Could he bring himself to barricade yet another door?

Ultimately, it didn't matter what he felt like doing. It was about what had to be done. He pitched in, following Max's orders, as Max didn't seem to have his own mild PTSD about making barricades. It took a good thirty minutes of work, which had them sweating and peeling their sweatshirts and extra layers.

They'd all added what they could— "Wear instead of carry," Joule had told them, and then reminded them that the rain was cold, and they couldn't afford illness. With no real medical supplies available, everyone had quickly put on whatever they could wear and still move in. Cage himself had managed two pairs of jeans. There'd been a moment when the snake went over his boot that he'd wondered if two layers of denim and good rubber rain gear might be enough to stop a bite. Then again, Ginnifer had made it clear that one layer of denim and thin plastic rain gear was useless against fangs.

He'd peeled several items of clothing as they'd piled furniture in front of the doors and windows on the lower floor. They'd rationed the pieces, planning it out so they didn't have to move anything too far. They'd put all hands on the bed in the back guest room and shoved the head-board to where it covered the windows. They'd piled things on top and covered most of the exposed glass, hoping that any creatures that couldn't see inside wouldn't want to come inside.

Near the back door, Max sat on the edge of the antique sideboard they had pushed up against the dining room window. They'd pulled the curtains and turned the beautiful teak table sideways, blocking as much of the glass as they could. Then they'd pushed the sideboard behind it, before adding weight to the top.

It had been hard work when he hadn't been fed well enough, hadn't slept in far too long, and was already exhausted.

Thinking that if he sat in the middle of the room, he might not get back up, he surveyed the space around him and then tugged on his friend's sleeve. He shook his head and told Max, "Come on. We're not done."

When his friend frowned at him, he said, "I'm assuming the house was closed up before we got here and there's no wildlife inside. But I don't know that."

He watched Max's eyes roll and he heard the word "Crap!" even though Max didn't say it out loud. He watched as his friend's eyes darted back and forth. He was clearly wondering if anyone else had heard their conversation.

Cage shook his head tightly, as if hoping to convey that he didn't want to alert anyone else. At least not until it was necessary.

The two began working their way through the home, splitting up and systematically clearing room after room. Cage didn't know if he should feel better that they didn't find anything or if he should be afraid that he and Max simply weren't qualified to do the search and they'd missed some important sign.

He came across a gun safe under one bed. The unlocked door had swung open easily to reveal a lone nine-millimeter, loaded and ready. Cage pulled it out and checked the safety before tucking it into the back of his waistband. It was a stupid place to keep a gun, but right now, the stupider place to keep it was under the bed.

"I think we're clear," Max told him, finally sounding as beaten down as Cage felt. Cage straightened and nodded his agreement.

Then he followed Max into the hallway on the second floor and watched as his friend leaned against the wall and slid down until he was sitting. Whatever Max's limit was, he'd reached it. "At least I hope we are."

Cage joined his roommate and sat there for five minutes before his sister came up the hallway. He must have been asleep because he jolted when she said his name.

"Are you okay?" She squatted down to look him in the

eyes, bending in a way he thought he might never bend again. Then again, she'd slept. *Through a bear attack.*

"I guess." He tried to offer a smile.

She wasn't taking it. "Everyone is in the main room." She stood easily, motioning for him and Max to follow, as if her movement was enough to make it happen. Slowly, Cage pulled himself to his feet and headed down the stairs. She was out of sight before he and Max even started down the steps.

In the main room, only a few of the refugees remained awake. When they'd come in, everyone had piled their backpacks and bags in the center of this room. They'd brought the things they'd packed at the dorm as well as any undestroyed food from the other house.

Though Cage and Joule had found a handful of canned items in the cabinets here, this place was nowhere near as well-stocked. There were no perishables in the refrigerator. The pantry was relatively barren. But at the moment, the kitchen didn't have gaping holes left by bears, and that was a huge plus.

He now saw that his friends had rearranged the room. One long wall featured a section for each of their personal things, as well as an area for group items. He spotted his backpack and rain gear easily and he felt his heart mush a little in his chest. He and Max might have been checking for rodents, but no one had left them to work alone.

There were a few remaining chairs that weren't useful for barricading anything. They had gathered pillows and blankets, making pallets for everyone. He counted nine— four already filled with sleeping friends. A fire roared in the fireplace, and the room was relatively barren except for what he was discovering mattered most. For a moment, his thoughts flicked back to the students remaining at the dorm.

What had happened to them? But he pushed the thought forcefully aside.

He found an empty pallet near the fire. He could use the warmth. When he motioned to Joule, she only nodded. Cage couldn't tell if she'd planned for him to sleep in this spot, or if he'd just usurped the place she'd staked out for herself. He was too tired to ask.

As he curled into the blanket, he realized that while they had barricaded everything else out, they had also barricaded themselves in. Though his brain had been rolling into the abyss of sleep a moment before, his thoughts popped him wide awake again.

Blinking hard, he tried to get tired. But a few moments later, he heard a voice that he hadn't expected to hear.

"It's midnight," Ginnifer said, more clearly than he'd expected. She must have been feeling better.

"We should sleep," he replied, finally feeling the pull of unconsciousness. "We're in for the night."

"The toilets do flush, right?" Her eyes darted from one corner of the room to another, and she was alert and sharp, as though she hadn't just been practically carried up the hill. As though she hadn't been out cold for almost twenty-four hours. As though they hadn't feared she would die from the round puncture holes with cleanly sliced X's over them.

As though Marcus hadn't died saving her.

She worried about the toilets flushing.

Cage felt his eyes narrow. Joule was right about this one.

Ginnifer began speaking again. "We still need the generator. But the good thing is, now we know where it is. So in the morning, I think we'll have to go out and get it."

She said it with authority. Each word felt like sand under his eyelids. It was all Cage could do not to dive across the room and strangle her. And he wasn't really certain if what stopped him was his own self-control or his complete exhaustion.

She was opening her mouth again, when the thump came at the door.

In the room, six of the heads popped up at the sound. Cage stilled. But it wasn't a bear. The heavy sound came again, and it was definitely human.

56

The thumping at the door came again. It demanded an answer, though no one spoke.

Cage's gaze darted from friend to friend, to the professor, to Ginnifer and Holly. He saw all eyes open wide and overly alert, except for Max. Only Max managed to remain asleep through the sound of someone almost trying to break through the door. This didn't surprise Cage.

The knocking came again. This time it was loud enough to even make Max stir. After the third hammering noise came, Cage decided for himself it sounded most like a fist on a door. He thought he heard the knob twisting, but he couldn't be sure. No one could see the door because they'd barricaded it so well.

Joule threw off her covers, clearly done waiting, and headed toward the door. Maybe because he was her brother —her twin—he could read it in the way she walked, but she was getting ready to negotiate. He felt his eyes squeeze shut. The thought of her slightly high-pitched, feminine voice being the only one intruders heard bothered him. So he, too, stood, only he bolted the few steps after her and grabbed her shoulders.

Being Joule, none of this shocked her. Cage was shaking his head at her, telling her *No, don't say anything* as the pounding came again.

This time a deep, masculine voice demanded, "Who's in there?"

Cage waved to Dr. Kimura, motioning him to the door. As the only actual adult in the group, maybe he could garner respect. After all, the man outside the door probably lived in the neighborhood.

"Can I help you?" Kimura called through all the pieces of wood and plastic and upholstery-covered chairs.

"Who are you? This is the Tamblyn house, and they're not home right now. I know you're not the Tamblyns."

"Correct. My name is Dr. Daishin Kimura. I go by Dean. I'm a professor of marine biology at Stanford."

Once again, the door rattled behind all the furniture they'd piled against it. For a moment, Kimura looked startled. Cage suddenly wondered if maybe Kimura wasn't quite fast enough on his feet to be their spokesman. But it was too late now. No point adding extra voices—and information— to the conversation.

The students had all crowded in close until they stood in a tight knot, listening at the door. Cage had the horrid thought of a shotgun blast coming through and injuring his friends.

Trying not to raise an alarm, he slowly motioned everyone back slightly.

"I'm here with several students," Dr. Kimura added to his earlier words. "We've barricaded ourselves inside."

"What on earth for?"

Kimura proceeded to explain that they had escaped

from the flooding in Stanford, and that possibly the neighborhood would see more refugees from the school. He simply didn't know.

For a moment, Cage wondered: *In a school that was supposedly as elite as Stanford was, were there any other people as smart as Joule? Had anyone else bought boats ahead of time?* Or maybe they'd been smart enough to scrounge some up after the flooding had started.

But he hadn't seen anyone else out on the water.

"There are bears roaming the neighborhood. We were in a different house—" Kimura took a half-second to suck in breath and yell again. "Three California Black Bears came through kitchen and ransacked the place. We hid upstairs."

"Are you fucking serious?" the voice came back, startling Cage and apparently most of his friends.

"Yes," Kimura replied calmly, maybe a better spokesman than Cage had given him credit for. "Absolutely. If you go look at the other house, you'll see where the bears came through the door on the back deck."

"Which house?" At least this time, the man on the outside didn't sound quite so angry. But Cage was getting concerned. There was wildlife out there, and some of it was dangerous, even deadly. Did the man not know?

Kimura suddenly shook his head and shrugged at the students. But next to him, Joule had already found a pencil and a small scrap of paper, though Cage had no idea where she pulled it from. She was scribbling down the address and handing it to Kimura, who shouted it through the furniture piled at the door.

"The Winchester house?"

"I don't know," Kimura yelled back.

It suddenly occurred to Cage that, while they had broken into the house and used the belongings, they hadn't once looked to see if they could find out who owned the place. That information had simply been for "later," and "later" had been broken and splintered by bears.

"Look, you have to get inside. There are snakes out there, too!" Kimura told the man they still hadn't seen, only heard. "We saw close to one hundred. Maybe more. They were sidewinders, I think."

"Sidewinders don't come up here." The doubt came right through the door with the words.

Kimura shook his head, as though the other man could see him, but at least his reply was steady as he yelled back. He was working hard to make his voice heard through all the things they'd shoved into place and over the sound of the relentless rain beyond the walls. "They do when they've been flooded out of the low grounds."

He paused, and when no accusations came back, Kimura told him, "All the wildlife seems to be out in numbers. All the species have been shoved out of their territory. They're angry. They're probably injured. And they're hungry. You need to find shelter now! Go back to your home!"

There was no reply. But no sound of heavy footsteps moving off the porch, either.

Cage held up his phone, indicating another gambit, and Kimura caught on. "Here's my phone number—No, wait. My phone is dead. Hold on." Turning to the group, he looked at the others, hoping someone would volunteer. It was Ginnifer who quickly rattled off her cell number and replied, almost smugly, "I still have juice."

That's because you slept for the past twenty-four hours while we carried you, Cage thought angrily. But better that the strangers have Ginnifer's number than Joule's. Or his.

"Go home!" Kimura demanded after making sure the

man got the number. "Get somewhere safe and give us a call. I'm happy to talk!"

"All right." That was it.

Cage pressed his ear to the wall beside the door. It was as close as he could get to understanding what was happening on the outside. Even the window next to him had been covered and barricaded. But at the top, where they'd left a small gap, he thought he saw a sweep of a powerful flashlight. Then it was gone. Had the people left?

The group waited out the tense moments. Cage thought through the possible scenarios—from shotgun blasts coming through the doorway to bears coming through the walls. Had the people standing on the porch, probably with lights and making who knew what noises, attracted more predators to their new home?

The group had come here earlier in the day, very deliberately not wanting to be out with the nocturnal creatures. Kimura wasn't wrong that every last animal was hunting. Their food stores had been lost, their hunting grounds possibly destroyed. Burrows and caves and open land were now flooded and unsafe. Would these people, who were out in the middle of the night banging on doors, even make it back to their own home safely?

He didn't know.

He didn't even know if the man would come back or not.

But as they all finally began to relax, Ginnifer's phone rang.

She put it to her ear and answered tentatively, her eyes darting around the group for reference. "Hello?"

She paused. "The man gave you this number?... I'm sorry. You said your name is... what?"

When Joule heard it, she grabbed the phone from Ginnifer's hands.

57

"**M**oonbeam?" Joule almost shouted the name as she grabbed the phone out of Gininfer's hands.

Much to Gininfer's consternation, Joule twirled away with no intention of giving one of the few working devices back to her. But Joule gave exactly zero fucks.

"Moonbeam?" she asked again, even as the voice tentatively replied, "Hello?"

Joule couldn't tell if this was the chemist she'd met and borrowed sweatshirts from or maybe someone else. But who else would be named Moonbeam? And the man at the door had said the other house they'd broken into was the Winchester house. Joule began explaining at a mile a minute.

"Moonbeam Winchester. Chemist at Stanford. Yes?" And before the other woman could even answer, she clarified, "My name is Joule Mazur. You let my twin brother Cage and me into your apartment during the first flood. This is the same Moonbeam—"

"Oh my gosh, yes! You're okay?" The voice cut her off.

The animation sounded exactly like the woman they'd met during the first, smaller flood. Happy, chipper, and genuinely pleased to find out they were doing well.

Joule returned the sentiment. "Yes, we're safe. I'm so glad you're okay, too. You're not at your apartment now, are you?"

But if she was, how would she have called Ginnifer? Wasn't the man at the door supposed to call? Joule's confusion must have shown on her face, and as she looked up at the group, she realized theirs mirrored her own. She turned away, only to have them all crowd around her again.

"Apparently, I'm several houses over from you right now," Joule explained.

But if Moonbeam's father owned a house here, couldn't she have come up here when the flooding started? Joule wondered.

Moonbeam was still talking, and Joule realized she should pay attention.

"—uncle and I came out and knocked on the door. Someone, a Stanford professor actually, gave us this phone number. But it's not yours?"

"You were at the door?" Joule asked, bypassing all the other concerns. For a moment, the two talked over each other.

"I have family up here. We saw someone had broken into the Tamblyn house..."

"When were you in your own house? I thought we were in your house?" Joule asked, growing confused again. This time, she paused and tried to do a better job of listening.

"I came up when the rains started. But then when the power went out, we headed up the street with my uncle. He already had a few people in with him, and it seemed better to be in a group. The address the professor gave us—where he and a few students stayed—was our house. That was you?"

Joule was nodding, though the rest of her group was looking at her as though they couldn't quite make everything out. "We must have arrived just after you left." She didn't add that she now understood why the place had been easy to break into and had a reasonably stocked pantry.

"You must have left just before my uncle and I went back to check on it last night. By then, the place had been broken into and it looked awful. That's why we went knocking on doors, to see if anyone was hurt. Then, your guy said it was bears."

"Yes, at least three of them, together," Joule said. Everyone was looking at the phone then at her. She considered putting it on speaker, but she wanted to conserve the battery and didn't want her conversation any more public than it already was. Moonbeam was her friend. "I can't believe you were outside at night. Have you not seen the wildlife?"

"No." The word came back tentative. "I mean, we did see a handful of raccoons and definitely some trash cans turned over, but we thought it must be the storm. We saw skunks and a few stray dogs that we tried to get to follow us home, but no luck."

Dogs? Joule thought as her stomach turned. Domesticated dogs weren't going to last long with what was out roaming the streets right now. She pushed the unsavory thought down. "There are at least black bears and snakes out. We saw both sidewinders and rattlesnakes."

"Nothing we saw seemed like it would do real damage." Moonbeam paused. "I mean, we didn't see anything we haven't seen before. We certainly didn't see bears. I know they're around—"

"They are out in force," Joule explained, hoping her voice held the gravity it needed. "The rising water has pushed everything out of its habitat. They're angry. My friend—" Maybe she shouldn't have used the word "friend" to describe Ginnifer "—got bitten by a rattlesnake."

Shit, she thought, how could she tell Moonbeam about Marcus's body? They'd simply left him in the upstairs master bedroom.

"Can we meet?"

The words had barely left her mouth when Holly broke in. "I don't know if we should go outside at all."

"We shouldn't," Joule agreed, "but do we have much option?"

"It's dark now," Moonbeam countered. "If things are out and about like you say, we shouldn't go. If they're nocturnal, we don't stand a chance." There was a pause before her overly-cheery friend said, "And maybe the rain will let up tomorrow."

Joule wasn't sure why she liked the chipper woman as much as she did. But Moonbeam was right, and Joule could hope. Though personally, she thought it was getting pretty Biblical out there. "Tomorrow is better. We haven't slept in... I don't know how long." Some of them had been awake for more than twenty-four hours, and she wasn't confident that anyone had slept one full stretch yet. Hell, they'd all been lying down at last when the knock had come at the door.

"Well, let's all get some sleep tonight."

Maybe tomorrow she could figure out how to tell her friend about Marcus' body. Was it better that the house belonged to someone they knew? Maybe they could get him back. Or maybe all hell would break loose.

"How is ten in the morning? We can come to you. Hopefully, there will be some decent light, even if it's still raining."

"That sounds good—"

But Joule didn't finish her answer. Ginnifer was already cutting in. "Do you have a generator?"

"No. We've been using the fireplace."

"Tomorrow, all of us go together to get the generator," Gininfer said, her eyes darting around the group, meeting each gaze as though to challenge them to say she was wrong. Then she added, "Safety in numbers."

Joule scoffed. Their numbers hadn't stopped the sidewinder migration they'd seen. When there had been four of them to one rattlesnake, Ginnifer had still been bitten and Marcus was still dead. Joule did not like those numbers, but they did still need the generator.

She agreed. "We'll un-barricade the door at ten a.m."

"Can everyone show up fed and ready to go?" Cage asked.

Moonbeam consulted with her group, however large they were—Joule hadn't asked. And they hung up.

Joule caught the look in her brother's eyes. "We'll figure out what to do and how to do it. We found a generator. We can have power if we can get it running."

"I can get it running," Ginnifer cut in.

Yes, yes, Joule thought, but she said only, "There are wild animals out and about. We'll need a plan to go get it."

The look she saw in Cage's eyes said something else. They really didn't need the generator if they could stay here and wait out the storm. They could barricade the doors and windows and wait for the rain and floods to pass. Or until they could signal a rescue crew.

No, they needed the generator because there were still students back at the school.

58

J oule stood back as Max helped Cage and Dr. Kimura lift the heavy couch from in front of the door. Were they playing the "manly men" card? She didn't comment because she was relieved that she'd finally slept a full night and didn't have to lift anything. She was well-fed and finally felt ready to accomplish something. Despite the rain that continued to drone outside, she felt better than she had in days.

"Hey," she commented and dove for a silver object at Dr. Kimura's feet, "this fell out of your pocket."

It was a wristwatch, heavy and possibly expensive.

Kimura took it back and quickly pocketed it again. Something in the way he did it made Joule press for an answer. He looked to the three of them and sighed.

"That's why I had to get out of the Bass Building. Why I emailed you. You were the only ones I could think of who might come get me." He paused. "There was another professor there. But he waded down into the lower floor after it flooded. I told him it was a bad idea."

Kimura's eyes darted around, mostly at the ceiling. "He

handed me his watch. It was ridiculous. But he said it was insurance that he was coming back."

He didn't come back.

Kimura didn't have to finish the story; he had the watch. And he was the only one they'd rescued from the building. So he hadn't seen the sharks, but he'd lost someone along the way, even before Marcus' death. Joule sucked in a deep breath of understanding and they all turned back to the job at hand.

They had just moved the last heavy object away from the door, when the knock came. Leaping up, Joule turned the knob and threw the door open wide—although that was a mistake. She should have used the peephole or at least asked who it was. But who else would show up precisely at ten a.m. and knock nicely on the Tamblyns' door?

Barely able to get a glimpse of the group crowding the front stoop, Joule was pulled into a massive hug by Moonbeam. Her friend then managed to catch Cage in the embrace too, though he didn't seem quite as enthusiastic. "It's so good to see you guys. I'm so glad you're safe."

Their reunion didn't impress her companions, who huddled under the small overhang that protected the front step. The relentless rain forced the small crowd to move. Several large men, all holding weapons, pushed their way into the living space, bringing water and a sense of trepidation with them.

Only two looked like what Joule had imagined from the voice at the door last night. Even though the neighborhood was rather posh, they had rough beards and big heavy coats. They looked ready for the elements. One held a shotgun, the other an axe.

The other two were more polished, and their coats were nicer—more expensive, more for looks than actual protection.

They appeared to have suffered more from the rain they'd walked through. One of them had on gloves, but no hat, his hair and head were wet from the trek over. Joule didn't think much of his decision-making skills. The other had a hat but lacked gloves. His neatly trimmed, and almost-too-shiny fingernails marked him as a businessman rather than a woodsman.

"Get inside and close the door!" The words, with their panicky edge, came from one of the more mountain-looking men, as they all shoved their way into the main living area. The businessman with no hat introduced himself as Phil, sticking out his hand to shake Joule's even though he still clenched his baseball bat in the other.

As he made his way around the room, repeating his own name and appearing to memorize everyone else's, Joule saw that the bat bore the signature of a famous baseball player. Now it had been dragged out into the storm, the signature less important than the protection it might provide.

Joule looked up at one of the burlier guys as he finished throwing the bolts on the door and looking around the room, as if checking out their barricades.

"Bobcats," the other mountain man volunteered, as though he were trying to be calm about it.

"*Bobcats?*" Cage made a face showing he hadn't processed all of it yet, but Joule was beginning to understand. They must have seen a large mountain cat—or several—on their way over, though they'd only heard about the bears and the snakes from her group. Last night, they hadn't been sure if anything more concerning than the flood was still out and about. This time they'd encountered something truly dangerous.

"Not a bobcat. It was a puma—mother and cubs. She did not look happy to see us," Phil countered as he dropped

Kimura's hand from a slightly over-enthusiastic shake. "I think she licked her lips when she saw us. Like she was going to feed us to the kits."

Shit, Joule thought. The last thing they needed was more wildlife. She should have known there were mountain cats up here. What else was up here that they hadn't already seen? Had Kimura's phone battery not died, he would have looked it up and told them all the options.

Casually, the two burlier men slid the couch back into place blocking the door. It had taken her a little effort to convince her friends to barricade their own doors last night, and she still wasn't sure if they had done it. But she was confident they would do it tonight.

"What's this about a generator?" one of them asked, and Joule watched as Moonbeam held her hand up.

Her friend looked around the rest of the group. "Can we introduce ourselves? I'm Moonbeam Winchester. Yes, related to the Winchester rifle company, and I had a hippie mother." She must have seen an expression on several of their faces. "This is my father, Robert."

She motioned to the other businessman. Clutching a handgun, he didn't appear dangerous with it and he did not look like he'd name his daughter Moonbeam. He'd been quiet since coming in the door.

"We own the house that I think you guys were in, the one the bears got into," Moonbeam continued. "These are my uncles—Phil and Chester." She pointed to the other businessman, and one of the more effective-looking men, then the other. "And his friend, Mickey."

Joule cut in then and went about introducing her group. She almost said, "And this is Marcus." As her chest tried to implode, she explained to them about Marcus.

Moonbeam's father, Robert, looked up with shock. "Come again? You left a dead body in my house?"

"We left our friend behind, sir." Cage stepped forward, an undertone of anger tinged his words. Joule could hear it, but she wasn't sure anyone else would pick it up. "He died saving Ginnifer's life. Ginnifer—" he waved his hand back toward her, "—got bitten by a rattlesnake while we were out looking for a generator. Trust me, we did not want to leave him behind." Something about his words or his tone, or maybe just a comprehension of the directness of the situation, made Robert back off.

The older man only nodded and offered, "Once the roads are clear, we'll take care of him."

"Thank you." Cage nodded a short head bob of agreement, almost military style, and in that movement Joule caught shades of their mother in Cage's unwillingness to budge.

Ginnifer, seemingly fully recovered now, pushed her way to the front of the group again and demanded information. "Who else is up here on this mountain?"

"I don't know." Mickey spoke this time. He still held onto his shotgun. Apparently, sighting hungry mountain lions would make you hold on a little more tightly. "We haven't seen any evidence of anyone else."

"Why did you come over here last night?" Ginnifer's suspicions weren't unfounded. It was a question they should have asked before, but she'd do well to dial her tone back a bit.

"Moonbeam and I went out and knocked on all the doors to check on—"

"Holy shit!" Joule couldn't hold back her surprise. "You were out and about late at night, and you didn't see anything?"

"We had a bright flashlight," he offered, sounding a bit chagrinned. Then he added, "It may have kept the animals back. But now, I'd guess everything saw us." His sour expression told Joule that idea didn't sit well with him.

"I'm glad you're safe," was all she could offer. When the conversation lulled for a moment, she added, "I'm glad that there are more of us now." *More adults*, she thought, though she didn't say it.

She and her brother had really been functioning as adults since last year. They had no parents to fall back on, only grandparents who provided a place to stay during the holidays but weren't like actual parents. Grandma and Grandpa Mazur offered a familiar house to go home to on school breaks, but they couldn't replace having a mom and dad. They certainly could never replace *her* mom and dad.

Something about the bulk of Mickey and Chester, about the surety of Robert's gaze, and even Phil's willingness to use his prized baseball bat gave her a little bit of steadiness. Or maybe it was seeing Moonbeam's face again and knowing that someone she knew had also survived.

So far...

"I don't know this is the safest place to stay," Joule dove in again. "Ginnifer's right. We need a generator. We need to get power... And we have two rafts. I think we need to go back to the school and see who we can save."

59

"Which house is yours?" Holly asked, but Cage had also wanted to know. Despite being outside in the rain again, he had questions.

There are too many of us, Cage thought as he stood to the side of the group. Ten was a lot for getting things done and staying organized. They'd lost Marcus, but gained five others—five who'd been functioning as their own group.

He watched the others warily, the weight of the gun heavy in his palm. Cage now knew it belonged to George Tamblyn. It had been a rough moment admitting to Joule that he'd had it for a while. But she'd eventually sighed and said she was glad they were better armed.

Together, Ginnifer and Joule—an unlikely combo—had argued in favor of heading out and getting the generator. Mickey had agreed with them, backing up the idea that power for phones and small appliances was necessary to alert rescue teams, either that they needed to be rescued or that they were safe and time shouldn't be wasted on them.

Moonbeam's group had all shown up ready to go on a trek for supplies, so all they'd needed was the argument for and against what they were after and a little bit of organization. The generator had proved an easy decision. But it was not the first stop.

Though Joule had brought her bow and arrow and Cage had the gun he'd found, most everyone else needed to be outfitted with something they could use effectively in a fight. This had involved pulling a few items from the Tamblyn home, but they only needed enough to get them across the street and up two houses, to where Phil lifted the door on his shed and allowed Chester to rifle through the garage.

They'd all stepped in from the rain and admired the tools and general supplies.

If only he had a generator, Cage thought.

Holly and Ginnifer had gotten their hands on machetes and looked just a little too eager to use them. Roxie had picked several sharp sticks that she was mostly using like a bow staff, though she lacked any formal martial arts training. And one by one, common household tools had become weapons, all the way down to Sky sticking a set of throwing axes through loops in her belt.

"I'm good," Gabby told the men, showing off the dagger set she'd brought with her. There was no trace of blood from the shark.

Phil looked impressed as he held out two canisters, which Cage readily recognized as bear spray. "Take this. I only have two more."

"What about you?"

Phil didn't blink. "We each already have one."

Cage nodded softly, his eyes darting outside the open front of the garage. Though he wasn't getting rained on, this would be a bad place to be caught unaware. And Phil had just proven that he wasn't handing out weapons equally between the groups. Cage didn't know if that was truly a bad thing. He wouldn't have handed Ginnifer bear spray, either, and probably not Max. But... he put the thought in his back pocket for later as they all stepped back out into the rain.

It hadn't let up, and though it was definitely brighter than it had been at midnight, he still hadn't seen the sun. He was beginning to understand the kind of depression that came with the weather.

This time, it was Joule who led the group. They had to get to the house that had the generator... and the rattlesnake. It was in between the two Winchester homes.

It was Phil who first piped up, "Isn't that Garrett's place?"

Robert was about to answer him, and Moonbeam looked like she was throwing her own answer over her shoulder to add her own reply. This was far-too-casual a conversation for the situation, and Cage was grateful when Kimura interrupted them.

He must have borrowed someone else's phone, because he was tapping and scrolling on a screen. Also, because it had pink rhinestones on it.

"Black bears," he said stoutly to anyone in earshot. "Mountain lions—puma, if you want to call them that. Rattlesnakes. All are indigenous to the area." His eyes made contact with the adults in case the deadly animals he was listing didn't make his point well enough. "We also saw sidewinders—a very large number traveling together. So just because something isn't native to exactly this area, doesn't mean we can't find it... or that it won't find us."

He paused a moment, but this time no one asked questions or pondered the ownership of nearby houses. Just because Phil and Robert were homeowners didn't mean they would lead this little expedition. Kimura continued. "I don't think the black bears are going to sneak up on us. But the rattlesnake that got Ginnifer certainly did. We need to stop talking and keep our eyes peeled."

Interesting development, Cage thought. It was strange seeing Kimura, who'd mostly been along for the ride and more than content with his role as librarian, step up and tell the big burly mountain guys they needed to shut up.

It worked, too. All five of the "others" were nodding along, but apparently the good professor wasn't done yet. "There are also brown recluse and black widow spiders in the area. We're heading into a shed and around the back behind it—"

"That's where they keep the spare fuel," Ginnifer interjected, though her voice wasn't necessary. "Unless," she turned to face Phil and then Robert, "You have fuel, but not rattlesnakes?"

Her tone was sharp. Then again she'd survived a rattlesnake bite and Marcus hadn't, even though he hadn't been bitten. That fact had to shake her to her core—and Ginnifer's core hadn't been all that great to start with.

Maybe a generator or a shed that didn't have deadly spiders would be nice, Cage thought. He'd certainly known the spiders were here, but it had never been a real worry on campus. Don't curl your fingers under the lids of the garbage can. If you turn a rock over, do it slowly and be prepared to step back quickly. But it wasn't like this, where everything was now a corner made dark by the rain. Everything was obscured, and all the animals were angry and ready to lunge.

Phil and Robert looked to each other and shrugged, but it was Chester who answered. "We have a fuel can, but it's low. If I had known this was going to happen, I would have..." he trailed off.

Cage thought, *If we'd known, we all would have done things much differently.*

Joule raised her hand and pointed, her fingers getting wet in the rain. "Then we need to go into that shed, and we need to get around back for the fuel."

"If you don't mind, I'm going to let someone else do that," Ginnifer stated pertly, though no one contradicted her.

Yes, Cage thought, *We'll do it, if only because you've demonstrated your poor ability to fetch fuel cans in the past.* He knew the rattlesnake bite wasn't her fault, but he still struggled not to blame her for Marcus' death.

Ignoring the chatter and Ginnifer's requests, Joule started walking. Like a flight of starlings, the group shifted almost as one, heading in a new direction. But fifteen feet farther down the road, a rustle came from the bushes off to their left. A big noise.

As they all turned in unison to gauge the threat, a large number of rabbits came bolting out from the woods. Cage put his hand out beside him, stopping Roxie and Sky as though he was a mother with kids in the car next to him. He hadn't needed to do it. Everyone has seen the family come out of the bushes at high speed. Or maybe they'd all heard the wrestling and—hyperaware—had turned to look.

Surely the rabbits didn't just think it was a good idea to hop as a group toward the heavily-armed humans? Something must have spooked them, something scarier than the people.

Cage looked up and over the furry heads to see what had frightened them. Whatever it was, it was certainly more of a threat than the rabbits themselves. But nothing emerged.

Instead, a large shadow overhead caught his eye as it swooped toward them.

60

"Jesus—" Joule bit her tongue before taking the name of the Lord in vain in a way that would have offended even the most casual of Christians.

The shadow that had loomed over their heads had first registered in her brain as possibly a pterodactyl—*a fucking pterodactyl*. Apparently, that was where her brain went when something passed overhead with a massive wingspan. Before she even identified the creature—because it couldn't be a real pterodactyl—it dive-bombed them.

The move happened quickly enough that her brain hadn't had a chance to process. She'd watched as the huge bald eagle swooped down and snatched up one of the helpless rabbits in front of her.

"Fuck my life," Joule whispered, shaking her head as the eagle soared out of sight. Having what it wanted, it disappeared as quickly as it had come, though the rabbit's terrified squeals were likely something she would not get out of her head for some time.

Could nothing go according to plan? Could nothing be executed without some heart stopping danger?

Probably not. They were in a severe weather alert and had been for days. They were in a flood—not the kind that washed out roads, but the kind that drowned cities. They still hadn't gotten word about rescue crews because the rain and strange winds were kicking up too much to put the pilots at risk.

Things are this scary, she thought, *because everything around us is like us*: scared, hungry, driven out of its home, and not sure when it would eat again.

As the eagle had swooped in, she'd seen Phil out of the corner of her eye. He'd choked up on the very expensive shiny baseball bat, and Joule was simply glad he was ready to knock the bald eagle out of the park if it got too close to them. Majestic as it was, the huge bird had been petrifyingly close.

"That was a bald eagle, right?" Holly's voice caught on a squeak that was partly due to her heavy breathing. Though Joule thought it was obvious what the creature was—at least at the end—she was more than glad that someone else found everything as startling as she did.

They'd hustled their butts after that. No one wanted to be the eagle's next dinner. The thing had appeared huge enough to carry off at least the smaller humans among them. The rabbits had scattered, making Joule hope the threat was gone, but she was tense waiting for the next one as they spread out around the shed that held the generator they'd found.

They'd set four members along the back perimeter to watch for bears or anything else that might come out of the woods. Mickey and Chester had volunteered to take point on that, and Joule was grateful. She didn't want to lose Gabby or Sky to a bear and she didn't want her friends to have to put themselves between the group and a hungry attacker. Mickey and Chester, at least, stood a chance of intimidating the animal. And with the shotgun and axe, they stood a chance—a small one—of winning a fight.

She and Cage had been assigned to go through the stacked wood and along the back wall with long sticks. They poked all the crevices, around the fuel cans and behind the woodpile, under the old mower engine. Not pleasant work, but luckily, nothing had jumped out at them. The twins had then quickly reached down and picked up the fuel cans. The one Joule grabbed was no longer perfectly situated in its dried grass spot. Ginnifer seemed to have knocked it over before getting bitten last time.

Suddenly worried, Joule leaned down and rubbed the bottom of the can on the wet grass, hoping to dislodge any spiders as her brother caught on and did the same. Then she picked it up, turned it over, and felt the heavy liquid slosh. The smell of gas wafted up to her nostrils. Normally, it wasn't a pleasant smell, but this time it was comforting. The can was full.

Motioning to those who stood guard at the back of the woods, she and Cage had trekked toward the street. The grass was just as slick and as sloped as it had been last time. They made their way slowly, but they met up with the others at the top of the hill.

Max's hands were full now with the handle of the generator as he rolled it slowly along behind him. All around him, the girls seemed to be guarding it as though the thick metal canister and its metal-rod carry cart needed their protection.

"Back to the Tamblyn house?" Joule asked.

But a quick consensus had Phil shaking his head. "My house."

For a moment, Joule's heart twitched. They'd gathered

the generator and the fuel. There were nine of them in her group now. And clearly, eight of them were just college students. The other group was almost entirely adults...

Had the students just set them up with everything they needed? Were the items going to get stolen and set up at the Winchester house? Or were the new guys simply going to weasel them out of their find?

Beside her, Moonbeam wore a smile at their finds, and Joule had to trust that Moonbeam's affections weren't given randomly, and that her family was trustworthy. But she knew almost nothing about her.

They headed back up the street—the group surrounding Max, because he couldn't defend himself and pull the generator up the slope. Sky and Roxie had joined him in the middle, carrying the canisters of gas that Cage and Joule had found. Joule now walked at the edge of the group, keeping her eyes on the surrounding landscape as best she could through the downpour. Her arrow was nocked again, and the string pulled taut.

She reminded herself that though her things were at the Tamblyn's, Phil's house has the garage with all the tools. It was also his own home—they could stay there with permission, something they couldn't say for the Tamblyns. But Joule couldn't tell if her distress was an actual gut instinct, or whether it was a product of all the things they'd been through.

She couldn't help feeling that she was walking into a trap.

61

"We made it," Gabby said as she looked up at the front of Phil Winchester's house. Her tone was far more optimistic than Joule felt.

She'd walked all the way back from the Tamblyn's uncertain what she would find when they arrived. Her brain had run off in myriad directions.

Phil had suggested they all stay at his house and Robert, Mickey, and Chester had all agreed. Whereas Moonbeam had less been of the opinion that it was practical and more that she was excited to have the group all together. She was the only one truly welcoming to the college students and Dr. Kimura.

All the students had nodded along at the suggestion. Even Joule. Despite her feelings, it was hard to poke holes in the plan. Phil and Robert had even offered to explain to the Tamblyns later about what had happened, who had moved into their home temporarily, and why.

They'd all dropped off the generator and the gas cans and taken a moment to stop and get out of the rain and be warm. Then they'd formed a second plan.

Joule, Cage, Roxie, Sky, and Gabby all headed out as a group, back into the rain and possible danger, to return to the Tamblyn house and gather their things. They would also lock the building back up.

"Don't bother moving the furniture back," Phil had told them. "I know the Tamblyns. They'll understand and just be glad you guys were safe and that you found their house."

Joule had almost protested when he seemed to catch on. "They'll claim any damage on their insurance. It won't be a problem."

The reassurance was comforting, but it also nagged a little spot of worry at the back of Joule's brain. So much so that she was glad they were leaving Max at the Winchester house. Max had volunteered to join the group trekking back to the Tamblyn house, but Joule had persuaded him that he was needed to help with the generator and such. Max was larger than Kimura—if not Mickey or Chester—and Joule wanted to leave their strongest friend behind. Just in case...

"Oh good!" Moonbeam had said as she threw the front door open wide on their return. She'd sighed out the words with much relief. "You're back!"

Cage had given the agreed-upon three sharp knocks.

She ushered them inside quickly, saying, "I worried every minute you were gone."

Joule had tried to talk Moonbeam into coming with them, both because her new friend was smart and useful, but also because she'd feel safer having one of the other group join them—maybe as a bit of insurance.

Robert had protested heartily. Moonbeam didn't have anything at the other house. There was no need for her to go back outside, friend or not. Had that been merely the protest of a father protecting his daughter from the black bears, the snakes, and apparently the puma? Or was there something more at play?

The one thing that made her feel better was Robert's insistence that Cage keep the firearm he'd "borrowed" from the Tamblyns. Mickey had then handed over his shotgun to the small group.

"I'll be inside. You take this." He'd thrust it into Roxie's hands, as though recognizing she was the most likely candidate of three girls to actually be willing to stand something down and shoot it.

Despite tense vigilance the whole way there and back, they'd not encountered anything dangerous. At least, not that they saw. And as she now looked around the room, most of Joule's fears were laid to rest.

Everyone looked dry and happy, and there was food out. Most of them were eating or had already finished.

Moonbeam made a motion toward the meal waiting in the middle of the room. "We made enough for everyone. Please, eat!"

Joule nodded. She'd carried her own backpack, her bow and arrows, as well as several bags of food on her arms. Luckily, the neighbors had cloth grocery bags, which she could sling over her shoulders and carry easily. She'd needed her hands free for protection. They all did.

The five of them were laden with all the things they'd brought and quickly the others jumped up and help them remove the bags.

"Look!" Ginnifer smiled as she held up her phone. The screen was bright, but Joule wasn't sure what she was looking at.

Her expression must have made her confusion clear, because Ginnifer wiggled the phone and motioned to the cord connecting it to a converter connected to the generator that was chugging away in the corner.

Joule frowned again. She hadn't even noticed the noise when she walked in, though the thing wasn't quiet. Maybe her brain had simply registered that she didn't hear the rain anymore and that was enough. Now she walked over to it and admired the machine. She couldn't help but notice the bright silver flex tubing that came off the back.

The tape job was also silver—duct tape—but it made a good seal, and as she followed it, she found the trail led her to a propped-open window. They'd snaked the tube behind the makeshift barricade and added a tarp to stop the water from coming in. It had taken several of the silver tubes— maybe dryer venting?—duct taped together to make it work. But Joule had seen worse. And they had power.

"This little generator is high end. We found a good one. Pretty new even," Ginnifer waxed on, clearly pleased with the results. But it was Phil who spoke over her.

"We pulled our little handheld backup batteries from each of the cars—you know, the little charger things? We did that a while ago, but they're already running low." He scratched his head and shrugged one shoulder as though he didn't quite agree. "Ginnifer insists that they're square waves, though, and that's bad."

Joule could tell from Phil's expression that he wasn't sure why it mattered if his wave was square or not. Well, it wasn't her favorite thing to do, but she backed up her roommate's claim. "Square waves will charge your phone, but they'll wear the batteries down a lot faster."

Phil merely shrugged in response. He'd probably heard the same thing from Ginnifer or Holly and it hadn't made him think any better of it the first time. "Hopefully, this—" He waved his finger around his head in a circle, as if to indicate the world, the weather, and everything going on in the house, "won't last long enough that I care. If all I have to do is replace a phone battery, I'll consider that an easy escape."

Ginnifer laughed as though it were a good joke, and Holly joined her for an uneasy moment before slowly going preternaturally silent.

That's right, Joule thought. *We didn't all escape.* It was something maybe Phil hadn't quite figured out yet, despite the fact that they'd told him they'd had to leave Marcus's body in Phil's master bedroom.

Joule decided to let it pass and sank down onto a pillow to get herself a meal. She was suddenly starving. The two sets of twins and Gabby tucked into the food quickly and the conversation stalled as they all ate. Joule found it better than anything she'd eaten since leaving the dorm, but hunger and fear were good spice.

"We cooked it over the fire," Holly told them. "Even though we have the generator and two cans of gasoline, we thought it was smart to ration the fuel and use the fire whenever we can."

Joule didn't say anything, but it seemed a smart move, so she just watched the faces around her and enjoyed the heat. But it was still barely afternoon. They were unlikely to be asleep anytime soon.

Once she finished, she turned to Kimura, the keeper of all information, it seemed. "Is there any report on the weather for the next few days?"

She still held out the stupid hope that the rain would let up. But Kimura dashed it quickly with a shake of his head. "I even got the radar to pull up."

His phone also had a long, slim white cord heading into a converter that Ginnifer had set up. He must have managed to get charged enough while they'd been out to turn it back on. So Joule broached the hardest subject one more time. "We need to get back on campus. There are students there and there's clear land and houses here."

She paused but continued when no one fought her. "We can't just leave them stranded."

Beside her, Cage nodded in agreement. Gabby looked to her and Joule read the expression in her best friend's eyes as clear support.

But Phil waited a beat, and then protested—as she'd expected he would. "Why would you do that? Why go back out? You're here. You're safe."

When she didn't answer right away—because, honestly, she didn't *want* to go back into the rain, ever again—he punched another hole in her request.

"Do you even know where to look?"

It was Ginnifer who held up her phone. "There are messages all over social media. Most are more than a day old, but students were saying they were stuck on campus." She paused and tapped at the device, not able to move too far because she was still plugged in. Then she held up the screen as evidence. "This is from Meara... I know her. She's on our hall."

Joule didn't know Meara, but the message was clear.

Her roommate continued. "She posted yesterday from the roof of the dorm. Told anyone who read it to tell her parents she loved them. So, yes, we know there were students there—alive—yesterday."

"Why doesn't the Coast Guard come get them?"

Surprising Joule, Ginnifer almost exploded at him. "The rain! The winds! They can't get in safely."

"Neither can we!"

"Then don't come!" Joule and Ginnifer said the words in almost perfect unison.

Phil pulled back, his argument stopping at the brick wall of their vehemence.

"So the answer is, yes, we know exactly where to look. But ultimately," Joule replied, "we made a promise."

She couldn't live with herself, safe in a big house, when she'd left so many at the dorm. It didn't matter that they'd vowed it only amongst themselves. "I'm keeping that promise."

62

"Tie the boats together like we did the first time," Cage told them as all hands worked to inflate the rafts again and lash them together. No one wanted to be out in the rain any longer than necessary.

"Shove the one end into the water," he added, his limbs already cold, his fingers numb. It wasn't the weather. They'd been out and about in this several times. They'd had to inspect and repair the bite marks, check the boats over, and count the oars. Despite a good night's sleep, he didn't want to be here.

It would be easier to stay in the house and eat the food that the Winchesters seemed to have stockpiled. He could enjoy reading a book and seeing if his phone had charged enough to message his grandparents and let them know he and Joule were safe.

Instead, they were here, testing the idea that Joule had put forth. Kimura and Ginnifer had talked their way through the design. Holly had made it a reality, and Ginnifer had supplied the charge.

"Hold on to this end," Joule told the others, understanding Cage's wariness about getting back on the water. She was worried, too. But he could see determination in her eyes as well. She looked at him until she had his full attention. "I'll go out."

"No," he replied. "We'll go together."

"Do you have everything?" Dr. Kimura asked, and for a moment, Cage wondered about the professor. Why didn't he want to be on the end of the boat, over the deep water? Wouldn't he want to see his precious elasmobranchs? Shouldn't he want to count the fins? But Kimura didn't seem to feel the need to step foot into the boat at all.

Cage reached out and clasped Joule's hand before turning to check that his friends were anchoring their end of the tethered boats on land. Essentially, they'd made a floating dock, allowing them to get out over water that was deep enough to be meaningful, without ever stepping down into it.

For the first time in just over forty-eight hours, he felt the give of water and rubber under his feet. Cage felt the boat tip as Joule stepped in slowly beside him. It took only half a second to steady himself. He'd been in the boat for so long that this was second nature now. Within three steps, they'd dropped to their knees and crawled along, awkwardly holding their supplies.

They moved up and over the bump where the boats were tied together. Joule held up her Ziploc bag, showing off the shampoo bottle inside. It was her way of asking if he was ready. He didn't speak, just held his own bag in return. His held pieces of deli meat, definitely past their expiration date, and almost spoiled.

The Winchester's fridge had at least proved helpful here. He was more than grateful that someone had stocked the house before everything had gone to hell. So far, their new friends had given the group everything they needed. Now, the plan was simple.

Moment by rocking moment, they made their way to the far end and sat there, watching the water, neither of them speaking. Cage wondered if he would see a fin break the surface. He wondered if the sharks were swimming below him, or even what else might be moving around down there —something they hadn't already found.

He didn't see anything. And, after a short silence, tired of the rain coming down on his face and simply wanting to get this over with he nodded to his sister. "I'm going to throw it."

Opening the bag, he peeled the first piece of meat, wadded it up, and chucked it overhand as far as he could. It hit the water with a splash. When nothing happened, Cage thought it might all be a failure. They had to attract the sharks to know if everything worked.

He counted down. Three... Two...

He was about to tell them they could go back inside when the meat bobbed once suddenly and then disappeared. A small head appeared next to it, chomping at the water, before Cage could even comment.

Joule's face didn't change expression, and she only nodded as though this had been thoroughly expected. "Throw the next one."

Cage peeled the next piece of meat from the slick stack and did it again. This time he threw it to a slightly different location. And once again, a head came up and swallowed the food whole.

But this time, the first shark was butted out of the way by a second.

"Three," Joule whispered and pointed. Cage watched as a fin broke the surface near the other two. "Throw another."

He lobbed this one in between where the first two had

landed, trying to establish an area where the food appeared. Next to him, Joule began to move, her hands checking the bag and the strings they'd attached without puncturing the airtight seal.

"All right," she said. "It's time."

She rose to her knees and held the bag up in front of her face, as though the dim light and the rain would let her see anything of value. They'd closed the bag tightly, squeezing out as much air as possible. Inside, the shampoo container had been cleaned and fitted with a small piece of electronics. That was powered by a set of two nine-volt batteries that they'd pulled from the Winchesters' closet.

Joule didn't look inside the shampoo bottle now. She didn't dare open the carefully sealed bag. It was time to trust and throw.

"Here goes nothing." She said and used the string like a lasso to fling the bag and bottle into the water. It landed with a smack a good ten feet away from the end of the boat dock, almost in the middle of where he'd thrown the three pieces of meat. She'd nailed the mark.

Neither of them let their eyes stray from the surface around the bottle. Cage watched closely for any activity. When nothing happened, Joule didn't turn her head, but whispered above the sound of the rain. "Throw the meat."

The shampoo bottle was mostly air and the Ziploc bag it was sealed inside still floated on the surface where they could see it.

Cage tried to get the meat slice to land near the container and almost nailed it the first time. He waited and watched as the slimy meat sat on the surface, untouched.

Then he threw another slice several feet away from the shampoo bottle and waited and waited. But nothing rose up to eat it.

63

J oule rolled her eyes. The living room was warm and comfortable, but the conversation was a mess.

"You just have to get there," Ginnifer argued. "So you want to take as few people as possible—someone who can make the trip. That's all."

No, Joule thought, *that's not enough—*

But Ginnifer was talking over her. "Once you pick up the other people, they can help row back. They'll probably be very excited to be rowing. It will mean they're heading to safety." Ginnifer waved her hands around, palms flat and out, as if her idea was patently clear.

"No," Joule repeated, out loud this time. "We don't know that the people we pick up will be healthy. Chances are, they ran out of food a while ago. So even if they're healthy, they may not be strong enough to take on the hard task of rowing. They might need medical treatment, which means we need to take enough people to row there, row back, and take care of anybody sick that we bring on board."

"You also need someone on defense," Phil said, his hand in his pocket, likely still wrapped around his firearm. It bothered Joule how infrequently he laid it down. Even though they'd barricaded the doors and the windows, he seemed to think a bear might still tear its way through, and that his nine millimeter would be an adequate response.

She almost asked the man what kind of defense he had in mind. They were already going in with a good offense. Or at least, as good as they could come up with.

Ginnifer sighed, but finally stepped back from her rally for the skeleton crew.

"The question is," Joule continued, "What are the numbers that we need? Can four people row out there and back?" She paused a moment and then added, "It was a hard row on the way out here. We were exhausted."

"But we went out of our way and picked up Kimura," her brother added. For a half-second, Joule thought he was blaming the professor for their extra work, but then her brother continued, "And we might need to take that same kind of route when we go back. It was good practice for what might happen on this trip."

Roxie chimed in next. "Conceivably, whoever goes may end up rowing all over campus. It just depends on where there are people to be picked up."

That was a huge task. Joule wasn't certain it was even possible. The hill here rose behind the area where their dorm was, but campus was huge if your mode of transportation was inflatable rescue rafts and oars... in the rain.

"We might also deal with the issue of a riot," Sky pointed out, her voice soft, but her logic solid.

"If only we had boats coming in waves." Joule could visualize it. Almost like the trams at amusement parks or buses in the city. When one left, you could spot the next one in the distance, already on the way. "It might help if they could see someone coming up behind us, ready to take the next round of stragglers." She didn't want to say survivors. Didn't want to think about what the numbers might really be.

So she turned to the group at large. "Can we do that? Can we make several trips with different crew? Have an A crew and a B crew? The first crew goes out. They pick up whoever they can. And as soon as they land, the second group launches."

She wanted that badly. Wanted to have something to tell anyone they found, if they didn't have enough room in the boat. Her heart was breaking just thinking about it. And that was given the best possible outcome. Her bigger—scarier—concern was that they would get back to campus and find nothing.

"I think that works." Mickey nodded along as though thinking. Though, from the look on Mickey's face, he wanted to be neither A crew nor B crew. Joule imagined that he would quickly volunteer for the C crew—the one that stayed at home to cook the stew and defend the place against bears.

If they managed to bring enough people here, maybe he would help them open another house or two up the street. But as they hashed out the logistics of rescuing their fellow students, Joule began to wonder...

"Why haven't more people been arriving? Surely someone else would have found a boat or a way off campus. This is high ground. Some of them would have come here. Right?"

"I don't know," Moonbeam replied, looking thoughtful. "Could they have swum here? It's not that far, and when you're determined—" She cut her own thought off midway.

The Winchesters had fetched Moonbeam when the flooding was still low. Mickey and Chester had run into town in Mickey's jacked-up truck, plowing through roads awash in dirty water. It was the same truck Joule and Cage had seen drop her off the first time they'd met her. So they'd not seen water deep enough to have to worry about what was swimming underneath. They seemed to believe the students about the sharks—but from their reactions, they'd seen nothing of it. Their belief was tenuous.

Joule didn't want to say it, but she didn't think anyone would survive a swim that far. Even if they managed to make most of it, sooner or later, one of the bull sharks would get them. They would get tired and become easy bait. Or something else they hadn't even figured out yet would end them. There was no easy path through the water.

"You weren't there when we tested the devices. Throwing a piece of meat into the water sparked a frenzy. A swimming person... well..."

For a moment, the conversation lagged. Then, once again, it was Sky who piped up. "Maybe they *have been* arriving."

Joule frowned at her friend. "We haven't seen anyone."

"We haven't seen much of anything," Sky pointed out quickly. "We wouldn't have seen anyone arrive, unless they arrived on this street." She pointed to the ground, as though talking about the place where they'd put the boat into the water. "We aren't going outside and we've barricaded all the windows. We won't see if anyone walks by. We would never have known that Moonbeam and Mickey were on our porch if they hadn't knocked. Also, the streets are lined with trees. Remember when we came up, it almost like running a gauntlet? So, unless they came specifically up this street, we wouldn't see them at all."

"Unless they were in our direct line of sight..." Joule was catching on. So was Roxie.

Roxie continued nodding at her sister as she picked up the thread. "We probably wouldn't see them even if they were directly *in* our line of sight. The rains have been coming down so hard for so long, visibility is very limited. So maybe they came up another street. Maybe they're here and we just didn't see."

"It's possible," Sky added, "that people have been escaping the flood all along."

Joule desperately wanted to believe that.

"Does that mean we don't have to go back?" Phil looked around the room, wanting an answer from the group. "If we don't even know that somebody's there, what's the point?"

Joule still wasn't overly confident of this man, though he'd done nothing to raise her suspicions since they'd come back and stayed in his home. But she looked him in the eye. "You don't have to go." Then she looked around the group. "Everyone can make their own decision based on how they feel, on how important you think it is. But when we left, I made a promise to myself. We left too many people behind in our dorm, and that whole street was filled with dorms, and the campus was relatively full, because no one expected the water to get this high. So I have to go back."

She couldn't leave someone behind. She and Cage wouldn't have survived the last year if the people in her neighborhood hadn't stepped up. And the flooding almost certainly wouldn't be the last disaster they faced. People wouldn't survive if they didn't go back for each other.

Something settled in her chest just then, some kind of knowledge or acceptance about what she was going to face, even though she didn't know yet what it was.

64

She was breathing far too heavily, but Joule dipped her oar back into the water, using the rhythmic motion to keep herself going. She wanted to check the time but had no way to get to anything unless she stopped. And she wasn't going to do that.

Cage and Joule, Roxie and Sky, Phil, Moonbeam, and Holly were the "A Crew." They were the ones braving the first route back. They'd settled in the middle of Ginnifer's skeleton crew idea and Joule's all-hands-on-deck approach. So now, four were rowing, and Joule was one of them. She wouldn't ruin the rhythm the group had going for something as trivial as an unnecessary time check.

They'd put all their phones in Ziploc baggies. Everyone was charged up, and they'd all ransacked the Winchester and Tamblyn houses for every backup battery they could find. They were all now stored in plastic zip baggies, too, ready for use as needed.

After a while, when she'd worked her ass off even more, Joule couldn't stand not knowing how long she'd been at this. Everything looked the same, despite all their hard work to move forward. "How are we doing?"

She had to practically holler to be heard, even though she was at the front left of the boat, close to where Sky was sitting with her phone glowing in front of her. Her friend was on navigation duty, following the map of streets below.

"So far so good," Sky hollered back. "Almost halfway."

Halfway? Joule thought. Well, she could manage that. She was the third person scheduled for break. When they hit the fifty percent point, she would get a short turn at navigation and a chance to rest for a bit. She would have said thank you, but all her energy was going toward pushing the water behind her and moving the boat forward.

Each of the members of Crew A were in their rain gear. Underneath everything, they each wore a Ziploc bag with some emptied household bottle and their battery device inside. It emitted an electronic field that they hoped would repel the sharks.

They'd talked at first about carrying the devices in their pockets, or simply tucking them under their raincoats. But if something happened, Joule wanted hers firmly on her person. She'd used a massive amount of duct tape to create a harness that held the device over a tank top, but under everything else. Though she'd not taped it directly to her skin, she had wrapped the tape around herself knowing the harness would have to be cut off of her later.

She wasn't sure now if it might have been a better idea to just tape it directly to her. She certainly should have field tested the makeshift harness first. The raw lines on her shoulders the duct tape straps had rubbed were super-fuck-ing-tastic. The burn reminded her of bad decisions with each movement of her arm. But she dipped her oar into the water and pushed it away again.

So far, they'd seen no fins near the boat. Joule wanted to believe that the six devices they were wearing were doing their job. But there hadn't been time for enough tests to be sure. All she could say was that it had worked well each of the times they'd done their trial runs.

Though they were on opposite sides of the boat, Moonbeam and Phil Winchester rowed in perfect tandem, like family. Phil would have happily stayed at home, but he was here, and he was committed. Joule figured he'd only come because his niece insisted that she was going.

Moonbeam had protested each time her father or uncles tried to tell her she should stay behind. "I know the students on campus. Some of them are mine. Some of my students live in those dorms. There's a very real possibility I will see the face of someone I know, and I'm not going to let them drown. I want to go to as few funerals as possible."

Joule had understood the argument, though at no point had Moonbeam suggested that she wouldn't be going to any funerals.

She pushed her thoughts aside and watched Phil's strokes in her peripheral vision. She wanted to make it easy for any of the crew who was following her to match her strokes. So she matched her speed and work to Phil and kept her thoughts away from funerals.

He rowed hard and kept a steady rhythm, pulling his oar with more force than just about anyone else. If it were up to Phil, they would already have a boat full of students and be on their way back to his house.

She rowed for another five or so minutes before Sky turned and said, "My time's up. It's all yours."

Joule didn't stop yet, she had to keep the boat moving as Sky slowly crawled over toward Joule's position to trade out. Scooting to the center front of the tied-up inflatables, Joule began to watch the navigation to make subtle course corrections that didn't tax the rowers too much. She also kept an eye out for fins.

She hadn't seen them when she was rowing. But now, at the front of the boat, without her eyes trained on her oar going in and out of the water, she could see a little further. They were out there, though they didn't come too close. She also didn't feel the bodies bumping the boat or rubbing along the bottom like she had the first time. Maybe this was going to be better. Safer.

Still, the sharks were out there and, given the number of fins she saw, their ranks were strong. She watched the streets slowly move by on the digital map and stayed focused. Her time was up far too fast.

Turning, she handed the navigation phone to Phil. But, with a short shake of his head, he refused it and jerked his head over his shoulder, indicating she should give it to his niece.

It took Joule another moment to carefully crawl further back in the boat though it was only a few feet difference. She didn't want to shake anything or rock anyone. It then took her another few minutes to explain to Moonbeam that it wasn't her turn, but that her uncle had handed it over to her because he hadn't expected to navigate them in.

When Joule had to indicate which buildings they were going to, where they were on the GPS, and so on, Moonbeam nodded and took the phone from her. Then Joule was rowing again as her friend headed toward the front of the boat.

It took effort to turn her thoughts back to the work. She was now sitting behind Sky, once again on the left side of the boat. Though she understood that Phil wanted to send his niece up to the front, she was beginning to regret letting him make the change.

Had she traded with Phil, she would be rowing on the opposite side as she had before. Being here put her in the same position. She strained the same muscles, rubbed the same blistering spot on her shoulder from her makeshift harness, and cramped her legs into the same position from before. It was a design flaw they'd not thought of, but one she would correct on the way back.

Even as she thought that, she heard Moonbeam yell out. "Look! There."

The shadow of what had to be a building jutted up out of the water as if it had suddenly appeared in front of them. Maybe Joule saw it because she was familiar with campus. But Phil seemed confused. "What?"

"There." Moonbeam pointed. "It's the roof of one of the dorms."

"Are there people on it?"

Moonbeam looked over her shoulder to address Sky's question, but Sky kept rowing. From her body posture, it looked as though Moonbeam couldn't tell. She shrugged her shoulders and leaned a little forward. "I don't see it. Wait... there."

She repeated that word with her arm outstretched, and her finger pointing toward the shadow that was one of the shapes they'd been looking for. They weren't close enough to read any details, but Joule was watching carefully.

She almost missed it, but the movement caught her eye and she watched it all as it happened—the snap of jaws, the raising up of a brown-gray body, sleek as it cut through the water, aiming for Moonbeam's outstretched arm.

Moonbeam yanked her arm back, but the chemistry postdoc's uncle was faster.

He let go of his oar and dove for his neice, grabbing her around the waist hauling her backward into the boat. He moved her too hard, too fast. They might be injured from their tumble. The boat rocked precariously, but the rows of teeth had snapped at nothing.

Joule was almost taking an easy breath that they landed inside the perimeter of the boat. But her relief was too soon. She watched as they pair rolled as they landed and Phil and Moonbeam crashed into Sky, knocking her over the side of the boat.

65

"Sky!" Cage screamed as he scrambled to reach his friend. But he was too late.

He heard Roxie's voice. Though his own was saying his friend's name, Roxie's scream was primal. This was her sister, her twin. Roxie and Sky were identical, closer even than he and Joule.

He wasn't sure if he dropped his oar inside the boat or out. It wasn't important in that moment. Phil and Moonbeam were scrambling to get away from the inflated edge of the boat. Her uncle pulled her up, revealing that Moonbeam's hair had swung over the rim and into the water when Phil had tackled her. Cage wasn't sure if they even realized yet what they what they done.

He was climbing over Phil's outstretched legs. Over the large body wrapped in the rubbery plastic of rain gear. He didn't care.

Sky was in the water, and Cage barely felt his hands hit the edge, pressing into the pressurized rubber of the boat. His hands had smacked down; his sister's hit right next to his, with Roxie pushing into the space between them. She had not stopped screaming as her sister sank steadily under the surface.

As the three peered down into the murky water, they saw nothing.

Cage tried to suck in air, but his lungs wouldn't move. He'd seen the splash. The ripples still broke the surface of the water where she'd gone in. His only hope came from knowing that Sky had her device on her body. Joule had insisted that everyone wear it is close to the skin as possible. It was turned on.

It should be making an electrical field around her that should keep the sharks at bay. Simultaneously, he was afraid that the splash would attract to them. He'd counted on the sharks, but not on drowning. Not on one of them hitting the water and sinking like a rock.

His eyes scanned the surface looking for any clues, but he didn't dare push his hand through to see if he could feel anything. Next to him, Roxie didn't hesitate to plunge her hands into the icy water. The surface was so cloudy, it looked as if they disappeared below the waterline. Cage grabbed her shoulder and held on tight, afraid she would be pulled under herself.

As Roxie swirled her hands around, the colors in the water changed. Something moved just below the surface. For a moment his heart cracked. Surely, it was a shark coming up. He wasn't prepared for what he might see. But what he did see was a pale hand, reaching upward through the water.

He watched as the changing colors just under the water began to resemble his friend and Sky came up. Her hand disappeared as she stroked upward, aiming for the air. He could see her face, her hair, her arms battling to break the surface. This time, he and Joule both plunged their hands into the water, hoping to grab onto her.

He felt her hand smack at his as she reached up, but he didn't quite manage to catch her. Her hood was dragging against her. Her heavy rain gear made her fight to the surface ever more difficult. She could not possibly have been dressed worse to go into the water, unless she'd been in a mid-eighteenth century gown and corsets.

Finally, Cage's hand contacted hers and he grabbed hard. Holding tight, he pulled. It took all three of them hauling her upward to bring her face into the air. She was heavy with water and excess weight. But she was alive.

Sky didn't smile, but her mouth opened. She didn't even seem to have gulped water. Somehow, she'd managed to take a good, deep breath before she hit the water. She'd also somehow managed to figure out, under the murky water, which way was up and head toward it.

He wanted to believe it was a miracle—and that part might have been—but the sharks not getting to her was science. He was convinced that the device she was wearing had saved her life.

Slowly, they worked to haul her up and over the edge of the boat. Hand over hand, they first got her shoulders out of the water. Then her torso. Phil and Moonbeam scrambled backwards, only able to help by getting out of the way as the rest dragged Sky the last little bit.

"Oh, thank God!" Roxie was reapeating as she reached to hug her sister, even before her legs had cleared the water. "Oh, thank God."

As she repeated it the third time, she let go, allowing Cage and Joule to try to haul Sky the rest of the way in. Looking to his sister, Cage took a breath and coordinated his pull with Joule. Together, they pulled upward, as suddenly Sky was yanked from their hands.

One good tug from under the water was enough to rip her away from them. Their grip hadn't been strong enough, and they had not been prepared to have her stolen.

Cage stared at his now empty hands. Sky had been in their grip, almost fully out of the water. The work of dragging all the water with her had slowed them. But somehow, she was gone.

The last thing he saw was Sky's face, contorted in a scream as she was suddenly snatched away, hauled beneath the surface.

66

C age sat with his head in his hands. His lungs tried to suck in air, but continually failed. He was still here so he must have gotten something. The rain continued to come down hard, puddling in the dent he made in the base of the boat. He sat in the water, unable to think or paddle or continue with their plan.

"Sky?" Roxie asked, as though her sister might answer.

It wasn't the first time she'd asked. Joule answered her a few times, softly saying, "She's gone" or "There's nothing we can do." But after several of these pointless consolations, his sister moved to just rubbing her hand across Roxie's back each time she asked. He wondered if Roxie could feel anything through the layers and the rubbery raincoat. Or through the numb haze of her grief.

Even while he was trying to think through everything, his brain catalogued the rocking of the boat under him. With no one rowing, the boat was probably drifting backward, away from their goal. But he couldn't quite put the effort together to get up and do something about it.

"Sky?" Roxie's voice cut the air again, only this time, she

moved. Diving for the edge of the boat, she plunged her hands beneath the surface of the water. They disappeared into the darkness, almost the exact reverse of when Sky's hand had appeared and they'd pulled her out.

Without thinking, he and Joule and even Phil jumped to catch Roxie. All their hands grabbed at her jacket and hauled her backward. But it didn't work.

Three of them suddenly moving toward one side of the boat made it dip precariously, threatening to send them all spilling into the water. He knew now that their devices wouldn't really protect them. That was a hard lesson. But Cage didn't let go of his friend. He'd learned a year ago that he couldn't live with himself if he didn't at least try his best. It was why they were out here in the first place.

Phil was smart enough to yank Roxie backward and down. He practically shoved her face into the base of the boat, but it balanced things a little bit better as Cage and Joule suddenly let go and scrambled to the other side. Phil had Roxie under control, so she wouldn't go over. They had to keep the whole floating mess upright.

Quickly, Phil lifted Roxie up, making sure her face was out of the water. It wasn't the kindest of rescues, but it kept her safe.

It had been necessary. Cage watched the shark fins break the water right beside the boat, exactly where Roxie had shoved her hands underwater just a moment before.

Sitting back, Cage hoped his breathing would even out on its own, but it just didn't seem to. His brain tried to reconcile the time they'd spent looking for Sky. They'd leaned over the side of the boat, trying to send things underwater to snag Roxie's sister and pull her back up—almost like fishing. Though, honestly, he wasn't sure what they might bring up... if they caught anything.

Then they'd seen something on the surface of the water, grabbed their remaining oars, and paddled over. The movement had been good for the stunned rowers. The sudden need for action spurred them back to life.

"What is it!" It hadn't been a question but a demand from Roxie.

Joule fished the item out of the water, the edges jagged and torn. "It's part of Sky's coat." She'd held it by her fingertips as though she didn't want to touch it, and Cage had understood. Before she could fling it back into the water, Roxie had reached out and snagged the fabric scrap, holding it as though she could read some mystical writing on it. As though she might cross to Narnia and find her sister.

Cage was only grateful that there was no blood on it. It had likely been washed away as quickly as it had appeared. No, Sky was gone.

Breathing again, after the mad rush to get the scrap of floating plastic raincoat, Cage stopped and pulled his oar in. No one was rowing, so neither was he. He looked at the others in the boat, trying to figure out their next move. They couldn't just sit here and float in the rain.

Phil still held tight to Roxie, making sure that she wouldn't go over the side and join her sister. Cage could not imagine what his friend was feeling. He could only remember the night he'd locked the door with his sister stuck outside with the Night Hunters. His sister had come back though. Roxie's blank, dead-to-the-world stare indicated that even right now, she truly understood that Sky wouldn't.

"What do we do?" he asked, "Go back? Give up? Do we go forward and see if we can find the students we came for?"

He realized, even as the words came out of his mouth,

that he'd pushed out a biased question. Still, he was in no mood to expend the effort to fix it. And he already had his expectations. Phil would likely want to go back immediately, declaring the mission a dismal failure. But it was Phil who first answered, and said, "We go forward. We came this far. We lost one of our own members, but if we go back, we lost her for nothing."

Beside her uncle, Moonbeam offered a small but somber nod of agreement. Joule also nodded, as did Holly. Only Roxie didn't vote. Cage didn't force her to.

Apparently, she was going along on a rescue mission when her own sister couldn't be rescued. Looking around the boat, Cage assessed what they had to do first.

They'd brought extra paddles, just in case they lost some while they were out. He could count all the ones they brought, though one of them was a good fifteen feet away, floating on the surface of the water.

Pointing at the floating plastic, he asked, "Can we get it back?"

It was Holly who confidently replied. She'd brought along a pair of what she called "old-lady-pinchers." She'd found them in the Winchester house, an extended arm with a squeeze handle at one end and pinchers to pick up stray objects out of reach at the other. She clicked the handle twice, indicating she was ready to grab their tool out of the jaws of a hungry shark.

He wished they could have saved Sky as easily, but said nothing as they slowly reclaimed their oars and the small boat began moving with Roxie curled up in the middle. Her knees were under her chin and her eyes occasionally closed. Cage reasoned the best thing they could do for her was get her out of here.

He and Phil maneuvered them closer to the floating oar,

but he felt his muscles tighten in fear as Holly leaned just a little bit too far to scoop the plastic implement out of the water. The moment passed as his gut wrenched tighter, but nothing happened.

When she had the oar again, all her limbs remained attached. Her hands were wet but still usable. She ran her fingers over the paddle, pausing halfway down the shaft, at which point Cage realized she'd discovered a bite mark. It didn't stop her, and she shifted her hold on the thick plastic and dipped the end into the water. "Let's go."

It took almost five minutes to arrive at back to the point where Sky had been pulled under. Though he knew Roxie probably didn't need to hear about it, Cage also knew it was imperative to the safety of those who were still in the boat to know. So he turned to Holly and asked, "Sky was wearing her device, so what went wrong? Why didn't it work?"

67

"Ellooooohh."

Joule heard the sound as if she was hearing something beyond a wall. Something from a dream. But it was a word, and it was being yelled to them. Someone had seen them!

"Hello!" Joule yelled back, a surge of happiness blooming in her heart. As she pinpointed the location of the calls, she saw what must be the outlines of students huddled along the top line of the dorm roof. Only the center ridge remained above the water line but there were so many. Far more huddled bodies crammed the small island than Joule had hoped to find.

Her heart surged a little at the thought. These were the students they'd left behind. The same ones who'd poked and prodded the first shark's body when she and her friends brought it up to the second floor. The same ones who'd shared it on social media and warned everyone of what was in the water. They were still here...

The heavy rain still fell steadily and the wind was harsh enough to keep the rescue choppers out of the sky. But these students were alive. At least this, though tainted by Sky's death, still felt like a victory.

The small group in the boat began rowing harder as the very top of the building began to materialize out of the mist in front of them. Slowly she could find the edge of the roofline, and the people became humans rather than just blobs as they moved down the slope toward the edge of the water.

"No!" she yelled as everyone in the boat begged them to stop. Immediately dropping her oar in her lap, Joule held her palms up for them to quit moving forward. Even as she did it, she wondered if they could see her clearly, and if they could interpret the tiny motions of the people in the boat. Would they stop moving even if they understood?

"Do not go in the water!" They each yelled various phrases of the same idea, their voices climbing on top of each other.

"We know!" Joule heard a voice come back. "Trust me. We know."

As she saw more clearly, Joule counted and realized that there weren't enough students up on top of the dorm. Though it was more than they had intended to take back with them, it was still far fewer than the number they'd left behind. What had happened to the other dorm residents?

She couldn't answer that. Not yet. But the thought of just leaving two or so of them behind was something she couldn't stomach. She quickly calculated the numbers and what the boat could hold. She felt like vomiting as she realized they had an extra spot now without Sky.

Jesus, she thought. She could not continue thinking that way. She could grieve Sky later.

Hell, she still hadn't sufficiently dealt with the fact that Marcus had died or even quite how it had happened.

Training her thoughts back to the immediately pressing problem, she realized their careful calculations were difficult to stick to when faced with leaving actual students here on the roofline.

She yelled out to the stranded students, "We'll pull up right onto the roof and, one by one, walk you slowly into the boat."

Joule called out each instruction as carefully and clearly as she could. She thought about telling them the boat was headed back toward Reservoir Road, but she didn't think they would care. They'd been on the roof for several days. *Off* was the best place they could be. Exactly where they landed wouldn't matter.

"Can anyone help row?" Cage asked right on the heels of her own words.

Several nodded. Several didn't.

Joule continued pushing her oar against the water, as did Holly. They had to keep the boat from sliding backward down the slope of the roof. They couldn't lose anyone else to the water today.

Roxie stayed in her tiny ball but moved out of the way as Phil and Moonbeam carefully took hands and helped the first students crawl onto the rafts. Cage did his best to steady the boat while the students gingerly spread themselves around the small space. The boat rocked with each movement, but it didn't stop them from moving and shifting as they found places. A few of them spaced themselves at the edges and picked up the remaining oars as Holly began explaining logistics.

She seemed the least affected by Sky's sudden and tragic death. Then again, she hadn't known the other twins before this trip. She and Ginnifer had only seen them when they stopped by the room and Holly happened to be there. The dorm room—though this was physically the closest they'd been in days—seemed a million miles away.

Joule told herself that Holly was merely being logical in the face of an emergency, and that was a good trait. She would suffer her traumas later—they'd all seen Sky die. Friend or not, that was traumatic.

Either way, Holly's attitude made things run more smoothly. And for that, Joule was grateful.

"You can sit here or here," Holly told the newcomers. "On your knees." And, "You'll be wet."

"We've been wet for days," came the reply. Several of them shivered. Most looked borderline hypothermic.

Joule realized they needed to get the boats back and get these students into a warm house quickly. They'd had no supplies on the roof, or else they'd run out some time ago.

"Here." Holly continued her mission work, handing out grapes, as if she'd thought it all through. The grapes were a little on the old side, but she wasn't about to hand them any solid food when they likely hadn't eaten for a while.

Smart girl.

In no time, they launched off the roof and turned around. Aimed back toward higher ground and the Winchester house, they left a desperate group on the roofline with promises to come back.

"My brother's in Lyman Commons," one of the girls offered in a smallish voice. Her eyes darted around the gray mist as the top edge of the building disappeared behind them. "Can we pick him up?"

Joule fielded this one. "No. Our boat is already too full. But we have another crew who's going to go out after this. Was this group all that's left of FroSoCo?"

"There was another group that left. They engineered a raft out of branches. They made it out of sight, but we haven't heard from them." No one added to that story, but their slow, somber nods told her everything she needed. "Then we'll tell the other crew to go to Lyman. You can give them your brother's name. Tell them what he looks like."

The girl nodded, her wet hair plastered to her head. Her raincoat was pulled tight around her torso, but her legs and most of her body were drenched anyway.

Holly, having made sure that all the students had grapes and all the crew had half an energy bar, began handing out water bottles. They'd voted to suffer the extra weight in the boat to carry almost double their expected need for water. They couldn't drink anything that they found along the way. And they knew they might find students in bad shape.

One of the girls leaned over the edge right next to Joule. She'd been rowing, and Joule had no idea what she might have seen or if she was merely delirious. Either way, she followed Phil's method and grabbed the girl's coat roughly. With the plastic in her fist, she yanked the new student backwards and down, keeping her weight toward the center of the boat. "Do. Not. Reach out."

The threat in her voice extended further than she'd intended. The boat had stopped, and they all turned to look at her. The new students outnumbered the A Crew and a few looked at her as if she'd abused the student who's raincoat she still clenched.

Joule decided to set them straight.

"We all have devices on our chests that emit an electrical signal. It should keep the sharks at bay. However—" she paused as her voice cracked. "We just learned a very hard lesson that as we pull someone out of the water, the signal comes up with them. In the air, it does nothing, and the sharks will come for whatever part of you is still underwater."

She took a breath. All eyes were on her still, but she'd let go of the girl and their terror was no longer aimed at her actions. When she steadied her voice, she continued. "So if reach your hand into the water, or lean over too far, they will come for you."

Though they all nodded their heads as if they understood, they didn't. One of the girls had just put her hand out toward the water. *Damn it, they aren't thinking straight.*

Joule hardened her voice further. "Listen to me! If you so much as lean over the edge, you're not protected." She was practically growling the words as she relived the moments when they had thought they had Sky safe, only to have her yanked back under. "Stay in your spot. Stay low on your knees. The boat will rock. Do not get startled. We're taking you somewhere with heat and a little bit of power. Are you ready?"

They all nodded at her.

She was still searching for the face that looked just like Roxie's. It wasn't there. With a very heavy heart, she put her oar back in the water and aimed for Reservoir Road.

68

R oxie had not come along on the second run. When the first boat had arrived at the Winchester house, they'd let her get about the business of grieving her sister. She seemed to periodically wake up in her sleep, calling out for Sky and realizing all over again that her sister was truly gone.

Cage had let someone else handle it. Since there was nothing he could do for his friend, he headed out on this trip to do what he could for others. He could bring home more students. And he would do that.

The B Crew had gone out and come back. They'd saved the rest of the students from the FroSoCo dorm and then paddled over to check on Lyman house. The conversation at their return had not gone well. Even though they'd brought back another boat full of students, they had not found Melissa's brother. Telling her had not been easy.

"He wasn't there?" She was the one who'd set them in the direction of Lyman dorms. The words had floated from her throat with both great expectation and fear in her voice.

She'd been answered by Robert, who'd gone out on the second trip. "We asked around...

Cage had felt his heart squeeze at the pause. He knew what was coming. It wasn't just that her brother wasn't there...

Robert filled in the words. "He didn't make it."

It seemed to Cage, as he rowed now, that the losses his group had suffered had been miniscule compared to what others had lost. Though he'd slept most of the time he'd been back in the warm house, he still heard snippets of conversation when he was awake. That had been more than enough.

The students from the rooftop talked about other students going crazy, no longer able to stand the rain and deciding that they were going to try to swim to safety. They mentioned the guilt of trying to hold other students back and not having the strength to do it, and feeling the desire to die with them as they were dragged toward the surface of the water. It still rang in his ears, how they had eventually let go, and their friends and dormmates had jumped into the water and only made it so far before they went under, or worse...

Jack—one of the other students rescued off the roof of Lyman—commented, "A few of them made it far enough for us to hold out a ridiculous hope that they found land or a tree or something."

Cage had heard the underlying subtext in Jack's words and felt it deep in his own core. Even though those few swimmers had made it out of sight, the chances that they had arrived anywhere alive were slim to none.

So he'd hopped back into the boat, and pushed the oar in rhythm with the others. Joule had been ·one of those insisting they go back out and run more rescue missions. The first time he'd tagged along, not wanting to be separated. But on this trip, he'd felt the drive to go back out, if not the desire to do so.

"I think I see it!"

Cage felt his head pop up at the excited tone in Holly's voice. Looking around at the gray surroundings, he tried to make out geometric shapes through the visual static of the constant rain. "Over there?"

Using one hand, he pointed to the darker patch of gray he saw. He had to let go on the upstroke of the oar and then had to re-grab the shaft again on the downstroke. He couldn't just stop rowing to ask Holly what she saw.

He felt both better and worse on his second trip out. Better, because they'd made it back with the first batch of students. Though they'd lost Sky, they'd saved all the students they'd brought back from the roof of Freshman Sophomore College dorm. The trade had not been worth it, but the value of that couldn't be measured. He'd slept soundly for a good few hours while the B Crew was out.

Joule said she had slept, too. But from the start, the tension on the crew's second trip had been higher. They no longer held the belief that the devices would fully keep them safe. The signal was a stop-gap measure at best. They rowed now with four more devices, already turned on and weighted and ready to toss into the water next to anyone who fell in. But they'd not been fully tested, and Cage's faith had been shattered in the worst way.

His mind wandered the entire time, traveling far enough that he sometimes wondered if he was even rowing as he was supposed to. He thought about Joule's fantastic foresight to buy these boats. They'd not seen any others like them out on the water. It didn't mean they weren't out there. It simply meant they couldn't see.

He thought about Sky and Roxie and how it would feel to lose a twin. He thought about Kimura and his tanks in the basement of the Bass Science Building... how the place had flooded while they stood in it. It felt like so very long ago.

Now the crew rowed the last leg of the trip to Yost, in hopes that some of the people in the nearby guest cottages could have made it into the upper floors of the dorm. Cage began to push a little harder as Holly urged them on. "I definitely see it. It's right there!"

Maybe she saw it because she knew where it was on the GPS. But she hadn't steered them wrong before, and they had to get these students. Cage pushed harder on the oar.

So far, no one else had gone overboard. And though it wasn't rational to think they would do so, the fear remained in every beat of Cage's heart. He was confident the others felt it too. This was virtually the same crew that had gone out the first time, though they'd replaced Sky and Roxie with Mickey and Chester.

Ginnifer had gone out with the B crew, but first she'd fiddled with all the devices, pulling them out of the plastic as they came off each person. She replaced all the batteries and reset them to make a larger electric field.

"It should hopefully work better," she announced as she gestured with the one in her hand. She clearly felt awful that the first iteration hadn't saved Sky's life like it should have.

It could work worse, for all Cage new, but it was all they had. And they did know that when Sky went overboard—when the device was underwater—it had worked.

So he rowed until he heard the faint shouts and began to

see the outlines of the students standing on the roof of Yost dorm. They waved their arms and jumped up and down, scaring him as they came perilously close to slipping off the slanted roof and plunging into the water.

"Over here, over here!"

69

"I think you're right." Joule had stopped rowing. They were almost halfway back to Reservoir Road, and she was counting that they'd picked up another batch of students without any mishaps as a win.

"What did she say?" Mickey's deep voice questioned from behind her. Still rowing, he didn't miss a beat, despite leaning forward to hear what Holly had said to Joule.

Joule leaned back and repeated what Holly had told her. "We think the rain is getting lighter."

"Oh my god." Mickey's voice held a hard swath of awe in it and she saw in her peripheral vision, as his face tilted upward to look at the sky, there was maybe a little bit of light in the distance.

"Lighter rain" didn't mean too much in the grand scheme of things. They still had to have several of the students they'd picked up at Yost dorm bailing the boat. It was an ongoing process. Bailing kept them light—the work of bailing meant that those using the oars had an easier time pushing the boat forward.

Hope bloomed in her chest.

She punched it down with every stroke she took.

Joule could not afford to get excited about something that was not guaranteed. She could not afford to shift her attention. None of them could.

Even so, she heard the sound ripple through the boat, excitement at Holly's words.

"The rain *is* letting up."

"Look, you can see it over there. The sky is brighter."

She couldn't resist turning her head and looking when the rest of them did. And sure enough, a line seemed to cross the sky with the dark rain over their heads and to their right, a gray that was merely paler. But it was enough to offer hope.

"It's your turn." Chester surprised her by shoving the GPS at Joule and making motions with his hands to take the oar from her.

Joule slid to one side, her butt splashing into the several inches of water in the base of the boat as she let her knees slowly unfold. She'd been nearly locked and cramped into position. Though she'd made sure everyone took turns rowing on both sides of the boat, it still wasn't easy work. It had left her aching in her bones in a way that felt far beyond her years. Then again, all of this had been beyond her years.

She told herself that the pale light off in the distance didn't matter, and she crawled toward the front of the boat. Holding the phone with the GPS, she checked it out for a minute, getting familiar with the layout where they were. The phone was not her own and was connected through USB to yet another backup charger that Ginnifer had made sure was working.

Joule had become more impressed with Ginnifer as the days went by. Marcus had tried to save her—and honestly, had probably succeeded. Ginnifer would most likely be dead without his intervention. He shouldn't have died from the venom, but he had. Or maybe it had been something else. They wouldn't know for some time.

While Joule wanted to believe that it was Ginnifer's fault for getting bitten by a rattlesnake in the first place, no one had predicted at that point just how wild the wildlife would be.

And Ginnifer had surprised her yet again by coming out and rowing with B Crew. She'd insisted that she was healthy enough, and she wanted to do her part. Joule wasn't quite ready to trust her roommate fully, but she was grudgingly stepping back from her anger. It was hard to lose Marcus for someone she didn't like very much.

"A little harder on the left," she called out, her finger pointed in the correct direction in front of her. She stayed crossed legged, down in the water, because she simply couldn't sit on her knees another moment. "Aim to the right."

Her fingertip did not cross the edge of the boat when she pointed. Nothing did anymore. When they put the new students in, they trained them quickly to stay within the boundaries and smacked down anybody who dared to reach over the side.

As the person who was navigating, she was on fin alert. Though she did see several, she also saw what she thought were black, swimming snakes. The last thing they needed was another threat in the water. The rain might be clearing, but the water was never going to be safe.

They were passing the halfway mark when she spotted the large building on their right. That was their landmark. She geared them around it, working on not getting stuck in any trees.

"Holy shit," Cage said, his voice feeling closer than where he sat in the boat.

"I know. The water level is definitely dropping."

"Maybe they opened some locks or something," one of the other voices in the boat offered a theory.

Joule didn't think that the Bay itself had locks that could be adjusted, but maybe the rivers and waterways around here did. Maybe it had been enough to change the levels. When they picked up each batch of students, the water had been noticeably lower to the roofline. Both buildings were the same number of stories, so the water should have been similar in height as it had been at the Freshman Sophomore College dorm. And yet, they'd had to have students carefully hang off the edge of the roof and drop into the boat.

It had petrified Joule, having them drop in like that. The boat had rocked and threatened to eject students each time someone landed. But they'd all made it, and the drop meant the water was at least seven or eight feet lower.

Now, the buildings jutting up around them showed more above the surface than the last time they'd been by. They could see the top edges of the windows on the upper floors.

The water was definitely going down.

She looked forward again, still aiming them the last leg of the way toward Reservoir Road, when she heard a droning, cutting-type sound on her right.

She found herself trying to keep her eyes on navigation and yet wondering what the mechanical-bee-like noise might be. It wasn't something new in the boat that a student had brought in. She ignored it until the tiny dark patch that had formed up and to the right became something more than just a blob in her vision and Joule saw what made the sound.

It was a helicopter.

70

"Are? You? Safe?"

The words had come through as individual syllable chunks, loud and grating over the helicopter's bullhorn.

The next set of instructions told them to wave their arms for "yes" and stay still for "no." Cage and the others lifted their arms and made bold motions to the helicopter. The students they had just picked up were perhaps the most enthusiastic of all.

The bullhorn cut on again, a sharp click cutting through the air before the words reached him. "Do you have a safe place to go?"

Again, the entire boat erupted, this time, led by the crew. The students they had just picked up had been told about the Winchester house, and the Tamblyn house, but had not yet seen land.

"Good." The bullhorn word was bracketed by clicks again. But then the next part came in a more conversational tone. Words flowing together as the voice from the helicopter attempted to explain that it had medical injuries on board to attend to, that the Coast Guard was going to leave them to row on their own way.

Cage, for one was glad. He didn't think it would be safer for the helicopter to try to medivac any of them up in the basket. They'd all watched, stunned, as the helicopter moved and hovered over the house that pushed up out of the water just ahead of them.

First, people emerged from the windows, leaning out and waving their arms. It had taken a good while for the helicopter crew to instruct them to go back inside and cut a hole in the roof.

The little boat's crew had watched with bated breath as inside, someone used an axe to chop through the roof. Then five people crawled out of the hole, birthing themselves onto the slick, wet shingles. One by one, they were hauled up in the basket as it swayed precariously in the wind.

That had to be terrifying, Cage thought. They'd listened as the helicopter spoke back and forth, asking how many there were in the house. What were medical injuries they needed tended. One of the people looked as if he was in very bad shape, one leg covered in blood and maybe not fully attached. He didn't move well, either.

The chopper hovered low and close enough to the surface of the water that it was blowing their tiny boat farther and farther away, farther and farther off track. But they'd waited in case something happened, in case somebody rolled off the roof. They were closer than the helicopter, all of them ready to row hard and fast if something went wrong.

Still, Cage wasn't sure that they could save someone with the rotor wash constantly blowing against them. But they'd all agreed to stay and try. The helicopter crew finally got all the people on board and said goodbye to the boat. The chopper and its heavy noise receded farther and farther into the distance until the chopper was just a change in the gray, and then gone.

"Joule." He looked at his sister. "Shall we head on?"

She nodded, and slowly she directed them all to begin rowing in a slightly different direction, this time to make up for how far they'd been blown off course. But the hope that surged in his heart was real now. The rain must be lighter, because the helicopter was out.

They saw two more rescue teams out and about before they ran the boat up on the road to the Winchester's house.

"Look!" His sister jolted in her seat as the front end of the boat ground itself into the pavement. "We're much farther down than we were last time."

The walk will be longer, he thought. But Cage welcomed walking on pavement over rocking in the flimsy little inflatables any day.

When they had returned from the first trip, they'd instituted a new protocol. Two people took the newest arrivals as a group and walked them up the road to the Winchesters. The goal was to get them dry and fed as quickly as possible. The rest remained behind to man the boats.

As they deflated each one enough to get it out of the water until the B Crew came along, Cage noticed that his sister—for whatever reason—looked exhausted this time. Was she coming down with something? He wanted to send her on ahead, but he knew that those who went ahead were already heavily armed and he struggled to think of an excuse to change protocol for her.

In the end, he didn't say anything and just went about

the task of securing the boats. He kept his hand on the gun he still carried. The water might be receding, but it didn't mean the wildlife was any less hungry. And he didn't want to be separated from his sister.

71

J oule woke slowly, eyes peeling open one at a time.
She couldn't quite focus, so she lay there. The
soft sounds of the bedroom that they'd decided to
camp in eased her into the world around her.

It was dark. The windows were still barricaded. While
she knew that hadn't really made a difference before, she'd
realized when she went to sleep that it did now. The world
was getting brighter.

Rolling her head over slowly, she looked to the upper
edge of the glass where they hadn't quite managed to cover
the entire window. And, yes, light was coming in. She tossed
back the covers and stood up, her knees still protesting from
having knelt in the boat for so long. Her shoulders whined
from too many strokes with the oar. Switching sides had
helped, but her muscles still balked from doing work they
weren't used to.

She looked at the small phone by her bed. It was hers.
There was something comforting about carrying it. The
generator Ginnifer had set up was doing its job and keeping

them all charged. They'd found more gasoline when Mickey and Chester had gone out, and they managed to keep the little machine chugging along.

They found and plugged in a high-efficiency/low-output space heater for use in this room, something they'd been able to do by venting the generator outside. It would have been easier to leave the generator itself outside and run extension cords, but Ginnifer and Mickey had fought hard to keep it inside. They'd argued that they didn't want anyone to have to go out into the rain and the wildlife if it needed any troubleshooting. They'd won that argument.

Joule frowned at the time. It looked too late in the day. Had A Crew gone out again without her?

Tip-toeing to the door, she tried to not wake up the sleeping students. They'd probably dozed some while they'd been on the roof, but the snores and the deep breaths now told her they'd not had much real rest in days. Still, she dashed away, afraid she would find her brother gone. But when she stepped into the living room, she saw him immediately, sitting on the couch, staring at his phone. Likely reading.

"We missed our shift," she told him.

"I know. I got up and Kimura and I talked. Everyone else was asleep." He stopped for a moment, tipping his head as though thinking what to tell her. "And, well, we decided not to go back out."

When she frowned at him, mad that the decision had been made without her, Cage raised his hand and pointed to the top of the window.

"Holy shit," Joule said. The living room faced a different direction than the bedroom window. From here, the world outside appeared practically sunny. "Did I sleep through the end of the rain?"

Cage shook his head. "It's still coming down. But it's so much lighter that it seemed like things are changing."

Joule was still startled by the idea. Unless the water was gone, people would still be stranded. She was opening her mouth to protest. Surely there were more students waiting. Every time they'd gone out, they'd come back with a boatful of people.

"B Crew went again. After they got back, they hauled the boats all the way in. They said it was getting more difficult with the water receding. There are new currents and eddies, and they are getting stronger as the water level goes down. It's a much farther walk to get to the water now. B Crew said they had to hike almost a mile up the road."

Joule felt her jaw drop. When they'd first arrived, the water had been five houses away from the Tamblyn house.

"It's not safe for us," Cage continued. "And the official rescue crews are out now. We might only interfere. B Crew saw those little motor-powered inflatables—"

"Zodiacs," she added.

He nodded. "With Coast Guard and National Guard volunteers."

"Wow." Joule took a moment to sit and absorb the fact that her brother was right. They didn't need to make another trip. They would hurt more than they helped. And she did not want to go on to the water again.

But something about Cage's expression made her wary.

Kimura sat in another chair, tapping on his phone, not reading. Probably researching. He was tethered to the generator, the short cord making him lean awkwardly over the side. He didn't look up until Cage specifically said, "Dr. Kimura? You should tell Joule what you wanted to do."

When the professor looked up, the light in his eyes

should have been reassuring, but it only made her more worried.

Oh hell no, Joule thought.

72

W*hy am I here? Why am I here? Why am I here?*
Joule felt the words roll through her brain over and over. They almost masked the instructions Dr. Kimura was giving them.

Holly, of all people, had jumped up and volunteered to be part of the "specimen collection committee," as Kimura had dubbed it.

Joule wished Roxie would have volunteered. Her friend was wonderful at tasks like this—organized and clear-thinking. But Roxie still hadn't really moved from where she'd sat on the couch. Joule understood Roxie would likely not be volunteering for a while.

She was deep in her grief, and Joule could not imagine losing a twin, let alone a twin who shared your face. Lord knew, she looked in the mirror and saw her own mother and father often enough to be startled by it. What would she do if her own face was also theirs?

So they'd made sure that Roxie ate and that she slept as she could. They all took care of her the best they were able. Then they made sure that Dr. Kimura had a team with some scientific practice, and they headed out into the rain, once again.

B Crew had deflated the boats and brought them up to the garage, thinking their use was done. Now the small "science team" had to haul them back down to the water's edge. Bulky and heavy, it was no easy feat to carry them along. Even though the winds had died down a good bit, a small gust could lift the boats.

Joule had been pleased when Mickey suggested that they use the wheelbarrow. The boats still didn't quite fit. But with a few people balancing them, and two others holding the handles, it did make the trip much easier.

They inflated them, lashing them together and rolling them out over the water, using them like a floating dock again. Once they were in place, the four of them shimmied their way out to the end.

Twice, Joule had rowed out in the boats with Ginnifer's electric-field devices strapped to her chest. This time, they wanted the sharks to come to them. So they had no devices at all.

Kimura had talked Phil Winchester into letting them use some of their precious food as shark bait. At first, Phil had not taken kindly to the idea. "We've already raided all of my neighbors' houses. We broke windows, damaged their homes, and stole their food. We can't waste what we have."

Kimura had only replied with, "It's a national emergency. People have died. I'm having a hard time imagining your neighbors are going to be upset that you fed people with the food that would otherwise have rotted in their pantries."

It wouldn't have rotted, Joule thought. That was the thing about pantries: they were long-lasting. And she wondered if the people who lived in the nice houses up here were generous with their belongings, or if they had nice houses in the first place because they tended to hoard their own things. She didn't say any of this aloud, however, just listened as Phil commented, "You're not feeding people, and I'm the one who has to live here after they all get back."

Maybe he didn't have to, Joule thought. But picking up and moving wasn't as simple as many made it seem and Kimura did tend to think only in scientific terms. He'd argued back as such. "We have to figure out what these creatures are, if they're different, and why this happened."

"It's over," Phil countered quickly. "Why do we need to know these things?"

"It's not over." Joule watched as her brother hopped into the argument and felt herself compelled now to join.

"Flooding is occurring all over the US, especially in the coastal regions," she added, knowing they were teaming up on Phil and that it wasn't fair. But she kept talking. "These are bull sharks. We've always known that they're willing to swim into brackish waters."

"There's a photograph from Hurricane Sandy of a shark in the water beside someone's porch. It's been examined, and no one can prove it's a fake. Biologists say the outline is that of a bull shark, which is consistent with what might have swum into hurricane waters. That's the same species we saw in the water here. So, no it's not over." Cage picked up her thread.

"This wasn't the first time and it won't be the last. We have to know what we're dealing with, or other coastal cities will have this same problem." Joule pointed at the floor, as though it indicated everything that had happened in the last week.

Somehow, her words had gotten through to Phil, and the argument went quiet. He didn't concede immediately, but after neither Cage, nor Dr. Kimura, nor Joule commented further, he ceded.

"What kind of bait do you need?"

"Meat seems to work," Kimura replied, not seeming to understand that it was their most precious resource food. Taking meat meant the students ate peanut butter instead.

Phil paused again, before leaving the room and coming back with a deli bag in his hand. "I think it's going bad."

Sliced ham, salted within an inch of its life, hung from his fingertips. A few slices seemed to be all Phil was willing to part with. Kimura was opening his mouth—almost certainly to ask for more—but Joule tapped him on the arm. Luckily, he'd taken the hint and shut up.

So, they'd headed out with the meat slices and now, as they worked to ready the boats by the edge of the water, small waves lapped at the toes of their boots. When they unrolled the boats and turned on the motors to inflate them, Kimura said, "I'd like to bring back as many as I can. I'd like to bring them back alive."

73

"Oh, hell no!" Cage had replied harshly when Dr. Kimura had originally pushed his idea to take the sharks alive.

The reasons why it was so wrong poured out of his mouth. "Where will we keep them? We already know they're dangerous—deadly, in fact. How will we keep people safe? We'd have to feed them, and we have so many people to feed first. How would we transport them?"

Kimura looked up at the sky and shook his head. "You're right. It was wishful thinking. I guess it's not possible."

Only then did Cage feel a little like a balloon flubbering about as it deflated. Kimura seemed to be after the specimens for the pure love of science, which he understood, but Cage was definitely coming down on the side of leaving the things that killed people far away from people.

However, Kimura's logic for needing to capture and keep a few of the sharks was solid. They were at the water now because the professor had argued them into the ground. He'd kept going until even Phil had believed they needed a specimen.

"We need to study this." "If I go back to my lab without sharks, then all the data is lost." "What if no one believes what happened? Where's the proof?"

Fuck, Cage thought again as he'd readied himself for yet another venture outside. Why couldn't he stay in and stay warm? Though he'd agreed, he now felt as if he'd been argued into something. Had Kimura pushed for the live capture, knowing that he'd lose, but that this task would seem a little more palatable? Cage didn't know. He only knew he'd agreed.

When Kimura had declared himself ready a little while later, Cage was surprised to see the professor had assembled quite a crew. As they headed down to the water's edge, he explained who was to take each position. Holly and Kimura were excited. Mickey and Chester seemed trepidatious but willing to help.

So now Moonbeam's uncle and his friend planted heavy feet on the road and stayed just back from the water's edge. Their task was to hold the tied-together boats steady as it functioned as a dock. They used ropes and spare webbing to protect their hands, rather than simply kneeling and holding on, which didn't provide much strength. This was better. Even so, Cage felt a bit uneasy as he stepped onto the boats.

He, Joule, Holly, and Kimura had somehow become the actual catching crew. The four had crawled forward on their elbows and knees, army-style. Up and over the hump they went, one by one, crossing between the two boats where they were tied together. They arranged themselves out at the far end, over the deepest water, barely fitting across. Cage wondered how they were going to get a shark up into the boat, too.

But Kimura thought he had it all worked out. He held

Marcus's old fishing reel. Cage's friend had brought it with them, surmising that they might need to fish for dinner. Now it would serve as a way to get the bait out over the water and hopefully to haul the fish in. They'd added one of Marcus's larger hooks, and Kimura tossed the line out with little skill.

It took less than three minutes to catch something big— and less than thirty seconds to snap the line.

"Good thing he has extra hooks." Kimura reeled the remaining line in and tied on another hook, smiling as though none of this was a problem. He looked the same way he had back in his lab when he and Joule had been talking about the specimens of unidentified eggs his sister had found.

"Also, it's good that we only used half a slice for bait," Holly quipped as she tore another half piece in half again and slid it onto the hook. Together they tossed it out quickly, then wound the reel, skipping the meat across the surface until another mouth came up and grabbed it.

This time, as Cage watched, Kimura exhibited more finesse. Using the hook, which was still far too small for the task, he tried to guide the shark toward them, rather than simply overpowering it and hauling it in. That had been the problem the first time: In a game of Shark vs. Anything, shark seemed to always win. Kimura was now just using the tug of the hook to make suggestions.

As the shark got closer, Cage could see the snout, aimed upward but staying just below the water. He was nearly face-to-face with a killer. His stomach churned, but he didn't refuse when Kimura handed him the fishing pole. Cage began turning the reel, trying to exhibit the necessary finesse to bring the shark closer—even though "closer" was the last thing he wanted to be.

It is impressive, Cage thought. How much pressure was on the stick in his hand? The shark was definitely alive and kicking on the other end.

"Closer," Kimura practically whispered, and Cage watched as his sister's hands wrapped around the handle, helping him hold it steady, freeing one of his hands to work the reel. Very, very slowly, he brought the shark in toward the edge of the boat and toward the hammer that Kimura had picked up.

The professor reached far out over the water, a dangerous place, but at least he did it quickly and Cage didn't have enough time to tell him how stupid the move was. Cage was also glad Kimura had not asked him or Joule to do this dangerous task.

With one sharp strike, the professor dropped the hammer onto the center of the shark's head.

Clearly, the man was a marine biologist. He managed to strike the shark in exactly the right place, and it went still, instantaneously dead.

"All right," Kimura said, sounding as if this were an everyday occurrence. It dawned on Cage that this man probably did pull things out of the Bay, quickly sacrifice them, then dissect them in his lab on a regular basis. Kimura knew these creatures were deadly, but still he hadn't seen anyone die... *had he?* Maybe Kimura just thought of them as strange specimens.

The professor picked up a third implement, motioning to Holly to help him. He'd crafted a hook from a bent hanger he'd duct taped onto the end of a broom handle. Together, the two maneuvered it into the shark's gills while Cage and Joule tried to keep the fishing line from breaking.

The shark kept wanting to sink now that it wasn't moving. At least it wasn't sinking quickly. After a few tries,

Kimura hauled the front end of the shark out of the water. He got very excited and hollered out, "I've got it!"

Then he and Holly—while Joule and Cage kept the tension off the line—used the hook to slowly drag the shark up and over the edge and into the boat. As it came forward, Cage scrambled backward. Despite the fact that it was dead, it was still a killer.

It had taken Sky.

It had taken the woman at the door.

It had taken the first students who had disappeared, when Joule had found the head, and later they had found a severed leg.

None of those were likely *this* shark, but in Cage's mind, they were all the same.

Despite his rampaging thoughts, he saw his sister reach out. Grabbing for the backside of the dorsal fin, she helped guide the shark further into the boat. When at last they had it lying in the boat between the four of them, Kimura stopped and looked satisfied.

Cage wasn't. He and Joule were on one side of the creature, Holly and Kimura on the other. The shark had separated them. Dead or not, Cage didn't feel good about the situation. He looked to Mickey and Chester who still held the boat with the strong straps wrapped around their arms as an anchor. He could hear them swearing like sailors at the size of the thing.

Cage would have joined in, but he was too stunned to say anything. Being so close, he could see the shark was longer than he was tall. Kimura was examining it, running his hand down the back, up and over the shape of the dorsal fin, then toward the front. Kimura prodded the skin around the eye and then the top of the skull where he'd struck it. His finger dipped into the little well where the hammer had broken the cartilage that protected the shark's brain. The professor leaned in for a better look.

As he did, the eyes popped open, the shark jerked, and the mouth flew wide. Kimura was too close and too slow for the predator. Teeth clamped down on Dr. Kimura's arm, and Cage watched as blood spurted from the bite.

74

J oule screamed, loud and long, before she acted. She could feel that it wasn't a cry of terror, but one of anger. Without thinking, her hands were reaching toward the mouth of the shark, as though she could pry it off of her professor's arm.

"No!" Cage pushed her backward, almost over the side of the boat, but even as he pushed, his fist closed into the rain jacket and held on tight. Given what they just pulled in, they knew the water was more than deep enough to be dangerous.

Kimura had yet to make a sound. He seemed stunned as the shark's jaws clamped down and the head thrashed side to side, pulling him with it.

With one hand still holding onto her tightly, Cage reached for the hook that Holly and Kimura had been using and worked to jam it into the shark's jaws.

Joule saw what he was doing and shoved his hand from her jacket. She grabbed on, helping to aim it, the two of them working miraculously well together. With adrenaline as their friend, they shoved the plain end into the shark's mouth. While her idea had been to push it all the way through and pry the jaws open, it jammed. There were too many teeth.

"Lift!" She yelled to her brother, jamming the end down into the lower part of the shark's mouth and pulling up.

Even as they did this, a rebel yell came from the other side of the boat. Holly was in the fight and she'd found the hammer. With a high swing above her head and the scream that got their attention, she brought it down onto the crown of the shark's head.

Her work was directly counter to theirs. Her strike pushed the jaw down harder onto Kimura's arm. But as Joule watched, the hammer sank halfway into the shark's head, and the creature suddenly went limp again.

Despite the blood and gore of Holly's hit, it lacked the precision of Kimura's first strike. It seemed as though Holly had done what Kimura hadn't. Still, Joule wasn't taking any chances.

"Lift!" she yelled to Cage again, and together they pushed on the pole. Using the edge of the shark's mouth as a lever against it, they used the bar to pry the teeth open. Maybe it was simply because the shark was no longer actively biting down, but the mouth lifted open, and they all watched as Kimura slowly wiggled his bloody arm out of the way.

The professor flopped backward, his butt plopping onto the inflated edge where the boats were tied together. Not quite oriented, and holding his wounded arm gingerly, he fell backward into the first boat. At least there was water under it, and he wouldn't also hit his head.

Letting go of the broom handle, Joule tried to scramble back toward him to help. He was bleeding profusely. But Cage was in her way.

As her brother realized what she was doing, he too began to move and both of them scrambled toward Kimura. She heard rather than saw Holly whacking the shark, again and again, making sure that this time it was truly dead. She was damaging Kimura's specimen, but right now, no one cared.

Joule reached into her back pocket, pulling out the folding knife she'd found at the Tamblyn's house and had carried with her since. When Ginnifer had been bitten, they'd wanted to cut her pants off of her legs. Though Ginnifer had been awake enough to protest and remove her pants herself, Joule had realized the need to have a knife in hand should someone not be alert.

So now, without asking, she reached out and sliced Kimura's sleeve open. First the rain gear, then the jacket, and she followed it last by opening the sleeve of his shirt all the way past his elbow. He didn't protest at the sharp shred of cotton hitting the laser edge of the small knife and giving way.

"Oh my god." Row after row of bites covered his skin. All were leaking blood and some flowed far too freely. A flap of skin threatened to fall away from his arm where the shark had bitten deeply enough.

"He's going to need stitches." She said the words out loud, though the idea that she needed to say that was almost laughable. Hysteria roiled through her system, buzzing along skin, down to her fingertips and up to the follicles beneath her hair. But she fought it.

"Come on. Come on." She hauled Kimura to his feet, not asking if he could make it. They took wobbly steps in the base of the boat. As Cage grabbed onto Kimura's side, Joule ducked her head under his good arm and began supporting him.

In front of her, she could hear Mickey and Chester swearing like sailors, but thankfully not leaving their post and letting the boats drift out into the water. Behind her, she heard Holly still hitting the shark. Sick thuds accompanied small grunts as the girl put her whole body into it.

"Holly, Leave it!" Joule yelled it as loud as she could, unable to call back over her shoulder, as her head was locked into place under Kimura's arm.

Kimura sagged against her and she jerked to the side, trying to look at his face.

"He passed out." Cage was remarkably calm as he made a jerking motion to try and lift Kimura's now motionless body a little higher.

She felt the boat rock as Holly stood and joined the three of them in their wobbly exit. Then, Joule steadied the professor's weight and stepped up and over the edge, her foot finally solid on the ground, as she left the boat for what she knew would be the last time.

75

It was almost a week later that Cage pushed the box into the back of the car and watched as his sister set a full laundry basket into the trunk. Placing it on top of the box, she gave it a small shove to wedge it in.

Next to them, Ginnifer and Holly carried a full trash bag and a comforter, bulky with items wrapped inside, and pushed them into the back of the car as well. The large SUV held all of Roxie's things that they'd been able to salvage, wash, and save from the flooded dorm room. It also held all of Sky's. The twins' parents alternately looked somber and shell-shocked at the horrible task of packing up both of their daughters but bringing only one of them home.

Mrs. Sanders' eyes darted momentarily to Cage, but landed again on Joule, as though she didn't quite understand that they had all been friends, and gender had not played a part.

"We're going to have a funeral for her." The woman's voice wavered. But both Joule and Cage nodded in return. "You're welcome to attend. I know it's far away, and we won't hold it against you if—"

Cage reached out and put his hand on the woman's arm. "We'll be there. We'll all be there."

He said it with the conviction of someone who had a bank account holding both of his parents' life insurance policies. His mother and father had set them up when he and Joule were very little. His mother once told him they'd planned the money so the remaining parent could pay off the house and not have to work until the twins went to college. Then, they added enough to cover college, since the remaining parent might not be working at all.

The money would keep him and Joule stable and steady for some time to come. And it meant that they could afford to fly all of Sky's friends to her funeral. Cage made a mental note to call Max, who'd already left campus and headed home to be with his family.

They'd once again lost numbers, even if they hadn't lost everyone literally.

Mrs. Sanders nodded, not understanding the force behind Cage's word, but appreciating the sentiment. She climbed into the large SUV, pulled the door shut, and disappeared behind the heavily tinted windows. Roxie had said her goodbyes and closed herself into the back seat some time ago. Cage watched as the car drove down the road.

The school staff, though much smaller now, had managed to clear the roads. Charity organizations and FEMA had come in. Tents were set up on the sides of some of the roads. The professors had gone in and begun the monumental task of clearing out the buildings.

Cage had thought about offering to help Dr. Kimura clean the marine sciences lab. Many students were gone from campus, but some were here and volunteering where work was needed. But Cage wasn't quite ready to pick out the dead bodies of the rays and the sharks that surely littered the lower floor of the Bass Sciences Building.

As the water had risen, they would have easily escaped the aquariums where Kimura was growing them. If they'd escaped the building, then the professor might have released new species into the bay ecosystem. In fact, anyone with live fishes in the area had done so. The San Francisco Bay had several aquariums which reported that most of their fish were missing. Many were freshwater and therefore likely had not survived—but given the mix of rain and sea water, it was hard to tell.

And that didn't account for home saltwater or freshwater tanks. For pet shops and all those fish and animals. The muscles between his ribs tightened involuntarily and he tried to push the thought aside. No, he had not volunteered for that cleanup. Maybe none of the students would.

He and Joule had taken part of the day yesterday to drive to the Bay and look for themselves. The water had slowly receded, leaving flotsam and jetsam everywhere. Mostly it was branches and fallen trees, but the ground still sported random car bumpers and the occasional, telling piece of clothing. So they'd gone out and looked at the water one more time. He wanted to be sure that it had returned to its rightful place.

As he stood there, he was irrationally afraid that the liquid would simply rise up and claim him. What had once been a peaceful body of water was now a dark mirror surface over a world of monsters.

Cage pushed that thought aside. The Bay wasn't here on campus—not anymore. And the Sanders' car was almost out of sight. He continued waving as they drove away, but it was time to turn around and find the next thing to do.

The school was mostly closed down. Administration was

figuring out how to handle grades or finish teaching the courses. They hadn't decided whether they could simply call the quarter a wash or if it was early enough in the term that they could regroup and make something out of it. Most of the students had survived. As it turned out, many had managed to get off campus during the early stages of the rain.

Cage had been surprised to learn that, though the students came from all over the country and even the world, many had ties to the area. He and his sister seemed to be the oddballs with no family connections. Most of those who had stayed on campus—like them, like Roxie and Sky—had not had nearby family or friends to escape to. Those who did hadn't wound up stranded on campus and hadn't had to face the worst of it.

He stood now in the middle of the road, where he and his sister and Gabby had been watching until the black SUV became a dot in the distance. It turned the last corner, leaving him with only the view of the road rolling away from him.

Campus was still wet. Ruined and broken trees were down. Roads were closed. Power was still intermittent at best. He turned to Joule. "What do we do now?"

"I don't know."

They didn't have a dorm room.

They'd been into the building and managed to salvage a handful of things. Clothing was mostly thrown into the wash. Extra machines had been brought onto campus and students were handwashing to make up for the fact that there would never be enough machines. But most of what survived was what they had carried with them.

Joule's bow and arrows. The small amount of clothing they'd packed. Their phones.

The computers were lost, but they'd both managed to log in to some temporary setups and see that their backups were in place. The car was dead, the engine drowned. Though they hadn't called their insurance yet, those who had filed claims found that their companies weren't even investigating. Cage expected no less when he called in.

Just then Joule's phone rang.

"Moonbeam!" she answered, holding the phone out where Cage could be part of the conversation.

The voice on the other end now felt like a familiar friend, like Gabby and Max, and even Holly and Ginnifer. Moonbeam had stayed steady through the worst of times.

"What's campus like?" she asked. The Winchesters had not come down off the mountain when things had cleared, preferring to stay and clean their house after the onslaught of more than fifty students who'd wound up sleeping, eating, and living in the place. Phil had commented that he needed to, "make amends with his neighbors."

"Campus is a mess," Joule told her.

"I'm assuming your dorm room is shot."

Cage nodded, though he knew he couldn't be seen.

"Well, we have the house up here. You and your friends are all welcome to come and stay." Joule was opening her mouth when Moonbeam added, "My Dad agreed. I mean, you've already lived here for a while, and you know your way around."

Cage blinked a few times at the idea, and then decided it sounded wonderful. They'd returned to campus the day before and found the dorm completely trashed by the water, the two of them had wound up staying in the gym in a temporary shelter the school had set up.

Temp shelters, he now knew, were hideous. They were necessary, and life-saving, but they were noisy. Bunking with almost a thousand other students, none of whom could sleep at the same time, had not been pleasant.

"We don't have a car," his sister replied.

"We'll come get you." The friendly voice was soothing and the idea of staying in a home lifted a weight off his shoulders, one he didn't realize he'd been carrying. "Stay up here with us. They expect to have the power back on tomorrow, and we have the generator." There was a pause, then an excited addendum. "Oh! Kimura came back today and got his shark."

That is good, Cage thought. It meant the stitches had been okay and the hospital had released him. He'd messaged them the day before from the ER, letting them know that the wounds weren't as deep as they had thought. Though it had been too long since the injury for the hospital to close the wound, they'd been able to work with what the students at the house had done to save the professor and his arm.

Luckily, one of the students had been an EMT. Kimura had been stitched with thread from Robert's ex-wife's sewing kit—definitely a home job. But if he was driving up the hill and fetching a five-foot-plus shark body, then his arm was going to be okay.

"Thank you, Moonbeam." Cage jumped into the conversation for the first time. "Was there any word on Marcus?"

The Winchesters had called for a removal of the body, and they'd all watched as the team had zipped Marcus into a black bag and drove him away. Phil had promised to pull whatever strings he had to be sure an autopsy was performed and to get them the results.

Moonbeam's voice faded a little. She must have turned away from the phone, and it sounded like she was talking to her father. Then her voice came back, directed at the twins.

"The autopsy isn't officially finished, but Dad pushed the Medical Examiner, and they think he had a congenital heart problem no one knew about. It's likely that the venom stressed his system too much."

"Thank you." Cage pushed the words out of his mouth, though it hurt to do so. When Joule thanked Moonbeam as well and then hung up, she sighed.

"So we stay with them," he said. "Then what?"

"We wait it out."

Joule nodded along with his thoughts as they turned and walked back toward the shelter. Mickey would likely come and get them there, bringing the big truck that could splash through any remaining puddles. "We finish. We get our degrees. It's what Mom and Dad would have wanted."

"You're right." And something settled in his heart.

"They'll be here in about an hour. So we need to gather up anything that we can." They'd have to figure out what was worth taking up the mountain with them. Joule turned to her brother. Then she looked around at the campus, which was still damaged by the flood but beginning to recover. "We can do this. It's only three more years. We're survivors and we won't let this stop us."

"Yeah, Mom and Dad would be proud of us." He was turning to head back to the shelter but then he stopped and looked his sister dead in the eyes. "But at the first sign of rain, we're leaving."

76

Cage felt his pulse race as he pulled the envelopes from the small box. Three today. It wasn't the envelopes that made him happy—he was getting several of those each day that he mostly just threw away—it was the logo on this one...

It had been three years since the flood, and he could still feel the world changing. He and Joule had fit their school-work to that model. Without family waiting at home, they had no pressures to marry and have kids. No pressures to join any family business. And no location pulling them back to settle down.

Their grandmother had passed the year before. And their grandfather had refused any and all attempts they made to come stay with him. He was "just fine" and they had "lives to live." Cage smiled. Grampa would make it to one-hundred-and-ten. Or so he hoped as he ripped the envelope open.

They were one month from graduation. Joule had already been offered a job with Helio System Technologies. As an about-to-graduate engineer, she was head-hunted and snapped up quickly. But they were still trying to stick together, so she hadn't yet accepted the position. It began in September and she had until July to make a decision before they dropped her from the roster.

That meant Cage had until July to get his own offer on the Alabama project she was already assigned to.

It's not just that Joule will be there, he thought as he looked at the other envelopes. The first was for a credit card he wouldn't be getting. It seemed to have the card already in it, though he hadn't signed up. He tossed it. The second was a missive from the school. Waiting on the important envelope, he opened it next.

Scanning the letter, he found it listed ways to get his appropriate cap and gown from a specific location on campus. He already had that. It reminded him to check in with his advisor—already scheduled. And to go online and check some box that said he was planning to graduate... as though he hadn't checked a thousand things already.

He tossed the envelope and held onto the letter, though he was pretty certain he'd gotten all the same information online the day before. Then, he took a breath and wedged his finger under the edge of the Helio System Technologies letter and held his breath.

Dear Faraday Mazur,...

His eyes scanned the entire thing before starting over. He thought... but he hadn't really read it. Then he grinned.

"Yes!"

He must have said it out loud, because several other students in the mailroom looked sideways at him. One even raised her eyebrows.

"Job offer," was all he replied as he fished his phone out of his pocket. "Joule!" He didn't wait for her to answer, just started speaking at the click. "I got it. I got the Alabama project."

"*Yes!*" she shrieked into his ear. And he listened as she explained to whoever was now eyeing her oddly that, "My brother just got a job offer at the same place as me!"

Then her voice came back into his ear, albeit a little too loudly. "Hang up. Call the number. Accept the job. I'll do the same."

Click.

She was gone. Instruction given, Joule was acting.

With a grin on his face, he dialed the number at the bottom of the letter. He knew most brothers and sisters were ready to be on their own in college, and certainly after. But he and Joule were twins. They'd been together before they breathed air. Their parents had told him, "She's the one who will always be there. She will always be your sister. That's the best friend you want." They'd told Joule the same thing.

And their first year here, he'd learned the hard way that twins aren't always going to be there. He had no other family left except Grampa. So he and Joule would stick together until they couldn't. Today was not the day they had to go separate ways.

The line clicked and he used his best professional, not overly-excited voice to speak to his new boss and accept the job offer. They spoke for a while, confirming several things that had been in the letter.

"Cage!" He heard his sister behind him and turned at the sound, surprised.

She looked as though she'd been running. Her breath soughed in and out, but she wasn't on the phone. Had she already accepted her job? Had her call gone faster?

He held up a finger, trying to listen to the voice still talking to him on the phone. "—really glad you called today.

I know you need to finish the term, but we are bumping up the start date. We need you here right after graduation."

"That should be fine. One second, please..." He covered the mic and relayed the information to Joule, who only nodded at him, her expression worried. She hit a few buttons on her phone and held it up for him to see, just as the voice on the phone spoke again.

"We've had to move all the dates forward. Just last night, we had a massive tragedy here, and our company is rapidly moving into position to help rebuild rather than alter existing systems."

Cage frowned, but the voice continued. "Did you see the news?"

He hadn't, but Joule was now playing a video on her phone of a massive tornado moving through street after street. The bar across the bottom read "Montgomery to Birmingham, F6 tornado sweeps several cities."

He frowned and spoke, but whether it was into the phone or to his sister, Cage didn't know. "F-Six? I thought the scale only went to five..."

It was the voice that replied. "It used to only go to five."

ABOUT THE AUTHOR

A.J.'s world is strange place where patterns jump out and catch the eye, little is missed, and most of it can be recalled with a deep breath. In this world, the smell of Florida takes three weeks to fully leave the senses and the air in Dallas is so thick that the planes "sink" to the runways rather than actually landing.

For A.J., reality is always a little bit off from the norm and something usually lurks right under the surface. As a storyteller, A.J. loves irony, the unexpected, and a puzzle where all the pieces fit and make sense. Originally a scientist and a teacher, the writer says research is always a key player in the stories. AJ's motto is "It could happen. It wouldn't. But it could."

A.J. has lived in Florida and Los Angeles among a handful of other places. Recent whims have brought the dark writer to Tennessee, where home is a deceptively normal-looking neighborhood just outside Nashville.

For more information:
www.ReadAJS.com
AJ@ReadAJS.com

Made in the USA
Monee, IL
21 June 2020

34238566R00246